THE CRIMSON QUEEN

Book 1 of The Raveling

ALEC HUTSON

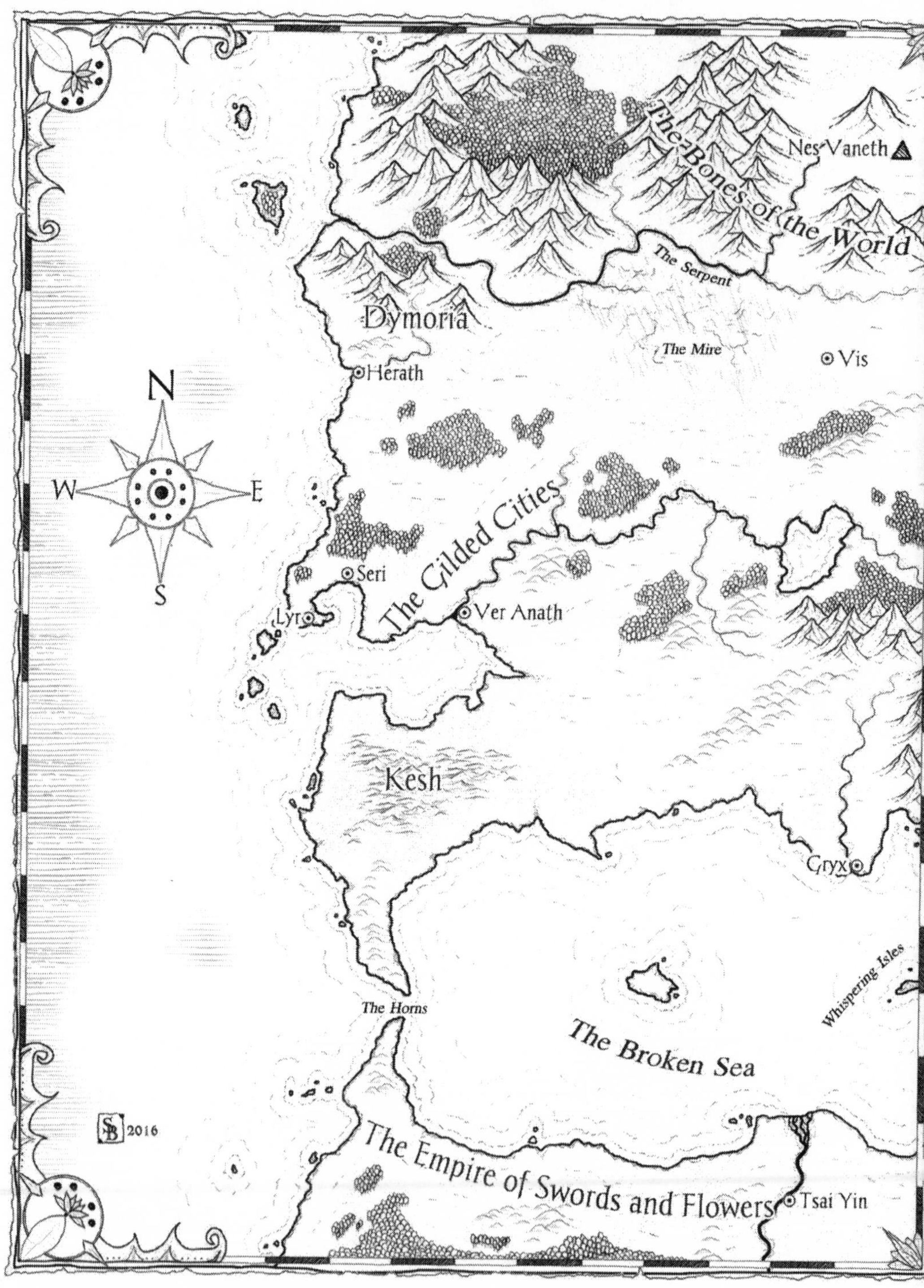

The Bones of the World
Nes Vaneth
The Serpent
Dymoria
The Mire
Vis
Herath
N
W
E
S
The Gilded Cities
Seri
Lyr
Ver Anath
Kesh
Gryx
Whispering Isles
The Horns
The Broken Sea
SB 2016
The Empire of Swords and Flowers
Tsai Yin

ARAEN
The Frostlands
Telemach
Menekar
The Menekarian Empire
The Fens
The Blightwood
The Spine
Theris
The Shattered Kingdoms
Uthmala
Palimport
Whispering Isles
The Thread
The Eversummer Isles
SB 2016

The Crimson Queen © 2016 by Alec Hutson
Published by Alec Hutson

Cover art by Jeff Brown
Cover design by Jeff Brown
Map by Sebastian Breit

Proofed by Jessica Parker
Interior layout and design by Colleen Sheehan

First Edition

ISBN: 978-0-9982276-0-3 (print)
978-0-9982276-1-0 (e-book)

Please visit Alec's website at
WWW.AUTHORALECHUTSON.COM

For my mother, who read to me

PROLOGUE

THE OLD MAN waited, shrouded in darkness, alone in a room carved from the mountain's heart.

How long had he been waiting? He knew, and yet he did not know. Time bled differently down here, so far removed from the sky and sea; usually it became thinner, more attenuated, moments stretching into eternities. But on rare occasion it seemed to bunch and swell, thundering through these passageways like a mighty river seeking the ocean after the spring floods, sweeping them all along whether they wished it to or not.

That is the danger, he mused, of living in such an immutable place. Change, when it did come, seemed too hurried, too discourteous.

And a great change was coming; he could feel it thrumming in the rock around him. They had a bond, he and the mountain. For one hundred and seventy-six years he had lived almost every waking moment within, one hundred and twenty of those as the daymo of the kith'ketan. The slightest disturbance reverberated through the halls to him like a great drum beating deep down among the mountain's roots.

So he was aware, even before his steward told him, that the Undying One was coming to see him.

The air in his room eddied, ever so slightly, and he knew he was no longer alone. The old man closed his eyes, embracing the shadow, and in his mind the contours of his sanctum materialized. He sat cross-legged atop a dais carved from a giant femur – not a dragon's, as his old master had once told him, since such remains held queer properties, but another beast from lost antiquity, one whose bones had turned smooth and hard with the turning of the ages. Five walls enclosed him, perfectly symmetrical, curving to come together far above, where a great iron bell was suspended. A silken cord dangled down, almost brushing his hand. A single tolling and his steward would appear. Two and any kith'ketan in the mountain of high enough rank to bear a shadowblade would hurry to attend him. Three and a dozen of his followers would burst through the chamber's entrance and slay whoever had displeased him.

He kept his hands in his lap, perfectly still.

The presence in his sanctum did not speak. The silence stretched between them for a time – *A moment? An eternity?* – and then the daymo pulled from his voluminous sleeves a long, thin object, something he had sent his steward searching for as soon as he had felt this one approaching.

"May I?" he asked, and at another time he would have choked on such a request. The thought that the daymo of the kith'ketan, within his own sacred mountain, would ask permission to do anything was galling – but, he chided himself, remembering his own teachings, pride was an illusion, an artifice that could be set aside when circumstances warranted.

And conversing with their most honored guest was just such a circumstance.

"Yes." The Undying One spoke softly, without inflection or accent. An unmemorable voice. Yet there was power behind it – the old man felt the reverberations.

Light flared in the darkness. Not a warm, golden glow, but a harsh, pale flickering that painted the room in shades of charcoal and bone.

The daymo set the corpsetallow candle in a twisted black-metal stand. The white flame writhed and danced like a creature in pain

– which, in a way, he supposed it was. Could a soul feel pain even when ripped from its body? A metaphysical question, and one he suspected no man living could answer.

The old man studied his guest. Tall, with pallid, unlined skin. Black ringlets that fell to his shoulders. Large, dark eyes and a thin mouth. The man was dressed in the traditional garb of their order, even though he was not truly a part of it – a black tunic lacking any design or symbol, loose black trousers cinched by a wire that could be used as a means to kill, a cloak and cowl. And it was as he suspected: the man matched perfectly with the image he still held in his memory from well over a century ago, when he had attended his own master in this very chamber as that ancient daymo had met with the Undying One to discuss the murder of a padarasha.

"You are leaving us," the old man said, passing his hand over the candle. The flame shied away from him, as if afraid.

The Undying One nodded. "I have been summoned."

That surprised the old man, but he did not let it show. "A man cannot serve two masters."

"I have no master," murmured the Undying One. Then his thin mouth quirked slightly. "And who said I was a man?"

True enough, thought the daymo. Considerations of who or what this creature was had consumed more of his time than he would ever admit. His master, the previous daymo, had confided in him once that he thought the Undying One to be an avatar of shadow, a physical manifestation of the philosophy that guided the kith'ketan. Brought into being, perhaps, by the intense devotion of those that lived under the mountain.

But the old man did not believe that. He now thought the Undying One was merely a visitor to their home, though his purpose for living amongst them for so many centuries remained inscrutable.

"Before you go . . . I wish to see your blade. I have heard many stories."

Did the Undying One hesitate? Had the old man said something unexpected, deviated from whatever scripted dance they were engaged in?

Then he stepped forward and drew his weapon. There was no sound, no rasping of metal like accompanied the drawing of traditional swords. Nor was there the faint whisper of silk, as when a shadowblade was flourished. The sword slid out as silent as a grave and the corpsetallow candle quailed in its presence, guttering.

The Undying One held out his sword so that the old man could study its curved blade. It looked like normal steel, notched in places, with a few faint cracks threading the metal. But the hair on his arm lifted when he reached out to touch the weapon, and the Undying One shook his head firmly.

"Do not touch. You are strong, but I cannot guarantee that it will not take you."

The daymo withdrew his hand, and the Undying One sheathed the sword.

Surprisingly, he found his mouth was dry. He swallowed. "Will you return to us?"

"I do not know. The world above is changing – surely you have felt the tremors. And now an old . . . friend asks for my counsel and help. She would not do this unless great events were unfolding. Perhaps the kith'ketan will be drawn into what is coming."

"We do not wish to guide the course of history. That has never been our purpose."

The Undying One shook his head slightly. "No, you would rather be the tools of those who would change the world. But perhaps you should consider another role for your order. Perhaps it does not conflict with your . . . philosophy as much as you believe. A new age is dawning, and the bold will shape it to their desires."

Those last words echoed in the old man's thoughts long after the Undying One had turned and departed, leaving after many years the darkness under the mountain and emerging again into the world of light and life.

1: KEILAN

KEILAN LEANED OVER the side of the small fishing boat and dipped his fingers into the dark water as his father pulled hard again on the oars. They slid forward through the swells that were trying to push them back toward land, his father grunting curses with each strong stroke.

"Can I help?" Keilan asked, settling onto one of the boat's seat-planks. Across from him his father grimaced a smile through his beard.

"The day I can't row out against the breakers," he said, his face flushed, "is the day I hang up my nets and give this old tub to you."

Keilan nodded. The same answer, returned every day to the same question. Endless identical days, it seemed, different only in the size of their catch, his father's mood, and the vagaries of wind and water.

Keilan glanced at the southern horizon, that thin seam where sea joined with sky. Wind and water. He didn't share his father's old fisherman sense of the changing weather, but still he could tell that this day would not be exactly like most others.

"Aye, you can feel it too, then," his father said as Keilan continued to stare off into the distance. "A storm's brewing out there.

Something's maddened one of the Shael, t'be sure. They'll be lancing the sea before nightfall, looking to spear a serpent or two."

Keilan saw it, a faint bruising in the hard blue sky that warned of distant storm clouds massing. He turned back to his father and was surprised to catch something glinting in his slate-gray eyes.

"Your father's not so old yet, boy. The rowing's hard because the sea's starting to work its way into a fury. You'll have to wait a few more years yet before you can call yourself the captain of this ship."

"How long until the storm comes?"

His father squinted, lines scored by years of sun and salt cracking his face. "We should be all right if we get back around the late tide, but I also don't want to tempt Ghelu. So we best start filling this boat with fish." He paused his rowing, holding the oars suspended over the waves; water streamed from the blades, drops glittering like jewels in the sunlight as they fell. "You best do your dowsing trick."

My dowsing trick, Keilan thought, rolling his sleeve up. His father likened what he did to a man finding water . . . though of course, out here, water was easy enough to find. Other things were more difficult.

He leaned again over the side of the rocking boat, this time farther out, and plunged his arm into the water up to his elbow. It was cold, but not bracingly so. Behind him he heard his father set down the oars with a clatter, and then a moment later the susurrus of nets being pulled from beneath the seat-planks.

Keilan stared into the shifting blackness. The sounds of his father dwindled as he concentrated on the sea and the feel of his hand drifting in the gentle current. Gradually the sun on his neck and the wind tugging at his hair also faded away. He dissolved into the water, spreading out into the yawning abyss below.

He was there. Under the water, floating, coddled by the freezing darkness. In the Deep. As always, the immensity beneath him was briefly, terrifyingly overwhelming, and he had to tamp down the panicked desire to kick for the surface and sunlight.

Keilan mastered himself. He was not alone; down here, he was never truly alone, if he looked long enough. He felt them then, surprisingly close, pinpricks of warmth skittering through the dark, rising from the depths . . . stars falling up. They were close, but not quite close enough.

With a gasp he returned to the boat, pulling his arm from the water. Below his elbow the skin had turned ashen.

"Well?" his father asked. "Is this a good spot?"

Keilan swallowed and shook his head, massaging his numb arm. "No . . . but not far. There's a fair-sized school coming, a bit more that way." He waved vaguely to the east, where a rocky spur thrust out into the bay.

His father grunted and dropped the net he'd been baiting, picking up his oars again. "Ironheads, are they? Must be chasing the minnows round the rocks."

Keilan shrugged and shivered, reaching for the sealskin blanket his father now kept for him in the boat. They lurched forward as his father pulled hard at the oars, straining to get them positioned quick enough. Keilan kept his eyes fixed on the bottom of the boat, but he could feel his father watching him with concern.

"You all right, boy? You don't feel the falling sickness coming on again, do ya?"

Keilan shook his head. "I'm fine."

And he would be. This was normal, a momentary weakness. Nothing like what had happened a fortnight before. When he'd almost died.

He put the thought of that awful day out of his head – otherwise, he'd be too scared to even accompany his father out here, let alone attempt his . . . dowsing.

His father rowed in silence, the rocks swelling larger behind him. They were black and jagged and veined by red strands of seaweed. When Keilan was a bit younger, before he had started coming out with his father almost every day, he and Sella would sometimes carefully pick their way along those same rocks, collecting fresh seaweed for Mam Ru to put in her soups. And there'd be other treasures, too, if they were lucky. Blue-shelled crabs tossed up by the waves and caught in the small pools that sometimes formed where the rocks came together, pale luminous sea-glass of different colors, and driftwood that must have come from one of the many ships that foundered on the treacherous rocks hidden farther out at the mouth of the bay. Every time he'd found one of those chunks of wood Keilan had wondered if it had been torn from his mother's ship, perhaps even if she'd clung to it before his father had pulled her from the churning waters.

"Da, where did you find her?" The words slipped out, unexpected, and immediately Keilan regretted his question. There was an unspoken rule between them, never to talk about her.

His father's face slackened in surprise, then grew dark. He didn't respond for a long moment, studying Keilan with eyes that almost looked reproachful. Finally, he sighed and gestured with one of the oars out beyond the end of the jumbled rocks.

"There. Clinging to that damned chest so hard I wasn't sure which was keeping the other afloat." His eyes passed beyond Keilan, looking at something else. "Lightning was rippling the sky, an' I saw her in the flash, bone white like some wraith come to drag those poor sailors down under. The waves carried me closer, and then there was another big strike, and I could see that she'd seen me, and that she wasn't no ghost, just a girl, and that she was scared. Scared and beautiful and fierce to keep on living. She was refusing to let these waters drag her down." His father cleared his throat and spat over the side. "I reached my hand out, and she took it, and I pulled her up and into this very boat, but with her other hand she stayed holding on to that chest, and she didn't let go until I hauled it out of the water as well. What foolishness; almost capsized us bringing it aboard. Then I put my back into the oars and rowed for shore like the Deep Ones themselves were tickling at my hull. Your Ma stayed huddled at my feet watching behind us as the Shael kept lancing the water, giving us these glimpses of her ship as it finished breaking up on the rocks, and then one time it was just gone, like it had never been."

"Did the rest of them die?"

His father nodded. "Best we in the village could tell. There were a few bodies that washed up the next day, along with some things from the ship, shards of wood and shreds of sail, a crate of broken pottery. Old Tannin found a silver bracelet studded with green stones big as walnuts. Thought he was rich as a prince, but a passing peddler later told him they was just colored bits of glass."

Keilan smiled, imagining Tannin strutting around town, proud as a rooster, and what his face must have looked like after the peddler had dashed his hopes. Knowing the old fool he had probably had the bracelet appraised in front of as large a crowd as possible, just so everyone could envy his good fortune.

His father stopped rowing. "About here, boy?"

Keilan glanced around, trying to estimate where the school he had sensed would be by now. "This should be a good spot," he said, with only a trace of uncertainty.

His father might have noticed his tone, but still he grunted agreement and bent to his nets. Keilan helped him thread a few more pieces of bait into the mesh, then took the far end of the net and brought it to the back of the boat. At the count of three father and son tossed the weighted corners out into the ocean and watched them sink, fastening the other ends of the nets onto iron hooks driven into the side of the boat, while also holding tight to the lines that ran down to the weights suspended in the deepness. Now they just had to wait.

Sometimes it could take an hour before they caught anything, or his father grudgingly gave up, but today Elara's bounty was swift, and almost immediately they felt the lines begin to thrum with the feeling of thrashing fish.

"Up boy, pull it up!" his father cried, hauling on the line that ran down to the net's weights. Keilan did the same, and slowly the net cinched closed, rising toward the surface. His father let out a whoop when he saw how many squirming, silver bodies they had snared, and with a great heave father and son dumped the wriggling fish into the ship. Each was about as long as Keilan's arm, and his father's guess had been right, as their heads were large and black and bony, almost as if they were wearing helmets. Keilan jumped back a step, wary of their snapping jaws. He'd watched his father's cousin lose a finger to one of these fish before.

"Ironheads! Ten, eleven . . . twelve! Just about the best first cast I've ever had. Elara smiles on us today, boy."

Keilan grinned broadly, more for his father's good humor than for the catch they'd brought up. In the past year there had been too many days of sullen silence trapped together on this boat, followed by nights of drunken rage and sadness. Since the night they'd lost her.

They dipped their net a handful of times around the rocks, bringing up a few more ironheads and also a small shark that must have been stalking the school. His father offered a quick prayer to Ghelu for the pardon of killing one of his most beloved children, then slid his boning knife into the shark's eye and finished it off with a twist. Shark meat was popular in Chale these days.

His father didn't ask him to dowse again for fish, and Keilan didn't volunteer. Doing so more than once in a day left him with a splitting headache the next morning.

Finally satisfied with their catch, his father took up his oars again and began rowing for home. The sun had started its slow descent by then, burnishing the bare slopes of the eastern hills so that they gleamed like sheets of beaten gold, while to the south the purple stain in the sky had faded to an ominous black.

Keilan began stuffing the fish they'd caught into a large sack; although almost all of them had stopped breathing, he was still careful of their hooked jaws, as even after death they sometimes snapped shut with a terrible strength. His uncle had told him this was a last attempt at vengeance by a lingering spirit, but Keilan secretly thought that the fish were simply too stupid to know that they were dead.

As they approached the beach Keilan saw that most of the other fishing boats had already returned and been dragged up into the tall grass where they could better weather the coming storm. Shadowy shapes milled around on the sand, and tarps had been laid out displaying each fisherman's catch. Long before he could make out faces Keilan recognized the spindly legs and barrel chest of Pelos, the old fishmonger from Chale, who traveled to their village most evenings in his great, rickety wagon to sift through Elara's bounty. He was gesticulating fiercely with a tall, stooped man that Keilan thought was probably his Uncle Davin.

When the boat's bottom scraped against the sand, Keilan hopped over the side into the surf and began hauling on the rope tied to the prow. His father joined him moments later, and together they wrestled the boat partway up onto the beach. Keilan spread out the tarp they used to display their catch, and his father pulled from their boat the sack bulging with ironheads, then began to lay them out carefully in neat rows. While he was doing this a few of the other fishermen who had already concluded their business with the fishmonger hoisted his father's boat onto their shoulders and carried it up into the beach grass, setting it upside-down beside the others.

Pelos strolled over, trailed by Keilan's Uncle Davin, and whistled appreciatively after a moment of careful inspection. "By the Ten, Farris, you had a good day. Two dozen ironheads and a decent-sized snapper." The fishmonger jerked his thumb over his shoulder to indicate the other catches. "Your brother here insisted there was nothing to find out there today, and I'd just about given up hope that this trip would be worthwhile."

For the first time, Keilan noticed that the other catches on display seemed unusually small, both in quantity and the size of the fish, and that his uncle's mouth was set in a thin, hard line as he watched the fishmonger peruse what they'd caught.

"There was nothing," his uncle insisted, with more than a trace of bitterness, "Farris must have brought up everything in the bay worth catching."

His father finished laying out his fish and then stood, wiping his hands on his tunic. "I whistled to the fish and they came. Old fisherman's trick."

Davin snorted, gesturing with a bony finger at Keilan. "It's the boy. He's just like his mother."

Keilan felt a hand on his shoulder, and then his father moved in front of him. "He's a good lad. He's a true fisherman's son." There was an edge to his voice, and Davin must have heard it as well because his uncle stepped back, muttering to himself.

Pelos brushed past his father and tousled Keilan's rain-slicked hair. "Well, if you helped bring up these beauties, I thank you kindly. So do the good people of Chale, as they'll be happy to have a bit o' fresh ironhead on the table tomorrow." The old fishmonger's face creased in sudden confusion. "Wait, what's this?" he said, tickling the back of Keilan's ear. "I think . . . I think you've got something caught back here . . ."

Keilan grinned, knowing what would come next. With feigned amazement the old fishmonger withdrew from behind Keilan's ear an iron bit, then with a flourish held it out for him to take. "By the Ten, lad, you best be careful where you put your money. All kinds of disreputable folk around these parts."

Keilan knew that some of the others his age in the village would have sneered at the fishmonger, trying to show how they were too old for such children's tricks. He'd seen fifteen winters, after all. Another few moons and it'd be the mid-summer solstice, and he'd have to night-dive for Elara's bounty and prove to everyone that he was ready to be considered a man of the village. But Pelos was almost family – he'd been pulling the same trick for a dozen years, since Keilan's mother had first brought him down to the beach to watch and wait for his father's return.

Pelos gave him a sly wink and then turned back to his father. "I'll take the lot. Three imperial drakes and a dozen bits."

"Four drakes even, and throw in a few pinches of that salt I know you keep in your wagon."

"Three drakes, fifteen bits."

The haggling settled into a familiar rhythm, with Pelos offering up outraged protestations and his father refusing to budge from what he thought was fair.

While they bargained, Keilan allowed his thoughts to wander a few months hence, when he'd have to stand at midnight on the rock with all the other boys on the cusp of manhood, and then leap into the freezing waters of the bay. He wouldn't be able to return to the village until he brought back something of Elara's bounty – most others scavenged sea urchins or crabs, whatever small thing they first found so they could get out of the water as quickly as possible, but Keilan had seen a few others return carrying spiny lobsters, which was considered especially blessed, and that's what he had once told himself he would hold out for.

Now though . . . the thought of the night-dive had been weighing heavily on him for the past two weeks, ever since his . . . accident. Keilan shuddered, and not from the cold drizzle that was slowly starting to strengthen. Swimming down into the water, pushing into that blackness . . . there were things in the Deep. He had touched one.

It had started innocently enough. They had been out in the boat, a high summer sun beating down mercilessly, and not a breath of wind to give relief. His father had been hunched at the prow with his cloak drawn up, still smelling of the bottle of spiced rum he'd finished off earlier that morning. While they drifted on that glassy sea Keilan had trailed his hand in the water, idly searching. But there were no fish that day that he could feel, at least anywhere nearby, and his father was in no condition to row them elsewhere, or even finish baiting the nets.

So Keilan had stretched himself farther into the water, pushing his senses past the rocky mouth of the bay, into the true Deep. There he had found things. Bright, swift-moving shapes he was familiar with, a great school of fish that twisted and turned as if of one mind. And on the edges of that huge constellation hung cold, clear lights he knew to be sharks, and when he drifted closer he had seen one dart into the school. The lights had swirled and eddied, moments later reforming as if nothing had happened.

Keilan had known he should have stopped then – already he had felt himself starting to tingle with the strain of reaching so far, but he had continued on, into the blackness.

Several times he had passed small, bright, darting things, and once a languid, undulating form, and then his breath had been stolen from him as a collection of vast, ponderous souls pushed past, angling upwards.

Whales, he had murmured, as the giant creatures surged around him. They were different than the other things he had felt in the bay, not warm and clear and predatory, but blazing with inner fire, and almost gentle, their hugeness encompassing him as he floated, awe-struck.

He had sensed his body back in the boat, so far away, begin to shake, but he wasn't able to stop now, not after seeing such wonders. So he had dived deeper, his speed quickening, thrusting himself forward into the darkness.

And that's where he'd found it. Down there, in the true black, where sunlight never reached. He'd thought the whales were huge, but it had reared out of the gloom like a sudden mountain, vast beyond the limits of comprehension. Terror had sluiced through him, and he knew from whatever tenuous thread connecting him with his body back aboard his father's boat that he had just emptied his bladder, a distant trickle of warmth running down his leg.

It did not move; it did not glitter like fish or sharks or pulse with the slow majesty of whales. But Keilan had known that it lived, and then, impossibly, an eye bigger than a wagon wheel had slid open in the blackness and found him, flensed his soul open like with a boning knife and peered into his depths. And he had fled, screaming.

His father had lifted from his stupor when Keilan had slumped to the floor of the boat, twitching, blue veins etched against milky skin and his wide eyes staring at nothing.

He had seen a Deep One. And it had seen him.

2: KEILAN

THE NEXT MORNING as Keilan pulled on his boots, his father clapped him on the shoulder and told him he could rest, that he would be going out into the bay alone today. Keilan started to say something, but then he glimpsed the bottle tucked into one of the pockets sewn into his father's cloak, and instead swallowed away his words. This was a reward, Keilan knew, for the excellent catch they'd brought up the day before, but he wondered if there wasn't something else as well. Yesterday, after his father had finally settled with the fishmonger, he had caught a few of the other fishermen glancing his way as they made the long walk back to the village. These were men he'd known his whole life – Big Benj, Uncle Davin, Cord, Seven-Finger Soman – but in their faces he hadn't seen a trace of the old friendliness, just thinned mouths and squints of hard suspicion. He'd lain awake much of last night, listening to the storm raging and thinking of the last time he'd seen his mother, of her empty eyes as the same men with the same expressions had taken her away from their small hut, down to the beach and the waiting sea.

Thoughts of his mother always led to him spending time with her books, so after filling a bowl with some of the leftover fish stew he'd prepared for dinner the night before he dragged out the box from behind his sleeping pallet and began removing its contents. He handled the books reverentially, making a circle of them on the hard-packed dirt floor of their hut with him sitting cross-legged in the middle. Fourteen books, the treasures his mother had refused to live without, the contents of the chest his father had rescued with her from the sea. He felt like he knew every word they contained by heart; his mother had taught him to read using them, and in the years since he'd finished each one two-dozen times. Keilan stroked their dark leather bindings, tracing the letters that flowed in silver and gold script across their covers. *The Metaphysics of Reason, A History of Menekar Volume I, When Blood Sings: The Poetry of Dzin keth Dzari.*

To Keilan's knowledge there were no other books in the village. He would be surprised if anyone else could read, actually, although Old Tannin had made a show of studying the Tractate the last time a wandering mendicant had passed through bringing a copy of Ama's holy book. That sacred text had been written in Menekarian, like most of the volumes spread before him now. His mother had told him that the language of Menekar was the most widely written in the known world, even outside the borders of the empire. It had become a thread binding together cities and people separated by vast distances, a common basis for trade, scholarship, and diplomacy. But it was not the only language among his books. Two of the titles, *The Physiology of Man* and *Folk-Tales of the Middle-North,* were written in High Kalyuni, a much more difficult and ancient script. Even the mendicants who came and preached in the village brandishing their copies of the Tractate wouldn't be able to understand the delicate, looping writing of the lost Mosaic Cities.

His mother had taught him so much. While most of the other villagers only knew about this tiny sliver of the world, their homes and the nearby town of Chale, the waters of the bay and the dun hills to the east, his mother had told him stories of the vastness that unfurled in every direction. Farther east, over the Bones of the World, lay the ancient cities of Menekar, where white lions curled at the feet of ruling satraps; to the far north was a frozen waste pocked by crumbling holdfasts locked in ice and sorcery; to the west the Gilded Cities glittered on the coast; and to the south, beyond the sea, was where the mysterious Shan ruled in their Empire of Swords and Flowers. Thoughts of such places had stirred him when he was younger, and he had spent countless hours imagining himself as a bravo of Lyr or a Skein thane.

He hadn't indulged in those dreamings since his mother's death a year ago. No, not her death. Her murder.

A rapping at the door startled him.

Keilan hurriedly repacked the books and slid the box back behind his pallet. Reading was looked upon with some suspicion by most of the other villagers.

He crossed the hut's one large room and opened the door a crack, then flung it wide when he saw who was standing there.

"Sella!" he cried, bending over to embrace the little, blonde girl. Her hair was matted and dirty, and as always smelled like she had slept in a barn – which was possible, as her father worked one of the farms clustered along the road running north to Chale. She hesitated a moment, and then Keilan felt her small hands on his back.

When he pulled away she glanced at him reproachfully from under long lashes, shifting her weight between her feet. "Thought you'd forgot all about me." Her mismatched eyes, one green and one blue, looked hurt.

Keilan took her by the hand and pulled her inside. He led her to one of the sitting mats, and when she flopped down he walked over to the hearth and removed the lid from the big iron cook pot. "Do you want some stew? It's cold but tasty. Even got a pinch of salt in it."

Sella nodded gratefully and accepted a bowl. As she slurped it down he studied her, looking for how she'd changed in the months since he'd last seen her. Sella's dress was a bit more ragged than he remembered, and she must have grown, as her sandals now appeared painfully small. She was only a few years younger than him, maybe eleven or twelve, but she still looked like a child, with her smudged cheeks and scraped elbows and thin, knobby arms and legs.

She finished with a satisfied sigh and handed the bowl back to him. "You never come round no more. You getting too big to play?"

Keilan smiled and shook his head. "It's not like that. I got to help my da out on the water."

Sella's face soured, her mouth drawing down into a pout. "But the other boys your age don't help their das. How come you have to?"

Keilan drummed his fingers on the side of the bowl she'd passed to him, thinking of the best way to explain things to her. "Well . . . you know, Sella, that working the nets needs two. After . . . after my ma was gone, my da didn't want to fish with Uncle Davin anymore. So he asked me to come help him. I know it's not natural for boys to fish the bay before they do their night-dive, but my da never really gave much care to how things are supposed to be done."

She was quiet for a moment, chewing her lip in thought. Keilan had other suspicions as to why his father brought him out onto the water almost every day – to keep him close, keep him safe. But he didn't think Sella would understand, so he didn't mention that.

Sella's expression relaxed as she arrived at some decision. "Well," she said, "you're not fishing today, yeah? So how about we go down to the rocks, see what the storm tossed up?"

Keilan felt some tension he hadn't even known he'd been holding leak away, and he grinned. "That sounds great."

Sella took the lead, as always, slipping through the grasping branches and brambles like some forest spirit, while Keilan followed behind, pausing constantly to unhook something that had snagged his clothes or tangled in his hair. The path had been worn clear back when they used to go down to the rocks most every day, but the stunted little forest that separated the village from the rocks had spilled into it over the past year. Or maybe he'd just gotten bigger and clumsier.

"You still go to the rocks sometimes?" Keilan asked, scrambling over the rotted remains of a dead tree, beetles the length of his thumb vanishing into the scarred wood.

"Sometimes," Sella called back over her shoulder. "It's not as much fun without you. But no one bothers me, which is nice. Don't have to weed the garden or muck the pens, and the others don't ever come here."

The others. Keilan knew she meant the children of the village, the sons and daughters of the fisherfolk. The relationship between the village and the northern farms was frayed – scratching sustenance from the ground and raising pigs was no way to live, and Keilan suspected that the farmers thought the same of those who reaped Elara's bounty. The farmers had arrived ten years ago, refugees from one of the interminable wars that always seemed to be simmering somewhere in the Shattered Kingdoms, bringing not only their plows and horses but also the golden sun of Ama. Many of the villagers had even begun wearing the copper discs of the faithful in the years since, and Keilan had heard more than a few fisherfolk grumble that the poor harvests brought out of the bay recently was a sign of the Deep Ones' displeasure with this encroachment by the eastern god.

While the enmity between the farmers and fisherfolk was usually confined to hard looks and muttered words, their children held no qualms about open conflict. A lone child found in enemy territory would be taunted and chased, and perhaps even beaten if tensions between the two were running particularly high at that time. Keilan knew his friendship with Sella was a rarity, but it had happened because they were both outcasts within their communities, he because of his mother and she due to her eyes, which were considered unlucky, a curse by some vengeful spirit.

Lost in his thoughts Keilan tripped over an upraised root and went sprawling onto the moss and soft loam of the forest floor. Brushing dirt from his face he glanced up just as Sella vanished in a flash of golden hair through the thicket ahead.

Sighing at his clumsiness Keilan stumbled to his feet and followed, crashing through the tangle where she had disappeared and pushing into the clearing beyond.

"Sella! Sella, wait . . ." the words died in his throat.

They were not alone. Sella stood a ways off, head down so that her hair obscured her face. She shuffled her feet and did not look up.

Leaning against a tree was Keilan's cousin Malik, the son of his Uncle Davin, and flanking him were Fen and Tharin, two other boys from the village. Malik was only a few months older than him, but he overtopped Keilan by a head and weighed at least two or three stones more. He looked very different from his father – where Davin was thin and crooked and burnt brown by endless hours at sea, Malik was broad and fat, with sloping shoulders, his skin a pasty white. He grinned when he saw Keilan's surprise, showing where his two front-teeth had been knocked out.

"Now give me," Sella said into the silence. Keilan noticed that her hands were balled into fists.

"Give you what, grub?" Malik shared a smirk with Fen, pulling something from his belt. It looked like a doll whittled from wood, crudely painted. Malik stroked its straw hair in mock tenderness.

"Give me Esmi! You promised!" Sella cried, her voice cracking.

Malik snorted a laugh and tossed the doll at her feet. Sella made no move to pick it up, and Keilan could see that she was shaking.

"Why are you here?" Keilan asked, taking a step back as Malik pushed himself from the tree.

"Wanted to talk to you," his cousin said, strolling closer. "Haven't seen you in a while."

"Been busy helping my da."

Malik stopped a dozen paces away, hooked his thumbs into his belt and whistled. "Yeah, you're a big fisherman now. You must be pretty happy you got out on a boat before I did."

"I never even thought about that."

Malik's piggish black eyes narrowed. "I did. And it don't strike me as being very fair, what with you being only half-fisherman. Half-fisherman and half-whore."

"Me and my da caught more fish than yours did yesterday."

Malik reached down and scooped up a rock. "Heard about that. Da says that's because you're like your ma. That you do some spell and all the fish go swim over to your boat. And then my da and his da and his da," Malik pointed to the others with him, "don't have anything to sell to that ugly old fishmonger, and we get hit when our das come home and our mas ask why there's no money." He glanced over at his friends. "Now does that sound fair to you two?"

"Don't sound fair at all," Fen said, staring hard at Keilan. There was a fresh bruise darkening his freckled cheek.

"What we gonna do about this, Mal?" Tharin said softly. Of all the boys in the village, Tharin made Keilan the most uneasy. He'd never caught him smiling or laughing, except when hurting others, and his gray eyes were always strangely empty, almost lifeless. He'd seen the same look in the eyes of the shark his father had brought up the day before.

"Me? I think we should beat him raw."

A coldness settled over Keilan. He thought about running, about turning and dashing through the woods back to the village, barricading himself in his house and waiting for his da to return. But when he looked at his cousin and his friends he didn't see the children he'd grown up with; instead, he saw their fathers, the men who had taken his mother. He felt himself tense, but not to flee.

Malik seemed to notice this, and something like uncertainty flitted across his face. Then his expression hardened.

"You know, my da told me that the only thing worse than a whore is a witch. A whore dirties her own body, but a witch dirties the world itself. The way I see it, though, your ma was both a witch and a whore, so that's got to be worse, right? Isn't that right?" Malik stepped closer, hefting the rock in his hand. "Ain't that right?" he screamed, rearing back.

Keilan ducked as the rock whistled past his head, and then had only a moment to brace himself before Malik's bulk slammed into him. They fell in a tangle, knocking the breath from Keilan, and blows hammered his stomach and chest. The bigger boy tried to pin him, but Keilan managed to squirm out of his grasp and throw his fist out blindly. He hit something soft and Malik squealed in pain and rolled away holding his face, shouting out curses. Keilan scrambled to his feet, steadying himself against the trunk of a tree, his heartbeat loud in his ears. Fen rushed over and helped Malik stand as blood spurted from between his fingers.

"You broke my nose! I'll kill you!"

Ignoring the pain in his ribs, Keilan reached down and picked up a fallen branch, a hard length of old wood. There was a rage in him, and he stalked forward toward the two boys. Their eyes widened in sudden fear as he lunged closer, swinging the branch hard. Fen raised his arm to try and ward away the blow, but the force of it nearly knocked him over, and he shrieked loudly, clutching his shoulder and stumbling backward. The second swing caught Malik in the head, and he fell like a sack of grain, his legs suddenly boneless.

Then Tharin was between them, iron glinting in his hand. "Careful, careful," he said, his voice barely above a whisper. He handled the boning knife with an easy familiarity.

Keilan stepped away, holding Tharin's blank gaze. His grip on the wood was suddenly slick with sweat.

Grimacing in pain Fen helped the dazed Malik find his feet. He flashed Keilan a look of hate and fear as he led his cousin into the woods, and they vanished quickly, the sounds of their blundering through the underbrush fading.

Tharin lingered, expressionless. Then a smile slowly spread across his face. "I'll see you again," he murmured, and turned and sauntered into the trees.

Keilan stayed standing in the clearing, breathing heavily, his grip on the length of wood white-knuckled, until a light touch on his arm made him jump. He whirled around and found Sella, her face miserable. In her other hand she clutched the little wooden doll tightly to her chest.

"Kay . . ." she said softly, "I'm sorry."

Keilan blinked, as if seeing her for the first time. He was surprised to find that the anger he had expected to feel from her betrayal wasn't there, and he managed to force a little smile. She tentatively returned it, her mismatched eyes starting to water.

"Hey there, don't cry," Keilan said, wiping away a tear as it trickled down her cheek. "I'm all right."

She sniffled loudly, even as her smile widened. "You beat them good."

"I guess I did." Keilan dropped the branch and gently prodded his aching ribs, wincing. "Maybe I'll be a mighty warrior yet."

"I think you're already a mighty warrior," she said, so seriously that Keilan couldn't hold back a little burst of laughter, which only made the pain worse.

"Ha, ouch, thanks."

"Should we . . . should we go back to the village? Will they be waiting for you?"

Keilan shrugged. "I'm not scared of them. Yes, back to the village."

"Okay." Sella moved next to him so he could lean against her, which he really didn't need, but the attempt to help was so earnest that he allowed her to bear a little of his weight.

"So," he said as they passed into the trees, "tell me about Esmi."

3: KEILAN

"**MAM RU GAVE** her to me," Sella explained during their walk back to the village, guiding Keilan with exaggerated care around where a tangle of roots had squirmed onto the path. "Said Esmi's really old. Used to belong to her own daughter; she died of the weeping a long time ago. I brought her some nightswort I found in the woods, and she said I looked so lonely these days, what with you gone, that she rummaged around and pulled out Esmi, gave her a spit of paint and some new hair, and said I didn't have to be alone no more."

Keilan held out his hand, and after a moment's hesitation Sella passed him the doll. It was carefully made of hard, pale wood, with clever interlocking joints that still moved smoothly despite the doll's evident age.

"I think Malik must've seen your da leave this morning without you," Sella continued, taking back Esmi. "Then he went lookin' for me. I was picking daisies for my ma and suddenly I looked up, and he was there with those two big ugly aurochs, Tharin and what's-his-name, ah, Fen. He took Esmi from me and said I got to go bring you to the rocks if I wanted her back. Said he'd smash her to bits if I told anyone. I was worried what they were going to do to you when we got there, but I couldn't go back to Mam Ru and tell her that her daughter's doll was gone."

Keilan patted her arm reassuringly. They had passed out of the small forest as they talked and now waded across a field of scratchy, knee-high grass. A flock of dark birds hidden in the scrub rose into the air around them, screeching. Keilan watched as they dwindled into the distance, becoming a line of ink scrawled against the gray sky.

"Well, Esmi's back and Malik has a bloody nose so I think everything worked out pretty well. I . . ." He trailed off, squinting ahead at their village. Something was happening there. Between a few of the dirt-walled and reed-thatched huts he could see a crowd had gathered around the rock at the village's heart.

"Mendicant," Sella said, shielding her eyes from the sun.

"Your eyes are better than mine. What do you see?"

"There's a man with black hair up on the Speaker's rock, dressed all in white. He's waving his arms around something fierce. You wanna go see?"

Keilan gingerly touched his ribs. The pain had already started fading to a dull ache. Nothing broken, at least. "Yeah."

Most of the village seemed to have come out to hear the mendicant preach. Men too old to help on the fishing boats had set aside their tzalik boards and mugs of grog to listen, many with sour expressions that spoke eloquently enough as to what they thought about this interloping eastern god. More excited were the children that clustered around the base of the rock, hoping for one of the Tractate's many stories about warring heroes, crafty demons, and wicked sorcerers. Then there were the village's women, hovering on the edge of the square as if feeling guilty about not attending to their chores. Their expressions were guarded, lacking the open hostility of the elders or the unrestrained exuberance of the young, but Keilan saw more than a few amulets bearing the red-gold sunburst of Ama.

The mendicant was almost a boy himself, maybe just a few years older than Keilan. His white robes were spotless, the only color coming from the shimmering gold bands than hemmed his sleeves and hood. Around his neck a copper disc flashed like the sun itself when it caught the light. He was just finishing a story, almost dancing up on the rock as he acted out some argument or battle. The children let out a collective gasp as he finished the tale by throwing up his hands and praising Ama.

Once, a few years ago, a group of the more traditional villagers had expelled a wandering mendicant from the village, sending him scurrying back to Chale bruised and terrified. A few days later the mendicant had returned, accompanied by a dozen warriors from the local temple, who had arrayed themselves around the rock and stood silently with their hands on their swords as the cleric preached. When one of the braver fishermen had loudly cursed Ama two of the warriors had strode across the square and struck him down with the hilts of their swords. There hadn't been an attempt to stop the mendicants from telling tales of their shining god since then.

The youthful cleric took a swig from his water skin and addressed the children seated in the dirt before him. "Tell me, little ones, which holy story should we remember next?"

A chorus of requests went up. "Jenna and her cloak of gold!" "Pellus Wyrm-Tamer and the father of dragons!" "The ship of lost children!"

The mendicant held out his hands to beg for quiet. "Ah, I think you all know these stories better than I do!" He pointed at a small boy seated close to him, Seven-Finger Soman's youngest son, Gevin. "You, child, what story would bring the light of Ama into your heart?"

"I wanna hear about the Pure," Gevin mumbled, concentrating on the ground while he pulled on some of the few tenacious blades of grass that had managed to survive in the well-trodden square.

"Aye, the Pure! The Pure!" echoed some of the other children, and the mendicant smiled indulgently.

"The Pure it is, then," he said, spreading his arms wide and drawing himself up taller. The children quieted, staring at the cleric with wide, expectant eyes.

"I know this story!" whispered Sella, tugging on Keilan's sleeve.

"Everyone knows this one," he hissed back, "I doubt there's a more famous tale in the world."

The sun vanished behind a bank of swift-moving clouds, casting the square into shadow. He was a true showman, Keilan decided, as the mendicant seized this moment to start speaking, his voice heavy with dramatic power. The children muttered and shifted, glancing excitedly at each other.

"Long before the Sundering, before the black ice swallowed the north, before the Star Towers shattered and fell, before even the waters of this sea lapped upon the shores of these lands, holy Menekar shined like a beacon, casting far and wide the light of blessed Ama. From his alabaster throne the emperor sent forth his legions, and the princes and chieftains of the cities on the plains knelt in submission, welcoming Ama's blazing presence into their hearts. For we are all His servants, as the Tractate teaches us, all His children, and it is the emperor's holy task to bring His light to every nation, every people." The mendicant stretched wide his arms, encompassing the watching children.

"But the souls of men are not pure. Within us all a spark from the Void smolders, a remnant from the beginning of time, when Ama hammered the world from the darkness. This spark makes us more than the beasts – some scholars say it is even what makes us pale shadows of Ama himself – but it also allows for us to perform the most terrible, unholy acts. The Void is hunger incarnate, you see, and so within every man this spark is constantly gnawing, always unsatisfied. Dominion, wealth, the trappings of power – all men desire these things, but to seize them is meaningless, and as empty as the air.

"There arose, during the Second Age, a new breed of man. Creatures of hunger, children of the Void, removed from Ama's sheltering radiance. They had discovered how to mine the spark inside themselves, how to coax power from that tenuous thread connecting them to the dark beyond. Sorcery slid like water beading upon a strand of spider's silk, from the endless Void and across unknowable distances, into the bodies of men. And thus the Warlock Kings of Menekar rose, in all their terrible glory.

"The emperor was cast down, then hung broken above the Melichan Gate. The legions, led by treacherous men, swore their swords in service to their new masters. The mendicants and satraps who remained loyal to the old ways were slain in terrible fashion, their heads festooning the walls of the holy city. Ama, the tyrants proclaimed, had gifted them with sorcery; their power was a mark of His favor.

"But that was a lie, and upon His golden throne Ama grieved, turning away from the wickedness of His children. A world He had given them, fashioned from the terrible emptiness, a refuge from the darkness, and they had betrayed Him, ushering the Void into His creation.

"Darkness fell upon the world. It was a time of war and plague, hunger and fear. The Warlock Kings commanded terrible powers, but they knew only avarice and refused to waste their sorcery helping those they deemed little more than chattel. In the countryside the crops failed. Babes were drowned at birth, lest their deaths be long and withering. The weeping arose then, and fathers laid their children in the ground, wiping clean tiny cheeks stained by bloody tears. Locusts covered the land, and unquiet spirits wandered the plains, howling and raging at the follies of their descendants.

"Into this time of evil a child was born. It is said that a mendicant found the baby in the charred remains of a village, surrounded by the burnt bodies of his kin. Raiders had torched the town, but the flames had not touched a hair on his golden head, and in wonderment the mendicant returned with him to his lonely monastery in the foothills of the Bones, the child swaddled in his own spare robes. Tethys they named him, 'The Unburnt' in one of the first tongues, though the meaning of that word would change in later years. They raised him in the old ways, free of the taint of the new, corrupt faith that held sway in the cities. His feats awed them: by his tenth birthday he could recite the Tractate, by his fourteenth he was said to be able to wash disease from a body like the great healers of old. Villagers brought to him their sick, asked for his blessing, begged for him to settle their disputes. His fame spread, until even in distant Menekar his name was heard.

"A servant was dispatched, a man steeped in the unholy powers of his masters. Ambitious and cunning, he saw in the boy a weapon to use back in court, a means to elevate himself among his rival black sorcerers, perhaps even to the side of the Warlock King. If, of course, the stories they said were true. So he arrived at the monastery cloaked in the guise of a leprous old man, begging for help from the famous boy. Tethys frowned when he saw the hunched stranger, feeling something was amiss, and knowing he was discovered the sorcerer let his illusion melt away. The watching mendicants gasped, the abbot himself falling to his knees and pressing his forehead to the cold ground, for in that cursed age even the holy men of Ama were forced to pay obeisance before sorcerers. But Tethys stood tall, and matched the visitor's stare.

"'It is good you do not grovel,' the sorcerer said, 'for you are not sheep.'

"'I bow only before Ama,' Tethys replied, and the sorcerer's smile turned cold.

"'You would not bow before your emperor, then, the chosen of Ama, His vessel in this world?'

Tethys shook his head sadly. 'The emperor is dead, his anointed line extinguished long before my birth. Ama has turned away from Menekar.'

The mendicants pressing themselves to the ground gasped, and some could not hold back burning tears, because they knew that their boy would now die a horrible death, a traitor's death.

But the sorcerer laughed. 'You have listened too carefully to the teachings of these fools. They are animals to men like us. We are gods to them. Come, return with me to Menekar. The emperor will want to meet you, and with my help you could rise high, perhaps even one day carry a thorned flail of the Seven, command great armies, and give counsel to he who sits the alabaster throne.'

"'And if I refuse?' the boy asked, and at that question a fell wind rose, rippling the robes of the prostrate men, but leaving Tethys and the sorcerer untouched.

"'Then I shall tear down these walls, and feed the souls of those I find within to a creature of the Void, a demon of great and terrible power.'

The boy nodded. 'Very well. Give me one more night here. I would meditate at the shrine atop this mountain, and ask Ama for his guidance.'

"'As you said, boy,' the sorcerer snarled, 'Ama has abandoned us. He fears us now, and what we will become.'

"But he allowed the boy to leave, to start upon the long and winding path to the mountain's top, where in another age a famous holy man had once lived. Then he commanded the abbot to bring forth wine and to slaughter the fattest calf, and dispatched another mendicant bearing the imperial seal to a nearby village, demanding that the youngest and most beautiful women be sent up to the monastery.

"The night passed, and in the cold, clear light of morning the boy returned, striding into the monastery's great hall. What had happened to him atop that mountain has never been said, but now his eyes shone with the radiance of Ama, and in his hand was a sword of pale, white metal.

"The sorcerer cast aside the girl he dandled on his knee and stood, blazing with dark power, an invisible force overturning the altar he sat behind and scattering the remnants of the previous night's feast. 'What trickery is this, boy?' he boomed. 'Do you truly hope to challenge an initiate of the Black Dawn?'

"Tethys said nothing as he approached. The sorcerer marshaled his strength and flung it at the boy, a torrent of shadowy fire that washed over the hall. Tables and chairs burst asunder, the great metal sun of Ama that hung down from the rafters dripped in the unnatural heat, but the boy walked calmly through the raging maelstrom, and without hesitating plunged his white metal sword through the sorcerer's wards and into his heart!"

The mendicant suddenly leaped from the Speaker's Rock into the crowd of seated children, thrusting out with an invisible sword. Laughter and cheers rippled through his audience as he danced among them, hacking and slashing at imaginary foes.

"Word of what had transpired at the monastery spread quickly, and many flocked to see the child who had slain a sorcerer, whose belief in Ama shielded him from dark powers. The most pious, the most resolute of his new followers, Tethys brought to the shrine atop the mountain, and if they were found worthy they would return after a night of prayer with the holy light of Ama spilling from their eyes. And so were the Pure born, the paladins of Ama, warriors who moved through dark magic like fish swim in rushing streams.

"Tethys led the rebellion that would consume the Warlock King and his depraved court. With his white-metal sword he opened the throat of that false emperor as he cowered upon the alabaster throne, forever staining the white stone black with the demon's blood. And when the people wanted to lift up their hero, gird him with the imperial mantle, and set the diadem upon his brow, he refused, and vanished forever into the Bones, journeying west. But the Pure endured, the greatest warriors our world has ever known."

The mendicant bowed, to scattered applause. An old man in the shade near Keilan snorted and shook his head, turning back to his tzalik board, gnarled fingers idly stroking one of the dark, sea-smooth stones.

"Do you think we'll get another story?" Sella asked excitedly, the shadow of the morning's events finally gone from her voice.

Keilan watched the village's children clutch at the mendicant's robes as he waded through them to get back to the Speaker's rock. "I'm not sure if they'll let him leave."

The mendicant stooped to unhook particularly tenacious little fingers from the golden hem of his clothes, then paused as the child said something in words too soft for Keilan to hear.

The young cleric tousled the boy's hair and straightened, turning to address his audience again. "The child offers a wise question. He asks whether sorcerers still walk this world, and if the Pure will protect us." The mendicant paused theatrically. "Black magic is practiced in these lands! We should be ever vigilant. If you suspect sorcery you must tell me, or another mendicant, so we might bring the Pure here to cleanse the foul taint!"

The mendicant moved to climb the rock again, but the tugging on his robes was insistent, and with a slightly less patient expression he once more bent to listen to the child. Soman's boy again, Keilan realized.

Something passed between them, and the mendicant's smile faded. He turned his head, following the boy's outstretched hand, towards where Keilan stood beside the old men playing tzalik in the shade. A cold wave washed over Keilan as he met the mendicant's surprised eyes, and he reached out to steady himself against Sella.

"What is it? What's wrong?" she asked.

Everything, Keilan wanted to tell her. *Everything*.

4: THE EMPEROR

THE ROOTS OF power, mused the emperor Gerixes Meneum III, were sunk deep in perception. An army was important, of course, the visible trunk holding aloft the rest, but without the fear and awe engendered by the imperial mantle, the tree of empire would most certainly topple at the first strong storm. Invisible, but the foundation of everything else.

And similar to how the roots of a great oak might be glimpsed rippling beneath the forest's surface, perceptions of his authority could only be measured in the reverence shining in upturned faces as the imperial palanquin passed by, or the way in which the crowds shrank back when he rode among them, resplendent in silver-flashing armor, accompanied by the Pure. He was the center of all this pomp and grandeur – divine, august, remote yet personal, offering to his subjects both the open hand of the mother and the closed fist of the father. They loved and feared him, as was the way in every family.

Which was why he did not allow his boredom to show through when he sat in audience, no matter how weary he was of state affairs. The imperial mask must be without cracks.

Today had been particularly tiresome, however. First that obnoxious Calliphon of House Belicau had come and fairly demanded – demanded! – that several more legions be dispatched east to protect his herds from the lizardlords. Gerixes had gritted his teeth to keep himself from ordering Velimus to collect the insolent satrap's head there and then, and had instead held up his imperial scepter to show that he had heard. The emperor had become remarkably adept at focusing the sunlight that poured through the window behind him with the aid of the nine-pointed crystal topping his scepter, and he had found that blinding those who annoyed him to be a much better way of expressing his displeasure than abandoning his serene composure.

Calliphon had shown only the faintest shiver of uncertainty as the light had played across his face – either he was braver than Gerixes thought, or his years away from the imperial court had left him incapable of reading into the subtleties of the emperor's actions. The last person Gerixes had raised his scepter on, a representative from the padarasha of Kesh come to collect on a loan, still wallowed in the oubliette he'd ordered him dragged away to. That reminded the emperor – he should set the fool free.

Gerixes gestured for his white vizier, Torrinis, to approach his throne. The ancient minister shuffled closer, his parchment-thin skin the color of cured vellum stretched tight over a strangely tapered skull. Torrinis had always seemed on the verge of death, even in the emperor's first memories. He remembered the morbid fascination he'd felt as a child watching this cadaver draped in robes of the purest white bend to whisper in his father's ear, and the comforting squeeze mother had given his hand when she'd noticed his unease.

"Torrinis," Gerixes said, trying not to wrinkle his nose at the sweet smell of decay that accompanied his white vizier, "we believe it is time to release that Keshian brat."

The old minister bobbed his bald, spotted head. "Your Grace is most wise. Unfortunately, cel Faraq caught a terrible chill and . . . expired yesterday."

The emperor frowned. "The padarasha will not be pleased. That fool was some distant relative."

"Should we repay the loan, then, your grace? Perhaps that would temper the padarasha's anger."

"No. Our coffers are still as light as they were a few days ago. Dispatch a delegation west with our condolences and a white lion for his menagerie."

"It shall be as you say, Your Grace."

Gerixes waved his white vizier away and beckoned for his black to approach. Wen Xenxing detached from the shadows and waddled closer, rolls of flesh trembling beneath his loose, dark robes. His up-tilted black eyes were fixed on the floor before the alabaster throne; despite thirty years in Menekar he still could not bring himself to meet the emperor's gaze – some lingering conditioning from his early years among the Thousand Voices of the Jade Court. Wen had been captured as a young boy at the Battle of the Shivering Stones, the greatest victory for the Menekarian legions over the Shan in centuries, and it had amused the old emperor to raise a child once being groomed to ascend to the Phoenix Throne in his own household. Wen had proven to possess a devious mind, eventually coming to don the robes of the black vizier.

While Torrinis dealt with the quotidian problems of the empire, Wen attended to the shadows.

"Your Grace," murmured the vizier, his words flavored by a slight accent.

"I'm sending a delegation to Kesh. I want several of your favorites traveling among the servants, ones we can trust in all matters. Perhaps a knowledge of poisons would be useful."

Plump fingers fluttered in acknowledgement. "Your words are like unwatered wine to this wretch's ears. I shall instruct them personally."

"And now are we finished for the day?"

Wen flashed a quick smile. "The delegation from Dymoria is here, if the imperial presence wishes to see them."

Gerixes sighed and rubbed his chin. He'd kept the Crimson Queen's men waiting since the early morning in an unventilated antechamber, attending to every tiny matter of state while they suffered in their heavy brocade and furs. The proud and the powerful often made mistakes when irritated. He'd been considering postponing the audience until tomorrow, but his curiosity was getting the better of him.

"Very well – send them in."

Wen pressed his forehead to the blue-veined marble of the top step and hurried down. The black vizier spoke quietly to Velimus, then melted back into the shadows as the captain of the Pure nodded curtly toward the emperor and moved to unbar the audience chamber's massive ebonwood doors. Gerixes glanced about, assuring himself that the dignitaries could not hope but be impressed.

The imperial audience chamber was the largest single room in the labyrinthine Selthari Palace, a forest of stone columns decorated with friezes extolling the glory of Menekar, mostly of legionaries with upraised swords cutting through the enemies of the Empire, and long lines of shackled prisoners winding toward stylized representations of the imperial city. Tattered mementoes of the legion's martial brilliance hung slack between the pillars: the bloody remnants of silken Shan battle standards, stitched with strange geometric designs that seemed to float up from the fabric; the pale, flayed hides of lizards once bonded to Qell warlords; brightly colored streamers flown by the mercenary armies of the Gilded Cities; and banners adorned with the heraldic sigils of Shattered Kingdom lords. Many of those countries and cities now considered themselves allies of Menekar, but no emperor would ever be foolish enough to return the captured standards. They served as very important reminders.

Glittering dustmotes floated in the late afternoon light shining through the huge window that backed the alabaster seat of the emperors; the throne crouched like a white lion of the plains atop a nine-tiered dais, each of those steps dedicated to a different facet of Ama, The Light Above. Flakes of quartz set into the marble floor painted a flashing avenue leading from the entranceway to the base of the throne, and flanking this approach was an entire cohort of the Pure, the elite warriors of the empire, armored in white-enameled mail. None wore helms, and copper-colored tattoos webbed their hairless scalps. The holy light of Ama shone from their eyes; this was the mark of the god's favor, the sight that allowed them to see the taint of sorcery. Nothing unnatural could approach the emperor while his Pure stood guard – and while this always gave him comfort, it especially did so now, as the delegation from Dymoria filed into the chamber. Wen had brought him strange tidings regarding this Crimson Queen.

They were only a dozen strong, with black beards forked in the style of the Gilded Cities, garbed in sumptuous many-colored robes. Sashes of black cloth cinched their waists, and silver flashed about their necks and fingers. They were large and burly, hairy as bears. Gerixes held his flail and scepter perfectly still and stared straight ahead, ignoring them as they approached. The delegation was not only men, he suddenly realized, his jaw clenching. There was at least one woman in the group, as heavy-set as her companions, her auburn hair bound into a long braid. The gall of these Dymorians! They must know that parading a woman before the Pure and the emperor without asking for permission first would be construed as an insult. He would have to punish Torrinis for not informing him of her presence.

One of the foreigners drew the emperor's attention: he was taller than the rest, young and clean-shaven, clad in a simple gray tunic with a bright red cloak secured by a golden brooch. His face was calm and his lanky body relaxed, but Gerixes thought he could sense an alertness, as if he was constantly taking the measure of his surroundings. This must be a member of the queen's newly-formed Scarlet Guard. Wen claimed she was building an elite fighting force without peer in all of western Araen – natural rivals for his Pure, long the finest warriors outside of cursed Shan.

Velimus stepped before the throne, facing the diplomats. The golden serpent bracelet coiled around his bared right arm flashed in the sun. "His Imperial Majesty, the Divine Light of the East, Chosen of Ama, Shield of the North, the emperor Gerixes of House Meneum, third of his name, welcomes the delegation from the far west."

An older Dymorian approached the throne and bowed deep. His hair and beard were clotted with gray, but the eyes under his heavy black brows were shrewd.

"Exalted emperor," he boomed, sweeping his arm to encompass his entourage, "we who have journeyed from distant Dymoria are honored to stand in your presence. Our hearts are filled with the wonders of your empire, the beauty of your people, and the flashing brilliance of your legions. Our queen Cein d'Kara, first of her name, gives thanks that such a mighty nation should count itself a stalwart friend of Dymoria."

"Old friends indeed," said Gerixes, for the first time looking directly upon the delegation, "but we see new faces. Where is Count d'Tarren?"

The speaker smiled, and behind his salted beard his teeth were very white. "Alas, Count d'Tarren was found guilty of fomenting rebellion against our queen, and has been put to death, along with other conspirators. I am Count d'Kelv, her majesty's humble servant." The count flourished another low bow, his beard nearly brushing the floor.

Gerixes, of course, knew exactly what had befallen the old count. Although many of Wen's sources had gone silent since the new queen's ascension, several reports had trickled back of the attempt to cast down the young monarch and install a distant cousin in her stead, and the bloody reprisals that had followed. The emperor was impressed with how smoothly this Count d'Kelv had both admitted to the plot and glossed over its significance. He was very confident, this one.

"A shame," Gerixes continued, "d'Tarren was well-loved by our father. They often hawked together when he visited, and the old emperor even bade us call him uncle. We are surprised and saddened by his treachery."

The perfect white smile did not falter. "It was a peculiar madness, Light of the East, and our queen realizes the old count was not in his right mind. Many suspect he had been ensorcelled, or manipulated by dark powers to go against his rightful liege. It was with a heavy heart that our queen called for his head – but as the emperor knows, mercy will be seen as weakness, and only embolden the enemies of the throne."

She has his loyalty, the emperor realized. He'd hoped to gain an ally in the court of this Cein d'Kara, but d'Kelv was too polished and clever by half.

The Crimson Queen. Gerixes restrained himself from sneering at the thought of her. Rumors had swirled for almost two decades that her father, Jeryme d'Kara, had fathered a bastard while adventuring across the Derravin Ocean, but not much credence had been paid to those whisperings until Cein had suddenly appeared at his side about ten years past, barely more than a child, sporting the same fiery hair that defined the d'Kara line. The sickly, childless king had declared her his successor, and she had formally ascended to the Dragon Throne two years ago when he had succumbed to a wasting disease.

Nothing to truly alarm Menekar – Dymoria had traditionally been a minor kingdom north of the Gilded Cities, a rolling, forested land in the shadow of the Bones of the World, raided by the barbaric Skein and in turn making war on the Gilded Cities to the south. But the kingdom's transformation over just a few years had been . . . remarkable. First, the young queen had led her army north to confront a feared Skein king, who had raided with impunity across the Serpent for a decade, and had dealt a crushing defeat to the northern barbarians. Then the poet-prince of Vis, with its iron walls and oracular birds, had offered his sword to the queen. Her northern flank protected, the new queen had turned her attention south, reclaiming territory lost over the centuries to other cities. In a few bold strokes Dymoria had become the greatest power in the West, and suddenly a threat to Menekar. Not since Min-Ceruth and the Mosaic Cities of the Kalyuni Imperium had immolated each other on a sorcerous pyre nearly a thousand years ago had such a nation resolved from the shifting chaos beyond the Bones, and the emperors of Menekar had played no small part in that.

The emperor raised his flail to show his appreciation for Count d'Kelv's words. They could have been lifted almost verbatim from *Beneath God*, Emperor Chalcedon's classic treatise on ruling, and a book Gerixes had grown up reading. *He knows my tastes, and tries to play to them.*

Indeed, usually these sorts of diplomatic exchanges devolved into bouts of mutual flattery, but this was no typical audience. He must try and knock the count off-balance, glean what he could about this queen's true intentions.

"Tell us, Count d'Kelv, why your queen has waited nearly two years to send her first emissaries to us. D'Tarren graced these halls at least once a year, bringing with him gifts of amber, ebonwood, and spices from across the ocean, and always remembered to thank us for our assistance during the Cleansing."

A tremor in the count's face at the mention of the Cleansing, almost instantly controlled. Satisfaction flooded Gerixes – he had hit upon something. But what, exactly? He had his suspicions, though it would be foolish to leap to conclusions.

And, admittedly, d'Kelv was showing little emotion standing within two columns of the Pure, the primary architects of the Cleansing. The sorcery-scenting warriors of Ama, immune to magic, their very presence debilitating to those who corrupted the natural order, had washed over the shattered western lands in the wake of the cataclysms that had ended the wizardry wars, helping to put all the surviving sorcerers to the sword. That had been the zenith of Menekarian power, with imperial legions spanning the continent, and if the Shan's black-bellied junks had not arrived in the devastated south, fleeing a mysterious disaster in their own distant homeland, then the empire would have long ago have fulfilled its destiny of bringing Ama's light to all of Araen.

"Menekar's help in restoring order after the destruction of the old world will never be forgotten." Count d'Kelv snapped his fingers, and one of his subordinates stepped forward, holding something in cupped hands. "As thanks we have again brought the riches of our land to you, amber jewelry for your concubines and great planks of ebonwood ready for carving. And this."

The younger Dymorian went to one knee, lowering his head and extending his arms towards where the emperor sat. Light glinted off whatever it was he held.

Gerixes gestured, and Torrinis tottered over to take the proffered object. The white vizier turned it over a few times, prodding it for hidden needles or other traps, and then climbed halfway to where the emperor sat and held out the gift. It was a tiny bird, ingeniously crafted from shining metal, with gems for eyes and copper-wire wings inset with chunks of colored glass. A silver key sprouted from its back.

"Wind the key," d'Kelv said from below, and after a quick nod from the emperor, Torrinis gave the key a few sharp twists.

The white vizier gasped and almost dropped the bird as it stirred to life in his palm. Glittering wings flexed, and as the tiny automaton's beak opened and closed Gerixes heard snatches of metallic-sounding birdsong.

The emperor cast a glance at Velimus, but the captain of the Pure shook his head. Not magic, then.

"Wondrous," Gerixes intoned flatly, "does it fly?"

That seemed to take the count aback. "No, Light of the East."

"Pity," said the emperor with a sigh, relishing the annoyance he thought he glimpsed in d'Kelv's carefully guarded face. "I almost thought it a worthy present for one of my nephews."

"If our gift displeases the emperor, my apologies. All know that the wonders of the west appear pale in the light from the east."

Gerixes shooed Torrinis and the strange, little bird away. He would have his learned men dissect the thing later, though he harbored little confidence that they could puzzle out the workings of its mechanical innards. Similar objects had come before his court and retained their mysteries, despite much interest from the astrologers and mathematicians of Menekar.

"It is good that you brought us such a toy. There have been rumors – vile and baseless, of course – that your queen has opened her arms to sorcery. Now we see that it is only the clever craft of the artificers that has fueled these malicious lies."

Gerixes leaned forward, trying to bring the entire force of his imperial presence down upon the Dymorian emissary. "It is a lie, isn't it?"

D'Kelv stiffened, matching the emperor's stare. "Dymoria has long been more forgiving of sorcery than other kingdoms. Without the windwarden's help we never would have crossed the Derravin and discovered the Sunset Lands. Soothsayers and bonewhisperers have plied their trades in our kingdom for centuries."

Gerixes waved away the count's words. "We are not referring to hedge wizardry. Minor village charms did not come within a hair's breadth of cracking open this world and plunging us all into eternal darkness." The emperor paused and breathed deep, trying to still his shaking hands. He was dangerously close to losing control. "If your queen should aid or abet the exploration of deeper sorceries . . ." The threat hung heavy in the silence that followed.

Finally, d'Kelv cleared his throat. "I assure you, Light of the East, that no one would dare court the same black arts that produced the cataclysms of the past."

Gerixes rose suddenly from his seat, and the count took an instinctive step back. Good – he felt fear. "Look!" cried the emperor, gesturing at the russet stains that marred his alabaster throne. "Do you see? The blood of the last Warlock King of Menekar, dead now for near two thousand years!"

The necks of the Dymorian delegation craned forward to glimpse this legend made real. "Once sorcerers ruled here, as they did in Min-Ceruth and the Mosaic Cities. Our souls fed their magics, our flesh their bodies as they pursued their dreams of immortality. We were but chattel . . ."

The emperor paused when he noticed Velimus climbing the steps towards him. The captain of the Pure's expression was strange . . . He looked almost uncertain, which Gerixes had never seen before.

"Your Grace," he whispered, leaning close to the emperor's ear, "there is something odd about one of –"

The world tilted, shuddered. A cacophony of shattering glass came from behind the throne. "My lord!" Velimus cried, knocking Gerixes to the floor and covering him with his body as shards from the destroyed window rained down.

The light flickered and dimmed as chaos erupted in the audience chamber. Gerixes watched in mute astonishment, his cheek pressed to the cold marble, as one of the Dymorians sketched a shimmering blue shield in the air while the Pure broke ranks and closed on them. Sorcery! In the Selthari Palace!

The count held up his hands, and Gerixes could briefly hear his voice over the din, "No! We did not –" and then he disappeared beneath flashing swords and swirling white cloaks.

Moments later the crackling blue barrier faded as a warrior of the Pure burst through it unaffected and thrust his blade into the wizard's chest.

Velimus's weight vanished from his back and Gerixes pushed himself to his feet, staggering slightly. "Kill them!" he shrieked, waving his arms at the few huddled Dymorians still alive. "Kill them all!"

At his words the Pure closed with ruthless efficiency. Swords rose and fell, and blood splashed the marble floors. Very soon only the Scarlet Guardsman remained, his back to one of the pillars, fending off three of the Pure with a sword he had managed to wrest from somewhere. His face showed no fear, only grim determination, as he struggled to keep the white-metal blades of the Pure at bay. He was skilled, no doubt, and facing death he fought like a cornered lion. A sword slipped past his defenses to score his side,and he stumbled to one knee; as the Pure lunged forward, Gerixes found himself yelling.

"Stop!"

As if of a single mind the white-clad warriors pulled back and raised their blades toward where he stood panting beside the throne. Behind them the Scarlet Guardsman leaned heavily against the pillar, clutching the wound in his side, his gray tunic rapidly darkening.

Gerixes steadied himself against his throne. Yes, best to keep this one alive. Wen had an amazing facility for extracting information from even the most conditioned, and there were many answers he wanted.

"Lay down your sword, warrior, and you will not be harmed," he said, summoning as much of the imperial command as he could muster.

Wincing, the guardsman straightened, meeting the emperor's gaze. His eyes were still calm, Gerixes realized, feeling his skin prickle. Without fear.

The warrior raised his sword in a mimicry of the Pure's salute, then without hesitation reversed the blade and fell forward. He made no sound, only twitched and was still.

Silence. Among the carnage the Pure stood motionless, staring up at him expectantly with pupilless eyes of shining gold. His small flock of advisors and sycophants poked heads from around the pillars they had fled behind, also watching him. There was something warm and moist in his left palm. He glanced down. A sliver of glass had sliced his hand, and without truly knowing why he did so, Gerixes held his closed fist over the alabaster throne of Menekar and allowed a few drops of imperial blood to fall and splatter among the ancient stains.

"Velimus," the emperor said absently as he studied the falling droplets.

"Yes, Your Grace," answered the captain of the Pure, hurrying to kneel beside him.

"You have failed me." Gerixes turned towards Velimus and struck him across the face, leaving a bloody smear upon his cheek.

The warrior did not flinch. "I have, Your Grace. I should have sensed the sorcerer long before he even entered this chamber. The Dymorians disguised him somehow . . ."

"Or perhaps Ama did not want you to recognize him," called out Wen Xenxing from below, daintily picking his way among the sprawled bodies.

"No." Velimus said with certainty, staring at something beyond Gerixes. The emperor turned.

Splayed upon the highest dais in a tangled heap of bloody feathers and long, stick-like legs was a white heron. Glass crunched beneath his slippered feet as the emperor approached the holy bird of Ama.

"Sliced to ribbons," Gerixes murmured, glancing up at the shattered window.

"It flew through," Velimus said, "there was no attack."

Gerixes whirled on his captain. "Bringing a sorcerer here, before me, is the same as a declaration of war."

"Why would their queen take such a risk?" Torrinis asked, crouched beside Count d'Kelv's corpse.

"This was a test," said Wen. "The Dymorians must have thought that they had uncovered a way to hide the taint of sorcery from the Pure."

Cold fear coiled in the emperor's stomach. For two thousand years the Pure had been the backbone of imperial rule, Ama's gift, the only advantage men had against the obscene power of sorcerers. And now they knew it could be subverted.

Velimus prodded the dead heron with his boot. "It must have escaped from the temple grounds."

"It did not escape, you simpleton," snapped the emperor, "Ama brought it here to unmask the sorcerer, since you and your brothers were failing me so spectacularly."

"Your Grace, I will gladly fall upon my sword if you give the order. But you should remember that the Dymorians' disguise was not perfect . . . the longer they were here, the greater the sense of creeping wrongness we felt."

"Ah, well then, let us just ask future assassins to dally so that you have time to uncover their plots." Gerixes fought to push down his anger. "No, no," he sighed, approaching Velimus and laying his hand on the captain's head. "You have served the empire ably for many years. Whatever new magics this Crimson Queen has birthed, we are certain that with the blessing of Ama the Pure will rise to meet this challenge."

"Thank you, Your Grace," Velimus said, his voice solemn, "I will never fail you again."

"Good," replied Gerixes, turning from the Pure captain. "Now I think we all have things we must do."

Much later, after hurried councils with his most trusted advisors and an interminable ablution ceremony performed by the half-senile High Mendicant of Ama, the emperor found himself upon the ceramic paths of his pleasure garden. Above him the final blush of day was fading to night, yet his way was clear, illuminated by brightly colored paper lanterns hanging from the branches of flowering dogwood trees. Away from the path, ethereal nightblooms shimmered palely in the dying light, unfolding for the moon just emerging from the darkness, and a warm breeze tinkled the chimes scattered among the lanterns, a sound that reminded him of her laughter. His heart quickened in anticipation.

Such a day! Assassins had come perilously close before to bringing the reign of House Meneum to bloody closure, but never had the threat come from inside the palace, with his Pure standing guard only paces away. Where was safe, if not the imperial audience chamber? Here, in the lavender-scented arms of his concubines?

Long, lean shapes moved seductively behind sheets of diaphanous cloth strung between the trees. Once he would have been tempted to slip within those silks belling in the wind and discover which beauty awaited him, but these days he hungered only for Alyanna, her cinnamon skin and eyes of liquid dark. Whispered entreaties followed him, promising delights that would make any man blush, but they fell on ears deaf to all but one voice.

Finally, he came upon her pavilion among the cherry blossoms, shining in the evening gloaming.

"Alyanna!" he cried, pushing through the hanging flaps.

She sprawled upon a wide, low bed, surrounded by mounded cushions, a single streamer of colored silk twined about her naked body. Smiling at him as he entered, she arched her back and stretched, and at this display of her full, perfect breasts his breath caught. She let out a throaty laugh when she realized what it was he stared at.

Alyanna, his flame, his ardor. She sat up, cupping one of her breasts, her eyes widening provocatively.

"Your Grace," she purred, "did you miss me?"

"More than a caught fish does the water," he replied, shrugging out of his imperial vestments and reclining beside his concubine.

She traced his nipple with a long nail; pleasure shuddered through him. "Such a poet's soul you have. These words should be set to paper, not wasted on ears like mine."

He lay back, sinking into the bed's luxuriant softness, and she settled beside him. Staring at her face he wondered again where she had come from. The old minister in charge of procuring concubines for the imperial harem had found her at the slaver's auction block in Palimport nearly five years ago, and even dirty and disheveled from weeks huddled below deck her beauty had burned through, gold shining among the dross. Shortly after purchasing Alyanna that minister had been gifted with a satrapy. Gerixes could be generous with those who pleased him.

Yet her time before the slave ship remained a mystery. Her first memories were of the reeking warmth of the hold, pressed against strange people speaking strangely flavored words. With her dusky skin she could have been Myrasani . . . but the half-dozen cities those slavers had purchased their wares in on their way to Menekar were all thousands of leagues from where that people lived beside the Bones of the World. He had seen others vaguely like her from the Eversummer Isles, and certainly the islands were much closer to Palimport and the slaver's other ports of call, but she did not speak their tongue, nor did they share her strangely shaped eyes and glossy black hair. He could only conclude that she was a gift from Ama.

"My Grace thinks deep thoughts," she sighed, snuggling closer. He breathed deep of her heady scent, better by far than any of the perfumes his satrap's painted wives drenched themselves with.

"It was an . . . interesting day," replied the emperor, stroking her hair.

"And why was that?" she murmured into his chest. "You know I find your stories so exciting."

"Well," the emperor began, pulling her tighter, "my vizier tells me that an archon of Lyr was killed in council over a courtesan."

"Oh, scandalous," she breathed, squirming against him. "How is it that women excite men's passions so?"

"Perhaps you all have a touch of sorcery in you. That could be why you make the Pure so uncomfortable."

She laughed again. "The girls think we make them uncomfortable because even Ama's light isn't as satisfying as the touch of a beautiful woman."

"Sacrilege. Best keep such musings from the mendicant's ears. I'd hate to have you all branded as witches. Now, what else happened?" The emperor watched her closely, hoping for a reaction. "Oh, yes, a sorcerous assassin penetrated the imperial audience chamber, right under the noses of the Pure. Ama Himself crashed a heron through a window to warn His beloved emperor of the danger. Here is my memento from the battle." Gerixes held up his hand, showing his concubine the livid, red scar.

Alyanna took his hand and brought it to her lips. Her tongue played with the wound, and he winced. She smiled wickedly when she saw this.

"Did you hear me? I said there was an attempt on my life today."

"I did, Divine Lord. But I know that no harm will ever come to the chosen of Ama. A higher power watches over you."

"Your faith is admirable," the emperor replied, not bothering to keep the annoyance from his voice.

His concubine laughed and pulled him closer.

5: JAN

THE CAIRN WOULD be simple, as she had been. Just a pile of rocks pulled from the stone wall that meandered around their farm, marking where she lay among the roots of the apple tree she'd loved so much. In seasons to come, her body would turn to soil and provide nourishment for the land, a final gesture for a place that had given her – given them – so much.

Jan sat back on his haunches and raised his face to the sky, squinting at the sunlight filtering through the latticework of branches above. Burying her had taken all morning; the earth was soft, almost as if it welcomed receiving her body, but despite the cool early-summer day his tunic still clung to him, and his hands ached from prying loose and carrying the stones that would mark where she rested. His fingers made patterns in the loose dirt. So strange to think that she lay only a few feet below him, her face mercifully free of the pain that had ravaged her these last few weeks. What would he do now? He could not stay here – twenty years of piled memories would prove too heavy a burden. Also, he was awake again. This was no fit place for an immortal.

What had brought him back to himself, after all these years? Had it been her death? Perhaps, but the awakening had not happened when the last trickle of life seeped away as he clutched her close, nor in the long hours afterwards when grief had consumed him utterly. It had come as a shock, in the very early morning as he lay beside her body; he could only compare it to being thrown sleeping into a fast-running, ice-cold mountain stream. One moment he had been Janus Balensorn, a crofter for nearly two decades on the lands of Ser Willes len Maliksorn, and the next he was Jan, the Bard. Again.

Frenzied barking interrupted his thoughts. He turned to find a piebald mare ambling toward his farmhouse, being challenged by his sheephound, Dragon. Jan whistled sharply, and Dragon bounded his way, tongue lolling and eyes bright with excitement, apparently content with having alerted his master to the intruder's approach.

"Good dog," Jan said, scratching hard behind his ears.

The visitor turned his horse toward the apple tree, and Jan recognized Robert Simeonsorn, the miller from the village. He looked much older than Jan remembered, having gained a steep widow's peak and a layer of paunch. How many years had it been?

"Janus Balensorn," Robert said, sliding from his horse. "I would say good day to you, but from the looks of it this day cannot be good."

Jan stood, wiping clean his hands, and stepped forward to clasp the miller's forearm. "Aye, you've the truth of it. But it's good to see you, Robert."

The miller shook his head, staring at the stones scattered about the grave. "A sad day. My nana always said that tragedy comes upon like a summer storm, when you least expect and fiercer than you bargained."

There was something in his tone. "What else has happened?" Jan asked.

A shadow passed across the miller's face. "Later," Robert said, squatting beside the mounded dirt. "After we finish. This is Elinor, yes?"

Jan crouched beside him, his eyes burning. "Aye, it's her. It was the weeping. Stole into her this spring; at first we thought it was just a chill, but then came the red tears . . . she was always a sickly thing. Goodwife Roesia tried her best . . ."

A calloused hand clapped his shoulder. "We all go to the light, Janus. Ama will preserve her, and she'll be waiting for you in the golden city when your days are finished."

Jan nodded his appreciation at the miller's words, and then together they bent to the task of building Elinor's cairn. At first Robert was silent, no doubt out of respect for Jan's loss, but after some gentle prodding he opened up about some of the happenings in the village since Jan had last ventured out of the hills. A new smith had set up his forge in the square, giving old Gwynn some competition; there had been deaths and births, a wandering minstrel who played not half so well as Jan, Robert assured him, but like Jan had stolen the hearts of more than a few young lasses in town; and a nasty dispute between a few farmers over a straying boundary stone that had ended with a broken arm and the admonishments of a very angry mendicant.

"More or less," Robert said as he set the final stone atop the pile, "the same goings on as every season, every year. Until last night." The miller wiped a hand across his suddenly pale face, leaving a smear of dirt. "I've been trying not to think of it . . . but I rode out here to tell you and Elinor, and the others that live around these parts, and I have to do my duty, Ama protect me . . ."

Now it was Jan's turn to reach out and comfort Robert. "Tell me what happened."

The miller swallowed hard. "You've been out of the village for a few years, so you might not have heard, but Ser Willes's youngest, Tristan, had gotten himself knighted, and had been entering into a few tournaments, the big one they hold every Husking Day down in Tellindale, a few others. Had some success in the lists, too. Pleased his da right well, especially with the eldest choosing to go study in that Reliquary out west." Robert tugged on the ends of his drooping mustache, his agitation plain. "Anyway, young Tristan had been at the joust held to celebrate Lady Isabel coming of age; he'd been expected back today or tomorrow . . ."

"And? Was he killed in the tourney?"

"No, no. He left the grounds all right, even looked like he'd won a nice suit of plate off one of the Fen lords. He was almost home, must have woken up at daybreak to surprise his da, and . . . and something came upon him on the forest road, over those there hills."

Just before daybreak. "Something?"

"It wasn't . . . it wasn't me who found him. That was Hewan, drivin' his goats down to the brook. But I saw later, after we'd calmed Hewan down and made him lead us back. There was blood everywhere." Robert rubbed his face again; his hands were shaking now. "Not much left of young Tristan. He'd been cut apart. But not like with swords. In my . . . in my mill we keep a lot of cats; can't have mice burrowing in the flour, getting into the bread. Sometimes the cats don't eat what they kill; maybe they're full, I don't know. But they don't just kill the poor bastards. They take them apart, scatter them around. My Dolores is always screaming when she finds a tiny little head in her shoe. That's . . . that's what it was like. And not just the men. Horses, too."

"How many men?"

"Three. Tristan, his squire, and one of the freesworn knights that lives up at the keep. All with swords, though none drew their blades."

Three men, mounted and armed, and none had fought back? Jan sat back heavily, staring out into the dense bracken before them. The forest suddenly looked much more forbidding.

"The mendicant has already declared it a demon's handiwork and sent word to the east asking for the Pure to come and track down whatever did it. Ser Willes has locked himself in his keep, won't even let the townsfolk in, and there's many who want to be behind some stout walls right now. Dolores begged me to stay, but I thought . . . I thought you folks out here should know that there's something terrible in these woods. Probably not hungry anymore . . . but like I said, it didn't look like that was what it was after in the first place."

"You're a good man, Robert, and brave. Not many would have come."

The miller gave him a shaky grin. "It's the dog, actually." He reached out to pat Dragon, who had curled up between them.

"Animals know when something's not right. If there was a demon about he'd have his hackles up, I'm sure."

"There's truth to that," Jan said, thumping Dragon hard on his side.

They sat together in silence for a moment, and then Robert stood, dusting himself off. "Well, there's another three homesteads I need to visit before dusk comes, and I've already spent too much time here."

Jan climbed to his feet and gripped Robert's arm again. "Thank you."

The miller shrugged away his words. "Anyone who walks in the Light should do the same. And to be true with you, I had a bit of a debt to discharge, as well. You might not have seen it, 'cause certainly Elinor didn't, but I loved her deeply when I was younger. Course, I was just a pimply baker's boy, and she was our Queen of Summer, fresh-flowered and pretty as the dawn. I used to imagine winning her heart, though I never truly envisioned how I would so such a thing." Robert chuckled sadly. "And then you arrived, with your honey voice and lordly manners. Everyone thought you must have been castle-bred, some lord's get, yet no-one looked down on you as they did other bastards, even the most high-born ones. All us boys loved your songs and the way you carried that sword, but we hated how the girls watched you moon-eyed, and sometimes late at night I'd slip from my cot and fence with the shadows, pretending it was you." The miller smoothed his mustache, shaking his head. "Took me years to forgive you for stealing her away. But I saw how you doted on her, and loved her like I had. And now here we are, twenty years on, standing over her grave. Me old and fat, and you not looking a whisker older than the day you wandered into town."

Jan caught the miller's arm as he turned away. "Robert, I'm leaving. There's not much for me here, with Elinor gone. I want you to help dispense what I have among the needy. I have some good iron pots and shearing tools, Elinor's loom, Dragon and my sheep. I've settled with Ser Willes on the land until the spring, and he'll be needing a new tenant."

"Aye, that's generous of you, Janus." Robert reached down to ruffle Dragon's fur. "You know, I could use this pup to keep those cats in line down at the mill."

Jan smiled. "I'd be pleased to know he had a home with you. Let me talk with him." Crouching beside Dragon, Jan took the dog's head in his hands, staring into his soft, brown eyes. "Dog, Robert here is your new master. Serve him as you've served me, and I'm sure they'll be plenty of meat-bones in your future." Jan extended a sorcerous filament, reaching inside Dragon's mind to replace his loyalty toward him with the miller, linking all the good things in the dog's world – food and play, warmth and petting – with Robert's smell and sound. Such bindings were infinitely more complex with humans . . . even the greatest of the old masters would have had trouble doing the same to a person, but a dog's mind was refreshingly simple. Jan had found that among all creation, only dogs and children offered unconditional love – the crofter Janus might have thought differently, but Janus had died this morning. At the same moment, he suspected, as poor Ser Tristan.

And that needed to be investigated. After Robert had left on his piebald mare, Dragon loping along beside the horse, Jan went back into his farmhouse and began collecting provisions. A few loaves of brown bread, cured mutton from the larder, a wheel of cheese, and a sack of ghostcap mushrooms Elinor had gathered the previous spring. He traded his doeskin shoes for traveler's boots of hard, gnarled leather, and strapped his lute across his back.

Then he returned outside and went to where an ancient elm spread spidery limbs over the gate to the small pasture where his flock grazed. He knelt and began digging, and after a few minutes he had pulled from the shallow hole a wrapped bundle. Jan unwound the rotted cloth, his fingers tingling as he brushed warm metal. Steel rippled in the sunlight, flashing with silvery runes, and the fist-sized fire opal set into the hilt burned like a frozen flame. Despite decades underground his sword Bright was just as unblemished as when it had first been forged a thousand years ago, when Jan had watched it drawn hissing from the mountain-pure waters of Nes Vaneth and struck with hammer and spell.

He was ready now.

The sight of the ambush had not been difficult to find. It looked like a great fist had come down from the sky and smote the land: the flattened grass was already yellowing, dried and desiccated months too early, and the trees listed away from the road, many of their branches ripped away and splintered into kindling. The bodies of Tristan and his men had been removed, but what was left of the horses remained, and Jan suspected that much of the blood splashed about had once flowed through human veins.

There was a palpable sense of wrongness, obvious even without touching his magic. The air was cold and heavy, fetid with the smell of death and the bitter, coppery tang of blood. And when he unclenched his Talent . . . Jan shuddered. Dark sorcery had been unleashed here, something he had never sensed before. Or he thought he hadn't. His memory was . . . scattered, riddled with holes. He remembered his life as Janus, and a decade of wandering before that, but the time beyond was shrouded, and the harder he strained to seize his past the farther it receded. The forging of his sword was etched sharp in his mind, but little else. Some fragments floated through the mist – he stood on a balcony as morning climbed out from distant peaks, his arms around his lover's slim waist, gazing out over a great city of twisted stone. An obsidian-scaled dragon was silhouetted against the sun, answering the call of a bone-carved horn blown by a tiny waif of a girl, her black hair streaming in the wind. And women, many women, in different dress, from peasant blouses to silken robes, but all tall and willowy, with hair of spun gold – and they all bore more than a passing resemblance to his lost Elinor.

It was as if he had lived a hundred lifetimes, but all were as insubstantial as dreams. Jan shook his head and tried to focus. Puzzling out the riddles of his past would have to wait.

What had attacked these men? He crouched beside a severed horse leg. The wound had been cauterized, sealed shut, but that must have happened after all the blood had been drained and splashed about like a child playing with paints. And where were the horse's heads? Jan ranged the edges of the ambush, searching among the ferns, but it wasn't until birdsong made him look up that he found them. Staring down at him from where they had been wedged among the highest branches of a great sentinel pine were the heads of a pair of destriers, warhorses bred for combat, and that of a smaller garron, all of their mouths twisted open in frozen death cries.

It was intelligent, this thing. And sadistic. But it had not been subtle. A trail led east, easily followed . . . almost too easily. Jan's eyes wandered to the knife-blade peaks of the Bones, some already dusted with snow, others still clear. Was it there, having retreated back to the depths of the mountains, or beyond, in Menekar? And did he sense something else beneath the creature's pungent spoor, a sweeter, more familiar scent that tickled at his mind? He concentrated, willing up a name to match with the feeling, and grudgingly it came, echoing up from the well of his memories, a single word, meaningless now, but he could tell that once hearing it would have stirred great passions within him . . .

Alyanna.

6: KEILAN

"**YOU ALL RIGHT**, lad?"

Keilan blinked, surfacing from his thoughts. He turned to look at Pelos seated beside him and forced a smile.

"Yes. I was just . . . just daydreaming."

The fishmonger sucked on his teeth and snapped the reins, spurring his two old nags to trot faster. Keilan had to grab the wooden railing to keep himself from bouncing out of the wagon and joining the men striding along the path beside them. "Eh. Usually a look like that on a boy means only one of two things. So which is it: a fight, or a pretty girl?"

Neither, in truth. Keilan had actually been considering that last lingering look the mendicant had given him a few days ago, but he couldn't discuss such a thing with Pelos. That's about all he'd been thinking about ever since it had happened, and each evening when they'd returned to the village from the beach he'd been expecting to find . . . something. What, exactly? The mendicant, standing in front of a stake, with the village all gathered around to watch him burn?

He was being foolish. No mendicant would take the accusations of a child seriously. But still . . . that look . . .

"Ah, it was a fight," Keilan finally said.

Pelos nodded sagely. "Thought so. That bruise – someone hit you good."

Keilan reflexively touched his face. The pain had almost gone, but his cheek was still swollen from where his cousin had struck him. That whole morning now seemed like a dream, and he'd barely given it any thought since then, overshadowed as it was by what had happened when he and Sella had returned to the village.

"One of the other fishermen's boys?"

Keilan nodded. "My cousin. Davos's son."

"The fat one?" Pelos cleared his throat noisily and spat over the side of the wagon. "Did he say something about your mother?" The fishmonger grunted when he saw Keilan's look of surprise. "Not hard to figure out, lad. Your mother was different, like you are. And in a place like this, being different can be hard."

Pelos's expression suddenly turned serious, and he gripped Keilan's arm. He was surprisingly strong for an old man. "Listen to me, lad. I knew your mother for many years. We would talk, sometimes for hours, on the beach waiting for your father to return with his catch. Your mother . . . she was filled with light. She was too bright for this place. You and your father kept her here, but she wasn't meant to be a fisherman's wife. And you're not meant to be a fisherman's son."

"I am," Keilan replied softly. "I'm like my father."

Pelos shook his head vigorously. "No. You're a reflection of your mother, even though you look like your da. And you'll need to leave this place before . . . before what happened to her happens to you as well." Pelos indicated Keilan's father with his chin, walking up ahead alongside a few of the other fishermen. "I've talked to your da. He says you can read, and that you love books. I have an old friend, someone who left Chale many years ago because he was . . . also different. Reminds me a lot of you. He's a scholar now, at the Reliquary in Ver Anath. I could send him a letter, telling him about you. Might be your calling, I think, out there among the books and scrolls."

A scholar at the Reliquary? Keilan had never considered anything like that before. He was a fisherman's son, in a small village at the edge of the world. Was it possible? A life of reading and searching through dusty libraries. Sleeping in a goose-down bed, in a stone tower, with candles to read by after darkness fell, and maybe even ink and quill to write with.

What foolishness. And yet . . .

For the first time in years, Keilan dared to imagine a different future for himself.

He was still lost in fantasies of teetering pillars of books when they arrived at the village, and found the faithful of Ama waiting.

Pelos cursed, jolting Keilan back to the present, and pulled hard on the reins. The nags snorted and stamped their feet, one of the horses turning back to stare at the fishmonger reproachfully.

"By the Ten," Pelos muttered, the awe in his voice evident, "look at this, lad."

Just about the entire village had gathered around the Speaker's rock, turned toward where the fishermen were now emerging from the path down to the shore. They had formed a crescent around a dozen or so men, most of whom wore leather armor and carried weapons, swords or pikes, but also a few curving longbows. Their shields and the tabards that hung over their cuirasses were emblazoned with the copper sunburst of Ama. Keilan had seen their like before, warriors that served the temple of Ama in Chale. Lightbearers, they called themselves.

The mendicant who had preached in the village a few days ago was there as well, but Keilan barely noticed the cleric, his eyes drawn instead to the man standing beside him.

The stranger was tall and broad-shouldered, with striking silver hair despite his youth. His armor was magnificent: the chain shirt he wore was a fine mesh of purest white, and his greaves and bracers were enameled the same color. At his side his sword's hilt flashed like a tongue of copper flame, but that wasn't what caused Keilan's breath to catch in his throat.

The stranger's eyes leaked golden light.

He was one of the Pure.

In his village. Waiting for them to return. Keilan's insides turned to water as the implications of this washed over him.

Pelos must have shared his thoughts, as the fishmonger set down his reins and looked at Keilan, pity in his eyes.

"Ah, lad," he sighed. "I suppose it's too late for me to tell ya to run."

From the crowd of villagers Speaker Homlin hesitatingly stepped forward, casting a nervous glance at the silent paladin. The fat smith swallowed hard, his jowls quivering, and mopped at his forehead with a soot-blackened cloth.

"As you see, my friends, we have visitors. Distinguished guests from Chale and . . . elsewhere. They, um, they've come because Brother Julias believes there may be, well, um, *sorcery* in our village."

At the mention of magic the low muttering of the crowd started to swell. A few of the smaller children pointed at Keilan, while still holding tight to the legs of their parents. The fishermen ahead of their wagon turned and stared at him, including his father, who had gone deathly pale. Shame burned Keilan, and he felt his face reddening. The speaker dabbed at his forehead again; he looked more flushed and uncomfortable now, Keilan thought, than at any time he had ever seen the smith laboring over his forge.

"Boy," he continued, gesturing towards Keilan. "Come down. Come here."

Keilan slid from the wagon. Briefly he thought of running for the woods, but instead he found himself walking slowly toward the waiting mendicant and the shining paladin.

A sorcerer? He wasn't a sorcerer. This was a terrible mistake. He had a gift, certainly, for finding fish, but that wasn't sorcery. Sorcery was calling lightning from the skies, binding demons, setting curses. Not knowing where to fish!

Keilan calmed himself. This was a mistake, and the truth would be known soon enough. According to the stories, the Pure could feel if sorcery was present, and when this one felt nothing he'd be free. And all the whisperings and black looks from the others would stop as well when they saw proof that he didn't have any real magic in his blood, just some small hedge wizardry, like how Old Tannin could smell lightning in the air.

This could be a good thing, he told himself, as he came to stand before the Pure. He forced himself to look into the terrible shining eyes of the paladin, tamping down an almost overwhelming desire to turn and flee to his father. This close, his skin prickled from the warmth emanating from the Pure – yet a shiver still ran up his spine.

"I'm no sorcerer," Keilan said, and though he'd meant to impress everyone with the strength of his words his voice cracked, and he felt another hot flush of shame darken his cheeks.

The paladin stared at him for a long moment, his face impassive. The entire village seemed to be holding its breath, waiting. Finally, the warrior laid a gauntleted hand on Keilan's shoulder; he flinched, but the touch was surprisingly gentle.

"No," the Pure murmured, his strange accent rich and lilting. "You are no sorcerer."

Relief flooded Keilan, and he nearly collapsed in the dirt.

"Not yet," the paladin finished, the grip on his shoulder tightening.

Keilan's eyes jerked to the Pure's face again. "What?" he whispered, instinctively trying to pull away.

"I am sorry, Keilan Ferrisorn." The paladin's words seemed tinged with sadness – or was it pity? "The tainted flame inside you burns bright. You are no sorcerer, for you've had no guidance. But the taint is there."

"No," Keilan croaked, struggling harder against the Pure's iron hold. "No! I don't have any magic! I can't do anything except find fish! That's not what wizards do!" Keilan twisted, looking around wildly for support.

The mendicant beside the paladin sketched Ama's holy sun in the air and stepped back a pace, his eyes round with fear. There was a commotion behind them, his father yelling, trying to get to Keilan but the warriors of Chale were holding him back. Something burst from the crowd of villagers, a blur of dirty yellow hair that beat tiny fists against the white cloak of the Pure. Sella, screaming, but the paladin did not appear to notice her flailing arms, and he continued to stare implacably at Keilan.

The day seemed to brighten. Something was building inside Keilan, a wave growing larger as it neared the shore, a terrible, rising force that would erupt from him and –

"No," the Pure said simply, shaking his head. Darkness rushed over Keilan, drowning him in silence. He sank into a black sea.

Light, seeping along the edges. Slowly it bled into the abyss in which he floated. No, not floated – swayed. Back and forth, rhythmic, in time to the clopping of . . . hooves?

Shapes towered to either side of him, reaching out with bony arms. Shadows dappled the ground below, a blinding sky wheeled above. Slowly, slowly, his sight returned, the blurred world gradually sharpening.

He was mounted on a horse caparisoned in silver metal, a giant of a steed much larger than any he had seen before, even bigger than the plow-horses that churned the fields of the northern farms. Keilan blinked, trying to focus. A brown mane spread upon a cream-colored coat, broken only by a few dark blotches. Muscles rippled everywhere the armor did not cover.

With effort he sat up straighter, looking around. He rode through a forest, along a road rutted with wagon tracks. Light slanted down from between grasping tree limbs; where it touched, the wildflowers speckling the green grass burned a little brighter. There were men on the road as well, beside and in front, the sunbursts of Ama on their tabards seeming to stare at him like accusing golden eyes.

It occurred to Keilan, through his haze, that he should not be able to sit a horse in his current state. Then he felt the presence behind him, holding him steady so he did not topple over.

Keilan squirmed, trying to say something, but his mouth was full of cotton and he could only muster a dry, rasping cough. He felt himself start to slide off the horse.

A hand closed around his wrist, steadying him. A stranger's hand, long fingered and pale, but even without the gauntlet Keilan knew to whom it belonged.

"Calm, Keilan," the paladin murmured. "I do not wish to do that again to you."

"What . . . what did you do?" Keilan managed, struggling to swallow away the dryness in his throat.

"I felt your sorcery starting to build. I did not wish for you to accidentally harm anyone, so I reached inside you and severed you from your strength. The backlash of sorcery rendered you unconscious." The Pure's words were flat, emotionless. Keilan struggled to understand them.

"My da. Sella."

There was a long pause, and Keilan's heart fell. The paladin must have sensed his discomfort. "Do not worry, they are fine. The little girl . . . I had some trouble prying her from my leg after you collapsed." Was that wry amusement Keilan heard? "A fierce fighter, that one. Finally her mother came and took her away. Your father, he was distraught. The lightbearers who accompanied me restrained him, eventually. Before we departed I talked with your speaker, and told him that no harm should befall your father. That the taint inside you was not his doing. And I told him that when next a mendicant traveled to your village he would ask after his health, and that such news would eventually reach my ears."

Keilan considered this numbly. "Why do you care what happens to them?"

"I am no monster, Keilan, and it pains me that I must take you from your father and friends. You are an innocent, simply unlucky. I would have no harm come to anyone else."

"Anyone else?"

The paladin sighed heavily. "I will not lie to you, Keilan. You have a long and arduous road in front of you, and I cannot assure you that you'll survive the journey."

"Then let me go," Keilan said, speaking quickly. "I promise on my mother's soul that I'll never use sorcery again. I would never use it to harm anyone!"

The paladin reached around Keilan to brush away some twigs and dirt that had become tangled in his horse's mane. "And I believe that you would try to keep that promise, Keilan. But sorcery is most seductive. Very few can resist its lure."

"I can!"

"Truly, it grieves me that I cannot accept such a promise. But it would be a betrayal of my vows and everything I have pledged my life to uphold. No, I'm sorry, Keilan – you must go to your Cleansing."

"Will I die?" Keilan said softly, the dizziness coming over him again.

"Some live, and some die. Usually it is the pure of heart who survive, and because of this I do believe you should not be without hope."

A gibbon shrieked somewhere in the forest; Keilan felt the paladin stiffen, then twist his body, as if quickly looking around. "Jerrym," the Pure said, and one of the lightbearers turned towards him, "be cautious."

The warrior of Chale ducked his head. "My Lord Senacus, don't worry, it's only these forest apes. Nothing to be alarmed about. This time of year they're always chattering away, or fighting to see who's king."

Keilan heard the hiss of metal from behind him – the paladin must have drawn his sword. "That was no ape, lightbearer. Something else is in these woods."

Jerrym looked skeptical, but he nodded and faced the others. "Listen up, ye hairy – ah, men of Ama! Be wary, Lord Senacus tells me something is out there. Keep yer eyes sharp, and let me know if you see anything strange!"

"Something like me?"

"Light above!" Jerrym cried, scrabbling for the greatsword slung across his back. There was a sharp intake of breath from the paladin.

A girl, perhaps a few years older than Keilan, sat upon the branch of a great oak tree, smiling impishly. One of her legs was drawn up, and she rested her chin upon her knee; the other dangled carelessly, higher than a man could reach. She was dressed in leather the color of ash, and her dark hair was close-cropped – in Keilan's village, only boys would sport such a cut.

"Who in Garazon's black balls are you?" Jerrym yelled at her, in his surprise clearly forgetting the paladin's presence.

"A friendly forest spirit, good man," the girl called down in a strange, trilling accent, "wondering what brings you through my sylvan domain."

Jerrym's mouth worked soundlessly, as if he wanted to form some response but couldn't conceive of how to begin. He glanced helplessly at the Pure.

Senacus nudged his horse toward where the girl perched. "What is your purpose here?" he asked, sounding genuinely curious.

A dagger materialized in the girl's hand. It spun, glittering, as she tossed it in the air and caught it again. "My purpose? To rescue the poor lad you've abducted." She gestured with the blade's point at Keilan.

"You're going to what?" Jerrym said incredulously, finding his voice. "Save the boy? You do know who's sitting behind him, don't you, lass? That there's a paladin of Ama. The Pure."

"I'm very good with this knife."

The lightbearer scoffed loudly. "I don't care if you're a bloody shadowblade. One little girl –"

"Quiet," the paladin said, and Jerrym's mouth snapped shut.

"Are you willing to negotiate for your life," the girl asked, "or shall we see if I can put Chance here between those pretty little eyes?"

"Chance," the Pure said slowly, "is not a very confident name for a blade."

The girl threw back her head and let out a quick peal of laughter. "That's true!" she cried, "that's why I seldom leave things solely to

Chance." A second dagger flashed, appearing in the girl's other hand as if plucked from the air.

"And does that blade have a name as well?"

The girl grinned down at the paladin. "I call this one Fate. Is that confident enough for you?"

The paladin sighed. "Enough of this game. Reveal your friends."

"As you wish," the girl said with a wink, then whistled sharply. A few heartbeats passed, and the lightbearers shifted uneasily, watching the forest, but still they did not see anyone approaching until the underbrush shivered all along the road. Then suddenly a score of men emerged, each dressed in gray-green forester garb and holding a nocked bow carved of black wood.

The men of Chale cried out in alarm and reached for their weapons, but a shouted command from the Pure stilled them.

"Stop! There need be no bloodshed here today."

The girl looked up from the fingernail she'd been paring with one of her daggers. "I agree. Help the boy down from the horse and send him to me."

Strong hands gripped Keilan's waist, and he heard the Pure's voice in his ear. "Go to her. We will meet again, I promise you."

With effort, Keilan swung his leg over the horse's broad back and dropped to the ground, stumbling slightly. What should he do? He glanced from the girl to the dense underbrush. Could he escape back to his village? From the easy way the archers had moved through the forest he doubted he would get very far if he ran.

She beckoned for him to approach. "To me, boy. You're safe now."

"Is he truly?" asked the Pure, his horse stamping the ground as if sensing its master's agitation. "I can feel you!" the paladin cried out loudly, causing a flock of brightly colored birds to explode from the branches above. "Come out, sorcerer!"

The girl appeared to be about to say something, but then she swallowed away her words. Keilan found that he was holding his breath, and everyone seemed frozen, waiting for what would happen next.

Then he heard it, a faint rustling, as if someone was pushing through the undergrowth, coming closer. Keilan caught glimpses of something red approaching, and then a young man with black hair wearing a bright crimson tunic trimmed with lace shouldered his way between two of the much larger archers. He bowed slightly to the mounted paladin, the amulets and chains he wore tinkling in the silence.

"Greetings to the Pure," he said in the same smooth accent as the girl in the tree.

"Sorcerer," the paladin fairly spat. "What are you doing here?"

"I'm sure you've guessed by now. The boy will come with us."

"To where? Dymoria?"

The sorcerer shrugged. "Perhaps."

"Perhaps," the paladin echoed mockingly, in the same accent. "You sound like you're from the Gilded Cities, but these men with you all have ebonwood bows. Only the Dragon Throne of Dymoria could possibly arm an entire troop of archers with ebonwood. I think you must have come on the orders of that Crimson Queen. This is a flagrant violation of the old treaties; be assured, sorcerer, the emperor will hear of this outrage."

The sorcerer's smile deepened. "Oh, I wish I could see his face when you tell him."

7: KEILAN

KEILAN'S BREATH BURNED hot and ragged as they fled through the forest. A drizzle began as the shadows gathered in the fading light, making the leaf-strewn ground treacherous, and he slipped a few times, scraping his arms and hands bloody. The girl from the tree kept pace beside him, helping him back to his feet when he fell.

After the third time he stumbled, she sighed and shook her head. "You know, I'm city-born, and I'm able to keep on my feet. I thought you peasants would have spent all your time in the woods. Are you just naturally clumsy?"

"I'm a fisherman." Keilan gasped, trying to find his balance on the slithering leaves. "We don't often go into the woods."

The girl gave his arm a quick squeeze. "Well, close your eyes and imagine you're running on sand."

Keilan grunted and tried to push on faster. "Why . . . Why are we running?"

The girl scrambled up a steep incline veined with roots, then reached back to help Keilan. "I've seen the Pure fight. We were lucky that one was concerned about the lives of the men he'd brought with him; otherwise, many would have died back there. We need to put some distance between ourselves and him before he decides to come after us."

Keilan spared a glance over his shoulder at the dark forest. He glimpsed the archers slipping through the trees still holding their bows, but he couldn't see any other pursuit.

The Pure. His kidnapping. The ambush. Now a frantic flight through the woods . . . the events of this afternoon were like hammer blows, one after another. Before he could find his balance or fully comprehend what was happening, everything shifted again, too quickly. He wanted to sink down onto the forest floor and close his eyes and wake up tomorrow in his bed.

But the girl was insistent, pulling him along; farther ahead, Keilan saw the red wizard hurrying, the lacy frill of his collar plastered to his neck. A pair of the archers flanked him, fistfuls of arrows held at the ready, as if they expected the Pure at any moment to burst from between the trees astride his war horse and charge them.

At this point, Keilan wasn't sure that would have surprised him.

Again he glanced at the woods, wondering if he could vanish into the bracken before the girl or her friends could catch him. But the paladin had spoken of taking him to something called the Cleansing, and that it would probably kill him . . . at least his rescuers had made no such threats.

Finally, they emerged from the forest into a large clearing beside a shallow, swift-running stream. More of the gray-hooded archers were there, lowering their bows when they saw who approached and touching the knuckles of closed fists to their foreheads in what Keilan assumed was some kind of respectful greeting. Behind them many horses and ponies milled, laden down with saddlebags, snorting and shifting at the sudden excitement. It looked to Keilan like they had come a great distance, and had a long way yet to go.

"Who are these men?"

"Rangers of Dymoria. Usually they stay in the northern forests, protecting the kingdom from raids by Skein warbands. But we brought a troop south because we needed to move through wilderness quickly."

The girl led him to a piebald mare and gestured for him to mount. Unsure of what exactly to do, Keilan put one foot in a stirrup and awkwardly swung himself up into the saddle. The girl watched him critically.

"Have you ever ridden a horse before?"

Keilan shook his head, still struggling to find his balance. The girl rolled her eyes and gathered his reins. "I'll hold on to these, then. Best pray we don't have to move faster than a canter, or I think you'll bounce right off."

She led his horse through the chaos of two dozen men hurriedly securing bags and climbing into saddles. Keilan noticed that every man had a golden medallion clasping his cloak, a sinuous dragon eating its own tail.

"Lady Nel," a ranger tying his quiver to his horse's barding said as she passed him, "we must ride through the night. In the darkness will we be able to navigate the road you spoke of before?"

"We will have to," the girl replied, vaulting onto the back of a russet pony. "I want to put as much distance between ourselves and the paladin as we can, and I doubt he is familiar with the old ways. But we won't reach the road until tomorrow's first light, at the earliest."

The ranger knuckled his forehead and turned away. The girl kicked her pony into a trot and tugged on the reins of Keilan's horse, leading him along.

"Your name is Nel?" he asked as they splashed through the shallow stream.

The girl did not turn around. "It is."

"Just Nel?"

"Just Nel."

Keilan shifted, trying to get more comfortable in the saddle. "But that man called you 'lady.' Doesn't that mean you are highborn?"

The girl threw back her head and laughed again. "I'm about as highborn as you are, fisherboy. My mother was a two-kellic whore on the Street of Silk, and my father was someone with at least two kellics in his purse."

"Yet you command these men."

"In truth, they follow me because I am Vhelan's knife."

"Vhelan?"

The girl reined her pony up beside the man the Pure had claimed was a wizard; he looked about as awkward on his horse as Keilan felt. He slumped in his saddle in his sodden finery, bedraggled as a cat caught out in the rain.

"Boss!"

The sorcerer turned toward them. He was younger than Keilan had first thought, maybe about the same age as the girl. His fine red clothing seemed to shimmer in the gloaming. He sniffled loudly and inclined his head at Keilan.

"Greetings . . ." The sorcerer raised his eyebrows and glanced questioningly at Nel. She cleared her throat and shot Keilan a look of embarrassment.

"Ah, yes, we didn't actually get to that, did we. What's your name, boy?"

Keilan tried to answer, but his mind was suddenly a scrap of blank parchment.

The sorcerer turned to Nel. "Is the lad simple? That would be unfortunate."

"Keilan. Keilan Ferrisorn," he finally blurted out, running a shaking hand through his rain-slicked hair.

The sorcerer offered a crooked smile. "Well met, Keilan. I am Vhelan ri Vhalus, a magister of the second rank, and this is my knife, Nel. We've traveled a long way to find you."

"Why is this happening? What do you want with me?" Keilan struggled to hide the edge of desperation in his voice.

Vhelan must have heard it, because he reached out to pat Keilan's arm. "Be calm, lad. We came because you have a great gift, and there are many who would do you harm. Our queen in Dymoria provides safe haven for those such as us. We did not expect the Pure to find you first, but luckily we travel in strength these days, and so could effect a rescue."

"And speaking of the rescue," Nel said, casting a glance at the woods where they had come from, "I won't consider it a success until we put about a hundred leagues between ourselves and that paladin."

"Agreed," the wizard said, fumbling his hands free of his long sleeves. "Let us be off." He mumbled something, too quiet for Keilan to hear clearly, his fingers sketching a quick pattern. The whispers had a strange resonance, shivering in the air for a few moments after being spoken, like the fading tolling of a bell. Cold clear light blossomed in the wizard's hand and began to swell.

Sorcery. Keilan's mouth was dry, and his pulse thundered in his ears. It wasn't fear that he felt, though, to his surprise. It was excitement. *If what the Pure said was true, could he be taught to do that?*

The wizard cupped his hands around the light, molding it into a sphere, still muttering his incantations. He released the glowing object with a flourish, and it floated free, coming to hover in front of him and bathing them all in pallid ghost-light.

"This should be enough so that the horses won't lame themselves in the dark. We ride."

The company followed the stream for a ways, the light floating ahead giving the water an eerie sheen, and then when the trees thinned they turned into the woods. The rain stopped soon after, though water still dripped from the canopy in an unsteady drumbeat. Shadows skittered around them as the glowing sphere passed through grasping branches, and Keilan found himself peering nervously into the darkness, while beneath them the moss on the forest floor shone with a faint luminescence, illuminating nightblooms stirring to life as they mistook the light for a risen moon.

Questions roiled inside Keilan, but he couldn't bring himself to break the silence. Instead, he stroked the neck of his mare and tried to sort through what had happened to him. He felt a pang of sadness thinking of his father, and Sella, but otherwise there was very little he would miss about the life he was leaving behind. His books. Should he try and get back to his village? Keilan hunched in his saddle as he considered what had happened. Could he trust Nel and this sorcerer? Weren't those that drew forth sorcery wicked? He had to admit that they did not seem evil.

The company rode until shreds of a gray dawn were visible through the branches above, then one of the rangers called a halt, and most of the riders slid from their horses and began rummaging through saddlebags, pulling out strips of dried meat and bread. Keilan clambered down, every bone in his body throbbing with pain. He accepted a water skin from Nel and drank greedily, pacing back and forth to try and walk off the aching in his legs.

"Your first long ride is always the worst," she said, chuckling at his discomfort. "I could barely walk for a day afterward."

"The way you ride now, I thought you'd been born in a saddle."

Nel snorted. "Hah. Until I was about your age the closest I'd come to a horse was when I slit the saddlebags of some fat merchant as he was riding through the prosidium. Neither Vhelan nor myself had ever ridden before we left Lyr seven years ago. And he still looks like he's never been on one."

Keilan handed the skin back to Nel. "So you've known Vhelan for a long time?"

"Almost my whole life. He was my first friend in the Warrens. I told you, I'm his knife."

"You've said that before, but I don't know what it means."

"His knife . . ." Nel paused, seeming to grope for the right words. "It's like a lieutenant. In the Warrens, all the gangs have a boss, and every boss has a knife. Closer than brother and sister. I'd do anything for him, go anywhere. So when a sorcerer noticed him and offered to bring him north, I came as well."

Keilan glanced past Nel at the wizard, who was rubbing his legs furiously, as if to restore some life to them.

"He was the boss of a gang of thieves?"

Nel smirked. "He's changed a bit, certainly. But even in the Warrens his nickname was 'scholar.' Vhelan's always been a little . . . foppish.

He cultivates it, somewhat. It is better, we've both found, if your enemies underestimate you."

Nel took a final swig of water, and then stoppered the skin. "Come. We must continue. Tonight, if we make good time and there's no sign of pursuit, we can sleep."

Keilan stifled a groan as Nel swung herself back up into her saddle. "You can walk for a ways, if you wish. We can't move so fast in the forest, though when we reach the road you'll have to ride again."

He gave her a grateful look and gathered up the reins. His horse chuffed, as if insulted by his decision to walk, so he patted its flank and apologized. Nel rummaged in her saddlebag and tossed down an apple.

"She'll forgive you quick enough if you let her have that."

One quick crunch and the apple was gone, and Keilan imagined whatever reproach he had glimpsed in his horse's eyes vanished with it.

Morning faded, the light deepening as they continued on. The forest was as wild as Keilan had suspected the night before; the trees grew thick and tall enough that the undergrowth was stunted, but even still they sometimes had to carefully guide the horses through a tangle of great roots or around fallen trunks. Birds flitted above, and once Keilan caught a shadowy man-shape recede into the highest branches. A gibbon, the reclusive forest-apes. This was the deep woods, far different than anything he had explored around his village. Only a few hunters ever braved these depths, and Keilan found himself remembering some of Mam Ru's old tales, stories of green men who watched from the boles of trees, their mossy teeth hungering for the taste of child flesh, ancient white stags with glimmering silver antlers, mischievous telflings, wicked faeries, ravenous spirits, and haunted ruins. He didn't think he could find his way back to his village now, even if he somehow managed to slip away.

Keilan did not see the road until he'd almost tripped over it. At first he thought it was just a rill in the folds of the forest, but when he crested the raised earthen mound suddenly there it was, a wide avenue of gleaming black stone that stretched as far as he could see.

The trees did not encroach upon the road, almost as if they shied away from it.

"What is this?" he asked, crouching down to trace the thin grooves where the blocks of stone fit together flawlessly.

"The Black Road," Vhelan said, his tone faintly reverential as he urged his horse forward. Its hooves rang strangely on the stone, almost as if they were striking metal. "Built thousands of years ago by the sorcerers of the Kalyuni Imperium. Once it connected their glorious cities with the north, the holdfasts of Min-Ceruth and other lost kingdoms. I've read that if you follow it south far enough it vanishes straight into the waves of the Broken Sea. Perhaps it still runs all the way to the drowned Star Towers – the sorcery woven into this stone is strong. Can you feel it?"

"I can." Keilan whispered, pressing his palm to the road. It was a thin pulsing, like the faint beating of a distant heart.

"The things the ancients wrought are far beyond our present skill," Vhelan said slowly, almost to himself. "But perhaps that will change soon." He glanced at Keilan, and crooked a smile. "Rejoice, boy, for you could be a part of our rebirth."

With a cry the sorcerer spurred his horse into a canter, each hoofstrike on the Black Road sounding to Keilan like when Speaker Homlin used to hammer iron pulled white-hot from the forge. The rest of the men followed, creating a shuddering, tinkling cacophony, until only he and Nel remained behind.

"Time to mount up again, boy." Nel moved to take his reins again, but he shook his head and gathered them himself.

"No. I can do it."

She eyed him for a moment, then nodded. "Very well. Try to keep up."

They kept a good pace, the forest hemming the road becoming a dark blur. During the ride Keilan gradually became more comfortable controlling his mare, learning how to slow or quicken her stride through slight pressure from his knees or a gentle pull on the reins. Keilan suspected that the horse had been very well trained, and was subtly compensating for any mistakes he was making. He made sure to pat her neck and lean forward regularly to whisper his thanks, and after some deliberation arrived at a name to call her: Storm, for the swirling dark blotches on her coat reminded him of the sky before the Shael unleashed their wrath on the seas below.

The afternoon light was beginning to wane when they reached the second road. It was smaller than the one they'd been riding on, wide enough for only a few horses, while a half dozen could fit comfortably on the main road with room to spare. It vanished into the woods, the trees pressing closer than on the road they had been following. Keilan thought he could see something else through the tangle, strange shapes looming deep within.

They halted at the junction, the sorcerer beckoning for Nel and one of the rangers to approach. This warrior's dragon-brooch was red instead of gold, and a twisting horn banded with silver hung from his saddle. The leader of these men, Keilan guessed. He nudged his mare closer so he could hear the exchange, while the rest of the archers kept a discreet distance, talking amongst themselves.

"We can camp there tonight," Vhelan said, gesturing where the smaller road disappeared into the trees. "We need the rest, and we'll have shelter if it rains again."

The ranger's mouth was set in a thin line. "I say we press on. Any pursuit will expect us to stop in the ruins."

The wizard snorted. "Pursuit? We've come so far so fast. Did you see any imperial trackers with the Pure? The paladins are not trained for this kind of hunting."

"Nevertheless, we could hide our camp in the woods far enough off the road that we'd be invisible to any that followed. Why take the risk? What do you hope to find in the city?"

Vhelan plucked at his sleeves, scowling. "Find? Nothing, of course. The city has been dead for a thousand years. But I do wish to gaze upon it with my own eyes. What is it that you fear?"

The ranger's face darkened. "I'm entrusted with returning you safely to Herath and the queen. I refuse to take unnecessary risks."

"Captain d'Taran," Nel interjected, "we do appreciate your diligence. But you were not given command here. You are to protect Vhelan and follow his orders, whatever they may be."

The ranger gave the sorcerer and his knife a long, measuring look. Finally, he sighed. "Very well. It is as you say. But be wary, wizard. There are many stories about such dead cities, and what can be found within."

"Superstitions, I assure you, captain," Vhelan said, waving away the ranger's warning. "The bones of these ruins have been picked over a half-hundred times by scholars from the Reliquary or other looters. Whatever magics once thrived there have long since faded or been stolen away."

The captain offered a curt nod of agreement and wheeled his horse around, trotting toward where a knot of his men were waiting expectantly. He muttered something under his breath, too quiet for the sorcerer to hear, but Keilan was close enough that he caught what was said.

"Then what are you looking for, wizard?"

8: KEILAN

THEY FOLLOWED THE avenue until it ended, but this tributary of the Black Road did not trail off into shards of stone pockmarking the forest floor; rather, it appeared to have been sheared clean, as if struck by a giant's impossibly sharp sword. And over that last gleaming slab a great archway loomed, built of dark blocks of stone that seemed so precariously fitted together that Keilan felt a slight pang of nervousness as they approached. The deprivations of the wilds were evident: the stones were pitted with age, stained by lichen, and vines like arms knotted with muscles wrapped the structure, as if trying to pull it down. At the arch's apex, where the crumbling stones met haphazardly, a great eye had been carved, seeming to watch the party as they neared. When Keilan came closer he saw that the arch was actually festooned with innumerable eyes, most so faded with age that they seemed to have nearly sunk back into the stone from which they had emerged. Wide eyes, hooded eyes, slitted eyes, the eyes of cats and snakes and fish and other animals Keilan did not recognize. All watchful.

"The Unblinking Gate," Vhelan said softly as they neared the arch. "Eyes were a common motif in Kalyuni art and architecture. They represented clarity, knowledge, the piercing of illusion and subterfuge. Those that approached this city would be unmasked if their intentions were not pure."

A poem leapt unbidden to Keilan's lips:

"windows to the chambered soul
twinned jewels, their facets gleaming
in lustrous joy they witness my return
such guile she must possess
for her to hide the truth within such beauty."

As they passed through the shadowed archway Keilan felt the sorcerer and his knife staring at him.

"What was that?" asked Nel.

"That," Vhelan said slowly, "was, if I'm not mistaken, the poetry of Dzin keth Dzari."

"Who?"

"A functionary in the court of the padarasha of Kesh. He lived a century ago, during the golden years of that empire. He's quite fashionable even today, especially among the aristocracy of the Gilded Cities. I, ah," Vhelan cleared his throat guiltily, "I had a paramour back in Lyr who was fond of him, one of the, um, kept women of a doddering old archon."

Nel smirked. "I remember that one. Insipid creature."

"But beautiful," Vhelan added, "and a romantic. Hence the affection for Dzari's poetry. The question is, how does a fisherman's son know such words?"

"My mother taught me to read," Keilan murmured.

The wizard and his knife shared a quick look. "I would like to hear more about your mother later," Vhelan said.

The far end of the gateway had partially collapsed, so they slid from their horses and led their mounts around the massive blocks of tumbled stone. When he cleared the debris and emerged again into daylight Keilan had to reflexively steady himself against his horse, overwhelmed by the scale of the ruined city that spread before him.

A few years ago he had accompanied his father north to Chale when rumors had trickled to their village that a famous bard was staying in one of the town's inns. The bard had moved on before they'd arrived, but Keilan still remembered the awe he had felt standing on the cobbled streets, looking up at houses built of stone stacked upon each other.

It could not compare to what he gazed upon now: a vast, dead city, shattered as if struck by the fist of an angry god. Great square pillars carved with runes flanked a broad avenue now overgrown with milk-pale grass; whatever they had once supported lay scattered about, black stony islands emerging from a shimmering sea of white. To either side of this central road great piles of rock were mounded, the remnants of once-mighty buildings, their former grandeur suggested by the occasional wall or doorway that still stood within the devastation. The forest had not reclaimed the city, but here and there trees had grown up among and even on top of the ruins, long spidery roots threading the stones. Aside from the wind sighing in the highest branches of these trees the city was silent as a tomb.

"What is this place?" Keilan asked quietly.

"Uthmala," Vhelan replied, "northernmost outpost of the Kalyuni Imperium. The only city of any size to escape the great flood. Not nearly as grand as Mahlbion or Kashkana, so the histories tell us, but impressive enough for those of us who live in this faded age."

"A pile of stones," Nel said, shaking her head. "And as you said, picked clean of any treasure by generations of looters. Let's find a good place to camp, so at least we won't get wet again."

They followed the city's central avenue, the strange, pale grass whispering against the bellies of their horses. Keilan approached one of the pillars, tracing the squirming runes with a finger. There almost seemed to be a faint charring, as if the symbols had been burned into the stone rather than carved. The thought made his skin prickle.

The road finally ended at the broken foundations of a building unlike any other he had seen in the city. It was a great wall, smooth and curved, made not of stone but of some translucent substance. His father's friend had once shown him an insect locked in a chunk of clouded orange glass he had found in the forest, and Keilan was reminded of this as he gazed upon the wall. Amber, someone in the village had called it.

Vhelan reined his horse beside him. "The only one of the fabled Star Towers not at the bottom of the Broken Sea."

"What happened to this place?" Keilan asked, sliding from his saddle and crouching down to run his hand along the glass-smooth wall. "If it wasn't drowned with the rest of the Imperium, how was it destroyed?"

"Menekar," Vhelan said with more than a trace of bitterness. "After the two great cataclysms overwhelmed Kalyuni and Min-Ceruth, the armies of Ama poured over the Bones of the World, hunting down and slaughtering every remaining sorcerer they could find. This city and its Star Tower contained the last tattered remnants of Kalyuni wizardry, and legions commanded by the Pure destroyed it utterly a thousand years ago. So much was lost in the sacking – the Pure took great pains to make sure none of the knowledge of the Mosaic Cities survived. The paladins of Ama are nothing if not thorough."

Keilan suppressed a shiver. *What would have happened if he had not been rescued from the Pure?* Gazing out upon the ruins of this once-great city, he suspected he knew.

"There," Nel suddenly said, and Keilan turned to see her pointing at a bulge of stone rising above the rubble. "A roof. We'll stay there tonight."

Most of a roof, at least. They camped beneath a dome that had been partially staved in; how the rest remained suspended above them Keilan wanted to attribute to sorcery, but when he asked Vhelan about this the sorcerer had chuckled and instead referenced 'physics,' which sounded to Keilan like an equally arcane subject. Above them, a great mosaic spread across the parts of the ceiling that were still intact, the image of a four-armed, black-skinned man brandishing a different weapon in each of his taloned hands: scimitar, ax, mace and serpentine dagger. But it was below the man's waist that was truly striking – although chunks of the ceiling bearing that part of the mosaic had collapsed, Keilan thought it looked like the man had the hindquarters of a great insect, or perhaps a spider.

Gradually, as night fell, the image on the dome was swallowed by shadow, until it had vanished completely and only a few glimmering stars were visible above them through the gaps in the ceiling. The rangers busied themselves setting up camp: unrolling bedding among the debris, driving torches into the ground to mark the perimeter, and moving several large stones, so that if attacked they could take cover easily.

While they were doing this, Vhelan coaxed a small fire to life using flint and some fallen branches scavenged from outside, then beckoned for Keilan to join him. Nel also sat, perching cross-legged on an inscribed chunk of stone that may once have been an altar. The sorcerer produced three small cups from his travel bags and shared them out, then unstoppered a dusty green-glass bottle.

Nel whistled. "Sharing your Sevinka? You must be in a very good mood – or you think we'll be able to get to a decent wine merchant before much longer."

Vhelan chuckled and poured a draught of golden liquid into each of their cups. "Both, dear knife. Here we are, among the detritus of the old world, in a place I've dreamed about visiting so many times. We have a new recruit for the kingdom, stolen out from under the Pure, and within a few more days we'll be sleeping in the finest featherbeds in Theris. And then it's only a month or so until we return to a hero's welcome in Herath."

Keilan sniffed at the drink, his eyes watering at the heady aroma.

"Firewine from Gryx," Vhelan said, offering a toast to them both before tossing his cup back. He let out a contented sigh and settled himself more comfortably against a chunk of stone carved with intricate friezes. Keilan hesitated a moment longer and then sipped at his wine, surprised at its spicy richness.

"Good, yes?" said Vhelan with a smile. "Now, fisherman's son, I have to apologize for the last few days. It's rude, I know, to drag you at such a pace through such inhospitable wilds, with no explanations given. So here we are, catching our breath and sharing libations: ask your questions. And after, I have a few of my own for you."

Keilan spent a moment watching ribbons of smoke unwind from the fire and disappear through the rents in the dome above, wondering which question he most wanted answered from the tumult churning inside him.

He supposed he should start at the beginning. "How did you know about me?"

Vhelan nodded, moving to refill his cup. "A fair question. It is certainly true that untrained children with the gift rarely make an impression on the magisters of Dymoria from hundreds of leagues away. Let me ask you: did anything unusual happen a fortnight or so ago?"

Keilan considered for a moment, and then realization struck him like a blow to the stomach. "The Deep One."

Vhelan's brow knit together. "The what?"

"The Deep One," Keilan repeated in wonder. "You're talking about that. I always helped my father with his fishing, because I could tell where to put the nets if I just slipped my hand into the water. But one time I decided to push my senses as far as I could into the depths – to see what was out there, I guess. And down below and far away in the darkness I brushed against something immense." Even sitting beside the fire Keilan couldn't suppress a shiver. "A Deep One. In our village we believe in great gods that lie slumbering under the waves. Ghelu the Toothed, lord of sharks and orcas and wraithfins; Elara, mistress of the great schools we hunted, as generous as any of the Deep Ones could be considered; Many-armed Relav, Shen of the Shoals, the Jatterlings. The thing I felt down there – it must have been a Deep One. It saw me, and I felt like a fish that had just met a scaling knife. Utterly exposed."

Vhelan was nodding as Keilan spoke. "What you experienced matches with what we expected to find." He took a hurried sip from his wine, his eyes bright with excitement over the rim. "I will tell you something now, Keilan, that only a few of the most learned scholars and sorcerers know about. Perhaps it was common knowledge in the heyday of mankind, but this far into our twilight whatever was once known has almost totally been forgotten." Vhelan gestured at the fire, muttering softly, and the flames twisted higher. In their depths a hazy image formed, some great shape writhing within forest-covered hills so small they seemed to be but a cradle for the creature. "We are not the first, nor the greatest beings to inhabit this land. Ages ago this world was ruled by beasts so vast and terrible that they would seem as gods to our terrified ancestors. In Dymoria we call them the Ancients." The creature in the flames spasmed and stilled, then vanished as the land rushed up to cover it. "For reasons we do not know, these monsters disappeared or perished, though a few instead fell into eternal slumber. Perhaps you have heard of the White Worm of the North? That is the most storied of the Ancients, for travelers passing near its lair find their dreams invaded by thoughts and emotions so alien that they have been known to drive some mad. There are others, as well, though how many we do not know. The truly powerful and sensitive can feel them if they try, impossibly vast presences lurking on the edges of their minds. Our Crimson Queen is one such sorceress. Not long ago she was awoken in the night by one of these Ancients – not some dream tendril, mindlessly extended into our human existence as does sometimes happen, but an actual *conscious* thought that reverberated from the beast across the world. It stirred! Luckily, it rolled over and soon went back asleep, but not before our queen hurriedly sought out what had disturbed the creature. And she found, deep under the ocean, a filament of sorcery connecting what we call a sending to a small boy sitting in a fishing boat just off the coast of the Broken Sea."

Vhelan set down his again-empty cup and stared intensely at Keilan. "That is how we knew of you – because you almost woke a sleeping god."

"Close your mouth, boy," Nel said, chuckling, "unless you want to catch some flies."

Keilan blinked and shook his head, trying to shake away the creeping numbness he felt. *He had been right! He'd touched a god!*

"How could I do that?" he asked quietly.

Vhelan shrugged. "We don't know. In some of those who could become sorcerers their gift never manifests itself before they receive any instruction. Others experience odd coincidences or other minor happenings that usually could be explained away. To successfully send, without any training, is remarkable. I've never heard of such a thing before. Believe me, the queen is very interested to meet you."

"Who is this queen you keep speaking of? The Queen of Dymoria?"

"She is the beginning," Vhelan murmured, almost reverentially. "She is the hope of all men. For a thousand years those with our potential for greatness have been hunted down. Now, we have a haven again. A sanctuary. A place where we can work to elevate what it is to be human without fear of angry mobs or warriors cloaked in white."

"And she will teach me?"

Vhelan dismissed Keilan's question with a wave of his hand. "No, no, no. Cein d'Kara is far too busy ruling a kingdom and exploring the higher mysteries to instruct apprentices. But there are other teachers, fear not. We have nearly thirty students with the gift studying in Herath now, drawn from many lands."

The wizard leaned closer to Keilan. "And that leads me to what I wished to ask you. There are many roles for sorcerers in the court of the Crimson Queen. Some of us are teachers, some are researchers, some are historians. I am a hunter. My order is charged with discovering others with the gift, just like yourself. We roam the lands, trying to find the elusive ember of sorcery that with luck can be fanned into a full blaze. Sometimes it is like trying to find a speck of gold on a sandy shore – not everyone who is gifted goes around poking sleeping gods! But there may be a better way to ferret out future sorcerers than chasing down rumors and peasant's stories. The leader of the hunters believes that the gift, like the color of hair or eyes, can be passed from parent to child. So he is writing a great book about every wizard in

Dymoria – as he often says, a family line is much like a great river, with myriad branchings and streams that sometimes rival the original in size and strength. Already we have uncovered a few with the gift by fully mapping the family histories of sorcerers. So I must ask you about your mother and father. What do you know of their pasts?"

Keilan shrugged. "Not much, I'm afraid. My father's ancestors lived in our village for as far back as anyone could remember. They were all fishermen, and well-respected. I never heard of any with strange abilities."

"And your mother? You said before she taught you to read?"

Keilan shifted uncomfortably. "My mother . . . she was an outsider. My father fished her from the seas after her ship foundered on the rocks in a storm. They married, and I was born a few years later. I asked her, many times, about her family and the lands she'd sailed from, but she always turned my question away. She had some books that she'd rescued from the wreck, and she taught me to read using them. My mother taught me many things – she knew so much about the world outside our village, and before she died I imagined one day leaving with her to explore together the places she spoke of."

"Forgive me for asking," Vhelan said softly, lightly touching Keilan's arm, "but how did she die?"

"She was murdered," Keilan whispered, speaking past the sudden tightness in his throat.

Vhelan's expression suggested that he had expected to hear as much.

"She was different. Not of the village. Her words were flavored with a strange accent, she knew how to mix herbs to make drinks that could ease bone pains and bring down fevers, she sang in the evenings in a language no one else could understand . . . her hair was the color of moonlight on water. By the time I was ten years old or so I started to understand what others in the village were whispering about. That she was a witch, that she used sorcery to make her vegetable patch grow better than the neighbor's, or bring the best fish to my father's boat." Keilan wiped away a stray tear, surprised at the emotions he felt welling up. "I asked her once, if what the other children said was true, about her being a witch. She laughed and told me that the other villagers simply could not accept anyone who did things differently than how they had been done there for centuries. And then, when they finally came for her . . . it all just happened so fast."

Keilan paused, probing the memories of that day like it was an open wound. Nel and Vhelan were silent, waiting patiently for him to gather his thoughts. "There was another woman in town, a spinster. She hated my mother. Much later, Mam Ru told me that years ago she had loved my father; many thought they would get married before the stormy night when my mother's ship sank, and my father returned to shore with her. I remember she had a long thick braid that hadn't been cut for many years – since the day my father spurned her, Mam Ru said. This woman was always spreading gossip, terrible rumors that in the way of small villages quickly hardened into known truths. Then one day she sickened, an illness for which no cure could be found, and even as she wasted away she accused my mother of murdering her with sorcery. She died terribly, blood boiling out through her eyes and ears, and the death was so horrific and unusual that some in the village became convinced that dark forces actually were at work. So one night they came to our door. Men from the village."

Keilan stared hard into the flames, remembering the men clustered outside the door, demanding to come in. "They searched our house, looking for signs of witchcraft. If they'd found my books first I'm sure that would have been enough to justify what came next – but they found something else. A doll. A doll with a long, black braid. So they took her. I tried to go with them, but my father held me back. It was the only time I'd seen him cry, and it shocked me. He knew what would happen next, even if I did not. She did as well, though, and before she left she kissed me softly on the forehead and whispered that she loved me and would always be with me. Then the men – my father's friends and relatives, many of them – led her down the path to the sea and drowned her in the surf."

There was silence except for the hiss and crackle of the flames. Keilan saw that Nel's eyes, usually bright and mocking, had softened.

"I'm sorry, Keilan – my mother was murdered as well."

Vhelan prodded the fire with a long stick, causing it to flare higher. "I grieve for your loss. Tragedies like what happened to you and your mother have been too common for far too many centuries. That is why what we are building in Dymoria is so important. No more young boys should lose their mothers because of such ignorance."

Keilan nodded, trying to push down the welter of emotions that his remembering had stirred up.

Vhelan seemed to understand that he needed some time alone. "Well," the sorcerer said, twisting around to gather up his bedroll, "let us sleep. Tomorrow comes quickly. And the dawn will be bright, I promise you."

9: KEILAN

KEILAN WOKE. HIS face was pressed against a mat of woven grass, his legs tangled in a thin blanket. From somewhere in the distance, a flame painted the huge fragments of stone scattered around him in striations of shadow and light. His body ached, numb from sleeping on the hard, uneven ground, and his legs and inner thighs burned from riding Storm.

He found Nel and Vhelan's sleeping shapes in the semi-darkness; the sorcerer lay with his arms out-flung, his hand almost touching the remains of the previous night's fire, while his knife had curled herself into a tiny ball, her fingers resting lightly on the handle of one of her daggers. Keilan could hear a faint snoring, and to his surprise he thought it was coming from Nel and not Vhelan. He smiled in the darkness.

What had pulled him from his dreams? The snoring? He didn't think so. The light from the torches their guards had set along the edges of the ruin they camped inside? No. It had been something insistent, like an itch that demanded to be scratched. Perhaps his legs needed stretching. As quietly as he could, Keilan stood and began trying to massage the deep ache from his muscles.

With a start he realized that the snoring had stopped.

"Are you all right?" Nel whispered, uncoiling from her sleeping position and sitting up.

Keilan nodded. "Yes, just sore," he replied quietly.

But then he heard it, a faint scratching, like a cat wanting to come in. Now that he had noticed the sound he recognized it as what had dragged him awake. "Did you hear something?" he asked Nel.

She cocked her head. "Nothing unusual. Perhaps it is the men on the night watch?"

As if prompted, the faint sound of laughter floated up from the entrance to the ruined building.

"No," Keilan said, peering into the darkness pooled around them. "But maybe I'm imagining it."

Then it came again, louder, claws scraping against stone. "It sounds like an animal," Keilan whispered.

Nel nudged Vhelan with her foot, and the sorcerer snorted awake. "Yes? What is it?" he murmured sleepily.

"Quiet," Nel hissed. "Keilan says he hears something nearby. It sounds like an animal."

"That's preposterous," Vhelan said, not bothering to keep his voice low. "What beast would approach the light and noise of our camp? And anyways, if there was an animal prowling about we shouldn't be quiet, but loud so we can scare it off. Speaking quietly is fool . . . wait." The sorcerer bent his head, as if listening hard for something. "Wait, I heard it. Like a scratching, yes?"

Keilan nodded as Vhelan cupped his hands and began muttering an incantation. Light seeped from between his fingers, then briefly flared, and he released another glowing ball like the one that had preceded them during their night ride through the forest. Slowly it drifted above the dead fire, banishing the darkness and drenching the ruins in its pale, colorless light. Keilan looked around, expecting to glimpse the tail of a wild cat or fox vanishing into a chink in the wall, but saw nothing. The scratching suddenly became more frantic, as if excited by the light.

Another sound, this time the crunching of many boots on gravel, and Keilan turned to find a group of rangers hurriedly approaching.

"What's going on?" said the captain with the red-dragon medallion when he arrived, the magical light making the steel of the sword he held run like quicksilver.

"Shhhh," Vhelan said, gesturing for quiet. He crept closer to one of the walls and the glowing ball followed him, illuminating intricate carvings that seemed to show some kind of ritual: dozens of men and women, their heads bowed, shuffling towards a taller man wearing a faceted mask with many eyes. The priest – if it was a priest – had his arms upraised, and in one hand he held a curved dagger. In the other he brandished what looked to be a heart. Behind him was a pit piled high with tangled bodies, dark holes cut into their chests. Keilan was almost certain that the scratching was coming from behind this carving.

Vhelan reached out tentatively, brushing the ancient stone with his fingers. When he touched the heart held aloft by the priest there was a click, and with a faint grinding a square of the carving receded slightly.

"Wait, magister," the captain said, putting his hand on Vhelan's shoulder, but the sorcerer was already shoving the panel aside, and it slid away to reveal a square hole just large enough for a man to squeeze through. A draft of cold air pushed out, heavy with the musty smell of dust and age-rotted things.

Vhelan glanced back at them, his eyes bright with excitement. "Who wants to come with me?"

The captain of the rangers stepped forward, making a cutting motion with his hand. "No, I forbid it. This foolishness has gone on long enough, wizard. We need to break camp right now and put some distance between ourselves and this cursed city."

Vhelan clucked his tongue. "Captain, if you're afraid of sorcery you are guarding the wrong man, and sworn to serve the wrong queen."

Keilan imagined he could hear the ranger's teeth grinding. "I am a loyal soldier to the Dragon Throne. But just as there are some good men and some bad, so the same is true of sorcery. And this place has the stink of evil."

"The stink of evil," Vhelan repeated, chuckling. "What does that smell like? Old eggs? The only smell coming from this hole is the admittedly rather fetid stench of things hidden a thousand years ago and forgotten about. I am worried about traps, it's true, but luckily I have with me the finest eyes in Lyr at finding and disarming such things. Nel?"

With an exaggerated sigh his knife stepped forward. "You know, boss, you did hear something scratching at that wall just a moment ago. Maybe you should be more careful?"

"I have a theory about that, actually," Vhelan replied, running his hands along the outline of the hidden door. Dust sifted down, disturbed for the first time in centuries.

"I think there was some kind of spell set on this secret panel. It's been waiting a thousand years for a sorcerer to come close enough so that it could activate and reveal itself. I can only imagine what waits for us within."

Keilan found his own heart beating faster at the giddiness he heard in Vhelan's voice.

The glowing sphere floated through the secret entrance, revealing a passageway sloping downwards.

"We're going inside," Vhelan said, rolling up his sleeves. "Who else wants a share of the treasure we find?"

Several of the rangers glanced at each other, but none said anything.

"Go with him," the captain said, his frustration evident. "Do your best to make sure he comes back in one piece."

Three of the rangers moved toward the door, but Nel held up her hand before they started to climb inside. "I'll go first. I should be able to find any nasty little surprises the previous tenants might have left behind."

With effortless grace she vaulted through the opening, and after a moment of careful inspection she beckoned for the rest to join her. The rangers sheathed their blades and pulled themselves inside; Vhelan followed last, clambering through the raised door with grunting awkwardness.

The sorcerer straightened his tunic, brushing away a smear of gray dust. "Keilan, you discovered this place as much as I. You should come with us."

Keilan's heart quickened again, and though his head was emphatically telling him he shouldn't accompany the sorcerer he found that his legs were moving toward the secret door.

"There's a good lad," Vhelan said when Keilan had climbed through the entrance, putting a hand on his shoulder. "Bravery is one of the most important traits for any sorcerer. Now, let's see where this takes us, eh?"

Nel took the lead as they moved down the passage, her eyes darting everywhere as she examined the walls and floor for possible traps. They had gone only a little ways when a familiar grinding started from behind them.

"The hole!" Nel cried, sprinting back the way they had come. Keilan followed, a sinking feeling in his stomach. When they arrived at the entrance they found smooth stone, only the slightest of grooves to indicate that there was any kind of hidden door. Vhelan slapped the wall with the flat of his hand.

"Captain d'Taran! Can you hear me?"

"I can, magister," came the faint response, as if passing through a great length of stone, rather than just a few spans. "The door closed on its own."

"Of course," replied Vhelan, his shouted replies echoing in the tiny passage. "Can you touch the same stone I did? The one shaped like a heart?"

There was a brief pause, and Keilan held his breath, desperately hoping to hear again the sound of the stone grinding.

"Nothing is happening. It's like there's no door here."

Vhelan muttered a curse under his breath. "All right," the wizard said, rolling up his sleeves. "Let's see how the old magic of Kalyuni compares to what we are creating in Dymoria." His long fingers sketched a glittering pattern upon the stone as he chanted in a language that tickled at Keilan's memory, almost as if he had known it once and then forgotten. The sorcerer's words boomed louder as he approached a crescendo, and Keilan covered his ears and ducked back as Vhelan finished the spell and smote the stone with his fist.

Nothing happened.

"Hmmm," Nel said, "looks like the wizards of Dymoria still have a few things left to learn."

"Be quiet," Vhelan muttered, massaging his hand. "Gods, that hurt." He stepped back, studying the wall critically. "There's powerful wards here. I won't be able to breach them easily." The *if at all* hung unspoken.

"It's fine," Nel said, "I'm sure there's food and water further down this passage. We can just wait a few weeks to be rescued." The rangers glanced at each other, their faces ashen.

"Quiet, Nel, you're scaring them. Don't worry everyone, Nel and I have been in more precarious situations than this. Remember the tomb of the Leopard Prince, in the catacombs below Lyr?"

"I remember being so hungry we ate a rat raw."

Vhelan flourished something from his pocket, a chunk of flint. "See? Our situation now is improved. We can start a fire – cooked rat tastes much better."

Nel rolled her eyes, turning away. "Well, let's hope it doesn't come to that. Maybe there's another way out, or some sort of key down here. Whoever built this place would have left something like that behind, surely."

"That's the spirit, Nel," the sorcerer said, hurrying to catch up with her quick, little strides. "I've missed this, you know. Sometimes I think we should break into a few noble's mansions in Herath, just to keep life interesting."

His knife chuckled softly. "Who is to say I don't do that already?"

"You don't, do you?" Vhelan cried, but Nel ignored the sorcerer, staring straight ahead. "Oh, you traitorous little wench."

The bickering between the wizard and his knife continued as the party moved down the passage, which swelled larger as they walked, until the ceiling no longer brushed the hair of the tallest ranger. Several times it jagged slightly, though always it continued to slope downwards. The walls were engraved with the same intricate friezes as the ruins above; the subject matter had changed, however, as now they depicted two great armies clashing. On one side the soldiers wore pleated skirts and had pointed helms, and their generals rode in chariots pulled by giant spiders. Their enemies were clad in carapaces of metal that covered every inch of their bodies, spikes and twisted barbs emerging from the joints, and even their faces were hidden beneath stylized masks that resembled grinning demons. At least Keilan hoped they were masks. Looming over the battle, as large as the mountains in the background, was the four-armed man from the mosaic on the ruin's ceiling.

Vhelan paused briefly to better examine the carven creature. "I believe we are in a temple to this demon," he said, stabbing the image with a finger. "I don't know much about it, but I've read that one of Kalyuni's many cults worshipped a spider demon, and this must be him. Handsome fellow."

"So are we caught in his web?" Nel asked.

Vhelan shook his head. "No. This place is a bolthole, a refuge of last resort. There should be some way of getting out – otherwise it wouldn't make a very good sanctuary, would it?"

A little farther on the light passed from the narrow corridor into a wider space beyond. Nel motioned for them to be still, then crouched lower and crept ahead. Keilan kept himself motionless, but he craned his neck forward, trying to make out the strange shapes the light was illuminating through the doorway. Nel vanished within the room, and as the seconds crept past the rangers and Keilan shared a few worried glances. Vhelan, however, seemed unperturbed, and he even began to hum softly. When the sorcerer caught Keilan's eye, he winked.

Finally, Nel emerged again, striding confidently back towards them. "There's a room, with nothing dangerous inside. Come, you should see this."

It looked like it had once been the personal chamber of someone important. The ceiling was lost to the shadows, ribs of stone curving up to vanish into darkness. A great table of black stone dominated the room, around which were scattered the remains of chairs, all reduced to shards of wood and metal except for the great granite throne positioned at the table's head. A skeleton in scraps of finery slouched in this seat, its skull resting in the dust of the table and its hand still clutching a tarnished goblet. The glowing orb had come to hover above the table, and Keilan saw that strands of silver threaded the deep black of its stone, almost as if a great spiderweb was sunk just below the surface. Stone shelves were recessed into the walls, many filled with mounds of paper fragments. When Vhelan saw this he cried out in delight and rushed over to investigate. The rest of the room was filled with the detritus of furniture: some of it had long since rotted past the point of identification, but Keilan saw the collapsed outlines of a few chests pushed against another wall, and the rangers moved quickly in that direction.

Keilan jumped when he felt Nel's light touch on his arm. "What do you think those are?" she asked, pointing at large holes in the walls at the upper edges of the orb's light.

"Perhaps some way to run water here? Or get fresh air?"

Nel nodded, but from the set of her mouth he didn't think she was convinced.

"Look at this!" Vhelan exclaimed, carefully pulling an intact scroll from the mounds of disintegrated paper. Cradling it gently he rushed to the table and laid it down, gesturing for Keilan and Nel to approach.

"Given the age of this city, and the state of the rest of the parchment here, this should be in fragments. And yet it is not." Vhelan stroked the yellowed vellum lovingly, lingering on the rosewood rollers that bound the scroll. "That means it has been magically preserved. And *that* means that there is a fair likelihood that this is a spell scroll, inscribed with one or more of the lost sorceries of the Mosaic Cities." Vhelan gathered in a deep breath, and then let it out slowly, as if trying to master himself.

Nel frowned, fingering the tattered edges of the scroll. "It might be a spell scroll, or it might be the cult's collected holy spider songs. Let's not dream of lordships from the Crimson Queen quite yet."

"True, true," Vhelan murmured, unrolling the scroll slightly. "We won't know for certain until we get back to Herath and find a scholar who can read High Kalyuni."

"I can read High Kalyuni," Keilan said, bending closer to see what Vhelan had revealed of the writing. "Ah, the first few words are: "*As the black sun wanes* – no, sorry – *waxes*."

He straightened to find Nel and Vhelan staring at him. "You read High Kalyuni?" the sorcerer exclaimed incredulously.

"Yes, my mother taught me. We had a few books in my house."

"Who in the seven abysses was your mother? There can't be more than a half-dozen people in all of Dymoria who can read it! And you had *books* written in High Kalyuni? You probably could have bought your entire village several times over!"

"I . . . I don't know," Keilan stammered, shrugging helplessly. "She never spoke of her life before my father saved her."

"Magister," said one of the rangers as he approached them carrying the rusted remains of a metal strongbox.

With a final long look, Vhelan turned away from Keilan. "Yes?"

The ranger set the box on the table and flipped open its lid. "We've gathered what we could salvage from the chests here."

Nel came around the edge of the table and peered into the box, her eyes widening when she saw the contents.

"You can keep your scrolls, boss," she said, pulling out a necklace of glittering purple stones, "it looks like there's something here for everybody."

Quickly she spread the objects out on the table, pushing away the skeletal hand and its goblet to make room. Aside from the necklace, there were several other pieces of jewelry – a few gold and silver rings inset with colorful gems, a circlet of delicately wrought strands of silver studded with chips of lapis lazuli, and another necklace, a thin black thread from which dangled a huge smooth-cut blue stone with a white cross emblazoned in its center.

"A star sapphire," Nel breathed as she slipped the thread over her head, the stone settling just below her throat.

There were also loose gems, both rough and cut; from their colors, Keilan could guess that there were diamonds and emeralds and opals, among many others he could not recognize. Nel scooped up a handful of these stones and gave them to the ranger. "Your reward, for following us down here. Share it with your fellows."

"Yes, Lady Nel! The blessing of the Ten be upon you!"

As he hurried over to where the other rangers waited Nel continued pulling treasures from the box. A curved dagger with a faceted ebony handle quickly vanished into one of the numerous secret pockets that were sown into her leather tunic and leggings. More paper fragments that Vhelan stirred with his finger, looking for anything readable.

"What is this?" Nel asked as she drew out a wadded pile of white cloth. "Looks like silk, but that would have rotted away a long time ago. Any ideas?" She tossed the fabric towards Keilan; it was so light that it caught the air and floated into his hands.

Keilan unfolded the cloth, marveling at how slick and supple the material was, despite its incredible lightness. He recognized what it was almost immediately and slipped it on over his head. "It's a shirt," he said, smoothing the fabric against his chest, "though I don't think it would be very warm. It hardly even feels like I'm wearing anything."

Vhelan stopped prodding the paper fragments and turned to rub the edge of the shirt between his fingers. "Remarkable. I've heard of something like this, one of the lost artifacts of the Imperium. Shirts made of spider silk, as smooth and light as the finest gossamer, yet as hard as steel." The sorcerer drew forth a small dagger and gently pressed the tip into the shirt, which dimpled but did not tear. "A great treasure. If it's as light as you say, I would wear it always."

A magic shirt! Keilan seemed to have somehow stumbled into one of his old daydreams; a wave of dizziness washed over him, and he reached out to the table to steady himself.

He gasped and jerked his hand back – the stone was thrumming. Nel and Vhelan glanced at him sharply

"Touch the table," Keilan whispered.

The sorcerer frowned and put his palm flat on the surface. "There's some kind of vibration."

"It's not the stone," Nel said, pointing at the silvery strands sunk into the blackness. They were moving like the plucked strings on a lute.

A thought came to Keilan, and cold fear settled in his chest. "Vhelan, Nel. Have you ever seen what happens when an insect blunders into a spider web?"

"Of course," Vhelan said with a hint of exasperation, "the creature is caught, and the spider wraps it up and drinks its blood."

Keilan swallowed hard. He could see realization slowly dawning in Nel's face. "How does the spider know the prey is trapped? It lurks elsewhere, waiting to feel the thrashing in the web."

"It knows from the vibrations," Nel murmured.

Keilan placed his hands again on the table. He slowed his breathing, reaching for the same sense of tranquility he needed before he used to attempt his dowsing aboard his father's fishing boat; he felt the stone, cold and hard and smooth, and embedded within it the gleaming threads of silver, hard as braided steel but thrumming like catgut, running under the surface, down the table's legs, into the floor, branching and spreading like a great tree through the stone, the walls, the ruin. Keilan flitted along the strands, and the ruins unfolded for him: it was so vast, tunnels and catacombs spiraling into the darkness, rooms stacked with pyramids of skulls, a great pool of glistening blackness, headless statues guarding something terrible he did not want to see, so he turned away as he flickered past . . . and movement. He felt movement in the great web, cold glimmering lights that were racing through the darkness, skittering towards . . .

He gasped and reeled away from the table, his hand pulsing with coldness, as if he had been clutching ice.

"We . . . we have to . . . to get out. Things are coming here, quickly."

"What?" Vhelan said, but Nel was already moving, pocketing more of the treasure and shoving the scroll towards the sorcerer.

"Stow that somewhere, boss. I've got a bad feeling. You there," she yelled at the rangers, who were crouched on the floor dividing up their spoils. "Prepare yourself for battle."

Sighing, Vhelan shoved the scroll into his belt and shook his hands free of his long sleeves. "To me, boy," he said to Keilan, beckoning him closer.

Nel slapped the ebony-handled dagger on the table and slid it across to Keilan. "Stab anything with more than two legs," she said.

"Where are they coming from?" one of the rangers asked. He was the only one who had brought his bow, and he had an arrow nocked.

"There!" Nel cried, pointing with a dagger at the holes set high up on the walls. A black shape was creeping forth from one, long spindly legs emerging from the darkness.

The ranger loosed his arrow, and it struck true, embedding in the bulbous center of the beast with a fleshy thunk. Silently, the shape detached from the wall, its legs folding up as it fell. The sound it made when it struck the stone floor was like the ice on a frozen pond fracturing.

"By the mercy of the Silver Lady," one of the ranger whispered, "is that a spider?"

"A bolthole, he called it. A refuge," Nel said sarcastically, daggers Keilan recognized as Chance and Fate glittering in her hands. "But a web? No."

Vhelan fluttered his fingers, and the wizardlight brightened, bathing the room in brilliant white radiance. "Sorry, my knife. Even I can be wrong once in a summer's snow."

"Once in a summer's snow," Nel muttered to herself, leaping up onto the table and facing the hole from where the spider had emerged. "This could be the last 'once in a summer's snow' I hear you ever say."

"How many of those things did you feel? Was it just the one?" Vhelan asked.

Keilan shrugged. "No, not just one . . . I couldn't count. There were so many."

"Then where are –"

Before the sorcerer could finish a torrent of black shapes exploded from several of the holes, not slowly creeping like the first spider but skittering at great speed down the walls, their obscene legs blurs of movement. The ranger fired as fast as he could; his first shaft struck the wall and went spinning away, but the second embedded itself in one of the spiders and the creature again dropped, while the third hit the edge of a bloated abdomen, and although ichor splashed out, the spider kept scrabbling down the stone.

The leading spider touched the floor, took a few quick mincing steps as it gathered itself, and then leaped at Nel atop the table, mandibles spread wide. The knife twisted from the path of the spider and lashed out with a dagger, and by the time the creature had struck the ground its legs had already folded up in death, its entrails bursting from a long gash in its side.

"Gods," he heard the sorcerer breathe, and then Keilan also gasped as he glanced away from the dead spider and back at the wall. It was a black waterfall of hard chitinous bodies, a horde of spiders the size of large dogs rushing downwards.

Then the creatures were upon them. The sorcerer flung a bolt of red energy at the closest charging spider, and it jiggered and danced before collapsing. But the swarm behind it clambered over its body, eyes like black jewels glittering in the harsh wizardlight. Their front legs were upraised, covered in black fur and tipped with wicked, curving claws. The sorcerer sketched a shimmering blue shield in the air, and a spider slammed into it, threading the barrier with cracks. Vhelan grunted and speared the spider with another lance of red energy, bursting its abdomen and splattering the magical shield with lashings of black ichor.

A spider skirted the edge of the barrier, coming close to Keilan. With a terrified cry he sliced down with his dagger, cutting into one of the monster's legs. The spider danced sideways in pain, knocking over Keilan, who struck the back of his head hard against one of the legs of the granite throne. He tasted blood in his mouth and tried to stand, but the spider was looming over him, a great mass of hard black shell and flailing legs. Keilan screamed and closed his eyes, expecting to feel the spider's mandibles at his throat, but when nothing happened he opened his eyes a crack . . . then had to cry out again as the spider's horrific face was only a few span from his own. He saw clacking mandibles spread beneath rows of soulless, black eyes, each reflecting his own terrified face. Then the creature was gone, skittering away.

Keilan scrambled to his feet, stumbling as the spiders surged around him. But they paid him no heed, intent on throwing themselves at the others. Was it the spider-silk shirt he wore? One of the rangers was down, clutching a ravaged leg, while his two companions stood over him, desperately hacking at the spiders with their stubby swords. Nel was still on the table, dancing back and forth, dodging the spiders as they leaped to grab her. Several of the monsters were curled near her, fluids leaking from their stabbed abdomens. Vhelan had backed himself into a corner, a few of his blue crackling shields just barely holding the mass of spiders at bay. And still the horde came on, spilling from the holes above. They would be overwhelmed in a matter of moments.

Light flared in the chamber. Not the harsh wizardlight but a golden, blinding radiance that forced Keilan to cover his eyes. When he opened them, blinking away the burning spots in his vision, he saw the impossible.

The rangers they'd left above were flooding the room, loosing arrows into the churning maelstrom of carapaces and legs. Most of the spiders had stopped, stunned by the golden light, and charging amongst them was the Pure, the silver-haired paladin who had first taken Keilan from his village. His white-metal sword flashed as he laid about, splitting open the spiders, the light in his eyes blazing with a golden fury. A few of the spiders turned to meet him, but his blade was a scythe, and soon the creatures were fleeing before the Pure, crawling over each other to escape.

But still more were streaming from the holes in the walls, meeting the retreating tide and turning them back.

"Flee!" the paladin cried as he skewered a spider. "Back to the surface!"

Nel jumped off the table and hurled a dagger at the spiders pressing Vhelan. One of the monsters juddered and collapsed, the blade lodged in an eye. Then Nel was among them, ripping that dagger free and plunging it and its brother into the heads of two spiders heaving against the largest of Vhelan's shields, which was so riddled with cracks that pieces of glowing blue glass had already flaked away. Red light stabbed out from the sorcerer, but Keilan thought it looked much reduced, and on a few spiders the energy simply coruscated along their carapaces and vanished with no other effect. But Nel was relentless, and soon she'd carved enough of a gap that Vhelan could drop his shields and follow her toward the doorway.

The injured ranger and his companions who had followed the sorcerer below had been carried away by the others, and after Nel and Vhelan had passed through the door only a small force remained near the exit: a few rangers releasing arrows into the encroaching horde and the Pure standing before them, his sword a crescent of white light as he hewed through the spiders. Keilan paused briefly at the doorway, watching the tide break upon the paladin, but then one of the archers pushed him hard and yelled for him to go.

Keilan scrambled back up the passageway in darkness, having left the wizardlight guttering in the chamber below. A square of light appeared ahead, the secret door, and then he was out, gasping as strong arms pulled him through. He found his footing and turned back to the hole. The panel that had once slid closed behind them was shattered, wisps of smoke still rising from the blackened shards of stone. He watched the darkness, panting hard, clutching the ebony dagger to his chest. Every ranger above ground had nocked their bow and trained it on the hole, waiting.

Keilan found himself counting his breaths. Thirty. Seventy. One hundred. He felt hope begin to fade.

Then a ragged cheer went up as the rangers who had stayed behind to cover their retreat tumbled through the hole and into the torchlight. Quickly they were pulled aside to safety, and then the watch on the door resumed.

Nothing more came through. Keilan heard the captain of the rangers curse softly. "All right," he said loudly, "I'm going back in to try and find that paladin. Who is with me?"

A few of the other rangers stepped forward, including one of the men who had just burst through the hole – his face was pale and his long red hair wild but there was a hard glint in his eyes as he nocked another arrow to his bow and stood.

"Wait!" cried Nel. "Look!"

A light was moving up the passage, getting brighter. Keilan glanced at Vhelan, but the sorcerer shook his head.

"It's not mine. I kept my wizardlight suspended in the chamber."

"It's him," said Nel, and it was. Golden light spilling from his eyes and a white glow burnishing his sword, the paladin walked calmly up the passage, stooping to pass through the shattered remnants of the secret panel.

Another cheer went up, this time louder than the first. From his cuirass to his boots the Pure's armor was stained black by the ichor of slain spiders, and there were long rents in his chain-mail leggings, parts of which hung in tatters, revealing deep cuts beneath. He took two steps towards the men saluting him with upraised bows and then collapsed, the white-metal sword slipping from his fingers to ring hollowly upon the stone.

10: JAN

SOMEWHERE WITHIN THIS silken labyrinth lurked a monster.

Jan breathed deep, his fingers brushing Bright's pommel. The garden's air was redolent with the scent of perfume and flowers, but to him those smells were subsumed by the acrid foulness he had tracked here. The journey had been long, nearly a month, over the jagged spine of the Bones and across chalk-white plains, to the ancient city of Menekar and this sprawling palace. At times the trail he followed had faded, dwindled to nothingness, but inevitably there would be some thick accretion of the thing's spoor clinging to the eviscerated corpse of a plains lion or bison, markers he understood to be signposts, leading him on. It wanted him here, in the pleasure gardens of the emperor.

Iridescent silks whispered in the breeze. They hung from branches and filigreed copper poles sunk among the flower beds, soft shades of green, red, yellow, purple, as varied as the garden's exotic blossoms. And within each pastel prison cell waited a young, beautiful girl. Some reclined on divans, while others sprawled on cushions or sucked on tubes that snaked into squat metal contraptions, eyes heavy-lidded, smoke leaking from the corners of their mouths. A few glanced at him incuriously as he passed. Jan did not worry that they would raise an alarm – he had watched enough ministers and servants enter these grounds to know that he, in his stolen Menekarian finery, would not seem out of place.

He was more concerned about the Pure. Jan could sense them by their absences, holes cut into the fabric of the world, wandering points of nothingness. Could they feel him? At times it almost seemed so. The paladins of Ama would waver in their rounds, quest out with tendrils searching, and he would be forced to gather up his power and fold deep within himself – until, apparently satisfied, they moved on.

How had the creature he tracked avoided their attention?

A peach-colored pavilion rose before him, larger than any he had yet passed. The trail vanished inside. Shadowy shapes moved within, languid female forms; low voices and laughter spilled out.

An image of those mutilated horses came to him, their heads wedged among the branches, lips curled back in rictal death-grimaces. He banished it and pulled aside the flap.

Three young women lazed upon a rumpled bed, dressed in wisps of diaphanous cloth: a blonde giantess, slender as a sword, her long arms wrapped around the waist of a freckled, red-haired girl, who sat cross-legged. The dark head of the third was pillowed in her lap, turned away from Jan, her dusky hand reaching up to toy idly with the ringlets that lay upon the red-head's pale skin. When Jan entered, the blonde woman gasped, but the red-haired girl only gave him a curious half-smile, and bent to whisper something in the ear of the third. The hand of the dark-haired girl released the red curls and moved to lovingly caress a freckled cheek.

Jan's eyes darted around the room. Where was the creature? There were just these three girls, the bed they sprawled on, some wrought-brass candelabras, and a rosewood chest carved with what looked like Shan symbols.

The chest. Jan strode across the pavilion and knelt beside it, tracing the characters etched into the wood. There was a binding here, sorcerous filaments holding shut the lid, but the creature's foul residue coated everything, and a whiff of the miasma he had followed for so many weeks trickled from within. His heart quickened as he set his hand upon the lid, a spell to shatter the invisible chains forming.

"I applaud your bravery, but I don't think you truly wish to do that."

The magics scattered, as if the voice had reached within him and brushed aside the forming spell. Jan turned to the bed. The dark-haired girl faced him now, and although he recognized her, he did not know her; as he went to grasp his elusive memories they squirmed away, vanishing into his mind's still-shadowed recesses. But his emotions rose again, powerful and fraught, just as they had when he had first caught her sweet scent underneath the creature's spoor and the stale smell of horseblood. He swallowed, cautiously fingering the edges of that feeling. Had he once cared deeply for this Alyanna?

"Who are you?"

The redhead giggled.

"Behave, child," admonished Alyanna.

The blond-haired girl was staring at him fearfully, muttering under her breath, some repeated mantra in a language he did not know.

"Hush," Alyanna murmured, and the girl instantly quieted. Then she sat up. "Please excuse these two," she said, addressing Jan again. "Bex has been my favorite for far too long. I spoil her, and this has fed the insolence you now see. I shall have to discipline her." She reached back to cup the taller woman's chin. "This one is new to the gardens. She can barely speak the common tongue, and for all my years I've never bothered to learn Skein. I believe she thinks you're a demon. Certainly that's what she imagines I am." Alyanna laughed. "And perhaps she's right. What do you think?"

Jan turned from the chest and stood. "I don't know."

Her hand slipped from the blonde girl's face. "But you remember my name?"

"Alyanna."

She closed her eyes, smiling. "It's so good to hear you say my name again." She rose and swayed towards him, eyes still shut.

Jan instinctively took a step backward; she opened her eyes, laughing again. "The Bard, a high lord of Min-Ceruth, scared of me?" She clucked her tongue then drew closer, placing a tiny palm on his chest. She smelled of spices and lilacs, and something else, something almost animal in its muskiness. He felt himself stirring. Her breasts pressed against him; he could feel her own arousal through his thin linen tunic. "Kiss me, Jan duth Verala," she whispered, her lips almost brushing his, "I've missed your taste."

"No," he said, taking a few stumbling steps backward. She did not follow him – instead she shrugged, as if his rejection was of no importance to her, and then returned to the bed, reclining with a sigh.

"Well, you remember *something* at least."

"My memories . . . are there. I can feel them," he said shakily. "But when I try and hold them they slip away. I know things about the world, but no details of my own life, save my name and a few other fragments. Who was I?"

"Your memories might be truly gone this time. Certainly they've seemed to fade the last few awakenings. I've wondered if even minds such as ours could overcome so many purgings."

"This has happened before?"

She sank back onto the bed. "Every time you remember."

"Who does it to me? You?"

She laughed, rolling onto her side and burying her face in the red-haired girl's pale thigh. "No, foolish man," she said, her voice muffled. "You do it to yourself."

"I don't believe you."

Alyanna sat up, serious again. "I don't care if you believe me or not. But I like you better when you don't remember. Watching you drag yourself around wallowing in guilt and self-pity is not becoming."

"I keep dreaming of a woman with golden hair and eyes like the ocean. Who is she?"

Alyanna shook her head. "Poor Jan. We've danced this dance before, you know. And I shall tell you what I told you last time, in the coral temple of Lyr's Oracle: knowledge is currency, and if you wish for me to reveal your truths you must do something in exchange. Secrets for a service rendered."

He found he was gripping Bright's hilt with white-knuckled strength. "What would you have me do?"

She waved away his words and patted the bed beside her. "In good time, Jan. Come sit with me."

"I will stand."

She shrugged again, then groped in the tangled sheets for something, eventually holding up a small silver bell. "Wine? Sweetmeats?"

"Nothing."

She tossed the bell back among the blankets. "Don't pout. If it wasn't for me you'd still be covered in sheep-dung and sobbing over your dead wife."

"Then you *were* the one who awakened me."

Alyanna rolled her eyes. "Of course I did. This age is ending, Jan. The world's twilight draws to a close. Will a new dawn follow, or endless night? I could not let you sleep through such happenings."

"Those murders . . . just to jolt me awake?"

Her gaze drifted to the rosewood chest. "My new servants are enthusiastic, I know. They succeeded in their task, as here you are. But the means were not as subtle as I would have liked. I'm sure that more attention was drawn than just your own."

"Your servants mutilated three innocent men. I came here to destroy whatever did that."

"And I would suggest you put such thoughts out of your head, as I won't allow it. For my part I will keep them on a tighter leash, though not for any reason as paltry as a few mortal lives."

"What are they? My memory is riddled with holes, but I know I've never sensed anything like them before."

Alyanna wagged a finger at him. "Again – secrets. However, as we will soon be working together I will satisfy a little of your curiosity. You are right, incidentally, though they are at least as old as us this land is very new to them. They have spent the last thousand years imprisoned, and I gather that they are quite excited to taste freedom again, even if I still hold their chains." Alyanna gestured towards the chest. "They arrived after the cataclysms and the Cleansing."

"They are Shan."

"Are, or were, or perhaps they are something else entirely that the Shan encountered in their long wanderings before they arrived at our shores."

"Isn't it dangerous to employ such servants? If you do not know what they are, how can you understand their strength?" Jan eyed the chest warily.

"If you remembered more you'd know I've always been a gambler. And since here I still am, one of the few of us not dead or broken," she raised her eyebrows pointedly at him, "you must realize that the risks I take are well considered. I've kept the same spells in place that have bound these creatures for centuries – I've merely allowed a bit more slack, so that they can be of some use."

He considered what she had said. He had come here to destroy whatever had murdered the men of his village . . . but Alyanna claimed she could control them. How could he trust her not to loose them again? She would have no qualms about murdering other innocents if such actions benefited her, he was sure. And yet despite this, he could not think of her as evil, at least as most might conceive of the term. She seemed beyond the boundaries of morality. Or was that the very definition of evil? Had he once been like her? The thought disquieted him.

"Put them out of your mind," she urged. "Let me tell you why I called you here."

"You said this age is ending."

"Indeed. Here, look at this." Alyanna rummaged in the blankets again and drew forth what looked to be a small, metal bird inlaid with jewels and colored glass. She twisted a key set in its back and it shivered to life, turning its head from side to side as its wings slowly flapped. Jan heard tinny birdsong as its beak open and closed.

"What is it?"

"A toy. A metaphor. A harbinger."

"I don't understand."

The bird's movements slowed, the noise it made becoming stretched out, attenuated. "You see? Imagine this clockwork toy is this world. In the dim times long ago some entity cracked open the doors within us to the Void – a god, a demon, perhaps even Ama himself, so that his followers would have someone to persecute. And for thousands of years the pulse of magic thrummed in our world . . . yet since the cataclysms destroyed Min-Ceruth and the Imperium it has grown fainter and fainter, like the slowing of this clockwork bird, or a dying man's heartbeat. No sorcerer of real power has been birthed for five hundred years. Until now, perhaps."

"Perhaps?"

A troubled look passed over Alyanna's face. "Perhaps. I don't understand – I thought I did. I was certain magic was leaching from this world, never to return, that the stream feeding us power from the Void was slowly drying up. And yet the pulse has suddenly strengthened. Great powers are stirring again; in the north I can sense the White Worm edging toward wakefulness, and in the seas, only a month past, one of the other Ancients briefly surfaced from its dreams before subsiding again. My spies tell me that in the black pyramids of Xi the spawn of Rho-goreth are again thrashing in their fetid pools, and in the Shan's Empire of Swords and Flowers the cult of the Raveling has returned. In the far west a new sorceress has arisen: Cein d'Kara, the Crimson Queen of Dymoria. My attempts to discover information about her – whether she is a fresh incarnation of an old wizard, perhaps even one of us, or a new power – have been rebuffed. Is she the cause of sorcery returning to the world, or merely one of its products? Is she a threat or an opportunity? Will she be a piece or a player in this game?"

"You want me to find out what she is."

"Go there. Hide your Talent, if you can. Sing your songs and dazzle the court. Even if she pierces whatever glamour you weave I doubt she could destroy you, and even if she can I imagine she would be too intrigued to try. But be wary, she does have power. She has devised some method of hiding other sorcerers, not just herself, from the gaze of the Pure – she successfully concealed a wizard in this very palace, a dozen paces from an entire cohort of Ama's paladins. I had to compel a heron to fly through the window of the imperial audience chamber just to alert the light-addled fools."

Jan idly smoothed out the bed's wrinkles as he pretended to consider. In truth he had already decided – the answers Alyanna dangled were reason enough to do what she asked. He desperately wanted to bridge the vast chasms between his few scattered memories. If Alyanna could do that, he would perform this task for her.

He also found the mystery of this Crimson Queen more than a little tantalizing. Even the sheep farmer Janus Balensorn had heard stories of the young, beautiful monarch who was carving an empire out of the western reaches, and almost every wine sink and inn he had passed through on his way to Menekar had been abuzz with strange rumors. She was planning a great expeditionary fleet to the Sunset Lands; she had forged alliances with the Skein thanes to invade the Gilded Cities; her consort was an exiled Shan princeling, and she had born him a demon child.

Jan nodded towards the red-haired girl, who now rested her head on Alyanna's shoulder. "She's Dymorian?"

The immortal sorceress twisted her neck so she could kiss the girl's forehead. "Yes, though unfortunately Bex was born in the slave pits of Gryx, and has no knowledge of the queen. I've found that my . . . interests . . . tend to find reflections in my personal desires." She suddenly laughed, high and sweet. "You know, I first came here to unravel fully the mysteries of the Pure, and I ended up seducing more than a few of them into breaking their precious vows before I realized that none of them had any real insight into what they truly are. Boring creatures, really. Bex is far more entertaining."

"Is that why you've stayed?"

"I stay here because I control an empire through the fool that sits the alabaster throne. If you return telling me that this Cein d'Kara is a threat – or do not return at all – I assure you that the Menekarian legions will march over the Bones for the first time in centuries."

Her chin resting on laced fingers, deep in thought, Alyanna continued to stare at the pavilion's flaps long after Jan had passed through them. She felt him move through the garden, then the palace, his power shining bright among the dull, untalented servants and the few searing points of emptiness that were the Pure. The lips of her Dymorian courtesan nuzzled her neck as she considered what had just transpired.

"Your thoughts?" she said, not addressing the two imperial concubines.

The air seemed to shiver as a man stepped out from the impossibly thin shadow cast by one of the candelabras. The Skein girl shrieked and cowered, and even Bex's arm around her waist tightened. The man was tall and pale, with curly, dark hair that touched his shoulders, attired all in black.

He watched her without expression for a long moment, then spoke. "You play a dangerous game, Weaver. The Bard cannot be controlled, nor can his actions be predicted. You inject unnecessary risk by placing his piece upon the board."

"You cannot win the world without taking risks, Demian. We've proven that before, and we might have to yet again. Besides, you two and I are the last, that I know. I lost track of the others centuries ago. How could I let him sleep through the ending of the age we created?" Alyanna stroked Bex's hand, and felt her flinch away at the touch. She sighed. "You've disquieted them." Alyanna unhooked the Dymorian girl's arm from her waist. "Both of you," she said, speaking to the two concubines, "leave us."

Bex and the Skein girl stood and hurriedly left the pavilion. Alyanna leaned back, reclining on her elbows in the now-empty bed. She watched the man in black carefully. "You've changed. And it's not just these interesting new powers you're flaunting. Your time under the mountain has altered something within you profoundly."

Demian inclined his head in agreement. "It has."

Alyanna waited, but he did not elaborate further. Finally she snorted and stood. "The Undying One, ha. So dramatic. Fine, keep your secrets, swordsinger – or should I say shadowblade? Have you become one of them fully, or just enough of a disciple to walk between the darknesses?"

He paused before answering. "I have come to appreciate their beliefs. I do not embrace every aspect of their faith. But you cannot trick me into revealing any of their secrets, Weaver, so this questioning is futile." He crossed his arms. "I am not the only one – how did you say it – 'flaunting' new powers. You dreamsent to me, a technique I thought lost long ago."

The ghost of a satisfied smile touched Alyanna's lips. "I've had centuries to develop my strength while you were meditating under a mountain. I'm stronger even than I was before the sundering of the world."

The once-swordsinger of the Imperium glanced at the rosewood chest. "And these thralls of yours . . . are you sure you can control them? I've never felt creatures like them before."

"As I told Jan, they are from Shan. I heard them crying out from half a world away, begging for release from their prison. So I traveled to the bone-shard warlock towers of Tsai Yin to free them."

"You claimed that they are being pursued?"

Alyanna waved away his words, as if they were of no consequence. "Do not concern yourself. Demon-hunters from Shan search for traces of the creatures, but I have set my pet genthyaki on *their* trails."

"The shape-changer? I did not know it still survived."

Alyanna grinned wickedly. "It survives, and hates me as much as ever. But it cannot slip its leash – and that should answer your question about whether I can control these Shan demons. Do you honestly believe I would employ them if I could not?"

His gaze held hers. "No, but your weakness is your arrogance. Be careful, Weaver."

"How can I not be arrogant?" she said, smiling innocently. "I whistled, and you came."

Finally she saw some emotion in his blank face, a hint of amusement. "I am curious about that. Why with your new-found pets would you need my help?"

"Oh, Demian," Alyanna purred, fluttering her long lashes, "a girl can never have too many friends. And I'd like to meet a few of yours."

He frowned. "The kith'ketan? You must know how dangerous they are. What would drive you to seek their aid?"

Alyanna let her carefully maintained mask slip. She leaned towards Demian and placed her finger on the corner of her eye, squinting as she traced the creases she felt emerge.

"Look," she hissed fiercely.

"A very minor blemish," he said, but she heard the uncertainty in his voice, and she even thought he drew back a little.

"A wrinkle, Demian. Do you realize what that means?"

He said nothing, but from his eyes she saw that he did.

"I am aging again. We are no longer immortal."

11: KEILAN

"**MOST IMPORTANT IS** how you stand. Don't favor either leg; keep yourself balanced. And stay up on the balls of your feet, so you can move and react quicker."

Keilan tried to imitate Nel's stance, bending his knees slightly and leaning forward. She studied him critically for a moment, and then nodded.

"Good. Now, there are a few important rules about knife-fighting. The first is: if they have a sword, you run. A knife is no protection against a warrior with a blade."

"Have you ever run from a fight?"

Nel snorted a laugh, quieting the chirping of the birds in the gilded cages hanging from the branches above them. "I've run from more fights than I've fought. It's why I'm still alive. Men who carry weapons tend to have a strange belief that it is better to die honorably than live to fight another day. Foolish. If the odds are against me I flee – and I've never felt any shame doing just that. Now, stay still."

Nel circled behind him and put her hand on his left elbow, raising his arm. Keilan tensed and tried to swallow away the little surge of excitement he felt at her touch. If Nel noticed, she didn't let it show.

"You want to keep your off-hand up and extended. Knife-fights can be bloody affairs, and really the only way to avoid getting cut is to control your opponent's weapon. When they go for a strike push away their arm with this hand, but you must be careful about their counter."

Nel guided him slowly through a simple sequence, turning aside an imaginary slash and then thrusting out with the other arm. "A second rule: don't throw your knife unless you have another ready."

"You threw your dagger in the catacombs."

Nel slipped around to stand in front of him again. "I did," she said, pulling up her long sleeve to reveal a blade strapped to her forearm. "And I had this if I couldn't recover my dagger quick enough." She grinned, her cheeks dimpling. "Actually, I also had this," she touched her other sleeve, "and this," she bent down and tapped her shin, then her boot, thigh, and waist, "and this and this and this. I rarely run out."

Nel snapped off the tip of a low-hanging branch and tossed it to Keilan. "Let's see what you've learned." Stooping, she picked up one of the longer lengths of wood that littered the manse's walled courtyard. "A small test."

Nel settled into the knife-fighter's crouch she had taught Keilan, and he mirrored her. With a disgusted sigh she lunged forward, quick as a striking serpent, and tapped him in the chest before he could move. "Well, you fail. What should you have done?"

"Knocked your knife away?"

"My knife? Look at its length, this is a sword! You're supposed to run, remember?"

"Oh," he said, feeling his face redden.

She laughed again and reached up with her branch to rattle one of the bird cages suspended among the yellow and orange fruit of the persimmon tree. An indignant squawking burst forth, accompanied by the frantic beating of wings.

"I wonder which of these little bastards was the one warbling last night during the witching hour." Nel gestured to a small arched window on the sprawling manse's third floor. "That's where they've put me. See how that bower almost brushes the ledge? When that damn bird wouldn't stop romancing the moon I was sorely tempted to climb out onto this tree and start opening cage doors."

Keilan smiled, imagining her doing just that. "I don't think Count d'Veskan would have been very pleased."

Nel shrugged. "The birds belong to his wife. He'd probably be secretly happy if a few took wing."

There were certainly enough of them. When Count d'Veskan had received them yesterday in this courtyard, Keilan had tried to count the silver and gold cages hanging in the branches of the huge persimmon tree, losing track at around twenty, when he'd been formally introduced to the Dymorian merchant prince. The count was a large man, well past fifty, his belly straining beneath a doublet of red silk and his impressive forked black beard streaked by fingers of gray. He had clasped Keilan's arm like he was an equal, or a friend, which had been shocking. In the Shattered Kingdoms, nobles would never degrade themselves by even acknowledging someone from the lower classes. The count had noticed his surprise and chuckled.

"You're no longer a fisherman's son, boy. You'll be an apprentice soon, and if what Magister Vhalus told me the first time he passed through here is true then you should be a magister yourself before long. He said he was on the trail of someone with a great natural gift."

A magister before long. A sorcerer. Keilan was still having trouble accepting the idea that he could ever wield the arcane powers Vhelan had shown. But he had offered a weak smile and tried his best to match the Count's iron grip on his arm.

"And I'm very interested to hear about what happened in the south. My man who met you at the gate told me that you brought a wounded paladin to the temple of Ama. I've never heard of such chivalry being extended between such ancient enemies. It sounds like you all have a tale to tell."

They did, and it was a tale Keilan could scarcely believe. What would Sella think of such a story? From touching a sleeping god to being welcomed at the estate of a Dymorian merchant prince in Theris, he thought she'd scoff at nearly every twist and turn. *You be tellin' me one of the stories in your books again, aren't ya, Kay*? she'd have said from under raised eyebrows. Perhaps she could have accepted the last few days – at least, nothing too outlandish had happened since leaving the cursed ruin.

They had fled as soon as the worst of the wounds among the rangers had been bandaged. For the Pure they had quickly lashed together a sled that could be pulled by one of the larger horses, and Nel, being the lightest, had crouched beside him while they rode, making sure that the jouncing did not split open his hastily dressed cuts. The paladin had not awoken, muttering and moaning in a fever dream as they raced north along the Black Road. Keilan had been worried that the spiders would prove venomous, but the others who suffered bites showed no signs of poisoning, so he supposed that the Pure's condition was simply from blood loss, coupled perhaps with exhaustion due to channeling whatever power he had wielded within the temple of that dark god.

The rangers had spoken in some awe of how the paladin had approached the sealed secret door while they'd all been clustered around trying to figure out how to open it again, holding up his empty hands to show that he came in peace. He'd told Captain d'Taran that he had been following them and had felt a great stirring of dark sorcery beneath the temple. After a hurried council, the rangers had welcomed his help, and the Pure had proceeded to lay his hands on the carving, which resulted in the secret panel sundering with a great crack into dozens of smoking shards of stone. Then he had joined the rangers as they rushed beneath the temple, and the memory of his fighting prowess had made Keilan thank the Deep Ones that he had not resisted the Dymorians when he had been ambushed on the road near Keilan's village.

After arriving in Theris they had left the still-unconscious paladin with some very surprised mendicants at the temple of Ama. That had been a few days ago, and Keilan hoped that word of the Pure's condition reached them before they departed the city.

"Someone comes," Nel said, plucking a persimmon from the tree.

A servant in the red-and-gold livery of Dymoria's royal house was approaching, and when he stood before them he pressed his knuckles to his brow and bowed slightly. Keilan hastily returned the gesture, and then had to jump aside as Nel lightly tossed her persimmon at his head.

"You shouldn't give such respect to servants. The higher castes don't do such things in Dymoria, and it will only make the servants uncomfortable."

"But I'm a fisherman – I *am* from a lower caste. And anyway, you were a thief!"

Nel sighed. "And now we're the personal guests of Count d'Veskan, second cousin of the Crimson Queen and seventeenth in line for the throne. Soon you'll enter into the Scholia, which will put you on equal footing with almost everyone in Dymoria. Magisters are considered to be a noble caste – you won't be granted any lands or titles, but the queen does provide chambers in the palace and a small stipend, provided you swear fealty to the Dragon Throne. Keilan, your days of being a commoner are finished."

Nel turned back to the servant, who had been studiously ignoring this exchange. "Yes, what news?"

"My lord and lady, the count wishes for you to attend him in his solar." The servant made a sweeping gesture for them to follow him.

"Lead on," said Nel, jumping up to snatch another persimmon to replace the one she had thrown at Keilan.

They followed the servant through the manse's large ebonwood doors, elaborately carved with twisting dragon-shapes in the style of Dymoria, then down corridors covered with thick, colorfully-patterned Keshian carpets, and up several flights of curving stairs. Along some of the passages the heads of strange beasts adorned the walls, mouths roaring and glass eyes flashing in the light from the wall sconces. The count had been a passionate hunter in his youth, and he had named each creature when he'd first led them through the manse, though only a few had lodged in Keilan's memory. There was a northern tiger, which was famous for stalking the dark, cold forests of Dymoria; there a snarling sable wolf from the Frostlands; there a russet-scaled wyvern, which Keilan had read about in one of his books, *A Tinker's Bestiary*. Wyverns were the lesser spawn of true-blood dragons and some of the only evidence that somewhere in the wilds great wyrms still lived. For every hundred eggs a dragon laid, ninety-nine would hatch a wyvern, stunted and near-mindless compared to their vast and terrible parents.

Finally, the servant ushered them into the solar, a room which conveyed the count's fondness for dark wood, books, and over-stuffed armchairs. Tapestries depicting mythical hunts hung from the walls, and dust glittered like specks of gold in the light pouring through a great bay window. Beyond the estate's high walls, the red-tiled roofs of Theris spread like a blood tide until they lapped against the city's mighty keep, the Warding. For such a large and imposing fortress, the Warding changed hands with startling regularity. Such was life in the Shattered Kingdoms.

The count was seated in a high-backed chair carved to resemble a lion, its paws the arm-rests. Vhelan was beside him on a much less impressive cushioned stool, and between them was a tzalik board on a small table – from the looks of it, the sorcerer had chosen the water side, and he had been backed onto the edge by his opponent's imps and efreets.

"Welcome," Vhelan said, turning to them as they entered. Keilan thought he looked pleased at getting a reprieve from his imminent defeat.

Nel bowed slightly from the waist, knuckling her brow, and Keilan hurried to copy her. The count did not look at them, continuing to stare intently at the board as he stroked his forked beard. Eventually he picked up one of his efreets and waved it vaguely in the direction of an empty armchair.

"Sit, sit," he said, then set the piece down with exaggerated care in a space occupied by one of Vhelan's naga. The sorcerer made a small, strangled sound as the count leaned back in his great chair.

"Well, magister, I believe you've lost again," d'Veskan boomed, smiling broadly.

Vhelan hesitated a moment, his eyes flickering around the board, then with a sigh tipped over the jagged malachite piece representing his fortress.

"Congratulations, my lord," he said, dipping his head slightly. "I haven't lost that badly since the queen herself invited me to join her in a game."

The count chuckled. "Runs in the royal blood. We've always been uncommonly good at tzalik – legend has it that one of the first d'Karas to sit the Dragon Throne traveled in disguise to the Cinnabar Palace and played the padarasha himself to a draw."

"You called for us, my lord?" Nel said, perched on the edge of a chair, her hands resting prim and lady-like in her lap. She looked terribly out of place, Keilan thought.

"Indeed," d'Veskan said, moving to refill his and Vhelan's cups from a crystal decanter filled with a muddy brown liquid. "Some news you and the boy might find interesting. We just had a messenger from the temple of light here in Theris. The Pure you brought them has awoken, and the mendicants think he will live. He sends his thanks for saving his life and bringing him to this city. My ears in the temple tell me that he has mentioned nothing about being rescued by a sorcerer, oddly enough. Oh, and particularly he wishes to express his gratitude to you," the count inclined his head towards Nel, "as apparently he remembers you caring for him most tenderly during the flight from Uthmala."

Vhelan glanced at her with raised eyebrows. "Well, he did save our lives," she said defensively. "Perhaps this is the start of a new era between sorcerers and the Pure."

"Ah, interesting you should mention that," the count said, swirling his drink. "Because there's other news. Tidings that might make you regret the mercy you showed the paladin."

Vhelan picked up his fallen fortress and rolled the piece in his hands. "What is it?"

"D'Kelv."

Keilan noticed Nel and Vhelan both stiffen at the name. "Who is that?" he blurted, momentarily forgetting his place.

The count ignored his impropriety; instead, he sipped his drink and grimaced. "A relative of mine. One of the first with royal blood to declare for the queen when d'Palan named her an imposter. He passed through Theris about six weeks past, heading east, leading the first official delegation to Menekar since Cein ascended to the Dragon Throne."

Vhelan set the malachite fortress down with a clink. "You told me he was overdue when last we stayed here."

"Aye. Nearly a fortnight. The delay could have been anything: bandits on the plains, an avalanche while crossing the Bones, a sickness that forced them to stop and rest until they recovered. But now we've had word."

"And?"

Keilan was surprised by the strain he heard in Vhelan's voice.

"Dead," d'Veskan said bitterly, then drained his glass. "Slaughtered like dogs by the Pure in the imperial audience chamber while the emperor looked on. A great crime, murdering an ambassador and his entourage. Even the Skein would never do such a thing."

"Dead," Vhelan repeated numbly. He looked shaken. "And his companions as well?"

D'Veskan eyed the sorcerer shrewdly. "The same fate," he said, pouring himself another glass. "The story I heard of what happened . . . I cannot believe it. My source told me that one of our countrymen used sorcery in the Selthari Palace, and this is what brought down the wrath of Gerixes. A wizard, only steps away from the alabaster throne! If the tale is true, then I expect the winds of war will rise before long."

Vhelan was quiet for a long moment, staring at the pieces littering the tzalik board. Finally, he slowly shook his head. "We were so sure. The process had worked before, we'd brought a sorcerer in front of the Pure without them batting an eye. What happened? Ah, Benosh . . ." With shaking hands he lifted his glass and tossed back its contents. "Farewell, old friend."

"You knew of this?" the count asked, leaning forward intently.

Vhelan nodded. "I did. The queen . . . she has discovered a way to hide sorcery from the Pure. We had tested it a dozen times, even had a wizard dressed as a serving girl deliver a paladin his dinner, and the chosen of Ama hadn't suspected a thing. But they must have sensed something in the palace; there must be some flaw that hadn't yet become apparent. Benosh was among the best of us. Magister of the first rank, one of my own teachers when I first arrived in Herath. A true friend."

D'Veskan tapped his chin thoughtfully. "You think your magic to hide the sorcerer failed? Perhaps it never worked to begin with."

Vhelan's eyes narrowed. "What do you mean?"

The count leaned back and clasped his hands across his large belly. "I'm considering this as a lifelong hunter. There are two ways to conduct a proper hunt. The first is direct: using hounds or falcons you flush your prey from hiding and run it down. You get your trophy, but every other beast within leagues has heard the commotion and fled. The second way is more subtle: you find a place where the animal feels safe, such as a watering hole, or its den, and then you settle in a nearby spot where you are hidden and wait. The animal's guard is down, and it suspects nothing. The trick is to make the ambush quick and quiet, so as not to alert anything else in the area. While not as exciting or glorious, the second method yields far more kills if conducted skillfully, as the hunter can lure many more unsuspecting beasts out into the open."

Vhelan drummed his fingers on the table. "So Gerixes is a brilliant hunter? That doesn't conform with what our informants in his court have told us about him."

The count shook his head emphatically. "Not the emperor. He is just a figurehead. I doubt very much his advisors keep him well-informed. His black vizier, though, the captured spider-eater Wen – he is a cunning snake. And despite the best efforts of you magisters to keep up the appearance over the last few years that the Scholia is merely a collection of scholars drawn by the queen to rival the Reliquary, there are simply too many in Herath who know the truth. Wen certainly is aware that Dymoria is gathering sorcerers and exploring magics long since abandoned. My men have heard the rumors themselves at taverns here in the Shattered Kingdoms."

"So you believe d'Kelv's murder was the hunter finally breaking his cover?"

The count shrugged. "I cannot be sure. But, by Menekar ignoring what has been happening out west, the magisters have grown more brazen. If the Pure had moved against them five years ago, it would have driven the wizards underground and made them much more difficult to ferret out. Now, the true nature of the Scholia is almost an open secret in Herath. The magisters have become comfortable – beasts at the watering hole, ready to be slaughtered."

Vhelan plucked absentmindedly at the embroidery hemming his sleeves. "And here I was worried that my rescue of the boy from the Pure was too brazen. Little did I know that the first move may already have been played in Menekar."

"And what will your counter be?"

Vhelan's response was quick and decisive. "We must return to Dymoria at once. The Kingdoms are too close to Menekar; half of the lords here now wear the sunburst of Ama and allow the Pure free rein in their holdings."

D'Veskan nodded in agreement. "Lucky for us the Iron Duke in Theris is no zealot. Otherwise we might have already had a few light-bearers backed by the city watch come looking for you."

"Still," Vhelan said, rising to his feet, "I don't want to bring any danger down upon your household. We can't know when the paladin we brought here will inform his masters about us, and if you were known to be harboring a wizard even the Duke might have trouble tamping down the anger of a mob when their fear and hate is fanned by the preaching of mendicants."

D'Veskan heaved his bulk from the chair, nearly upsetting the gameboard, and clapped his hands together sharply. "Don't fear for me, I've plenty of friends still in the Kingdoms. But I appreciate your concern, and I agree that a quick retreat to Dymoria is the best plan. Whenever you can sense a storm brewing, best to get behind some stout walls. And I have a feeling this storm will shake the world to its foundations." The count slipped with surprising grace from behind his desk and went over to a side table scattered with paper. He found a scroll bound with red ribbon and turned back to Vhelan. "There's a large caravan preparing to leave for Herath in the next few days. The merchant leading it is an old friend; he and most of the guards are Dymorian, and when you show him my seal on this document he'll obey you in all matters – if you ask to leave immediately, he will, and protect you on the journey as if you were my own blood."

Vhelan knuckled his brow and bowed. "Word of your kindness will reach many ears when we are again before the Dragon Throne. Thank you, my lord."

D'Veskan smiled grimly. "The queen believes that the coming struggle will determine the fate of our kingdom. I am grateful for any part I might play. Now, let us find you some supplies." The count jabbed a thick finger at Keilan. "And you, my young friend, need some warmer clothes if you're on your way north. The forests of Dymoria are far harsher than the soft lands to which you're accustomed. Best prepare yourself."

12: KEILAN

RIBBONS OF PINK dawnlight were just creeping over the city walls when they arrived the next morning at the Maw, the huge gate that guarded Theris's northern flank, and through which travelers who wished to journey to the far east or west usually passed. Jagged shapes dripped from the gate's arched recesses, just resolving from the morning dimness: the spikes of an upraised portcullis, and where Keilan suspected the gate had gotten its name, as it truly did look like they were riding towards the fanged mouth of some great stone beast.

The fortifications above the Maw bristled with pennants and pikes, and perched like predatory birds on the ramparts were the hulking shapes of trebuchets and catapults, staring north.

"How did the city ever fall?" Nel asked as they neared the gate, guiding her horse around the steady stream of farmer's carts laden with vegetables and bleating animals that were heading to market.

"And yet it does," Vhelan muttered, his words still slurred slightly from a night spent drinking with the count and playing tzalik. The wizard hunched in his saddle with the hood of his cloak drawn up, as if the encroaching dawn was something that needed to be avoided at all costs. "The Iron Duke has held the city for nearly three years, which is an eternity in the annals of the Shattered Kingdoms. In the decade before he overthrew the boy-prince – what was his name, the one with the bloat – a dozen men had ruled in the Warding, although to be fair the city had never fallen in a siege. Usually someone in the city watch turns traitor and opens the gates to whoever is camping outside. Or an ambitious vassal puts a sword in his lord's back. Or there was that one earl who died face down in his onion soup – no one ever figured out who'd poisoned him. In all honesty, after a century of near-constant chaos and war I'm surprised that there's still anyone with noble blood left in the Kingdoms. The lords around here seem to come and go fast as mayflies."

"We haven't seen so much of that down south," Keilan said, unable to tear his gaze from the imposing walls that continued to swell higher as they neared the Maw. "My da said it was the western lords who had the hottest-blood and the deepest memories. Couldn't ever let a grudge die, and that just kept layering fresh grudges over the old ones, until no one even knew what started it all. The Fens are pretty torn up, he said, and up along the edges of the Blightwood the villages have all been razed and their people gone elsewhere, like the farmers who settled near our village. But the fighting hadn't come anywhere near us in a generation."

"Lucky lad," Vhelan said, fumbling a silver flask from his saddlebags and taking a quick sip, "and lucky us that the Iron Duke has turned this city and the northern roads into a little oasis of calm within the tumult. There were some years not a single caravan of any size made the journey from the Kingdoms to Dymoria. Just a few small traders who risked life and limb navigating a route infested with robber bands, unpaid mercenary troops turned feral, and greedy lordlings."

As if in thanks, Vhelan saluted with his silver flask the pair of grim-faced men flanking the Maw. Neither of the gate guards glanced at the slumped wizard, continuing to stare straight ahead, their hands gripping the shafts of the long-handled halberds planted in the dirt in front of them.

They passed into the dimness of the Maw's gullet, almost brushing the ancient, lichen-stained walls to avoid a large cart filled with squealing pigs. Keilan found himself staring into the deep blackness of a murder hole, wondering if someone was looking out at him holding a loaded crossbow. He shivered at the thought and kicked Storm into a trot.

Beyond the Maw spread a ramshackle collection of buildings, most only a single story tall. Chipped and crudely painted wooden signs hung above the doors of a few of the largest: a frilled serpent coiled around a foaming mug of ale, a pair of leaping goats, their horns locked, and the silhouette of a rose laid over the outline of a plate, or possibly the moon. Inns and taverns, Keilan guessed, for travelers who either did not want to pay the rates commanded in Theris proper, or were departing early in the morning. A few dark shapes huddled outside the entrance of the tavern with the flower emblazoned on its signage.

"Ah, the Rose," Vhelan sighed wistfully as they passed the sprawled drunks. "A shame we didn't get a chance to spend another evening there."

Nel glanced at Keilan and rolled her eyes. "Yes, a real shame. When we came through Theris last time this wizard and a certain disguised Dymorian merchant prince made quite the scene. Couldn't keep their mouths shut or their eyes off a few veiled Keshian ladies who were very clearly spoken for. Started a huge mess, which of course I had to settle. The owner, good pockmarked Rose herself, had to roll out extra sawdust to mop up the blood on the floor. I'm fairly sure we were banned from ever stepping foot inside again."

Vhelan waved away her words. "Oh, please, taverns such as this have short memories. Just a regular night at the Rose, really. Next time we push through those doors with a purse full of silver we'll be welcomed with open arms."

"Until next time, then," Nel muttered.

Beyond the dilapidated inns and alehouses was a large fenced meadow where a half-dozen different caravans had circled. Closest to the paddock's gate were three large covered wagons, the blazing sunburst of Ama painted on each side. Shaggy ponies were tied to a nearby hitching post, cropping grass as their Menekarian masters in loose, white robes busied themselves, preparing to depart.

"Look!" Keilan cried excitedly, pointing at a white shape lolling among the ponies, its long tail lashing. At the sounds of his voice the steppe lion raised its silver-maned head and yawned languidly, regarding them with sleepy eyes.

"A white lion of the plains," Vhelan said, leaning forward to get a better look. "The Menekarians have tamed the beasts, making them as docile as house cats. They can still be vicious killers, however. The beastmasters of Menekar bring them into battle, though we in western Araen rarely see these war lions. They are used on Menekar's eastern frontier, where the empire borders with the Qell wastes. What a sight it must be, watching a host of these lions race across the red steppes and leap into the snapping jaws of the pale lizards at the vanguard of a Qell horde."

Keilan couldn't tear himself from the lion's unblinking gaze as Vhelan led them towards wagons that were swarming with activity. Finally, with some effort, he broke the spell and turned to find a stocky, richly dressed merchant approaching Vhelan's horse. His forked black beard was bound with silver rings, and gold glittered on his fingers as he knuckled a respectful greeting. Vhelan reined in his horse and returned the gesture.

"Good health to you," the man fairly bellowed, his words accented in a flavor similar to d'Veskan, although to Keilan's ears he sounded a bit rougher. "You must be our guests who are in such a rush to be off that we can't wait till tomorrow . . . and for our last delivery of pear brandy."

Vhelan cleared his throat. "Ah, yes. We greatly appreciate you leaving early. We have pressing business in Herath."

The merchant squinted and rubbed his nose. "So d'Veskan's man said. Well, the count has been good to me and mine, so I don't mind doing him this favor. The name's Halan, out of the Slopes. Your men arrived earlier this morning, tough looking lot they are."

Keilan noticed for the first time a few familiar faces among the caravan guards. The rangers had shed their forester garb and golden dragon medallions and now wore unadorned leather armor and pointed steel helmets. Their captain, d'Taran, caught Keilan's eye and winked.

"We've quite the menagerie this trip," Halan said, gesturing at the wagons behind him. "Dymorians, a seeker, and a Shan all traveling together. Along with whatever you folks are. Sounds like the beginning of one of Jesaphon's Tales."

Vhelan's brows knit together. "There's a seeker from the Reliquary here? And a *Shan*?"

The merchant nodded. "Aye. Been with us since we came up from the Thread. Queer fellow, but keeps to himself. Normally I wouldn't truck with one of those spider-eaters, but he paid generously, said he needed to get north in a hurry. My guess is that some Visani lord wants some new silks for his mistress, but the Shan hasn't let on what he's carrying." Halan shrugged and spat. "And I haven't asked. Enough gold buys privacy as well as protection."

"And that one?" Nel asked, pointing to the last wagon in the forming train. It was the same pale wood as the Menekarian wagons they had passed earlier, and on its side was painted the same coppery sunburst. Keilan felt a small thrill of apprehension at the sight. An impossibly thin and tall man in flowing white robes was checking the harnesses attached to his two shaggy steppe ponies.

"Him? Newest member of our little troop, joined up just this morning. The rest of his fellows are headed west, to Gryx and then on to Kesh. This one's got business in Herath, something about the fur trade, I think he said."

"Wonderful," Nel muttered under her breath. "A Menekarian. We just can't get away from them."

Vhelan turned towards his knife and lowered his voice so that the caravan master couldn't overhear. "A solitary merchant, one without even guards of his own. Unless he's one of the Pure in a very convincing disguise I imagine there's not much to concern us."

"From the looks of it you don't have many supplies," Halan said, gesturing towards the saddlebags hanging from their horses.

Vhelan faced the merchant again. "Aye. But we've coin enough. When we stop along the way we'll buy provisions."

"Very good," said Halan, "and if we're caught between inns you're welcome to partake in my own personal stores. I've a few choice bottles of crystal wine; it pairs nicely with fresh-caught game dripping juices into a fire while a blanket of stars blazes above."

Vhelan's mouth quirked. "Good merchant, I believe we are going to get along quite well."

Halan clapped the wizard on his shoulder. "Ha, excellent. Sometimes I'm starved for civilized company out on the road. I've been out of Herath for nearly a year now, and I'd dearly love to catch up on the gossip I've missed."

For Keilan, the days with the caravan quickly fell into a familiar rhythm. He would wake just before dawn, either in a bedroll damp with morning dew, songbirds above him greeting the rising sun, or on a mattress of stale straw in the common room of whatever inn they'd stopped at the night before, the rich smells of baking bread and simmering gravy wafting from the kitchens. After breakfast he would saddle Storm and give her oats from the feedbag Halan used for his own horses. The mare would watch him with liquid brown eyes, ears twitching as he whispered to her. Sometimes he spoke of his father, or Sella, or even his mother, and sometimes he wondered aloud what awaited him in Dymoria and the court of the Crimson Queen. He would pour out his hopes and his fears, and in reply Storm would whicker softly and press her nose into his hand, asking for a second helping of oats.

Then he would lead her over to where the caravan was forming and climb back up into her saddle. By the fourth day the ache in his legs and back had almost disappeared, the callouses on his thighs having bloomed and wilted during their long days on the road.

Most often he stayed at the front of the wagon train, riding beside Nel and Vhelan as they chatted with Master Halan. The caravan passed through a sparse forest of stunted birch and pine, and then rolling meadows grazed by sheep and aurochs. Shepherd boys watching their flocks would turn and stare at them as they passed, sometimes waving their crooks in greeting, sometimes hurriedly urging their animals away from the road.

Yet despite the shepherds' wariness, Keilan at first struggled to reconcile the lands they traveled through with the dark picture painted by Vhelan. Gradually, though, he began to notice small signs of past troubles. Beside a fresh-timbered farmhouse he could see a charred foundation poking from the long grass. Elsewhere the road was lined with a score of small cairns, a few topped with rusted, split-open helms. On the third day they came to a fork, the road diverging around a massive oak tree. From one of its gnarled branches four men had been hung, their bodies bloated black and twisting in the breeze.

"Bandits," Vhelan said, wrinkling his nose at the smell. "Encouraging, actually. It means that either the Iron Duke's justice reaches this far north, or the local lord has decided that the coin gained from feeding and housing merchants outweighs what could be stolen from those same merchants at the point of a sword."

Keilan stared at the hanged men, unable to look away as the caravan passed beneath them. He'd seen the dead before – in his village, the bodies of those whose souls had slipped beyond the veil were wrapped in cloth and carried down to the sea. It was always a festive occasion, the children skipping ahead of the procession and scattering flower blossoms and seashells. Usually the faces of the dead were resigned and peaceful, as if their souls had departed willingly.

The souls of these hanged men had not departed willingly. The few eyes that had not been picked out by scavengers bulged wildly, and the flesh of their necks was patterned with livid purple and blue bruises.

"What did they do?" Keilan asked, swallowing away the dryness in his throat.

Vhelan shrugged. "Robbery. Rape. Murder. What always happens when men live in a land with no strong ruler. In Lyr, the people pride themselves on the freedoms granted them by the archons. On the Hill, in the Silk Quarter, beside the Salt, the touch of the watch is light, but it is there, and outside of bravos dueling there is little violence. In the Warrens, however, the archons long ago ceded authority to the criminals, and it is a deadly place. If you do not pledge to a gang you cannot survive. Since I left the Gilded Cities I've come to appreciate the strong hand of the Crimson Queen. Some freedom must be sacrificed for order."

Keilan learned much from Vhelan in those days. Quickly he came to realize why the once-thief had earned the nickname 'scholar'. He was a fount of knowledge about a vast array of topics, and anything could set the wizard off on a rambling lecture. A glimpse of a brooding keep on a distant hill led to a lengthy description of the major families of the Shattered Kingdoms, which was then followed by a detailed history recounting how the death of two princes had first plunged the realm into chaos, twin brothers who slew each other on the field of battle. Another afternoon was spent outlining in broad strokes the Incarnate theory of sorcery, how it was believed that wizards opened a conduit to the primal force of the Void, and through will and technique shaped it to serve their purposes. That explanation was peppered with arcane terms and references about people and places Keilan had never heard of, and most of it washed over him without illuminating very much, but he did manage to glean a few interesting facts about the Scholia's understanding of sorcery.

Foremost of which was that the mumbled incantations and fluttering fingers that accompanied Vhelan's conjuring was not what actually summoned forth sorcery. The magic was always there, bubbling within the wizard like a spring, but the actions and words allowed it to be used in very particular ways. That was why the ancient scrolls they had found beneath Uthmala might be so valuable, as possibly they contained the intricate formula to twist sorcery in a way that had been lost thousands of years ago. Once, Vhelan had sighed, staring off at some scene only he could see, sorcerers had walked on air, climbing into the sky to coax rain from the sky. What the wizards of Dymoria now knew was only a tiny fragment of the sorcerous knowledge of old.

When they stopped for the evenings, Nel continued her own instruction with Keilan. She would lead him away from the encampment, until they found a clearing hidden from the road, and then she would patiently walk him through the basics of knife-fighting. He learned how to balance on the balls of his feet, how to feint, how to strike quickly and powerfully, how to find the chinks and seams in most armors, and also, since Nel constantly stressed its importance, how to recognize when he was overmatched, and retreat hastily.

On their third night from Theris the caravan stopped early, having arrived at a rambling old inn that wrapped around a towering stone monolith. A ragged cheer had gone up from many of the merchants and guardsmen when the pale white spire had first appeared over the tree-tops ahead. "The Godsword," Halan had said, "finest establishment between Theris and Vis. No better inn along the entire length of the Wending, I'll stake my good name on it. They'll be music and feasting tonight, lads."

Keilan hurriedly stabled Storm, the playful skirling of fiddles calling to him from the inn's main hall, but before he could push through the ancient doors Nel materialized beside him.

"There'll be time for that later. We should take advantage of this light and get your practice in."

He turned to her, prepared to beg for a night's reprieve, but the words died in his throat when he saw that she was not alone. A man stood beside her, not tall but powerfully built, with broad shoulders and a barrel chest. His skin was dusky, and his dark eyes flecked with gold. He was dressed in polished leather armor, the cuirass and greaves of which were dyed a deep burgundy, its fasteners and buckles shaped of red copper. Keilan had seen this guardsman and a few others in matching armor milling around the ornate wagon of the scholar from the Reliquary.

The warrior flashed him a grin and sketched a shallow bow. "This one gives greetings to the young lord. This one is Xin of the Lapis Stables, Third of Five."

Keilan mirrored the bow, feeling flustered. "Ah, hello. My name is Keilan Ferrisorn." He glanced at Nel questioningly.

"Xin has agreed to train with us tonight," the knife said, and Keilan suddenly noticed the bundle of wooden practice swords she was holding under her arm. Nel saw where he was looking and held out one of the leather-wrapped handles for him to take. "Wielding a dagger effectively is a valuable skill, to be sure, but limited in usefulness unless you plan on skulking in shadows and sneaking up on your enemies. In a straight fight a swordsman will always have the advantage. I have decided it is time I learned a bit myself."

"But . . . I don't have a sword."

The warrior chuckled. "Little lord, this one will tell you a truth: there is no shortage of swords in this world."

Keilan took the wooden blade from Nel, surprised at the heaviness. "It's weighted," Nel said, hefting one of the swords herself and wincing slightly.

"You both will have to strengthen your wrists and arms," said Xin, plucking the last training blade from Nel's hand and flourishing it as easily as if it was a willow reed. "Fatigue kills as many warriors as poor technique." The sword became a blur, carving patterns in the air faster than Keilan's eyes could follow.

"We could ask for no better teacher," Nel murmured, also watching the dancing blade. "Xin is a Fist warrior. The others you've seen in the caravan dressed like him are his brothers."

Keilan blinked, surprised. The Fists were legendary, reputed to be some of the finest warriors in all the world. The stories he'd heard in his village were certainly embellished, but from the respect in Nel's voice at least some of what he'd been told might be true. They were the elite slave-soldiers of Gryx, renowned as incorruptible bodyguards. He remembered, though he wasn't sure where he'd heard it, the strange tale of their origins in the red-brick slave city of the Fettered. Five slave mothers matched to a great warrior of the fighting pits, five mothers who lived and ate and slept together, and finally gave birth together to five sons on the same hour of the same day, sons that forevermore shared an unbreakable bond. A Fist of Gryx.

Xin winked at him. "Come. This one has much to teach you."

13: JAN

DEEP IN THE mists corpselight flared, a fleeting burst of green and blue flame. Jan peered into the grayness blanketing the marshes, but he felt no tingling to suggest sorcery was the culprit. He pulled his black cloak tighter, trying to ward away the creeping chill of these wastes, and urged his horse into a canter. Perhaps the pale light had simply been marsh gas, as he had once heard a scholar claim, or maybe it was brigands warning others ahead of his approach. He kept himself alert. Immortal he may be, a thousand-year old sorcerer with a magic sword at his side, but an arrow in the eye would kill him just as easily as any other man.

He rode along the Wending, the ancient, rutted road that bound together the scattered settlements of the north. Bits of broken stone tiles embedded in the earth only hinted at the road's ancient glory. Memories like ghosts hovered on the edge of Jan's thoughts, haunting him with faint recollections of a distant time when great forests hemmed this very way.

Now on either side of the road spread the Mire, league upon league of frozen, desolate marsh. Hummocks of mud rose from reeds and water, invisible sinkholes lurked that could swallow a horse, and copses of twisted bloodbarks trailed their tangled roots into stagnant pools. During the day it was the same unending sight, while the last three nights he had camped on the relatively dry earth of the old road, huddled beneath his blankets, watching pale clumps of ghostweed shimmer in the darkness.

He kept his attention where he had seen the corpselight, but nothing further disturbed the gray murk. Jan slowed his horse. There were many miles to travel before he arrived at the kingdom of the Crimson Queen, and if his horse pulled up lame in this desolation then he would have to suffer a very uncomfortable walk. The Mire, then bogs and moors, then the vast tiger-haunted forests that spilled down the slopes of the Bones of the World's western reaches, and finally the Derravin Ocean and Herath. Weeks more travel, yet it was only a small distance when compared to how far he had already come, all the way from Alyanna's pleasure garden.

He had left Vis two days past. It was an old city, and he had been there before, he was sure, in his youth. The great, gleaming walls of black iron that girdled the more temporary buildings within had stood for thousands of years, the locals had assured him, predating even the last sorcerous age and its cataclysms. A chill had stolen inside Jan when he had passed through the teeth of the western gate, which had been shaped into a dragon's roaring mouth, the coldness of the encompassing iron seeping through his furs and leather and drawing the strength from his bones. Ancient defenses had been woven into those walls, powerful spells to guard against sorcerers.

A flock of birds rose shrieking from the tall grass fringing the road, his horse shying away from the unexpected commotion. Jan whispered encouragement, trying to calm his mount with a tendril of sorcery. The horse snorted, close to panic, and Jan was forced to harden his gentle touch before the animal could throw him. Surprised, Jan edged his skittish horse closer to where the birds had been feasting. He caught snatches of pale white flesh among the reeds, half submerged in the black waters. Jan grimaced. It was the corpse of a serpent three times the length of a man and as thick around as a small shield, though death had certainly bloated the snake somewhat.

The thing's eyes had been picked out, and at several points along its sinuous body the skin had festered and burst. Out of one of these openings several small, almost translucent snakes had spilled, and now floated motionless on the surface of the brackish swamp water.

Jan patted his mount's neck. "A good argument for finding shelter tonight, eh, boy?"

The horse whinnied and stamped its hooves as Jan pulled it away from the rotting serpent.

They rode on, their pace quickening as the gray day slowly began to darken. From the directions he had received in Vis he knew the marsh's border should be close, and there he would find a traveler's inn. The thought of a warm fire and a soft bed made his skin tingle in anticipation.

Twilight had nearly given way to true night before the marshes finally dwindled and vanished, replaced by rolling moorland. The eternal grayness became suffused with pink and purple, and long tendrils of mists coiled just above the ground, unsettling reminders of the dead snake. Sounds carried across the wastes, low and mournful. Possibly the wind, and possibly not.

The inn emerged suddenly from the darkness, bulked against the fading evening light. It was two stories, built of stone and surrounded by a low wall, the top of which bristled with iron spikes. Fingers of mist threaded between these points and tumbled like silken streamers to the ground. It looked more like a fort than an inn, but being just south of the Frostlands, and on the edge of the Mire, Jan could hardly blame its builders. Large torches flanked the open gate, dripping gobbets of burning pitch onto the frozen ground, and Jan could hear the faint sound of laughter from inside. Several wagons had been pulled within the safety of the walls, and he counted five big draft horses tied to a hitching post, along with a few donkeys. They grazed on a pile of mounded hay, where a young boy lay sprawled, his straw hat pulled over his eyes.

Jan slid from his horse and cleared his throat loudly; the boy shot upright, then scrambled to his feet when he saw the new arrival.

"Begging your pardon, master," he mumbled, pressing his palms together and ducking his head. "Rare t'have the lone traveler on these roads, 'specially at this hour."

Jan handed his reins to the boy. "Never mind, lad. You have rooms, yes?"

The boy scratched beneath his hat, glancing at something he pulled from his hair before flicking it away. "Not sure, master. Two caravans came through today. But if there's no rooms then there's always hearthspace."

"Or hayspace," Jan said, and the boy showed a gap-toothed smile.

"Aye, when the hounds curl up with ya its better than being beside the most blazing fire, that's for sure."

Jan rummaged in his coin belt and tossed the boy a Visani copper piece. "Give my horse some hay and a few apples, if you've any."

The boy tipped his hat. "'Course, master."

Jan offered a curt nod and then strode to the heavy oaken door and rapped loudly. Several voices inside were raised in song, and he had to repeat his knocking a few times before he heard the sound of latches being lifted and the door was slowly pulled open by a wiry old man. The graybeard blinked watery eyes at him in surprise, his toothless mouth hanging open. Beyond him the common room had quieted – it was a standard northern traveler's inn, with trestle tables filling most of the space, a bar against the back wall, and a raised area in the middle. A trio of dark-skinned Visani, their long black hair tied back into topknots, stood with arms linked upon the stage, staring at him. Their fellows clustered below, and a few who had not yet noticed Jan's entrance tossed out ribald heckles for the pause in the performance. A pair of young girls – one with long blonde hair and an ample figure, the other smaller and thin faced, with auburn curls – were being dandled, squealing, upon knees as roving hands explored the laces of their blouses.

Closer to the bar, a group of Dymorians huddled around a table, their bushy black beards almost dipping into the tankards set before them. Where the Visani dressed simply, in gray and black doublets and breeches, the westerlings favored garishly bright colors and enough silver jewelry to give a demon pause. The Dymorians spared him a disinterested glance, and then bent again to their talk.

The old man swallowed hard, the lump in his throat bobbing. "Ah, greetings young master. Come in, come in. Did ya arrive by yerself?"

Jan stepped inside, unclasping his mist-damp cloak and handing it to the doorman. A fire blazed in the hearth and he closed his eyes, enjoying the rolling waves of warmth. "Aye, from Vis."

The old man paled slightly. "Through the Mire? And only you?" He shook his head, turning to hang Jan's cloak on a peg driven into the wall. "Young master, you are either very foolish or very sure of that sword."

"Some of both, I imagine," Jan replied with a smile.

The old man pushed shut the heavy door with a grunt. "Well, go speak with Alomir about a room and some food. He's there."

Jan nodded thanks and made his way to the bar, the drunken Visani revelers returning to their songs as he passed. The stout bald man behind the length of polished oak watched him approach without smiling, yet still he pressed his hands together in the traditional northern greeting. Row upon row of stoppered green-glass bottles lined the wall, and mounted above these, almost brushing the rafters, was the cracked and yellowing skull of some massive lizard. It was fully half the height of a man, each curving fang the length of a child's arm.

"Welcome," the barman rumbled, "to the Demon's Mouth."

They clasped forearms, and the innkeep seemed to relax slightly.

"Well met. My name is Jan, once of the Shattered Kingdoms. Your inn is a welcome find."

The barman turned and spat something into a pot set beside him. It clanged hollowly. "Aye, I've heard that before. I'm Alomir, and this here's my house. Our rooms are full, but there's bedding and a place by the hearth, if you wish, and hot food on the spit. Ale as well, of course."

Jan placed a pair of silver pieces on the bar. "What's supper tonight?"

Alomir scooped up one of the silvers and studied it critically. "We've got a goat roasting for the westerlings." He indicated the

Dymorians with his chin. "And there's a bit for you, if you want. Also my boy netted a few fat frogs this morning, and the wife makes a savory black eel stew."

"The goat and a flagon."

The innkeep pulled out a tankard and bent to fill it from a cask. "You should give the eels a try. We swampfolk know how to cook 'em up right. Throw in some spiced leeches fattened on sheep's blood, and you've the perfect answer for a cold and wet night such as tonight."

"Another time," Jan promised, hiding his smile with a long draught of ale. It was bitter and strong, with more than a hint of the marsh.

"Mella!" barked Alomir, and the busty blonde girl disentangled herself from the arms of her Visani admirer and flounced up to the bar, ignoring the exaggerated pleas for a swift return she left in her wake.

"Yes, uncle?" she said sweetly, fluttering her long lashes at Jan and standing close enough that he couldn't ignore what her half-unlaced blouse revealed.

Alomir jerked his head towards a door at the end of the bar. "When the goat's done carve off a bit for Master Jan here. And a ladle of the eel stew. On the house."

She waited a moment longer, her gaze lingering on the fire opal set into Bright's hilt.

"Go, girl, get," muttered the innkeep, and with a pout and a flirtatious glance at Jan she disappeared into the kitchens.

Alomir shook his head. "Foolish girl. She wants out of the swamps so badly, but refuses to listen to me when I tell her that anyone she runs away with from here will just leave her at the next stop. I've had to break a few bones when someone's tried to take advantage." The innkeeper spat again and gave Jan a long warning look.

The bard tapped his nose to indicate he understood, an old northern gesture. Alomir grunted and set to polishing a glass.

"Where did the monster come from?" Jan asked, indicating the skull with his tankard.

The innkeeper paused and turned to regard the bones. "I'll tell you the tale I tell my boy," he said, clearing his throat. "One day his grandad was out fishing in the Mire, which for my pa usually meant long hours sleeping in his skiff with a bottle or two of old marsh juice, and nary a tickle on the string. But this day he feels a bite and gives the rod a good tug. What breaks the water then and dives back down was a swamp demon that hadn't been seen round these parts for about a hundred hundred years. Now his missus, my mama, was the stubborn kind, and had told him not to bother coming back if he didn't bring home something, so instead of turning tail he wrestled the demon up from the black depths and dragged it home. Mama didn't even blink, either, when she saw him straining to pull this thing through the reeds to our house, just chopped it up and set to frying some steaks."

The innkeep set down his glass and looked at Jan. "D'ya believe that?"

"There's a kernel of truth somewhere in that tale."

Now a slight smile tugged at the corner of the barman's mouth. "Aye, there's bit hidden away. My granddad did hook this beast out in the bogs, but it had already been picked clean, same as ya can see here. Pulled up a small piece of it, then returned the following season during a drought and claimed the rest. Been starin' down here ever since."

Jan silently toasted the leering monster. Perhaps it was a strange swamp creature, but from the cast of the skull he imagined it was in truth a wyvern, the smaller, beast-dumb spawn of dragons. Fragments of a memory drifted closer, and he grasped for it greedily. He remembered that decades had passed in Nes Vaneth between blessed clutches. When the great wyrm Xocl'etal had produced a royal egg the entire city had feasted and celebrated, the fire warden had made the sky burn with cavorting images, and the silver trumpets atop the Winding Stair had pealed the good news. And she . . . *she* . . . had been so happy, as she talked of a future where her daughter would fly beside her. *What was her name*? Jan lowered his head into his hands and concentrated hard, but the memory faded and was gone, leaving only the echoes of her laughter.

"Here now, son," said a gruff voice as a hand slapped his shoulder. "Surely it's not all that bad."

Jan raised his head, blinking away the shadows of his lost past. One of the Visani had slipped onto the stool beside him, a man well into his middling years, with a weathered face and hair almost totally gone to gray. The fellow gestured at the lute strapped across Jan's back.

"My boys are wondering if you know how to pluck that thing. We've been traveling for near a week now along the Wending, all the way from Ver Anath, without a decent song to lighten our hearts. Jerrym there," and now the Visani jerked a thumb at one of his companions, a scrawny, sad-eyed lad idly fingering a lyre, "had his voice crack just as we left the scholar's city, and it doesn't sound near as sweet as once it did."

Jan glanced at the innkeep, who shrugged.

"Yer supper will be little while yet, and I'll throw in a few extra flagons if you play half-decent."

A smile broke the Visani's creased face, revealing surprisingly white teeth. "It's settled, then. What better way to warm such a wet and frozen night than with a song in the air and ale in the belly?"

Jan pushed away from the bar, eliciting a small cheer from the watching Visani. He slipped his lute from the case strapped across his back as he threaded his way between the tables towards the raised stage, clenching and unclenching his hands to try and get the lingering marsh chill from his fingers. Empty tankards pounded tables as he climbed the stairs, and a few sharp whistles cut the din, but all noise quieted when he reached the top and faced the common room. Jan almost smiled. He had performed for Visani before; they were a loud, boisterous people with a love for song, but also respectful and generous. A minstrel's perfect audience.

His gaze swept the room, commanding attention. The Dymorians had paused their huddled conspiracies and now watched him, while beneath the roaring wyvern skull Alomir wiped down the bar distractedly. Jan caught a flash of gold from the cracked-open kitchen door. He ran his hand along the smooth wood of the lute's neck, enjoying the simple pleasure of holding it again. How long had it been since he'd performed for someone other than Elinor? Ten years? Twelve?

His fingers brushed the strings, picking out a simple melody. At first he kept his movements simple, letting each note hang shivering in the inn's silence before plucking the next. Ever so gradually he increased the tempo, layering another simple tune beneath the first, twining the two so that a new, more complex sound emerged. An appreciative murmur rose from those listening as the distinct melodies he had created on the upper and lower strings blended, and they recognized the song. The core of the ballad was as ancient as the north, though the words had changed over the centuries. He remembered suddenly, in a memory that came and then faded like a flash of lightning, that he had first heard it as a boy in Nes Vaneth, sitting in his sister's lap while a wandering one-eyed bard performed for his House.

Then it had been known as *The Lament of the Raven Prince*, and though he knew the modern incarnation of the song he decided on a whim to keep the old verses.

In Ferdelin, far Ferdelin
On the edge of the twilit sea
A tower rose from the stony shore
For which there was no key

A princess fair with sunset hair
Gazed out longingly
From the tower's cold high walls
And whispered forth a plea

"Oh Raven Prince, my light, my love
How could you abandon me,
After all the centuries we've shared
Why am I not free?"

The raven heard, that dark-winged bird
And flew unerringly
To that distant land of harsh black sand
On the edge of the twilit sea

He sang in a language his listeners could not understand, save for a few words that had survived down through the centuries, but by the third time the refrain came round the Visani were stamping their feet to the music and attempting to sing along. The thin, dark-haired girl squealed as she was bounced from lap to lap, her flailing arm upsetting a tankard and drenching the older Visani who had approached Jan in ale, which brought a roar of amusement from the rest.

Jan finished with a flourish and offered a bow as the audience applauded. To shouts of "another" he rubbed his throat and one of the Visani motioned towards the bar for a drink. Mella must have been waiting for this sign, as she appeared only moments later beside the stage with an overflowing tankard.

"You sing beautifully," she whispered into his ear as he bent down, her fingers lingering on his hands as he took the ale. She smelled like wildflowers and summer.

Jan nodded thanks and drank deep. Then he set down the tankard and strummed a few random chords before beginning *One-Shoe Suli*, a tavern favorite that by the end had the Visani standing and kicking up their heels in some peculiar hopping dance. He followed with *Frog's Eye Pie*, another popular tune, and then changed course, plucking out the first haunting melodies of *The Brother's Ballad*. The Visani settled back into their seats as Jan sang of the twin princes Conn and Celn, and the greed and madness that led to the brothers' deaths and the fracturing of their kingdom.

Finally he left the stage to a roar of approval, many hands clapping his back as he wended his way back to the bar and slipped onto a stool. Alomir set a fresh tankard before him as the sad-eyed lad climbed the stage and started in on a song. For a moment he sang sweetly, but then his voice cracked, and Jan winced as a groan rose up from the Visani.

"You'll be called up there again soon enough."

Jan shook his head at the innkeep's words. "I haven't performed in so long I doubt my throat could survive another round."

"You've a good voice. Best I've ever heard, I think. Maybe if I keep the ale flowing you'll gift us with a few more songs."

Jan raised his drink in thanks. "The more of these that are set before me, the more likely I'll sing again."

Alomir turned and spat, then leaned in closer. "That first song – I only understood a few words. It was like . . . it was like a dream I couldn't quite remember. Familiar, yet so distant."

Jan took a long swig. "Ah. I don't really know what it means, either. I trained under a bard who had grown up in the north and held some interest in the old tongue. He said the song was ancient – maybe even Min-Ceruthan."

"Min-Ceruthan," Alomir said softly, sketching a quick warding circle in the air. "A cursed folk. We sometimes get travelers passing through here, heading north to trade with the Skein squatting in their dead cities. One fellow . . . must have been a few month or so ago . . . he was coming south from the thane's hall at Nes Vaneth. He said what he'd seen still haunted his dreams – ruins of tumbled stone, white steps climbing into the sky, towers of glimmering crystal sheathed in ice. He said if you pressed your face to that ice, you could see shapes within, man-shapes, staring back . . ."

A tingling had spread through Jan as Alomir talked. He felt dizzy, and had to lean on the wood in front of him to stop from sliding off his stool.

The barkeep gripped his arm. "You all right, lad?"

"Aye, I'm sorry," Jan murmured, managing a weak smile. "I don't . . . I don't know what came over me. Mayhap your northern ale is a bit strong for this southerner." He shook his head, trying to clear it. What was wrong with him? Shapes in the ice, flesh turned to stone . . . something fluttered on moth wings at the edges of his memories.

Alomir was looking at him queerly. "Aye, well, have a rest, lad. You've come a long way, and if you're heading west you've a long ways to go still. I'll send the fellows from Vis a round if they try and pull you up there again."

Jan nodded his thanks and pushed away from the bar.

He stood at the entrance of a vast, blue-lit chamber. Once he had known this place, but it was different now. Sorcery coiled in the air, drifted between the silent ones with their dead, granite eyes – accusing, knowing eyes. How they cowered! There was Helmskjatter, breaker of dragons, his mouth open in an endless raging challenge, the golden whip that had tamed the Wild Wyrm looped at his side – now but cracked stone. And there was fair Elowyn, of whose fabled beauty the bards had sung. He had sung. Her hands were raised imploringly toward the wall of shimmering ice that filled the far end of the room, atop the stairs that had once climbed to the Dragonbone Throne. Was she begging, or praying? What had been her final thoughts as the magic had rolled over her and the blood had begun to thicken in her veins? Did she curse what her queen had laid within the ice? Jan approached the flickering blue wall. Dark shapes lurked within, but one in particular drew him closer, and he reached out trembling fingers to brush the ice . . .

He awoke to the smell of summer. Mella hovered over him, indistinct in the light from the hearth's fading embers, her golden curls cascading down to tickle his face. She leaned in closer and her lips found his, her tongue darting inside his mouth. For a moment Jan welcomed the kiss, and he had to fight the urge to pull her down on top of him and crush her soft body against his own.

Instead he pushed her away. "Mella," he whispered, stealing a quick glance to see if any of the other sleepers curled near the hearth had woken, "what are you doing?"

The girl bit her lower lip, her wide eyes pleading. Jan tried to ignore the warmth of her body.

"Master bard," she breathed softly, "take me with you. Please. I can sew and cook, and I'll never complain, promise." She tried to kiss him again, but he held her away.

"God's blood, girl. You've only just met me. I could be mad or dangerous or cruel."

Mella shook her head, her expression certain. "You're not. And I'm not foolish. I wouldn't try and run off with any handsome face with a shiny sword. There's something about you, I can sense it . . ."

Jan stared into her soft brown eyes. Then he pushed himself into a sitting position; she moved to give him room. He gently brushed her cheek, and she flinched away. There was something behind that pretty, round face, a glimmering of the gift. If she did not escape these swamps, then likely one day she would be named wise-woman, and sought out by other marsh-folk for her charms and advice.

Jan extended a tendril of magic. He could not compel her – especially one marked by sorcery, no matter how minor – but he could make her take notice of what he said now, and consider it deeply.

"Mella," he said gravely, cupping her chin, "I know you think of this place as a prison. That you yearn for a different world, like the one you've heard about in song and traveler's tales. But I've wandered this land for more years than you've drawn breath" – *much longer*, he silently added – "and I can swear to you before any god you can name that having a home where others care for you is what brings true happiness, not jewels to pin in your hair or servants to draw your bath."

Tears glimmered in her eyes. "I know they care for me here, Uncle and Nana and the cousins . . . but I want more than this. More than bringing ale and squirming in the laps of ugly merchants. I want to see Vis, and Farayne, and maybe even the Gilded Cities."

Jan withdrew his sorcery. "Aye," he said tiredly, rubbing his eyes, "truly, Mella, I can't blame you for that. But my path is my own, and too dangerous for a serving girl to travel. I can only give you some advice: be careful with whom you finally leave this place. Will you do that?"

Mella nodded, swallowing back her tears. "I promise," she murmured, then stood and dashed silently across the common room and through the kitchen doors.

Jan watched her go. He sighed and lay back down again, pillowing his head on his bedroll, and met the eyes of a Visani merchant who had turned towards him.

"Singer," the man said with a slight smile, "you've more strength than I. That would have been too much temptation for me."

"Almost too much for me, as well," Jan whispered in reply, rolling over to stare at the darkened rafters.

He tried to push away thoughts of Mella and the memory of her smell. He had been dreaming, hadn't he? Something about Nes Vaneth . . . a frozen chamber, a wall of ice . . .

Jan sat upright. He had been there, in the audience chamber beneath the palace. Some of the great lords had been turned to stone, others were entombed in the ice, the terrible ice that the Kalyuni had called down upon the north.

Jan threw aside his traveler's blanket and stood. North. He must go north, and find out what he could about his past. There was knowledge in the ancient holdfasts, answers to riddles he could not yet even ask. Alyanna had those answers and more, he suspected, but could he trust her? Perhaps, if he went north, he might discover who he really was, what had happened to him. What had broken him.

Jan quickly gathered his things and slipped from the inn into the gray dawn-light. The dogs curled beside the boy sleeping in the hay raised their heads and growled, but Jan calmed them with a flicker of sorcery. He untied his horse from the hitching post, and as quietly as possible opened the inn's gate and led his mount back onto the road. His horse whickered in what seemed to be exasperation when it gazed upon the endless gray waste resolving from the darkness, and Jan patted its neck. "Strength, boy. We've a long way yet to travel."

Fingers of pink light spread across the horizon as he rode west, and by the time he came to where the road forked, the rosy dawn had given way to a dull blue sky, the first Jan had seen since leaving Vis. One path led on through the moorland, vanishing far ahead among hazy, dun-colored hills. The other turned north, and Jan's eyes were drawn to the distant Bones of the World, soaring and snow-capped. That way was Nes Vaneth. His home.

He urged his steed onto the right branching, but at first the horse resisted. "You might have more sense than me," Jan muttered, pulling harder on the reins.

They had ridden only a few hours when he sensed the presence ahead. It stood half-hidden in the tall grass of the moors, a girl-child in tattered gray rags. Long, tangled hair veiled her face, and the patches of skin he could see through the shifting grasses looked bone-white. She waited silently. Jan halted and slipped from his suddenly skittish horse, his hand on Bright. A cold wind gusted, stirring his cloak and bending the grass around the girl, but her clothes and hair remained untouched.

His flesh crawled. He had felt this thing before, and had tracked it across Araen, only to be turned away at the last by Alyanna and her promises. Yet here it was, waiting for him. He drew Bright, blue light flaring as the spell-steel left its sheath. The creature did not move.

"Finally we meet, demon."

jan. His name seemed to come from everywhere and nowhere, spoken in the hoarse whispers of many children.

"You know me."

we do. you are known to our mistress, so you are known to us.

"I should destroy you for what you did to Tristin Willesorn."

The titter of children's laughter filled the air.

Jan approached the girl, but she retreated deeper into the tall grass. "What do you want?"

this is not your path. our mistress bade you to go west, to find the red queen.

"I will travel north."

no.

Jan snorted. "Are you going to stop me, demon?"

she feared your resolve would weaken when you neared the bones. the temptation to witness your folly would again be too strong. but you will not go north, not until you have fulfilled your end of the bargain you struck.

"And if I do go north?"

if you do, we shall visit the summer child you just left weeping behind you, and hang her in bloody tatters from her uncle's hall.

Then the girl was gone. Jan cursed and slashed at the grass with his sword, staring at where she had been.

14: XIN

"AND BEGIN."

Nel lunged forward, her wooden sword thrusting toward Keilan in a passable approximation of the first form of The One Who Strikes. The boy shifted from the second form of The One Who Waits to the first, catching her blade and turning it aside. Quick as a rabbit Nel jumped back, far enough that Keilan couldn't try any counter without extending himself. Xin felt a small flood of satisfaction. Three days ago, Nel's speed and aggressiveness had simply overwhelmed Keilan when they trained; gradually, though, the boy had improved at parrying and blocking her attacks, and now it often took her some time before she could find a chink in his defenses and score a winning strike.

Her initial foray turned away, Nel began to circle Keilan, looking for an opening. Xin marveled at how effortlessly she moved over the uneven ground of the forest clearing, stepping over rocks and roots without even looking down. She had incredible balance, and an almost preternatural sense of her surroundings. If she continued her training she could become a brilliant swordswoman, he suspected, perhaps even one that might someday challenge a Fist warrior.

Xin regretted that thought immediately, as he sensed a mental snort of derision from his fourth brother, Chandren. The others were trying to guard their minds, but Xin felt a mixture of curiosity, disapproval, and bewilderment leaking around the barriers they had erected. Chandren had been the most vocal opponent of Xin training these two in swordfighting, but his opinion was not unique among the brothers. One of the first lessons they had learned in the red-sand pits was that the martial knowledge of the Fists must never be taught to those who were not Fettered. The origins of the Forms could be traced to the swordsingers of the lost Kalyuni Imperium, and in all the centuries since the waters had swallowed the Mosaic Cities those secrets had never left the stables of Gryx's slave masters.

But as Xin had explained to his brother Delon, he was only teaching the most basic of the Forms, and since the seeker would travel with the caravan for only a few more weeks – then turn south towards Nes Vaneth – there was not nearly enough time to impart very much else.

The rapid clattering of the practice swords returned Xin's attention to the duel. To his surprise, Keilan had for once gone on the offensive, and he was pressing Nel hard. Soon her back would be up against a tree, and then the boy's size and strength would almost certainly force her to yield or suffer a thumping blow – much like the ones she often delivered to him, he thought wryly. Her face was a mask of concentration as she warded away his sword, but Xin could tell that her defeat was inevitable now, as she had lost the initiative, and there was no place left for her to retreat.

He pushed himself from the mossy boulder he was leaning against, and was just opening his mouth to call a halt to the duel when Nel threw herself forward, Keilan's wooden blade whistling over her head. She tucked and rolled, somehow keeping her sword in her hand, and as she came to her feet again she lashed his side with enough force that the boy's ribs would almost certainly be bruised, if not cracked. Xin winced as Keilan stumbled back a few steps, fully expecting him to collapse in pain.

"Stop! Enough!" Xin cried, hurrying toward the boy.

But Keilan steadied himself and gave Nel a rueful smile. "I thought we were supposed to stay with the Forms?"

Nel grinned back and shrugged. "What did I tell you? In a fight, there are no rules. Take whatever advantage you can. I have a few old knife-fighting tricks I draw upon when in a tight spot."

Xin stopped a pace from Keilan, looking at him in surprise. "Keilan, are you all right? This one thinks you should be on the ground, clutching at your ribs and trying not to cry in front of the girl."

Absently Keilan rubbed his side. "Really? It knocked the wind from me, but I barely feel anything now."

Xin stepped forward and gently touched the same spot, pressing on the boy's ribs. "Nothing, truly?"

Keilan pulled up his tunic, revealing a second shirt beneath. It was made from some strange silvery fabric, almost like silk, the threads so fine it appeared seamless. "Oh, I guess it's this. Vhelan told me it's special, from the old Mosaic Cities. He said it would be like wearing steel, yet the shirt's so light I usually forget I have it on."

Xin cocked an eyebrow. His instincts had been right: these three companions were far more than simple travelers.

Nel winked at Keilan. "So next time I'll be sure to rap you on the head."

"This one thinks our little evening lessons would quickly come to an end if I brought the boy back to camp unconscious."

"Speaking of getting back to camp," Nel said, glancing up at the darkening sky, "we should probably return soon."

"This one agrees," Xin said, taking back the wooden practice swords. Was it just his imagination, or did Nel's fingers linger on his hand when she passed him her blade? He felt a small shiver at her touch, and that surprised him. He had taken lovers before, of course – it was encouraged in the pits, to pass along strong bloodlines – but he had never felt the same tingle of excitement as when he brushed against Nel, or caught her looking at him.

She was not a great beauty like what was described in song or the *ghee*-poems of the Fettered – she was not tall, nor did she have many soft curves – but her teardrop face, with its large eyes, high cheekbones, and short, boyish hair, had started worming its way into his daydreams while he marched beside the seeker's wagon. His brothers had noticed this, of course, and he had suffered a fair amount of good-natured abuse over the last few days.

Xin was used to it. He had always been the curious brother, the one most likely to try the sour and spicy camel soup of Kesh, or to let the fluttering hands of a Lyrish courtesan administer the Ceremony of a Hundred Needles upon his aching muscles after a long day of training. This trait often brought rippling waves of exasperation from his more conservative brothers, but always this feeling was shot through with affection. They were a Fist of Gryx, bound together forever, different facets of the same soul.

Keilan led them through the sparse forest, back toward where the caravan had circled for the night in a small field just off the Wending. Before they had pushed their way through the last of the stunted trees, though, the boy suddenly stopped, listening intently. After a moment, Xin heard it as well, the ghostly sound of strings being plucked somewhere nearby. Each note hung quivering in the air for several moments before fading away, like the rolling of distant thunder across the blood-dark sea; this was not the hurried strumming of a lute or harp, but something new, something different. He almost felt like he could gain some insight into the soul of the musician just by listening to his playing.

Keilan glanced back at them, and Xin could see from his expression that he wanted to find the source of this haunting melody.

"It's coming from that way," Nel said, peering between the tangled branches.

"The Shan," Keilan whispered, and Xin could hear the excitement in his voice. "He likes to set up camp a little ways off from the rest of the wagons."

"Probably so he can eat his spiders in peace," Nel said, winking at Xin. "Otherwise he might have to share."

Keilan stuck out his tongue in disgust. "Do the Shan really eat spiders?"

"This one knows they do," Xin replied. "Two years ago this one and his brothers accompanied our old master to Tsai Yin. Along the big roads in that city vendors sell all manner of barbecued vermin impaled on little wooden sticks – spiders, scorpions, snakes. This one tried a spider as big as a man's hand. Truly, it was not bad. Crunchy, though sometimes the goo inside spurted out. And they have these spicy dipping sauces –"

Nel waved at him to stop talking. "Gah. Quiet, or I won't be able to eat later."

"I want to see him," Keilan suddenly said.

Xin shrugged. "If you wish."

The music paused before they had gone very much farther, and a moment later Xin glimpsed the shadowy bulk of the Shan's wagon through the trees.

"He has good hearing," Nel said, with a hint of admiration.

"You make more noise than a drunkard stumbling around in the dark," Xin replied, shaking his head.

Nel snorted. "I'm a city girl. I hate the woods."

The trees thinned, and then they emerged into the clearing where the Shan had set up camp. A small fire had already been kindled, and a pitcher with a long spout hung suspended over the flames by some clever contraption of interlocking metal rods. Their mysterious traveling companion sat cross-legged in the grass wearing a robe of shimmering green, behind a strange instrument that looked like a small, narrow table carved with an intricate flowing design showing birds in flight among shreds of clouds. A half-dozen strings ran the length of its surface, and the Shan plucked at one as he watched them stumble from the woods. When the ethereal note faded, he bowed his head in welcome.

"Greetings," he said, in the same accent Xin remembered from his journey south of the Broken Sea. "I welcome you."

Xin pressed his palms together. "*Nel soon, Xi Xu*" he said, hoping he remembered the proper honorific.

Nel and Keilan turned back to stare at him like he had grown a second head.

The Shan quirked a smile. "You know a little of my language. Please, be welcome and sit. I will prepare some tea." He rose smoothly and vanished through the black curtain that hung in the doorway to his wagon. Xin had watched his old master during several of these ceremonial introductions, so he knew vaguely what was expected of them: he sat, folding his legs like the Shan had been sitting, and motioned for Nel and Keilan to join him. Moments later the Shan returned, carrying a tray with four small green cups of glazed clay, and then filled each with a steaming liquid from the pitcher hanging over the fire. Finally, with a flourish, he placed the tray between them and sat, gesturing for them to take a cup.

"To new friends," the Shan said, lifting his drink high, "may the East Wind always blow upon our backs."

They mirrored the Shan by holding up their cups. "There's a purple flower in my water," Nel whispered out of the corner of her mouth.

"It's supposed to be there," Xin hissed back. "Now drink."

"Drink the flower? What kind of man drinks flowers?"

Xin tried his best to keep his voice low. "No. Drink around the flower."

"What kind of man drinks flower-flavored water?"

The Shan had sipped from his cup and put it down, and was now staring off into the forest, as if politely trying to ignore their mutterings.

"The kind of man who comes from the Empire of Swords and Flowers. Just be glad we're not drinking sword-flavored water!"

Nel snorted again and sipped her tea. Then she smacked her lips loudly. "Hm. Not bad. A little bitter."

"I'm Keilan Ferrisorn," the boy suddenly blurted, leaning forward, his eyes bright with interest.

The Shan nodded slowly. "Well met, Keilan son of Ferris. I am Cho Yuan, first son of Cho Han."

Xin shifted, watching their host carefully. Keilan had skipped a few steps of the ceremony and jumped straight to the formal introductions, but the Shan did not seem upset.

"This one is Xin, third son of Delemachus."

The Shan inclined his head, smiling faintly. Then he turned to Nel. She didn't seem to notice, instead studying something floating in her cup. Xin discreetly elbowed her, and she jerked her head up.

"Ah? Oh. I'm Nel, one of probably many daughters of someone who frequented the Silk District, but who fortunately didn't stay around long enough to introduce himself."

Xin chewed the inside of his cheek, certain the Shan was going to take offense at Nel's flippancy. But the Shan's slight smile deepened, and to Xin's surprise he bowed his head even to her.

"I bid you all welcome to my fire. It is good to meet my fellow travelers."

"Are you going to Vis?"

The Shan shook his head at Keilan's question. "I am not. My path leads to Herath."

"You're a silk merchant?" Nel asked, her finger in her cup as she tried to fish something out of her tea.

Again the Shan shook his head. "I am looking for something that was stolen."

"Stolen from Shan?" Keilan asked.

"Yes. I found traces of it in the Kingdoms. But there the trail went cold. I have heard that the queen in Dymoria collects such things as I am looking for. So I have decided to travel west, to her kingdom."

"And what will you do if you find it?"

Something flickered in the Shan's eyes, an emotion Xin could not quite understand. "If I find what I am looking for, young Keilan, I will destroy it."

15: KEILAN

THE OLD MAN was talking to himself again.

Keilan moved closer to where the scholar crouched at the bridge's edge, but the fierce wind whipping down from the north carried away most of what Seeker Garmond was saying, and the little Keilan could hear sounded almost like another language. *A perfect parabola . . . where is . . . keystone? Sorcery . . . or geometry?* The scholar was fiddling with some small silver instrument he had set on the bridge beside himself, minutely adjusting a set of scales and then scribbling down the results in a tattered black book. The wind suddenly gusted, plucking the scholar's gray pointed cap from his head and sending it fluttering out into empty air. The old man patted his head distractedly with the hand not holding his quill, but appeared otherwise unconcerned by his loss. Keilan watched the cap spiral down, down, down, until the scrap of gray was swallowed by the frothing river far below.

Keilan glanced at the bridge's far end, where the other wagons had already reached and now waited. There seemed to be an argument ensuing: Halan was gesticulating wildly back at where the scholar's wagon was perched, unmoving, upon the center of the arching bridge. Next to him stood Delon, another of Xin's Fist, his arms folded, apparently absorbing the Dymorian caravan master's abuse with stoic detachment. Delon had gone ahead with the rest of the caravan to ensure that they would not leave them behind after the scholar had halted their wagon halfway across the curved ribbon of stone. Keilan sighed and stepped closer to the scholar and the bridge's edge, careful to avoid staring at the distant river below and its tumbling, white-flecked rapids. He wondered again why whoever had built this bridge hadn't also put up some kind of railing.

"Seeker Garmond," said Xin respectfully, "we should hurry. The others are waiting."

The scholar paused in his manipulation of the silver instrument and turned his head toward Xin. Despite his lined face and bushy gray eyebrows his expression looked to Keilan to be full of almost childlike wonderment.

"My dear lads, have either of you ever seen a bridge such as this?"

Xin shifted his feet and shook his head. "This one has not."

The scholar traced the nearly invisible seams where the stones were joined. "At least a thousand years old, yet it appears as solid as if it had been built only yesterday. And barely weathered, despite the cold winds and snow flailing down from the Frostlands. Remarkable. If I'd known there were such wonders along the Wending, I would not have had us sail the Broken Sea to get to the Kingdoms in the first place."

Garmond gestured for Keilan to lean closer, a strange smile on his lips, and after a moment's hesitation Keilan crouched beside the old man.

"Here is the most amazing thing," the scholar whispered, tapping the pages of his opened notebook, "I think there might be no sorcery involved in its construction!" The scholar drew back a bit and raised his eyebrows.

Xin squinted at the very natural looking stone beneath his feet. "Sorcery, sir?"

Garmond made a cutting gesture with his hand. "None! Obviously I need to check my calculations, but if the mathematics hold true then we would know it is possible to raise such a wonder in a post-sorcerous age!" The scholar thrust his notebook towards Xin. "Here, lad.

Read my notes. Of course, you probably lack the numeracy background to check my figures . . ." The scholar paused, blinking. "Ah, please don't be insulted, I shouldn't make such assumptions. Perhaps you are an amateur student of the perfect art – math, that is – anyway, I've jotted down my findings, here they are, it would be good to get a second set of eyes on them."

Seeker Garmond continued babbling as Xin took the proffered book. Keilan, straightening up and standing beside the Fist warrior, also glanced at the jumbled numbers and tiny, crabbed writing.

"Well, what do you think?"

Xin snapped the notebook shut and handed it back to the scholar. "This one cannot read, sir. Our masters in Gryx discourage such knowledge among the Fettered. But I'm sure your findings are most interesting."

Keilan smiled at the scholar's horrified expression, and had to cover his mouth with his hand.

Seeker Garmond shook his head, the shocked horror in his eyes slowly softening to sympathy. "Ah, poor lad. Of course, of course. Tragic failures in your upbringing are the reason the Reliquary does not usually employ the Fettered, despite the excellent reputation of the Fists. A reputation, I should add, which I've found to be well-earned on our journey together." The scholar gathered up his instruments, secreting strange objects in the folds of his voluminous gray robe, then gripped Xin's elbow and slowly pushed himself to his feet with a pained grunt. "Eh, these old knees. Not so spry as I once was. You know, in my youth the Light of the Lore used to call upon me to retrieve books from the archives because I could take those thousand steps faster than any other apprentice." The scholar staggered slightly, and Xin helped steady him before he could tumble off the bridge.

"Careful, sir."

Seeker Garmond nodded thanks, and then his face broke into a puzzled frown. "Why are my ears so cold? Wait, where's my cap?"

"It blew off while you were doing your examinations," Xin said as the scholar glanced around the bridge.

"It fell into the river," Keilan added.

Seeker Garmond leaned closer to the edge, and Keilan had to restrain himself from yanking the old man back. Instead he tensed, prepared to grab a handful of the scholar's loose robes if he needed to be pulled to safety.

"By the Pen, that was my favorite cap. Gift from Seeker Merriam upon my publication of *The Codex Arcanum*. Mink lining, quite warm. A terrible shame." The scholar thrust his hand into the inner recesses of his robe and pulled forth another gray cap, an apparent twin of the one that now was floating down the river.

As the old man settled the new cap on his head Xin subtly began to steer the scholar back towards his waiting wagon. Keilan gave the crowd waiting on the far side of the bridge a quick wave. Even from this distance he could tell Nel's annoyance from her stance and crossed arms.

The old man twisted around as Xin was helping him up into the wagon, laying a hand on the Fist warrior's shoulder. "We must teach you how to read." Garmond stared past Xin, focusing on Keilan.

"You there, lad. You know how to read, yes?"

"Y-yes," stammered Keilan, meeting the scholar's guileless blue eyes.

"Excellent! I know Xin here has been teaching you in the evenings how to swing a lump of iron around so that one day you could split open some poor fellow's head like an overripe fruit . . . I think it would be a fair trade if you in turn taught our good Xin here how to pull meaning from those magical little squiggles."

Xin opened his mouth to say something – to refuse, Keilan thought from the look on his face – but the seeker waved away his words before he could speak.

"No, no – no thanks necessary. *We Are Candles In The Dark*, that's what's carved above the entrance to the great library at the Reliquary, looked at it for nearly sixty years. Illuminating dark corners, that's what we scholars do . . ." The old man's eyes widened again, and he quickly shook his head. "Wait, no, that came out wrong. You're no dark corner, Xin – a bright one, I can tell, I've had plenty of dullard apprentices, my goodness you should have met Ogden, or Ox, as we fondly called him –"

Xin gently guided the scholar inside and drew shut the heavy curtain. Seeker Garmond's voice faded as Keilan and the Fist warrior walked over to the pair of mules harnessed to the front of the wagon. Xin slapped the beasts lightly on their flanks to get them moving, and the wagon lurched forward.

The Fist warrior sighed. "The caravan master is not the only one unhappy with the delay. Your friends are complaining as well."

"How do you know that?"

Xin glanced at Keilan and tapped his head.

"Can you really hear them in your mind?"

"No. We brothers cannot whisper like that. It is not words that echo inside us. But we know, nonetheless, what each is thinking. This one can always feel them. We are different reflections of the same man, this one told you this already."

"And right now they're telling you to hurry?"

Xin chuckled. "No. Truly this one's brothers do not care if the scholar wastes time upon the bridge. We like the old man. He is kind to us, kinder than most masters."

The cold wind gusted, and Keilan drew the hood of the cloak down to shield his face. "Where did you meet him?"

"In Ver Anath. We traveled there as guardians for our old master's son, who told his father he had pressing business in the scholar's city. Pressing business was dealing in artifacts of the lost Imperium – this son knew that the thief prince of Ver Anath was an avid collector. But he did not know that the artifacts had in fact previously been stolen from this same thief, the man they call the Sorrow. He gave my old master's son a choice: give over our Fist to him, or the Sorrow would take both his hands and his feet and feed them to the wraithfins in the bay. So we worked for the thief for a year. A bloody year, this one did not enjoy it. Finally we were sold to the Reliquary as payment for some debt. And now here we are."

"Why were you in the Kingdoms?"

Xin glanced over his shoulder at the wagon. "The good seeker has many interests, but foremost among them is animals. Rare, legendary animals. We came to the Kingdoms chasing the rumor of a basilisk."

"And did you find one?" Mam Ru had told Keilan stories of basilisks when he was young, how the faces you could sometimes see in the rocks in the forest were victims of the beasts.

Xin grinned. "We found a big lizard covered in tar and chicken feathers, and a very enterprising farmer charging two bits for a quick look. Seeker Garmond was not happy, but he does not stay sad for long. Always there is something new to distract and interest him. Like this bridge. It is a good way to live a life, always learning."

"Do you want me to do what he said?" Keilan suddenly blurted. "Teach you how to read?"

Xin was silent for a moment. When he finally spoke, there was an odd tone to his voice, something Keilan hadn't heard before from the Fist warrior.

"If you teach this one how to read, our lives will be forfeit if we return to Gryx. The masters will hang us outside our old stables. They will cut off our ears and our noses and feed them to their dogs. They will flense us, slowly, until the red-brick dust of the city cakes our raw and bleeding bodies, and then we will hang there, twisting and burning in the merciless sun, before we are finally cut down, doused in honey, and staked to a fire-ant hill. We will die as examples to the other Fettered, so that they might know what happens when a slave dares learn how to read."

Keilan found he was holding his breath.

"Yes," Xin said, turning to him just as they approached the end of the bridge and the rest of the waiting caravan. "This one wishes to learn."

Despite the delay caused by the seeker the evening mood was festive for the first time in the weeks since the caravan had departed the

Godsword Inn and started on the Wending Way, the ancient road that connected the eastern empire of Menekar with the Gilded Cities on the shores of the western ocean. They had come far north, and now they camped in the shadows of the Bones of the World, among great tumbled slabs of stone. Perhaps the revelry that night was a response to the wildness they found themselves in, a rebuke to the cold and dark of the looming mountains and the Frostlands beyond. Possibly the good cheer was due to the large cauldron of rabbit stew the Dymorian rangers had provided for the caravan, or – and this was more likely, Keilan supposed – it was the case of firewine one of the merchants had broken open and passed around.

Keilan sat between Nel and Vhelan, close to the fire, watching the shadows from the flames crawl and dance upon the wall of rock that rose up beside their camp. He glanced at the wizard and his knife, and felt a warmth inside him that might have been the wine, but he suspected was not. His earlier thoughts of escaping and returning to his village – or striking out into the wilds – seemed like distant memories, the foolish impulse of a scared child. The Dymoria Vhelan spoke of now seemed like the only place where he could find a home . . . and find protection from the faithful of Ama. He swirled the sluggish red liquid that remained at the bottom of his own cup, savoring the wine's lingering spice.

"Not a bad grape at all," Vhelan said, saluting the merchant across the fire, the one who had shared the wine. The merchant returned the gesture, briefly doffing his plumed cap, and then after a moment's hesitation rose and made his way toward where they sat, skirting the fire and the cleared space where two of the caravan's guards were wrestling. The guards had removed their shirts, and despite the cold their darkly muscled bodies gleamed in the firelight. Lively betting was going on among the watchers as to who would finally be pinned.

The merchant unrolled a mat of woven reeds beside Vhelan and sat with a contented sigh, stretching out his long legs. Excitement rippled around the fire as one of the wrestlers broke a hold by flipping his opponent, nearly sending him tumbling into the flames. A flailing leg did kick a burning log, sending up a shower of sparks and ash. The merchant who had just sat with them brushed his pantaloons clean with a sniff of disgust. He was not as young as Keilan had first thought – thirty-five summers, at least – though he wasn't sure of the man's age exactly because his face had been whitened and smoothed by some cosmetic.

"Many thanks for the wine, friend," Vhelan said, toasting the merchant again.

"You are very welcome," he replied, and Keilan caught the quick glance shared between the knife and her wizard. "I am Elwyn ri Tannis, of the Goldridge Tannises."

"A fine Lyrish family," Vhelan said slowly, his fingers drumming the lip of his cup.

"Indeed. May I know your name? I must confess that I overheard you speaking earlier, and was surprised and delighted to find out that I shared this ghastly road with at least one other civilized man."

Vhelan dipped his head in thanks. "Ah, of course. I am Vhelan ri Vhalus, and this is my niece, and this my nephew."

"A Vhalus scion?" the merchant said, pressing two fingers to his temple. "I am honored to meet you. May I ask what brings you so far from the shining city? I noticed you have no wares to trade."

"Visiting family in the Kingdoms," Vhelan said quickly, tousling Keilan's hair. "The boy and girl's grandmother was the daughter of a baron. Terribly barbaric people, but they do own half the tanneries in Theris."

"Yes, yes," the merchant murmured, looking at Nel with new interest. She smiled back sweetly and fluttered her lashes.

Keilan swallowed hard and edged away from them, not wanting to be part of what he suspected was coming next.

But before Nel could throw the merchant into the fire a shadow appeared beside Vhelan, one of the Dymorian rangers.

"Lord, we found something in the woods."

"Some more rabbit, I hope," Vhelan said, taking another sip of wine. "Or another cask of this delicious vintage."

"No, my lord . . ." The ranger glanced at the merchant.

"It's fine, we are all friends here," Vhelan said, motioning for the ranger to speak.

"Ah, very well. We found claw marks on some of the trees nearby. Old, to be sure, from a season or more ago, but definitely wraith."

"Wraith!" exclaimed the merchant, nearly dropping his wine cup.

Vhelan held out his hand for calm. "Any fresh spoor?"

The ranger shook his head. "No, my lord. Nothing to suggest the beasts are still around. But it's rare that wraiths range out of the Frostlands. Captain d'Taran thought you should know."

"Wraiths!" the merchant repeated, looking out into the darkness. "I've never heard of those monsters near the Wending Way."

"Keep a tight watch tonight," Vhelan said to the ranger, who nodded and melted back into the shadows.

"Even if they are still prowling about, we're far too many to worry. Wraiths are scavengers, not raiders."

"Yes, of course . . ." the Lyrish merchant muttered, turning back to the flames.

A moment later someone threw a handful of powder onto the campfire, and it flared skyward, tongues licking a knuckle of rock protruding from the cliff-face. A few of the watchers clapped and hooted.

"God's blood," Nel said, gesturing across the fire, "did you see who threw that magician's dust into the fire?"

It was the Shan. He sat cross-legged beside Halan, his silken robes shimmering red and gold in the firelight. In his thin fingers he held a white, long-stemmed pipe carved into a curling dragon-shape, and as Keilan watched, a stream of sinuous, blue smoke issued from the dragon's open mouth. The smoke did not dissolve as it drifted over the flames; rather it remained as tendrils that twined together like mating serpents, eventually vanishing into the darkness above. His black hair was bound up into a tight bun, but it looked to Keilan like if he let it down it would nearly reach his waist. The revelry gradually ebbed as the others around the fire noticed the arrival of their mysterious traveling companion, until only the hiss and crackle of the flames could be heard. Even the wrestlers disentangled themselves and scuttled back into the circle, one cradling his arm and the other dragging a leg.

The Shan's lips quirked into a half-smile, then he leaned closer to Halan and began whispering. Surprise flashed across the caravan master's face, soon replaced with wry amusement. He beckoned toward where Xin and the other members of his Fist were sitting, and one of them rose and approached.

"What's going on?" the Lyrish merchant asked as Halan said something to the Fist warrior, whose turn it now was to look surprised.

Vhelan shrugged. "I have no idea."

The Fist warrior returned to his fellows, and after a brief consultation he nodded toward Halan and the Shan.

Halan heaved himself to his feet, coming to stand in the central area recently vacated by the wrestlers. He cleared his throat, turning to take in all those watching, then began to speak.

"Fellows! A request has been made. Our companion Cho Yuan has asked for a demonstration of an ancient art lost long ago. He has heard in his land that the Fists of Gryx remember one of the fighting styles of the drowned Mosaic Cities, the shadowdance of the Kalyuni swordsingers." Mutterings rose around the fire at these words, swelling when two of the Fist moved in front of the flames holding wooden practice swords.

Halan hurriedly sat again as the two warriors faced each other, the blades extended so that the blunted tips were lightly touching. For a long moment they were utterly motionless.

And then the dance began. In perfect tandem each pulled their sword back and lunged forward, incredibly fast, but when the blades came together there was no clatter of wood, no sound at all. Flashing routines, cut and thrust, spinning apart and colliding again with jarring force – yet somehow silent, except for the sound of their shuffling feet. Shadows dancing.

Their speed increased, the practice swords blurring together in the firelight, until the two Fist brothers ceased to be two and instead became one, a single fluid warrior that swayed and danced.

"How do they do it?" whispered Keilan.

"Practice," Nel murmured back. "Every strike is perfect, and though the swords seem to come together they never actually touch."

And just as suddenly they stopped, blades crossed, breathing heavily. Applause spread among the watching merchants and guardsmen. Keilan glanced at the Shan, curious about his reaction.

It was not what he expected. The Shan was clapping as well, but he was clearly distracted. He was not even looking at the Fists; rather he was staring into the darkness beyond them, his face creased with worry. Something seemed wrong.

Keilan started when he felt a hand fall on his shoulder, but it was only the Lyrish merchant, smiling broadly.

"A show to remember, eh?"

It retreats further into the blackness. Such eyes! Such piercing eyes the one from across the World Ocean has, sorcery unlike it has sensed in all its endless wheeling years, not strong but different, so different; soon the manling Shan will split its veil and see the truth, flense the skin and lay bare its hidden beauty. Something must be done. Mistress will gnash and rend if it returns in groveling failure; she does not care for it, never has, and now she has new pets to interest her. The Shan will die, as the mistress has decreed. There are others, though, that travel with the caravan. Warriors and sorcerers, too many to overcome. It must find allies.

Behind it the firelight dims, the shapes recede. Many centuries had tumbled past since last it saw the shadows sword-dance. The wheel turns; what was dead and dust has come again. Could it rise once more with this fresh age? It pushes the thought from its mind. There is nothing for it now except the mistress and her desires.

It moves through barren woods. Here, near the roof of the world, the moonlight tastes different, not as sweet as in the southlands. It extends its tongue, licks the night, savors the bitter radiance of the waning moon. Shivers with joy.

Faster. It sheds its skin, reveling in the power and the freedom – and oh, the beauty! – of its trueform. Twisted branches clutch at it, fall away. It flows over rocks, up precipitous cliffs, talons sinking into stone, waiting to catch a scent.

There. Faint so faint but unmistakable; it follows, squeezing through narrow crevices, along impossible paths, to a rent in the mountain's fabric. Inside they wait.

It enters the blackness. Shapes uncoil in the cave's recesses: dams and young, huddled, fearful; yes, it tastes their fear, shuddering in ecstasy. Larger shapes approach warily, the bulls, heaving with rage and terror; terror for this thing that smells unspeakably ancient, like the roots of the mountain. Do they remember the scent? In the dim race-memories of these fallen creatures is there a frisson of recognition?

The largest bull charges, leaps, claws extended. It laughs and catches the creature as it would a puppy, holds it by its neck, compares the ruined monster with what it remembers its people once were. The creature squirms, kicks its taloned feet.

"Do you still know speech?" it asks, slurring the word-sounds in a tongue it has not spoken for three thousand years.

The wraith gasps, scrabbling at its throat.

It loosens its grip, so that the beast may talk.

"Yes."

It smiles, runs its tongue over rows of serrated teeth. "Good. I have a task for you."

16: ALYANNA

SOMETHING NEW HAD arrived in the emperor's pleasure gardens.

Alyanna had learned this from one of her favorites, a dark beauty from the Eversummer Isles, as they lay tangled together in her pavilion. The girl had whispered to her like a maid confessing a secret love, describing in hushed tones a magical bird with a hundred glimmering eyes that servants had released just this morning near the quartz sculptures. Alyanna had laughed softly at the wonder in the girl's voice and kissed her affectionately on the cheek.

Later, she found herself on the ceramic paths, wandering through flowering copses of dragonblooms and stands of shimmering ghostweed, searching the gardens for this mysterious new guest. Red-tailed monkeys plucked from the jungles of Xi watched her warily with luminous golden eyes, and a large lizard basking on a rock flared its neck-frill and hissed a challenge as she passed. She hissed back, and it scuttled away with an indignant croak.

Finally she found the birds, a small tribe of them picking daintily through a bed of tiger-ear lilies, hunting for worms or insects. They were marvelous: their feathers were green and blue and gleamed iridescent in the sun, and set into their fanned tails were dozens of beautiful, staring eyes.

"What are you?" she murmured, half-tempted to compel one closer so she could stroke its glistening plumage.

"The Menekarians are calling these birds peacocks. We have another name for them in Shan."

Wen Xenxing stood on the path a few steps behind her, watching the birds without expression.

"My lord!" she said, dropping into a curtsy. "A thousand apologies. I did not hear you approach."

The black vizier shrugged his hands free from his robe's long sleeves and bade her to rise. "It is I who should apologize. I did not intend to frighten you – moving silently has just become part of my nature, I suppose. Too many years spent skulking in shadows."

Wen shifted his gaze back to the peacocks. "Beautiful creatures. I had not seen one since I was a boy in Tsai Yin. They roam free, there, in the Chalcedony City. In the Shan tongue their name means 'the eyes of Heaven', and it is believed that through the patterns on their tails the gods watch the mortal world. No man would dare kill such an instrument of the divine, yes?"

"Do you believe this, my lord? Are the gods of Shan spying on the emperor?"

Wen smiled. "While there are certainly sights worth seeing in this garden – such as you, my dear – I do not believe that Heaven has any power in Menekar. The only god watching our fumblings here is Ama, through the eyes of his blessed Pure."

Alyanna ducked her head in agreement. "Of course, my lord. To think otherwise would be blasphemy."

The black vizier grunted in reply and returned his hands to his sleeves. Watching him watch the peacocks, Alyanna was reminded of her recent foray into the Empire of Swords and Flowers, when she had stolen away the Chosen from the warlocks of Shan. He looked to her just like a mandarin of the Thousand Voices, the ones she had seen wandering among gilded pagodas, across soaring crescent bridges, and between the dragon-wrapped pillars of the emperor's court, their silken slippers whispering upon floors of polished jade.

"I notice, my lord, that only some of the birds sport beautiful tails. Why is that?"

Wen shrugged. "I am not certain. But I do know that the birds with tails are males, so perhaps they are trying to attract a mate with the display."

Alyanna crouched beside one of the peacocks that had wandered close to where she stood. She extended a tendril of sorcery, caressing the dim intelligence she sensed within its dark eyes, compelling it to take a few more tentative steps in her direction.

"I have heard the world is upside-down in the far south. So that would mean in Shan men must garb themselves in beautiful clothes and paint their faces, as the women do in Menekar? Does the emperor of Swords and Flowers labor to make himself more handsome for his concubines?"

The black vizier chuckled. "The women in Shan mastered the art of seduction thousands of years ago. No man can resist the allure of Shan's noble ladies."

Alyanna reached out her hand and stroked the peacock's head. "Then the concubines of Shan rule the empire?"

Now Wen turned to her again, the slightest of frowns touching his lips when he saw the way the peacock had dipped its neck to her. "The emperor has no concubines in Shan."

Alyanna allowed the tendril of sorcery she had twisted around the peacock's mind to dissipate, and the bird jerked itself away from her in confusion. "How can the emperor deny himself the pleasures of the flesh?"

Wen's eyes glittered as he watched her. "The history of the Shan people is riddled with stories of powerful courtesans who through their influence plunged empires into chaos. The Raveling itself was brought about by a concubine's poisoned advice to her emperor. So when the long years of the Empire of Wind and Salt ended, and the ships finally arrived on the shores of this new land, the mandarins decided that such a tragedy must never happen again."

"What did they do?" asked Alyanna, though in truth she knew the answer already.

The black vizier smiled. "Before every new emperor sits the Phoenix Throne he is transformed during the ascension ceremony into a eunuch. Thus he can better dedicate his life to ruling Shan, without distraction."

"How barbaric," Alyanna murmured, wrinkling her face in mock disgust.

"Perhaps. But others would say civilized. After all, what is civilization but man's attempt to separate himself from the animals, which are ruled by base impulses. The Shan emperor is now no longer a slave to this most powerful of passions."

Alyanna had during her long life known more than a few eunuchs, and she had found them just as petty as any other men – perhaps more so. Competition for women was replaced by competition for glory and riches. The eunuch order that had served the sorcerers of Kalyuni's Star Towers had been as bad as the women of any harem, expending vast energies in intricate plots to slightly raise their own status relative to their rivals.

Alyanna did not mention this to Wen. Instead she smiled and fluttered her lashes and pretended sweet insipidness.

Men were fools, whole or not.

Wen watched her carefully. Too carefully. She felt a little shiver of – what? Excitement? – under his piercing gaze.

"I will admit that my purpose in coming to the gardens today was not just to see these marvelous birds. I also came to find you."

"Me, my lord?"

"Yes. And after the history lesson I've just given you about the Shan, perhaps you can guess why."

Of course she could, but Alyanna kept her expression carefully innocent. "No, my lord."

"Our emperor is obsessed with you," Wen said flatly, reaching up to pluck a brilliant purple blossom from a low-hanging tree branch. "He speaks of you in our council meetings. He mentions you whenever there is word of new silks from Shan or gems from Xi arriving in the city. His servants tell me that he mutters your name in his sleep." Wen twirled the flower in his hands, then let it fall. "I hope you will use your influence over the chosen of Ama wisely."

Alyanna ducked her head, as if embarrassed by the black vizier's words, though in truth it was to hide her small smile. "I have no power over the emperor, my lord, I promise you. I am just a momentary plaything, a diversion that eases the great burden of ruling."

The black vizier stared at her for a long moment, his face impassive, but Alyanna sensed the unspoken threat growing between them. Then he turned and glided silently away upon the ceramic path, until he vanished among a tangle of vines hanging down from copper trellises. Alyanna wanted to laugh at the theatrics of it all.

The thought that this puffed up little worm could scare her! She had been underestimated by a thousand powerful men over a thousand years, and this Wen Xenxing would be no different.

A chill breeze shivered the flowers near her, and then one of them was there, peering out from behind the knotted bole of a banyan tree. The peacocks cried out in alarm and half-flew, half-hopped away, beating their clipped wings frantically.

filthy birds.

This one was a boy, Alyanna thought, though like all the Chosen it kept its face hidden behind matted black hair. "I appreciate their beauty," she said, strolling closer to the crouching demon-child, which flinched away from her.

filthy, evil shan things. and you speak to one, a shan. we wish to eat his heart.

Alyanna chuckled. "You may yet have your chance. But it won't be so you can exact some revenge for your imprisonment. And anyways, he serves Menekar, not the Phoenix Throne."

all shan are cunning. do not trust him.

Alyanna waved away their echoing words. "If the Shan were so formidable I would not have been able to steal you away from right under their very noses."

underestimate the warlocks of shan at your peril. their ways are as deep and as fathomless as your own.

"If you feared them so much, why did you leave such an obvious trail across the Kingdoms? There are Shan hunters out there, searching for you."

they will not find us. we will not go back. we will rend and scatter their limbs to the four corners of the world.

"They will not find you," Alyanna agreed, reaching out to brush aside the Chosen's tangled hair. The thing's face was smudged with grime, like a street urchin. It had no eyes, just gaping black holes, but she felt it watching her. She let the hair fall back. "You are not my only servants. I have set upon the trail of your hunters an old and powerful pet."

the false man. the so-chin-jeng

Alyanna let her surprise show. "It is familiar to you?"

they existed in the ancestral lands of shan, as well, before they were hunted to oblivion

Interesting. "They were also hunted here. My servant may be the last of its kind, then. When we found them living amongst us, feeding on us, we named them genthyaki – 'the hidden ones'. An ancient immortal race, slowly dwindling, having lost the ability to breed but still deadly strong, and wielders of great magics. The wizards of the north and the south united to root them out. I led a band of hunters at that time, and we took many of their heads. I wore a necklace of their teeth, and armored myself in scales I flayed from their still-living bodies. It was a wild age. The last we tracked was the strongest I had ever encountered; it slew my fellow hunters, and came close to besting me. But in the end it cowered before me, and begged for mercy, and I slaved it to my will." Alyanna remembered that moment vividly. She had stood over it in the lashing rain, in that remote northern forest among soaring pines, her face streaked with mud and her body laced with red claw-marks, her hair coiling like a nest of snakes as the air crackled with spent sorcery. A cat-of-nine tails drawn from the living darkness had squirmed in her hand, and with ancient words she had bound its soul to hers.

It would dispose of these Shan hunters. She was sure they had brought some sorcery to recapture the Chosen, but they could not possibly be prepared for the genthyaki.

"Leave me," she said, and the demon-child faded into the gathering shadows.

yes, mistress, it whispered in its chorus of lost voices, and was gone.

Such strange, artless creatures, so full of passion and power. Imbued with great festering sorcery, yet at the same time riven by weaknesses that left them in thrall to her. She could not restrain her fascination.

Alyanna shrugged out of her silken shift, letting it puddle at her feet as she stepped from the ceramic path. Fireflies were appearing as evening fell in the garden, sketching patterns around her and swarming the stirring nightblossoms. She breathed deep of the garden's smells. Cool grass tickled her feet, and a warm breeze caressed her body. Above her the emerging stars glittered like diamonds strewn across velvet.

A dark shape slithered through the grass away from her. Alyanna sunk a tendril of sorcery deep within the snake's cold brain, compelling it to approach. She closed her eyes as its smooth, dry scales wrapped her ankle and began to climb her leg. So alive. The garden, this world, herself. She should have died a thousand years ago, but she had refused to go meekly into the dark. Instead she had traded their world for her eternity – a bright, flowering world, to be sure, but she held no regrets. All that mattered was that she now lived, when the rest of them were dust and shadows. The snake's darting tongue touched her thigh. She shuddered with pleasure.

17: KEILAN

"**THE TIGER AND** the lion are oft . . . often compared with each other, as they are the largest spe . . . spe . . ."

"Specimens."

"Specimens of cats in our world. But they could not be more different. While the tiger is a soli . . . solitary flame burning in the dark forests of the north, the lion lives in close . . . close . . ."

"Knit."

"Close-knit families on the arid eastern plains."

Keilan leaned back on his stool in the scholar's wagon, unable to keep from smiling broadly. Xin buried his ashen face in his hands and groaned.

"This one feels like he's just run ten leagues. Then fought in a battle. And *then* been chased by a pack of hungry wolves. Up a mountain."

"That was excellent reading."

"This one's head hurts."

Keilan laughed and bent again over Seeker Garmond's copy of *The Tinker's Bestiary*. It was a beautiful edition, far nicer than the one he had kept in his mother's chest back in his village, the flowing script precise and perfectly proportioned, each page decorated with colorful illustrations of the beasts it described. Even the borders and blank spaces were inked with twisting vines and blooming flowers and small, bright birds.

"Come. Let's finish."

Xin waved his hands in surrender. "Enough. Enough for now. This one needs a rest."

Keilan grinned and twisted to face Seeker Garmond, who was seated behind a small desk littered with scraps of parchment and several strange objects – the jeweled skull of some large rodent, an hourglass filled with blue sand, and a tiered pyramid carved from red crystal. There was also a bottle of clouded green glass and a trio of matched tumblers in front of him.

"What do you think, Master Garmond? Has Xin done enough for the evening?"

In response the scholar uncorked the bottle and poured a dollop of honey-slow amber liquid into each of the waiting glasses.

The Fist warrior let out a long sigh of relief and pushed himself away from the table he hunched over.

"His progress has been remarkable," Garmond said, stoppering the bottle. "Barely a week has passed, and our Fist friend seems ready to enroll in the Reliquary. His teacher should be proud."

"I am," Keilan said, joining them at the seeker's desk. And it was true. Watching Xin progress from forming basic letter sounds – some of which, admittedly, he had already known – to stumbling through simple sentences, to reading entire pages in a book as difficult as the *Bestiary* had been incredibly fulfilling. He felt like he had revealed a whole new world of wonders to the Fist warrior.

"Then it is time for a toast," Garmond said, passing a tumbler to each of them. "We call this scholar's milk. It helps sharpen the mind."

Keilan sniffed the viscous liquid. It smelled like the dead whale that had once washed ashore near his village.

"This one doesn't want to know what teat this milk was squeezed from," Xin said, eyeing his drink warily.

Seeker Garmond tossed back his glass, smacking his lips loudly. "By the Pen, it's good. Now hurry up and drink yours, fearless warrior, before I make you read aloud to me from my seminal work on the arboreal mushroom of the northern Blightwood. I have it right here, two hundred pages describing that fascinating fungus in exhaustive detail."

"This one takes back what he said earlier about this master being kinder than the others," Xin muttered, and then drained his tumbler.

Before he could even set down his glass Xin was doubled over coughing. "Gods. Gods. What is that poison?"

"Scholar's milk. I already said that."

"Don't, lad . . ." Xin gasped, his face reddening, "It's a trap . . ."

Keilan swallowed and carefully set down his glass.

"My boy, you are wasted as a warrior," the seeker sighed. "You should have been a mummer."

"Master Garmond," Keilan said, trying to distract the scholar from his untouched drink, "I've been wondering what that is." He pointed at a large mirrored box pushed into a corner. Aside from a small cot, the desk, the table and its chairs, and a few large chests it was the only other furniture in the scholar's wagon.

"Ah," Garmond said, pulling a stubby bone pipe from the folds of his robes. He tapped out the ashes, then tamped a fresh pinch of dreamweed into the bowl. "That was what I came up with to transport our basilisk back to the Reliquary. A shame we'll never get to know whether it would have sufficed. But that's the life of the scholar, I suppose – endless hours spent researching and traveling and exploring, with no guarantee that anything will come of all your hard work. I've often wondered –"

Xin suddenly stood, knocking his stool over, his face twisted into a look of intense concentration.

"My boy, what's the matter?" Garmond said, frowning.

The Fist warrior blinked, seeming to notice Keilan and the scholar for the first time. "Something's wrong. My brothers . . ."

A scream from outside, high and piercing. "What's happening?" Garmond said, also rising to his feet.

"We're under attack," Xin said, whirling towards the door. "You both stay here." He reached for the sword at his waist and found nothing. "God's blood. Master, do you have any weapons in your wagon?"

Garmond blinked. "Perhaps . . . a cheeseknife?"

Another scream, cut off abruptly just after it began. "This one doesn't think cheese is out there."

The door was flung open, and Garmond let out a strangled cry, but it was only Delon, Xin's Fist brother. He had already donned the wine-colored cuirass of the slave-soldiers. The lanky warrior tossed a sword towards Xin, who plucked it out of the air with ease.

"What's going on?" Keilan asked, trying to keep the panic from his voice.

Delon looked behind him. "Wraiths. Swarmed into the camp moments ago. They are slaughtering the merchants."

"Wraiths?" exclaimed Garmond, "That's impossible. There's never been a documented case of wraiths attacking a caravan as large as this."

Delon shrugged. "First time for everything, I suppose."

Xin hesitated, glancing from the scholar to the open doorway and the darkness beyond.

"Well, go fight," Garmond said, making a shooing motion with his hands.

"But we are supposed to protect you . . ." Xin said, letting his words trail off.

Garmond *harrumphed*. "Killing those monsters would be an excellent way to do just that. Off with you."

Xin grinned wolfishly and dashed for the door.

Wraiths. Keilan knew little of them. He had asked Vhelan what they were after the rangers had mentioned they'd found their marks on nearby trees. The wizard had said that the creatures roamed the Frostlands in packs, and like the gibbons of the woods near his home they were man-shaped, though larger and thinner than the forest apes. He'd also said that they were scavengers, lurkers, and avoided all contact with men.

Outside, something thumped hard against one of the wagon's walls. Garmond and Keilan glanced at each other.

"Well, boy," the scholar said, "how is your weapon training coming?"

"If there's one thing my teachers have taught me," Keilan replied softly, "it's that running is often the best course of action."

The seeker glanced around his small cluttered wagon. "I suppose we don't want to be trapped in . . ." Garmond cocked his head, as if listening hard.

Keilan heard it then, and cold fear washed through him. There was a sound from outside, like knives scraping against wood. And it was moving, though not quickly, along the length of the wagon and toward the front. Keilan couldn't tear his eyes from the wedge of blackness beyond the partially opened door.

"Should we douse the light?" Garmond hissed, reaching for the oil lamp hanging from the ceiling.

Keilan's mouth was bone-dry, but fear forced him to reply. "Do you want to be in the dark right now?"

The seeker withdrew his hand and instead rummaged quickly through the piles of papers on his desk, eventually pulling forth a tiny blunt knife, specks of white still crusting the blade.

Keilan didn't know whether to laugh or cry.

The scraping had stopped. Keilan edged closer to the scholar, keeping his eyes fixed on the doorway's thin strip of black, and picked up the seeker's red-crystal pyramid.

"It's gone?" murmured the seeker, desperate hope edging his voice.

With agonizing slowness something emerged from the night. A long, blue talon, curved like a raptor's claw, curled against the doorframe. Another followed, and then another, as if the creature outside was deliberately stoking the fear of those within.

Then the door was flung fully open, ripping from its hinges with a shriek of torn metal, and the wraith loomed in the entrance, stooping to peer inside the wagon. Its long, dangling arms were roped with muscle, and its skin was gray-green and scabrous, bubbling as if it was covered in huge warts. Slitted red eyes peered from behind a ragged tumble of greasy black hair, and its mouth hung open as it panted, revealing yellowing fangs jutting at odd angles.

Keilan screamed and hurled the pyramid at the monster.

With surprising grace the wraith caught it between two of its blue-tinged nails and brought it close to its face, sniffing. A long, thin tongue flickered out and licked the pyramid. The creature's sunken features wrinkled in disgust, and the pyramid disappeared in a shower of glittering crimson dust.

"Savage!" gasped the seeker, and the wraith jerked its head to look at them again, its small red eyes narrowing further.

Keilan took a stumbling step backward as the wraith crouched, gathering itself, but before it could leap at them something caused it to glance over its shoulder. It hissed a challenge at whatever it saw there and turned, then digging its claws into the doorframe it vanished, thrusting itself back into the darkness.

The scholar and Keilan shared a wide-eyed look. Neither moved for what seemed like an eternity, and then both jumped as Xin filled the shattered entrance to the wagon. The Fist warrior's tunic and sword were splattered with black blood.

"With me," he commanded, and they hurried to follow him out into the night.

Keilan paused as he passed through the doorway, his breath catching. The seeker had set up his wagon a little ways from the others and atop a gentle rise, so much of the chaos that now gripped the caravan was spread before him. The fire that was kept burning every night had somehow spread, and flames crawled along several of the wagons. In the flickering light he glimpsed long, lean shadows moving quickly, chasing down the smaller stumbling shapes of merchants and guardsmen. The wraith that had entered the scholar's wagon now lay curled in the long grass a dozen steps away, still twitching and crooning softly.

"We must find Nel and Vhelan!" Keilan cried, grabbing Xin's sword arm.

The Fist warrior nodded grimly. "Where do they sleep?"

"Near the fire, most nights," Keilan replied, frantically searching for them, but around the campfire there were just scattered bedrolls and churned earth.

"Nel is smart and quick," Xin said, scanning the darkness as they descended the small slope toward the caravan. "She'll have found a safe place to hide your uncle."

"And your brothers?" Garmond managed between wheezing gasps.

"They are all fine. This one can feel no fear in their minds. We should go to them – the wraiths will quickly learn to give their swords a wide berth."

"Do you know where?"

Xin shook his head curtly at Keilan's question. "No. This one can feel the flood of their emotions, but cannot ask them where they are. Delon told me before we split that the fighting was fiercest around the Shan's wagon, next to the river, and that he was headed there. Perhaps that's where my brothers still are."

Xin stopped, eyeing the seeker and Keilan uneasily. "But if that's where the wraiths are thickest it will be dangerous . . ."

Garmond waved away his words. "We are safest with you and your brothers. Lead on."

"Very well," Xin said, stooping next to the crumpled body of a merchant. He slipped a small curved dagger from the dead man's sash and held it out for Garmond.

The scholar shied away from the weapon. "Give it to the boy. I have my cheeseknife."

Keilan accepted the dagger, swallowing hard. Its leather-wrapped handle was sticky and warm.

"That way," he said, gesturing towards a stand of slender trees. Keilan remembered them as white birch, but in the faint light cast by the fire they had been transformed into a jagged patch of deeper blackness. "I saw the Shan leading his wagon over there earlier. He usually sets his camp near water, if there's any nearby."

They skirted the edge of the camp, dashing across open ground to crouch beside first a rock, then the wheel of a wagon. Keilan didn't see any more wraiths flowing through the darkness, but there were bodies of merchants and guardsmen hidden in the grass, and he almost tripped a few times. They must have tried to flee when the wraiths had streamed into the center of the camp, but been overtaken and slain. Keilan remembered the fluid quickness of the creature back in the scholar's wagon. They were terrifyingly fast.

Xin stumbled and almost fell to his knees.

"What's wrong?" Keilan cried, trying to steady the Fist warrior.

Xin turned to him, and even in the dimness Keilan could see how stricken he looked.

"My brother is dead."

"Oh gods," Keilan whispered, "I'm so sorry."

Xin reeled away. "No, no, no . . ." he moaned, his body spasming violently one, two, three more times, almost as if he was being struck by unseen arrows or swords.

Keilan rushed to hold him up; otherwise, the warrior would have collapsed in the grass.

"All of them," Xin moaned, his voice wrenched by pain, "they're all dead. My brothers are gone."

Keilan lowered the Fist warrior to the ground. Xin's head lolled as if his neck was broken. "They were there, inside this one. Then . . . fear, pain. And now nothing."

"We must keep moving," Keilan said, shaking him hard. "We must find Nel and Vhelan. They can help us."

But Xin didn't answer, staring sightlessly up at the stars. He was like a puppet with its string cuts, arms and legs splayed uselessly.

Keilan caught a flicker of movement in the darkness. A shadow, flowing through the tall grass, coming closer.

"Xin!" Keilan screamed, clutching at the Fist warrior. He could hear its terrible crooning now, and there was nothing inside him except blind terror.

Xin stirred in his arms, as if coming awake.

Garmond cried out, cowering before the monster as it loomed out of the grass near him. The wraith swelled larger, like a serpent rearing back to strike.

"No!" screamed Keilan, wanting to turn away from what he knew was coming, but he could not tear his gaze from the scholar and the wraith.

Then Xin was moving. The Fist warrior surged to his feet, screaming, and the monster hesitated, twisting toward this new threat. They collided in a shadowy blur. The wraith's crooning sharpened into a piercing shriek, and Keilan heard the sound of metal striking flesh. The monster faltered as Xin hacked again and again; Keilan saw it raise an arm to ward away the blows, only to have the arm lopped off at the shoulder. The creature's keening wail stopped when Xin sliced sideways with his blade, separating its head from its shoulders. The body stood swaying for a long moment, then toppled forward into the grass.

Keilan rushed to the Fist warrior. Xin was panting heavily, heaving with emotion.

"Are you . . .?" he began, but Xin had already turned and started running before Keilan could finish. Running towards the river and the Shan's wagon.

Keilan grabbed the scholar and pulled him to his feet. "Come on, we must go with him."

The Fist warrior quickly outdistanced them, vanishing among the shadowy trees. Keilan and Garmond followed, stumbling through the copse with arms outstretched.

A faint red light was ahead of them, filtering through the lattice of trees. Keilan slowed, picking his way as carefully and quietly as he could, until he saw the Shan's wagon in the thicket ahead. "Wait," he murmured, putting his hand on Garmond's shoulder.

A red paper lantern hung above the curtained entrance to the wagon. The light stained the pale birch trees fringing the clearing, so it looked to Keilan like Xin stood in the center of a great room bounded by rose-colored pillars, the night sky above a vault of black stone. The Fist warrior was turning slowly, as if unsure where to go next.

Something moved in the darkness opposite where Keilan and Garmond crouched. Three wraiths stalked forth, crooning a challenge to the lone man that waited for them.

"Run, Xin," the scholar whispered, his gnarled fingers clutching at Keilan's wrist. "By the Pen, run."

But Keilan knew he would not.

The wraiths fanned out as they approached, showing the instincts of animals accustomed to hunting in packs. They feinted forward, and then drew back, trying to pull Xin toward one of them. As soon as he did that, Keilan knew, the other two would flank him and close with talons flashing.

The Fist warrior did not move, except to raise his sword into the fighting stance he had first taught Keilan weeks ago, the blade's point extended and leveled at the chest of the middle wraith.

Keilan was so intent on what was happening between the wraiths and the warrior that he did not even notice at first when someone else calmly walked across the clearing to stand beside Xin. It was the Shan, his black hair now unbound, gripping with both hands the hilt of a long, curving sword. Cho Yuan held the blade sideways above his head, and his knees were bent slightly, as if he was gathering himself to jump. The red phoenix unfurling along his green robes burned like a tongue of flame in the light of the lantern.

The wraiths drew back, hissing. Xin glanced at the Shan and nodded slightly. Then they attacked.

The two warriors could not have been more different. Xin charged the wraith nearest to him like a maddened bull, his sword raised, while Cho Yuan took small, quick, almost mincing steps, his blade-work a mesmerizing dance that sent another of the wraiths stumbling backward, its long knobby arms upraised, as if were trying to ward away the flickering sword. One style was like an avalanche thundering down a hillside, the other water flowing over smooth stones.

They were equally effective. Xin's speed took him close enough to a wraith that the monster could not scuttle back in time before the Fist warrior's blade lashed out and left a line of black blood across its ribs. The wraith shrieked in surprise and pain as Xin's following thrust buried a span of steel in its chest, the blade bursting from its back. The Fist warrior pulled his sword free and turned to face the remaining wraiths, but they were already down, the stumps of their necks leaking blood into the grass. The Shan slid his long sword through a silken tie at his waist and picked up one of the heads by its matted hair, frowning. The thing's slanted red eyes blinked stupidly, its mouth working soundlessly. After a moment its jaw slackened in death, the light fading from its eyes, and Cho Yuan let the head drop next to its twitching body.

Keilan moved to stand, but Garmond restrained him with a hand on his shoulder. "Wait, lad, look."

Another man emerged from the darkness, striding toward the two warriors. It was the tall Menekarian merchant that had joined the caravan back in Theris. His loose white robes were stained red, and blood covered his arms from his hands to his elbows.

"Are you hurt?" Xin called out.

The merchant paused, slowly looking from the sprawled corpses of the wraiths to the two warriors, shaking his head.

The Shan stiffened suddenly, then quickly returned to his fighting stance, his sword over his head. He said something in a tumbling language Keilan had never heard before.

The Menekarian regarded Cho Yuan without expression. "I do not understand you. But you speak the common language of this land, yes?"

"I do," the Shan replied, "I ask what you are."

The man ignored the question, crouching beside the wraith Xin had impaled. "Look at this poor broken thing," he murmured, stroking the creature's lank hair. "I remember an age when these sad beasts dressed in damask and silks and sipped from jeweled chalices." He glanced up at Cho Yuan. "Your race has fallen as well, though not so far."

"You speak of the Shan?"

The Menekarian chuckled, standing again. "No."

He seemed to see Xin for the first time. "Ah. Another one. Your death will bring completion – your brothers had delicious souls, but of course there was something lacking in the meal."

"My brothers?" Xin said hoarsely, raising his sword.

"Yes," the Menekarian said, making a show of studying his blood-drenched forearms. "What beautiful, piquant lives they'd lived."

Xin hurled himself at the merchant, his sword an arcing blur. With casual ease the Menekarian struck him down, a backhanded blow that snapped Xin's head back and sent his sword spinning into the darkness.

The Menekarian stepped over the motionless warrior and strolled toward Cho Yuan.

Garmond's fingers dug into Keilan's arm. "Look at his shadow . . ."

Keilan stifled a gasp. In the light of the lantern the man's shadow was clear – yet it was the shadow of no man. It was tall, much taller than it should have been, gaunt and emaciated and studded with curling black thorns. Its shoulders sloped down at an inhuman angle, and its dangling ape-like arms nearly brushed the merchant's sandaled feet.

As the man approached the Shan moved backward, his glittering blade sketching a complicated pattern between them. "You serve the Betrayers?"

The Menekarian cocked his head to one side. "Is that what you call them?" He barked a laugh. "They named themselves the Chosen. Vicious little creatures; I care not for them."

"Then why are you doing this? You must know the threat they are."

For the first time some tremor of emotion passed across the man's face. "Because my mistress wills it," he said, and lunged forward.

The sword flashed, too fast for Keilan to see clearly, but it was as if the Menekarian knew exactly where every thrust would come. He moved with unnatural grace, twisting slightly to avoid each strike, until he stood, untouched, only a span from the Shan. Then his hand found Cho Yuan's neck, and the Menekarian lifted him from the ground with terrible strength.

The crack of the Shan's neck breaking carried across the clearing.

The next few moments seemed to happen unbearably slowly.

"Keilan! Keilan!" It was Nel's voice from somewhere nearby, coming closer.

She burst into the clearing, brandishing black-stained daggers, a cut on her forehead smearing her face bloody. The Menekarian carelessly tossed the Shan's body aside and turned to her.

Without hesitating, Nel sent Chance and Fate spinning toward the false merchant, two more daggers appearing in her hands almost instantly.

The Menekarian caught one of the tumbling daggers by its handle; the other buried itself in his shoulder, and he hissed in rage, tearing it out and hurling it back at Nel in a single motion. She threw herself to the ground as it passed where she had been standing just a heartbeat ago.

Then it was moving toward her, all pretenses of its humanity flaking away, its skin melting like running wax and strange sharp barbs tearing through its white robes. It was like a fist unclenching – the man opened, swelling huge and lean, all scales and sharp-angles and tapering thorns, the nubs of wings unfolding from its back. It screeched raptor-like as it flowed toward the helpless girl, who seemed momentarily frozen by the man's horrific metamorphosis.

Keilan stumbled from the trees. "No!" he cried, raising his hands, feeling the great wave swelling within him.

The monster turned, its wide nostrils flaring in alarm.

Green light lanced from Keilan's hand, carving a burning path in the air and striking the creature in its scaled chest. It was flung back into the trees, smashing through the trunks. Emerald flames enveloped the monster; it shrieked and thrashed within the underbrush, writhing in agony. Then it lurched to its clawed feet and stumbled into the darkness, toward the river, a blazing green torch that suddenly vanished as it threw itself into the water.

Keilan sank to his knees. The last thing he saw before he was enveloped by the warm darkness was Nel reaching out towards him, and he smiled.

18: ALYANNA

THE RIFTSTONE PULSED, thin and fluttering, like a dying man's heartbeat.

Alyanna clenched it tight in her palm as she slipped between great slabs of quartz burnished gold by the early morning light, stepping over the slowly-closing petals of plum-colored nightblossoms. The tittering of songbirds, usually omnipresent in the gardens at this time of day, was faint, as no trees crowded near the soaring pillars of white stone. It was, in fact, a district of the imperial pleasure gardens that saw few visitors, feathered or not, so it suited her purposes this morning perfectly.

In the shadow of one of the quartz monoliths she opened her hand, studying the riftstone. It was an unblemished smooth and white circle, utterly unremarkable, something that could be found almost anywhere wind or waves had worn down rocks. But this was one of the great artifacts of the old world, an object of immeasurable power and value. Even her colleagues in the Star Towers had been unable to unlock its mysteries. The scholars who had dedicated their lives to studying it had believed the riftstone had been created during the age when the Warlock Kings had established the world's first sorcerous empire, in the very city where she now stood. It had tumbled through many hands in the centuries since then, but for the last thousand years it had been hers, and she was not about to lose it now.

Which meant she needed to collect the riftstone's other half while its bearer still lived, and from the thready, uneven pulsing, that might not be for very much longer. Also, she was very curious about what had happened last night.

Alyanna extended a filament of sorcery into the riftstone, sliding inside it like a key into a lock. She gave a twist, and the stone's power blossomed.

Before her a circle of air began to shimmer and undulate, as if it was a length of silk caught in a strong wind. The quartz pillars and awakening garden encompassed by this floating portal slowly faded, and was replaced by another scene from a very different place.

It was darker there, hundreds of leagues to the west, a few stars still visible in a charcoal sky. Shadows draped huge, tumbled rocks and pine trees, and the silhouettes of mountains in the distance bulked stark and black against the gray dawn. A chill wind slipped through the rift, and Alyanna shivered, pulling her cotton robe – the heaviest clothing she kept in the gardens – tighter around herself.

Sighing, she stepped through the portal and into the forest that bounded the southern Frostlands.

The grass was coarser, the dew colder. There was the faint sound of swift-running water from somewhere nearby, no doubt one of the countless small rivers that veined the north and carried snowmelt down from high in the Bones. She summoned a small orb of wizardlight so that she wouldn't trip over anything on the uneven ground, and cast about for the other half of the riftstone. It did not take her long to find.

The genthyaki was propped against a rock near the edge of a stream. It was motionless, its head slumped forward, an impossible tangle of scales and thorns and sharp angles. Alyanna brought her wizardlight closer, and clucked her tongue when she saw the state her servant was in.

What scales were left on its hide glistened wetly, but most had been sloughed off by some terrible heat, leaving charred black patches across its body. Under one of these wounds, which spread over much of its left shoulder, Alyanna could clearly see bone beneath the blistered flesh.

To her surprise, the creature stirred as she approached.

"Mistressssss," it hissed, with great effort lifting its ruin of a face.

"Slave," she replied, shaking her head as if in great disappointment. "You have failed me."

A harsh, wet coughing wracked the creature, until it finally spat up a wad of black phlegm that landed in the grass near her feet. Wrinkling her nose in disgust, Alyanna stepped farther away.

"Mistress, it burns . . ."

"I should think so. It smells like someone's bathed you in dreadfire."

"Burnssssss . . ."

A frozen wind gusted, and she knew that they were no longer alone. Three ragged shapes now crouched among the rocks, watching.

mistress, the false man dies.

"I can see that," she said. "But I need to know who did this."

Alyanna moved closer to the genthyaki and bent down beside it, trying to ignore the sickly-sweet smell of its burned flesh. She found the thin chain around its neck and ripped loose the other half of the riftstone, a crescent of black rock that fit perfectly with the white circle she already held.

"Tell me what happened," she said firmly, tightening her grip on the creature's will.

"The Shan you sent me to kill . . . is dead. The fool thought the Chosen he was hunting . . . were in Dymoria. The warlocks of Shan . . . had heard of the Crimson Queen, and must of thought . . . she was the one who had stolen them away. But there were others in the caravan . . . a boy, untrained but with Talent . . . traveling with a wizard to Dymoria . . . I sensed his gift, but did not appreciate the depth of his power. He lashed out with dreadfire." The genthyaki gasped, laboring to breathe through charred lungs.

"An untrained boy summoned dreadfire?" she murmured, standing again. Was it possible? Dreadfire was one of the strongest weapons wielded by the wizards of the past, but she had thought all knowledge of it among mortals had drowned with the Star Towers. A true Talent, even untrained, might accidentally in a time of great duress bring forth such magic, but a Talent like that had not been born for an age. This would be the first in a thousand years – or possibly second, since it seemed that Dymoria's Crimson Queen was similarly gifted.

Not so long ago she had thought there were only three such sorcerers in the great wide world. Now it appeared there may be five. Interesting times had come again.

She turned away from the genthyaki and began to pick her way carefully back towards the shimmering portal.

"Mistressss . . . you would abandon me . . ."

Alyanna paused, turning again. Idly she stroked the smooth riftstones, considering. "You don't think this fitting? The first time we met was in a place such as this, was it not?" She spread her arms, gesturing toward the pine trees and jagged rocks. "I could have ended your life then, if I had wished. I gave you a thousand-year reprieve – you should thank me for my mercy."

The creature gurgled. Was it trying to laugh? "Mercy . . . I was your dagger in the dark, the means to your endlessness."

"You were a tool, nothing more. And after many years of service you have broken. I do not know what sentiment you are trying to reach."

"Mercy. You speak of it, mistress. I will pass soon, and my race will end. And when you die even the memory of my people will be lost. As if . . . as if we had never been."

Alyanna shrugged. "Such is the fate of all living things. We can only strive to hold back the darkness for a time."

"The last . . . I should not die chained. Free me, mistress. I beg you. Let my soul rejoin my ancestors unclouded by your taint. Please. Pleasssse."

Alyanna chewed her lower lip as the huddled creature extended a shivering arm in supplication. She sensed the rapt attention of the Chosen.

Finally she sighed. "Very well. I am not a monster." Concentrating, she dissolved the sorcerous noose she had long held around the genthyaki's mind, surprised by the emptiness she suddenly felt as their wills separated.

It moved faster than she thought was possible. Uncoiling from the ground, lunging toward her, a blur of spines and flashing claws.

The sound of it striking her wards echoed in the empty forest. Its fangs splintered against an invisible wall only a half-span from her face, its talons scrabbling uselessly as it tried to reach her. She watched it, without emotion, as it gathered itself and flailed one final time against her power, and then slid to the ground, exhausted, black fluid smearing the air in front of her.

"I am not a monster. Nor am I a fool."

With a final, pitying glance she turned away. "You may do as you wish," she said, but not to her ruined servant. The Chosen's surge of excitement prickled the skin on her arms.

The genthyaki's screams followed her as she stepped once again into the pleasure gardens of the emperor.

19: KEILAN

HE DID NOT dream of monsters or fire or dead men scattered in long grass. Rather, there was moonlight on water, his mother's hair unbound, flowing around him in silver rivulets as she held him in her lap and sang. The words hung shivering, mysterious, yet still they could summon forth such an aching longing in his chest, and he knew that if only he could concentrate a little harder their meaning would become clear. He reached up with a tiny hand to brush her smooth warm cheek.

Slowly Keilan surfaced, coming awake on a bed so soft he felt he was sinking back down again into his dreams. Cool silks swaddled him, and over those sheets was another blanket of thick, deep fur. Swallowing away the dryness in his throat he tried to sit up, but it was as if his bones were made of iron, and he could only shift his shoulders and twist his neck weakly.

He was in a large chamber of dark stone, a bedroom lit by tall candelabras with a fire burning low in a recessed hearth. Several small, dark windows were arrayed along one wall, and decorating another were canvases covered with lashings of color, paintings of some kind. All the furniture in the room – his huge four-poster bed, the shelving, the table and chairs near the fire – were meticulously carved of the same dark wood, so black it seemed to drink the room's light.

She stood so quietly he did not see her until she gave a little gasp. A young girl, perhaps no more than ten, in a shift of fine gray wool and carrying a silver tray piled high with small orange fruit. When she saw he was awake she hurriedly slid the tray onto the table and scuttled for the chamber's only door, casting a nervous glance back at him before vanishing.

"Wait!" he croaked, but she was already gone. Keilan struggled to sit, and after what seemed like an eternity of effort managed to prop himself against the headboard. He pulled his hands from the sheets, and laid them on the dark fur of the topmost blanket. His hands looked unnaturally white. How long had he been sleeping?

The door creaked, and he glanced up to find that a man now stood in the room, watching him. He was about thirty years old, with fine, sharply etched features and a mop of unruly black hair. His pallor was unusually pale, which contrasted starkly with the rich black doublet and breeches he wore.

"Do not be alarmed, Keilan. You have woken among friends." The man's voice had an almost musical lilt to it.

"Who . . . who are you?"

The man approached the small table near the fire. He plucked a fruit from the tray and popped it into his mouth. "My name is Qwellyn Pelimana Chount-Adreth. You can call me Lyn. Or Prince Lyn, if we're constrained by formality."

"Prince Lyn? Of Vis?"

The man flourished a bow. "Indeed. Welcome to my city."

Vis. His mother had spoken of it, many years ago. How she had wished someday to visit the Poet's City and walk its legendary iron walls, to listen to its fabled players declaim upon the stage, or its bards compete in its mead halls. An ancient city, as old as any in the world, renowned throughout Araen for its song and art, for its celebration of beauty. And, Vhelan had told him, recently sworn to the Dragon Throne of Dymoria.

Keilan struggled to rise, floundering in the heavy blankets. "My prince. I'm sorry. I didn't know."

Prince Lyn motioned for him to sit back. "Easy, Keilan. You've been lying in that bed for three days, and from what your friends have told me you've been sleeping for nearly a week. I don't expect you to hop out of bed and throw yourself before me."

"My friends . . . they are all right?"

The prince's smile wavered. "They are alive, though not all are whole, it grieves me to tell you. I have called Magister Vhelan here, and he will tell you more."

"Thank you, my prince."

Prince Lyn waved away his words. "Please, it is I who must thank you. Without your heroics a caravan bearing a high-ranking scholar from the Reliquary and a Dymorian magister would have been lost just outside my city – you've saved me an endless amount of diplomatic trouble, truly."

"Keilan!" Nel burst into the chamber, flinging the door wide. When she saw the prince standing there she offered a deep bow. Vhelan followed a step behind her, lost in conversation with Seeker Garmond, but his eyes darted to the bed, and his grin could not be missed. Both he and the scholar also paid their respects to the prince before approaching Keilan.

Nel hurried beside him and tousled his hair roughly. The sight of her dimples made Keilan's chest feel heavy.

"Your head? Are you fine?" he managed, coughing to try and hide his sudden blush.

Nel touched the thin white line on her brow. "It's nothing. Won't even scar, the healers say." She winked at him. "Three dead wraiths, and I don't even get to keep a memento from the fight."

"If it was a keepsake you wanted," the prince interrupted, sauntering closer to stand beside Nel, "you could have done what the Skein do. They shrink the wraith's heads and wear them as necklaces. A charming accessory, and it would be quite the topic of conversation at any dinner party in Herath."

Nel ducked her head. "I'll remember that for the next time I'm ambushed by wraiths, my prince."

"Rub iron that it will never happen again, my lady."

Vhelan came to stand at the foot of the bed, leaning on one of the intricately carved posts. "Jesting aside, Keilan, how are you feeling?"

"Tired," Keilan admitted. "And thirsty."

"Of course, of course," Seeker Garmond said, materializing on the side of the bed opposite to Nel and the prince. He held a cup out for Keilan to take. "We dribbled water mixed with honey into your mouth as you slept, but certainly it would be the first thing your body demanded." Keilan accepted the ceramic cup and drank deep. He could almost feel his strength returning as the water trickled through his body.

"Slowly, lad. Your body is still weak."

Keilan paused; the cold water pooling in his empty stomach suddenly made him realize how hungry he was. He passed the cup back to the scholar and rubbed his face. "Is there any food?"

The prince clapped his hands, and the girl in the gray shift slipped into the room. "Mila! Bring supper for our guest." The girl sketched a quick bow and vanished again.

"While you are waiting," Prince Lyn said, retrieving the tray of fruit from the table and setting it on the bed beside Keilan. "Tangerines from my own garden."

Keilan had never tried these small firm fruit before, but he quickly decided that they were the most delicious things he had ever eaten. Soon his fingers were sticky with their juice, and the ache in his belly had subsided.

"What happened?"

Vhelan sat on the end of the bed and patted Keilan's legs. "You drained yourself by somehow conjuring up one of the lost sorceries. Dreadfire, it's called. A river of green flame that burns anything it touches. The histories of Min-Ceruth and the Imperium are full of tales of wizards melting stone fortresses with the stuff, armies of steel-armored warriors running like wax when struck by its power."

Keilan swallowed hard. "How did I do that?"

Vhelan flashed a crooked smile. "The same way you touched an Ancient with a sending. The truth of it is . . . I don't know. But your importance to the queen and our Scholia just rose even higher in my eyes, and I was able to impress this upon the good prince, who is a recent but stalwart ally of the throne."

Keilan considered Vhelan's words. How was he able to summon forth these great magics when a magister could not, even with all his sorcerous training?

"And the ambush on the Wending?" Keilan continued. "Why did that happen?"

"We have the same question, and we've been turning it over between us since the wraiths appeared. Certainly it was no random attack, but the reason and the true target are still unclear. What I am certain of is that if you hadn't struck down that monster we likely all would be dead. So you have my gratitude."

"What was that thing?"

Vhelan shrugged. "From the good scholar's and Nel's descriptions it sounds like nothing the wizards of Dymoria have seen before. Something new."

Garmond cleared his throat. "Or something very old. There are legends, from well before the Sundering, of creatures that vaguely resemble that monstrosity. Fragments in ancient texts, just veiled allusions, really, as if the writers themselves were not clear of what they wrote about. A race of monsters that could wear the skins of men like cloaks – the Reliquary has always treated such tales as folklore, to be honest. When I return to the archives I plan on collecting all the information I can, and seeing if it matches what we witnessed. In any case, that creature was the most remarkable I have ever encountered, in all my years of studying the beasts of this land. We do not even know if it was a monster in the form of a man, or a man who could become a monster."

Keilan rolled the last tangerine between his fingers. "Was it just a random attack? Were we simply unlucky?"

Vhelan shrugged. "It's possible, of course. But we know the creature you killed was intelligent, so I think we must assume it would only ambush a heavily-protected caravan if there was a compelling reason. And remember, the monster had been with us since Theris, in the guise of a traveler. Everything was very carefully planned."

"The last group with cause to be upset with us would be the Pure," Nel said.

The wizard rolled his eyes. "We've discussed this before. The mendicants of Ama tend to avoid employing demons."

"But its man-shape was that of a Menekarian merchant," Nel continued, pressing her point, "And it likely traveled west out of the empire with that other caravan."

Garmond drummed his fingers on his chin – a sign, Keilan knew, that he was thinking deeply. "That is an excellent observation. But I can't believe the same zealots brandishing their copies of the Tractate and spewing venom about wizards would consort with such a creature."

"Are we sure it was us that the demon was after?" Keilan asked.

Vhelan nodded towards Garmond. "How about it, seeker? Insult any denizens of the Void recently?"

The scholar looked mildly affronted. "Not unless they took umbrage with my most recent treatise on Blightwood fungi."

Keilan struggled to remember those last chaotic moments in the clearing. "What about the Shan? I think . . . I think the monster may have known him. They spoke, briefly. About something called the Chosen – or maybe it was the Betrayed? And the monster said he'd seen the wraiths dressed in clothes, a long time ago. I don't know; it doesn't make much sense."

The prince had watched this exchange with obvious interest. "I have my own resources we can consult – the Barrow of Vis is one of the world's great libraries, and our lorists remember in poetry and song things that have faded everywhere else from the memory of man."

"You would allow us into the Barrow?" Garmond said, clearly impressed, his bushy gray brows rising.

The prince nodded. "Under supervision, of course, for the library's protection and also your own. I would be a poor vassal of Dymoria if

I did not extend my help to the loyal servants of the queen. Now, we should probably let the boy rest. Perhaps with a bit more sleep and a full stomach he'll recollect more."

As they began to move away from his bed, Keilan concentrated hard, trying to scour his memories for any clue he could offer them before they left. The creature had spoken to the Shan, then killed him, but before that he'd said something to Xin about his brothers . . .

Keilan blinked. "Where's Xin?"

He couldn't miss the quick glances shared by the four around his bed. "Is he all right?"

Their solemn faces made his chest tighten. "He is alive," Vhelan finally said, slowly, "but he is not as you remember."

A short while after they'd departed, the serving girl returned with his dinner, and he managed to drag himself over to the small table to eat. The meal was the finest of his life: a braised leg of lamb so tender it seemed to dissolve in his mouth, swimming in a rich mushroom sauce that went equally well with the buttered carrots, potatoes, and leeks piled next to the meat. He sipped from a silver goblet a blood-dark wine that was tarter than the firewine from Gryx he'd tried before, though equally delicious. When he was finished his head was reeling from the richness of the food and the strength of the wine, and he collapsed back into his bed, asleep before he could even get under the blankets.

When he awoke again, Nel was there, sitting on the edge of his bed. She smiled at him, though it didn't seem to touch her eyes. "Feeling better?"

Keilan rolled over and sat up. "Much."

"Good, then. You seemed a bit overwhelmed before."

Keilan shook his head. "And how could I not feel that way? One moment I'm summoning fire from my fingertips, slaying a monster, and the next I'm in a bed in a palace, the guest of a prince."

"Slightly more exciting than being a fisherman's son?"

Keilan snorted and tossed a pillow at her. She caught it and clutched it tight to her chest, resting her chin on the lacy edge. "In truth, you are handling everything that's happened remarkably well. Spiders and wraiths and shape-changing demons. It's been an interesting few weeks, even for me. I'm proud of you."

"Thank you," he said, awkwardly, and she burst out laughing. He felt his face redden, and he buried himself beneath his heavy fur blanket.

"Don't bother being shy, Keilan. You're a good boy, but you're still just a boy. How many winters have you seen? Fifteen? I know I look young, but I'm at least ten years older than you."

"Sixteen, very soon," he mumbled, emerging again from the blanket. "My birthday is a few months hence. If I was still in my village I would have to do my night-dive when the mid-summer solstice comes."

"Night-dive?"

"It is tradition. You enter the waters of the bay a boy, and emerge a man. Then you are ready to fish for Elara's Bounty with the others."

"In the Warrens, you're not considered a man until you kill someone. I like your village's way better."

"So in Lyr you must have been considered very manly?"

Nel stuck out her tongue at him and threw back the pillow. "More manly than many, I suppose." Her voice softened, and she leaned in closer, enfolding his hand in her own. "Keilan, I've seen you watching me when you think I'm not looking. Set aside those thoughts. I am a woman, and you are still a boy." Her eyes sparkled. "But don't be sad, as I'm sure there's a few pretty little sorceresses your age studying at the Scholia." Nel held his gaze until he nodded. "Good, then," she continued briskly, pulling away. "But I didn't come here to break your heart. We need to go see Xin."

Keilan swallowed away the sudden dryness in his throat. "We can do that? I thought he might still be recovering from the attack, and that only healers were allowed to minister to him."

Nel chewed on her lip. "We can. His wounds are not of the body. But you are right – he is still recovering. I think . . . I think seeing you would help him."

"What's the matter?"

Nel pulled on the thick fur of the blanket. "I'm sure you know something of the Fists. Five infant boys, all sharing the same father, are born and raised together. Something happens to them, there in the red-sand pits of Gryx. Something almost magical, though Vhelan has told me that he could sense no sorcery when we were traveling with the caravan. An unbreakable thread binds their minds." She paused. "Well, unbreakable unless one of them dies. And though the death of a single member of the Fists is traumatic for the survivors, usually together they can persevere. Xin has no such support. He has lost them all, in one fell stroke. One moment he was whole – the next, alone and helpless."

"I want to see him," Keilan said, sliding from the bed. He swooned when he found his feet, still a bit weak, and had to steady himself on one of the bed's posts.

"Good," Nel said. There was a tone to her voice Keilan hadn't heard before – apprehension? Relief?

He followed her out of his chamber and into a hallway lit by gilded sconces, decorated by more of the same odd paintings that were in his own room.

"The prince does them," Nel said when she saw him looking. "Strange, eh? I've never seen paintings that weren't of *something* – portraits, a city, a mountain. I'm tempted to find one in a scarce-visited hallway, wrap it up, and take it with me back to Herath."

"I'm sure the prince would give you one, if you asked. He seems to have enough."

"Now where would the fun be in that?"

Keilan sighed and followed her down several corridors, until they came to an oak door patterned with whorls and banded with iron. Nel rapped on the door, and then opened it without waiting for a response from within.

It was another bedroom, very similar to his own but slightly smaller. The room was cold; the fireplace was filled with mounded gray ash, and the windows had been thrown open, letting in a chill breeze. The sounds of the city drifted in as well, the hum of many voices and the faint skirling of a fiddle. The blankets were drawn up, as if the bed had not been slept in recently, though Xin was there, sitting cross-legged on the furs and facing the window. He wore only a loose pair of gray breeches, and Keilan couldn't help but marvel at the muscles etched into his dusky back. A naked sword lay across his knees. He did not turn when they entered the room.

"Xin," Nel said, her voice strained, "How are you? I've brought a guest."

The Fist warrior did not answer. There was no evidence that he had even heard.

Nel motioned for Keilan to follow her, and together they slipped around the bed, until they stood in front of Xin.

Keilan shivered as fingers of cool wind touched his legs and back. Xin didn't seem to notice them or the coldness in the room; his jaw was tensed, and his gold-flecked green eyes stared past Nel and Keilan, as if they were not there.

"Xin!" Nel repeated, this time louder, waving her hand.

Slowly, the Fist warrior blinked, focusing on them. "Nel," he said softly. His voice was raspy, and he cleared his throat. "Keilan."

Nel turned to the windows. "May I close them? It's freezing in here."

Xin breathed in deep. "Yes. This one keeps them open because of the noise. It reminds me . . . it reminds me of what it was like before."

"Are you all right?"

Xin's eyes were empty, and the gaze the Fist warrior fixed him with chilled Keilan almost as much as the cold mountain breeze coming through the window.

"They are still out there, somewhere. This one can feel them. But when this one reaches for his brothers . . . nothing. It is like trying to grasp the air. Do you know what happens to many warriors when they lose a limb, an arm or a leg, on the field of battle or in the surgeon's tent? It is gone, but for the rest of their years they can still feel it there, itching or aching, hanging by their side."

"Xin," Nel said firmly, crossing her arms. "You are a Fist warrior, one of the finest and most loyal soldiers in the world. You have a duty to Master Garmond that cannot be discharged until he is returned safely to Ver Anath. You must set aside your grief and finish your task."

Xin ignored her. "This one can still hear them, too," he said softly. "So faint, like through a great span of stone. They are calling to me, asking me to join them."

"Your brothers would not wish you to die! That is your guilt speaking to you, not your brothers!" Keilan had never seen Nel truly angry before.

"Without me, they are not whole. We are of one soul, fractured into five parts. How can they pass into the Eternal City when this one is still here?"

Nel dismissed his words with a sharp cutting motion. "They can wait for you; time doesn't matter much to them anymore." She took a deep breath, controlling herself. "As you said, you're still here; you haven't used that sword to hasten your family reunion. I think you must know that there is unfinished work for you in this world still."

Xin's calm gaze shifted to Keilan. "This one has waited for you."

"Me?"

The Fist warrior nodded slightly. "Yes. Keilan, this one must thank you. You saved my life, but more importantly, you took revenge when this one could not. My only solace now is that this one knows the monster that slew my brothers has been banished back to whatever abyss it first crawled from."

Keilan swallowed. "You're . . . you're welcome, Xin."

Xin closed his eyes, the tension leaking from his face. "Then there is nothing left for me here."

Nel stepped forward and slapped his cheek hard. Redness bloomed, but the Fist warrior did not move or open his eyes.

"Nothing? What about the seeker? What about Keilan? What about *me*?" Her last words were wrenched by a sob.

She loves him, Keilan suddenly realized, watching Nel tremble in anger and sadness. Now it was clear, and he wondered how he hadn't seen it before. The way her eyes had followed him while he'd shown them the basic patterns of sword-fighting, how her fingers had lingered on his when he'd adjusted her grip on her hilt. He felt a little surge of something in his chest – jealousy? – but that was quickly washed away by sadness.

"Xin . . ." he said, "I know how you feel. My mother was murdered a year ago, drowned by people my father had always considered friends. Sometimes the anger and helplessness felt overwhelming, and I wanted to throw myself into the same waters that she died in, sink down and let the blackness wash over me. But that's not what she would have wanted. And your brothers wouldn't want you to kill yourself, either. You know this."

Xin opened his eyes. Was there a flicker of emotion now? "This one is sorry, Keilan. The evenings we spent sword-training together and reading in the scholar's wagon were some of the happiest of my life. But you do not know what it means to be a Fist."

"Make us your new brothers!" Nel cried, clutching at Xin's arm.

"That is impossible," the Fist warrior said sadly, shaking his head.

An idea came to Keilan, and he seized it. "You say I did you a great service, yes?" After Xin's slight nod he continued, changing the tone of his voice from pleading to commanding. "Then you are in my debt."

Xin watched him carefully.

"You must know that we are still in grave danger. Vhelan believes that creature was sent to kill us, but by what or whom we do not know. We need your sword if we are to get to Herath alive. Xin . . . you owe me. How could you go to meet your brothers when the one that avenged them still needed your help, and you could have given it? What would your brothers say to this?"

Xin was quiet for a long time. A tremor passed across his face, as if something had changed within him. Finally, he let out a long sigh. "Keilan, there is truth to what you say. This one has a debt to you that must be repaid before he passes beyond. This one will accompany you to Herath."

Nel let out a small gasp and glanced at Keilan. Xin saw this, and the sadness returned to his voice. “And then, when this one knows you are safe, he will go to meet his brothers.”

20: JAN

HERATH.

Jan's first glimpse of the Crimson Queen's city came as he crested a hilltop that had been scarred by fire, the trees that usually pressed close to the road and would have blocked his view reduced to blackened stumps. He reined to a halt, his horse whinnying in thanks at this unexpected reprieve. Jan patted the sweat-damp mane, rummaging in his saddlebags for some oats. They'd spent the past several days laboring up and down the hills that rippled out from where the Bones had sunk their roots deep in the world's roof, and his horse had earned a well-deserved rest when they finally reached the city on the Derravin. Not so much longer now.

Herath was a distant smudge crusting the edge of a dark bay; it had outgrown its old walls, as buildings spread in almost organic-looking arms from the shore and pushed into the surrounding forest. To the north the stain of habitation crept up a steep slope until it brushed against the walls of a mighty fortress. That must be Saltstone, the ancient seat of power for House d'Kara. Jan's gaze lingered on the jagged crenellations that soared stark and imposing against the cloudless sky. It was no wonder that the family that had built this keep centuries ago had managed to unite these notoriously fractious lands under their banner. He squinted, imagining he could see something. Was she standing on the battlements even now, slim white fingers resting on cold stone, a sea-breeze tangling her red curls as she watched these faraway hills?

His fascination with her had only grown during his long journey west. A young woman who had fashioned her small kingdom into an empire. A queen who had thrived without a king beside her, as once was common in his lost home, the doomed holdfast of Nes Vaneth. And perhaps most compelling – she was a sorceress that even ancient, immortal Alyanna feared to confront directly.

A black speck floated in the unblemished sky, some large bird. He remembered the old Min-Ceruthan superstitions – if that was an eagle riding the wind, good fortune would follow him into the city. A raven and he should hurriedly find some luck elsewhere, as disaster was threatening. And if it was a seagull, he might as well turn his horse around right now. Of course, seagulls couldn't be as much of an ill-omen in coastal Herath as they were in the land-locked mountains of his homeland. Perhaps eagles were what was rare here, and glimpsing one of *those* majestic birds was considered unlucky instead.

Jan watched the speck for a long time, until it spiraled down to the distant ocean and vanished. Definitely a seagull.

Herath was a young city, and much of its growth had clearly come in the past few years. The walls looked stunted when compared to the soaring black iron that girdled Vis, the last major city he had passed through, and the roads were churned earth rather than cobblestones or tile. Nevertheless, there was a briskness to the city, an undercurrent of energy among the travelers that jostled him as he approached the small city gate. Strange how the character of a people could be glimpsed in the way they carried themselves. The Visani had seemed to drift, unhurried, through their ancient stone city, while the citizens of Menekar glided aloof and imperial between their vast edifices of basalt and marble. But the Dymorians here strode with confidence and purpose, staring straight ahead as they hurried along roads hemmed by buildings of timber and sod that would have been considered mean and provincial in the older, prouder cities to the east.

Their dress, too, was different. Most wore brightly colored clothes, bordering on garish, vivid shades of blue and red and green. A few of the men on the road with him clashed so much it looked like they were wearing motley – Jan had heard of an affliction where you could not distinguish one color from another, and maybe that disease was epidemic here in Dymoria. He certainly stood out, in his drab brown doublet and gray traveler's cloak.

And perhaps that was why the guardsman at the gate stopped him, using his long spear to bar his way.

"Halt, friend. What business do you have in Herath?"

Jan reached up to touch the lute strapped across his back. "A wandering minstrel, sir. From the Shattered Kingdoms by way of Vis."

Another guardsman, leaning on a white kite shield emblazoned with the red dragon of Dymoria, looked him up and down. "A minstrel, eh? From Vis? Competition a little much in the Poet's City?"

Jan inclined his head, as if in agreement. "Many fine singers there, certainly. I was hoping the mead halls of Herath would prove more fortunate for me."

The guardsman's eyes lingered on the sword at his side. "Looks like you've seen plenty of fortune. The jewel in that there hilt could buy a tavern for yerself, I'd wager."

Jan allowed himself an easy smile. "A wager you'd lose, good sir. Just a bit of colored glass to impress the townsfolk."

The first guardsman snorted. "I bet it'd impress the townsfolk enough that they'd slit your throat for it. Damn foolish, swaggering around with that at your side. But it's your own neck, I s'pose." He waved for Jan to continue and lifted his spear. "Go on, then."

Jan nodded thanks and spurred his horse forward. He hadn't gone two dozen paces when he heard someone hurriedly following.

"Wait." It was the second guardsman, panting from running after him in his heavy armor. "Minstrel, hold. I near forgot. My uncle, Fendrin, owns an inn and eating house. He's been looking for someone to sing in the commons for board and a few coppers a night. Do you have other business, or would you be interested?"

"It sounds like fate to me."

The guardsman's plump face broke into a smile. "Aye, good news. Fendrin will be pleased, and if you've any talent I might get a few free rounds out of this. His inn is the Cormorant, just off the docks. Follow the main road here and then bear left when you see the farriers. Take your second right, another two hundred paces more and you're there. If you get lost, ask anyone. They'll point you true. And remember to tell him it was Benosh who sent you."

It was not as easy to find as the guardsman had made it seem. Jan had come to the farriers quick enough, a cluster of forges set at the confluence of two streets, one dedicated to blacksmithing, and the other to horses and their tack. He had stopped and had one of the apprentices check his horse's shoes to make sure the metal had not weakened, or any small stone become wedged during their journey where it could cause harm. Then he'd paid a silver to stable his horse for a month, patting her affectionately on the flank before the boy led her off into a low wide building. He hadn't asked about the Cormorant, as what the guard had said had still seemed clear enough, but after taking the road's left branching he had soon discovered that he was well and truly lost. His enquiry about the inn to a pair of fruit sellers had been met with blank stares, so since the guard had mentioned it was near the docks he had instead asked to be pointed in that direction.

And thus he found himself sitting on a broken wooden crate beside a rotted pier, eating the speckled white flesh of some ridged purple fruit he had never seen before and watching the sun slowly sink into the mauve sea. A dozen ships lay at anchor in the bay, their profiles shadowed against the fading light of day. They seemed larger and grander than he remembered. Most were caravels, crescent hulls sweeping up into high forecastles where trebuchets and ballistae bristled. One still had its sails unfurled, showing the red dragon of Dymoria in all its sinuous glory. These must be the breed of ship that had crossed the Derravin decades ago and found the Sunset Lands. It was a good reminder, actually, that the progress of man was not merely measured in the mastery of sorcery. Boat-building, architecture, mathematics, art – some called this age the Twilight, but in many disciplines it could very well be considered a dawning. Jan sucked the last bit of sweetness from the fruit's rind and tossed it into the water.

There were other ships, too, scattered among the Dymorian craft. A long, dark cutter, sleek as a shark, flying a flag stamped with the black eye of Lyr. Close to that ship were two large triremes studded with many oars, which made them look to Jan like those insects that skated upon the surface of ponds. And most impressive was the largest boat in the harbor, huge enough that it dwarfed even the Dymorian caravels, a behemoth that wallowed in the water so low it almost seemed to be sinking. This must be one of the famed junks of Shan, boats that centuries ago had arrived from shores far more distant and mysterious than even the Sunset Lands.

The sight of the Shan ship reminded Jan of Alyanna's strange demon child. That creature had appeared to have come from the Empire of Swords and Flowers, as the symbols of Shan had been carved prominently on the rosewood chest serving as its prison, and the sorceress herself had claimed the same. Unless, of course, Alyanna had painted those herself to mislead him as to the demon's origins. An interesting thought.

He was so lost in his musings that he did not hear the others approaching until they were almost upon him. Jan glanced up to find three men watching him with the predatory intent of cats that had stumbled upon a baby mouse. Two were large and balding and covered with livid scars that disappeared into the hems of their well-patched tunics. The third was much thinner and smaller, with a frizzy shock of red hair. He sauntered closer, grinning.

"Oi, friend. That there's my crate your arse is on."

Bemused, Jan slid from his perch. "My apologies. I did not know."

The small man blew his nose loudly into his shirt sleeve. "Course ya didn't, course ya didn't. Still means we gotta ask for some . . . ah, compensation. Ain't no free seats on Chol's docks, no sir."

Jan noticed that the bustle of activity nearby had stopped; the dock-hands and sailors who had been carrying goods and scurrying over the small boats tied to the pier had paused their work, and seemed to be watching what was unfolding out of the corner of their eyes.

"And are you Chol?"

The man brayed a laugh, turning to look back at his two companions. "Am I Chol, he says. Friend, you're not long for the docks if you don't know who Chol is. He's the big man around here, the boss. I'm just his strong right arm." He tugged at one of his long red curls, then jerked a thumb at the two large men standing behind him. "Actually, come to think of it, these lads here are Chol's arms. I'm more his brains."

"Quite the organization Chol has."

The man's eyes narrowed. "Yeah, he does. But running such a concern certainly ain't cheap. Lots o' folks need to get their bread."

Jan smiled, his hand going to his coin-belt. "Certainly. A copper for a moment's rest, that would be fair, yes?"

The small man snorted. "A copper? Seems a bit stingy for someone with such a nice sword. How about you toss a silver to me, and we'll all leave as friends."

Jan sighed. "Two coppers, then?"

"Ain't no bargaining on Chol's docks. Set price."

"Well, then," Jan said, starting to walk away, "I suppose I must, with regret, back out of this transaction."

One of the balding toughs reached out to grab a handful of his shirt as he passed. Jan caught his wrist and twisted it so that the man shrieked in surprise and pain, falling to one knee.

"I dislike such strong-arm negotiating tactics," Jan said calmly. As the other scarred man lunged toward him he let go of the wrist he held and jabbed his fingers into the throat of the onrushing attacker, knocking him backward, then in a single fluid motion kicked his legs out from under him. The man whose wrist he had wrenched scrambled to his feet and took a few stumbling steps backward, nearly falling over in his haste to get away.

Jan rested his hand lightly on Bright's hilt and turned back to the small man, whose mouth now gaped open like a hooked fish. "Next time, I'll draw my sword. Still want to try and collect from me?"

The man swallowed hard. "No, friend. Terribly sorry for the mistake. Thought you were someone else, actually. You're free to sit where ya like."

Jan watched them scurry away until they vanished into an alley's mouth.

"That was well done. Nice to see that idiot Gherv knocked down a few."

Jan turned to find a young woman in a frayed blue shift sitting on the crate where he had until a moment ago been watching the bay, swinging her legs and flashing him a lopsided smile. Her hair was gathered up under a cap, but a few stray red curls had escaped and dangled down to brush her pale cheeks.

"Best be careful, lest he sees you sitting on his crate. It's an expensive place to watch the sunset, apparently."

The girl giggled. "He'd have to catch me first, which he ain't doing." She looked Jan up and down appraisingly. "I ain't seen you around the docks before. You come on a ship?"

Jan shook his head and pulled from his bag another of the purple fruit. He tossed it to her, and she caught it easily. "No. Came along the Wending Way, from Vis. Just arrived today. I'm looking for the Cormorant, do you know it?"

The girl gripped the fruit with both hands, then with a sharp twisting motion pulled the rind off smoothly, revealing its white innards. "Sure I do. Follow that street there," she gestured towards the alley where the toughs had disappeared, "you'll see it on your left quick enough."

"Much thanks."

The girl scooped out a pinch of the fruit's flesh and popped it into her mouth. "You a minstrel?" she asked while chewing noisily.

Jan flourished a formal bow. "I am, my lady. Jan, once of the Kingdoms, at your service."

With a grin the girl jumped lightly from the crate and offered him her hand. He took it and brushed his lips against her fingers – the taste was sticky and sweet. She giggled again and dropped into a surprisingly good curtsy. "An honor to meet you, Sir Jan. My name's Serene. Serene o' the Tides, if you please."

"The honor is all mine, my lady." Now that she was standing Jan could see that she was not as young as she'd first appeared; her legs were long and shapely, and the gentle swell of her breasts under her shift showed that she was a woman grown.

Serene saw where he was looking and rolled her eyes. "I ain't that kind of lady, Sir Jan, though I can recommend a few nice lasses that live around here, if that's the kind of company you'd like."

To his surprise, Jan felt himself blushing. A thousand years old, and still a sharp-witted woman could disarm him utterly. He shook his head. "My apologies. It's been a long and lonely journey."

Serene leaned forward and gave him a quick peck on the cheek. "Well, you've arrived," she said, her lips quirking."Welcome to Herath. I think I'll have to come hear you play at the Cormorant one of these evenings. I hope you're good."

21: SENACUS

THE BELLS. HE still dreamed of the bells.

Senacus's steel-shod boots rang on the temple floor, seemingly in time with the deep tolling of a distant bell. So much of this place was indelibly etched into his memory – the endless expanses of pink marble, the haze of incense clouding the air, the pristine white robes of mendicants as they scurried about – but it was the bells that truly brought him back to his youth in these halls. They always seemed to be ringing, somewhere. Calling the faithful to prayer, usually, though they also rang for meals and deaths and births and holy days and study sessions and Cleansings. He realized now, many years late, that the true purpose of the bells was to remind everyone in the temple that Ama was always present, always watching. Sometimes literally.

Senacus glanced up at the Aspects staring down at him from their niches carved high in the walls. Joy, Rage, Grief, Lust, Compassion, Fear, Curiosity, Love, and Hate. The nine facets of Ama, the nine qualities He had imbued in His children, the sparks of godhood that separated man from the animals. Senacus's eyes were drawn to a shrouded statue with outflung arms, the most common representation of Compassion. It was the Aspect he had always tried to shelter in his heart and allow to guide his actions, even when confronted by the enemies of the faith; others among the Pure drew strength from Hate, or Rage, or Grief . . . but not him. And it might have cost him his life.

But what was done was done. He could not change his actions now – and he wasn't sure, honestly, if he would, even if such a thing was possible. Yes, he had saved the life of a sorcerer, an unthinkable crime for one of Ama's paladins. But he had rescued him from a much more ancient and evil magic. Did that not count for something, on whatever scales were being used to decide his fate?

To his right the wall with its images of the Aspects ended, allowing Senacus to look down between pillars at a large courtyard garden. He paused for a moment, leaning on the balustrade, enjoying the play of sunlight on his face after too many days spent inside the temple. A path of ceramic tiles was sunk into the soft earth below, wending between dripping ferns and colorful blossoms. Stone benches were scattered about for visitors to rest on; most clustered around the small pond at the garden's heart. From his vantage above, Senacus could see what looked like a smear of orange and white twisting beneath the pond's surface – a school of the koi fish that were stocked in the temple's gardens as food for Ama's tame holy birds. One of them was there now, Senacus realized, so still and silent it nearly blended with the spray of reeds and cat o' nine tails surrounding it. The heron's long neck was angled up, watching him. Senacus nodded in greeting. He almost felt like he should apologize to the birds of the temple – when he had been a neophyte here he had been tasked with scraping the heron's droppings from the galleries and gardens, and he had held such a sullen dislike for them, even at times doubting their holiness. But now he knew it to be true. One of these birds had crashed through a window in the imperial audience chamber to warn the emperor of a sorcerous assassin. Great events were stirring in the world when Ama intervened directly in the lives of mortals, the Tractate was clear on this. Were his actions beneath the cursed city somehow a part of whatever was unfolding? Would he be remembered as a hero, or as a traitor to the faith?

He would find out soon enough.

With some effort Senacus pulled himself away from the balustrade and resumed walking. He could not be late. Even if it was to his own execution.

Around him the rosy blush faded from the marble floor and pillars, until he walked down a hall of unblemished white stone. Nowhere else in the world had Senacus seen marble that was not the least bit stained or cracked – only here, in the inner sanctum of Ama's paladins. It had been many years since he had strode these halls, but nothing seemed to have changed. That arched passage led to the barracks, dozens and dozens of small stone cells that could house every member of the Pure if they were all ordered to return to the holy city. Senacus had his own tiny room there, just a cot and a chest to store his few meager possessions, but he hadn't even visited once since he had arrived in Menekar two days ago. He had immediately gone to confess to the High Mendicant of his sins, then had spent the rest of his time in meditative prayer, waiting for these summons.

He turned a corner and was there, at the door to the High Seneschal's quarters. One of his brothers stood guard outside, still as a statue, flashing eyes staring straight ahead. He was one of the palace Pure, as like all the other paladins who served the emperor directly he had shaved the silver hair that had resulted from his Cleansing, and now gleaming copper tattoos laced his scalp. He was also young, and must have been elevated to the brotherhood while Senacus had been across the Spine of the Bones, as he did not know him.

"Greetings, brother. I have been summoned by the High Seneschal."

The Pure did not glance at him, but he swung the door open. "He is waiting for you, brother."

Senacus nodded slightly in thanks and stepped inside, with some effort keeping himself from wincing as the door clanged shut behind him.

The room where the High Seneschal met with guests was decorated sparsely, reflecting the vows of poverty taken by the paladins of Ama. A large bronze sunburst was affixed to the far wall, roughhewn as if forged by a smith of very little skill, and next to that ancient holy symbol of Ama a sword of pale white metal hung. Beside that sword was another of slightly different make, and then another, and another, until the circular room was very nearly wrapped by a crown of blades. These were the swords of all those who had served as High Seneschal over the past two thousand years, and Senacus found his heart beating fast in the presence of such history.

In the center of the room was a simple table carved from some white wood, large enough for a dozen chairs to fit around. But today there were only two, and both were occupied.

The High Seneschal rose as he entered. He was an old man, but still tall and straight-backed, and he wore the same cuirass of white-enameled scales that all the Pure clad themselves in when they strode out in the world to contest with the enemies of Ama. His eyes did not shine with the blazing radiance of youth; their glow had faded over the long decades and now gleamed nacreous, reminding Senacus of the pearly luster of a sea-thing's shell. Senacus knew that this did not mean that the High Seneschal's strength was waning, or that he had lost Ama's favor. How the light of their lord manifested itself changed during the seasons of a man's life, but even in the fading days of winter Ama's gift lost none of its potency.

The other man in the room stayed seated, watching him without expression. Senacus had only a moment to glance at him before he dropped to one knee and bowed his head respectfully towards the High Seneschal. The man was some indeterminate age, his skin pale and unlined, thick black ringlets tumbling to his shoulders. He was dressed in black, all the more striking given the contrast to the room's unblemished marble walls and furniture of pale white wood.

"Rise, my brother." The High Seneschal's voice was as deep and sonorous as the temple's great bell.

"Ama's light be with you," Senacus said as he stood again.

"And with you," the High Seneschal finished the ritual greeting, lowering himself into his chair. He regarded Senacus for a long moment over steepled hands. "Many years you've been outside, brother. How long?"

"Five years."

"And Ama has blessed your efforts. Seven of the tainted he has revealed to you. Four you sent here to be Cleansed, and three entered the Golden City with souls unsullied by sorcery. The last has joined our brotherhood as a neophyte, and has taken the name Septimus, in honor of you."

Senacus had not known that, and it gladdened his heart. He had thought when he'd sent back the baker's boy that there was a chance Ama might favor the lad. There had been an innocence to him, a purity that those that survived their Cleansings often possessed.

"Tell me of the fifth you found."

Senacus swallowed, remembering chamber upon chamber of horrors beneath a manse in Theris. Walls that sweated blood, tiny blackened corpses.

"A sorcerer, full in his powers. I do not know where he gained his knowledge, but it appeared to me that generations of his family had kept the traditions of blood magic alive in catacombs carved below his family's ancestral manse. He was a rich merchant in Theris, from a long and distinguished lineage, and had been known for his kindness and generosity toward the orphans of the city. I found many of their remains that day. They had suffered horribly."

"Then you did a great thing, ridding the world of this foulness."

Senacus said nothing, but inclined his head in agreement. "Ama guided me, brother. I felt his presence with me that day."

The High Seneschal drummed his fingers on the table's wood. "And did you feel his presence when you gave up the sixth tainted one you found to the seventh, a fully-fledged sorcerer?"

A hot flush of shame darkened his cheeks. "I did what I thought I had to do to save the lives of the men with me. Followers of Ama had accompanied me to the village where I found the boy, local men with no real skill at arms. We were ambushed on the road back by a host of trained soldiers. Many innocents would have been killed if I'd resisted the sorcerer at that time. I thought it best to let them leave with the child, then follow and wait for an opportune moment to take him back. Perhaps even the chance to confront the sorcerer directly would arise if I could separate him from his guards. I had his scent after our first encounter; he could not escape me."

"And yet instead you saved his life."

Senacus opened his mouth, readying his justifications for his actions, but then thought better. "I did," he said simply.

"The wizard disturbed some dark sorcery that had long lurked in the ruins of Uthmala."

"Yes."

"He would have been destroyed."

"Yes."

The High Seneschal leaned forward, his eyes flashing iridescent. "But why do we care if one evil consumes another?"

Senacus had no answer for this. After a long silence he swallowed away the dryness in his throat. "I accept whatever punishment Ama believes is just."

The High Seneschal sat back, sighing. "If the High Mendicant had left this decision to me alone, I would have ordered you to open your veins across the radiant altar. You were given Ama's most precious gift, and you squandered it by saving the lives of those who would burn the world for their own selfish ends. I cannot forgive this."

Senacus felt his legs weaken at the High Seneschal's words. To hear the head of his order say that he would have ordered his death . . . the shame was overwhelming.

"But your fate is not in my hands."

"Who decides my fate?" Senacus whispered, reaching out to steady himself on the table's edge.

"Ama, of course," the High Seneschal replied, "through his chosen, the High Mendicant."

"Ama has spoken to him of me?"

The High Seneschal's lip curled. "Of you? No. But of someone you have met. Our bright lord visited the High Mendicant in his dreams last night. He said that the boy you let slip through your fingers has strength unlike any other, that if Cleansed he could become the greatest of the Pure, the greatest since Tethys himself cast down the Warlock King. The High Mendicant was gifted a vision that showed the boy as the shining general in the coming war against this demoness, this Crimson Queen and her profane school of wizards, and that he could be the man who finally expunges the taint of sorcery from these lands and returns purity to the world."

"Why me . . ."

"Because you have met the boy. You know what he looks like, you have spoken to him and tasted his scent. Now your holy task is to find this Keilan and bring him back to Menekar."

"But he must be in Dymoria soon, if he is not already. The queen and her sorcerers will sense me, or any paladin that approaches within a hundred leagues of Herath."

The High Seneschal placed a thin golden box on the table. "You underestimate the power of our lord." He snapped open the latches and withdrew from a bed of velvet what looked like a yellowing finger-bone. It dangled from a shimmering silver chain, seemingly fused with the delicate links. "Do you know the story of Tethys's final assault on the Selthari Palace?"

Senacus found he could not tear his gaze from the slowly twisting bone. "Yes."

"Then you remember how the Warlock King in his desperation opened a rift into the Void, and a demon of fell power slipped through?"

"I do."

"Tethys slew the beast, of course, but the Tractate tells us that he lost three fingers to the creature's slavering jaws."

Senacus gasped and quickly sketched the circle of Ama in the air in front of him. "That is from Tethys's hand?"

The High Seneschal nodded solemnly. "It is. It is one of the greatest treasures of our order." He undid the chain's clasp and slipped it around his own neck, so that the bone lay upon the gleaming white scales of his cuirass.

Senacus could not stifle a small cry. The silvery luster of the High Seneschal's eyes faded, watery blue pupils emerging. The faint aura that enveloped every paladin of Ama wavered and was gone.

"The bone takes away our strength?"

The High Seneschal turned to try and find his reflection in the bronze sunburst fixed to the wall behind him. "It hides it, from both men and sorcerers. But if you use the gifts of Ama then the charm is broken."

"Truly it is a mighty weapon against sorcerers."

The High Seneschal removed the chain and laid it again in its golden box, the light instantly flaring once more in his eyes. "It is. And invaluable. In centuries past we had three; now this is the only one that remains. You must not let an enemy claim it."

"I will guard it with my life. But . . . but how can I approach the boy to spirit him away? He will be held in Saltstone, protected by stout walls and a thousand warriors."

"He will help you," The High Seneschal said, gesturing to the silent, watchful man in black.

"And who is he?" Senacus turned to face the stranger. "Who are you?"

"My name is Demian," the man said. His words seemed to have been shriven of any accent. Senacus could not tell if he hailed from Menekar or Gryx or Ver Anath.

"And you can help in rescuing this boy?"

Demian smiled without humor. "A rescue? Is that what you would call it?"

Confused, Senacus looked at the High Seneschal again. "Who is this? Why is he here, privy to our order's secrets? He is not one of us."

The High Seneschal cleared his throat and shifted. For the first time he did not seem so absolute in his convictions. "He is not. He is . . . kith'ketan."

Instinctively, Senacus's hand went to his sword's hilt. "Shadowblade!"

The High Seneschal held up his own hand. "Calm, brother. Ama's ways are mysterious. The High Mendicant saw this man in his dreams, and our bright lord told him that he was our ally in the coming war. And now he appears to us, as Ama foretold."

"But he is an assassin!"

The shadowblade's thin lips quirked. "We are both killers."

Senacus drew himself up taller. "I kill those who would befoul the world and prey on innocent souls."

"Yes," Demian said mildly, "those children you sent back, the ones that spilled their blood upon your blazing altar, they were truly befouling the world with their presence."

"Enough!" commanded the High Seneschal, rising again to his feet. "Brother, are you so arrogant that you would question the ways of the Creator Himself?"

Senacus ducked his head. "No, forgive me. My thoughts have been clouded lately."

"Indeed," said the High Seneschal, sliding the gold box across the table. "Go to Herath. Find this boy and return with him, bring him into the light and give the faithful of Ama a new champion. You leave on the morrow."

22: KEILAN

"THE MOST IMPORTANT thing to remember when dining with a prince," Vhelan said as they approached an imposing set of doors, one of white wood and carved with a sun, the other of gleaming black and inscribed by a crescent moon, "is always to laugh at his jests."

"Unless, of course, he doesn't smile at his own wit," Nel added, plucking irritably at the lacy fringe of her dress's neckline. She had been fidgeting since they had left their quarters, clearly uncomfortable in the finery she wore. "Because that means it might not have been intended as a joke. It's embarrassing, being the only one laughing at a formal dinner. Vhelan can tell you all about it, actually."

The sorcerer scowled. "How was I to know the padarasha's father had just died?"

"The mourning wreaths? The black veils? The hundred-horse funeral procession we had seen when entering the city?"

"Could have been for anyone," Vhelan muttered. He glanced over at his knife as she let out a little growl of frustration and tugged at her clothes. "Comfortable?"

Nel shot him a withering look. She wore a slim-fitting blue dress of some expensive fabric, trimmed with lace, her shoulders and arms bare. Her short black hair had been brushed down, and someone had even applied faint purple blush to her cheekbones, which matched the glittering jewels she wore around her neck – the same jewels they had found in the hidden sanctum beneath Uthmala. She looked like a beautiful noble lady, Keilan thought.

She looked miserable.

"Comfortable? In this? Do you know how hard it was to find someplace for my daggers?"

Garmond, in his formal seeker robes of deep forest green, stumbled and nearly fell. "You are bringing weapons to a dinner with a prince? What if the guards find them?"

Nel snorted. "If they can find where I've hidden them, they deserve to be stabbed."

Vhelan sighed. "You can take the girl out of the Warrens . . ."

"Please. I have noticed little difference between eating in a thieves' den or around a royal dinner table. Nicer table-settings, maybe – the quality of the company is about the same."

"Quiet," the sorcerer commanded as they arrived at the doors to the banquet hall. The guardsman outside was garbed in silver and black livery, a silver tree emblazoned on his tabard. He raised his long ceremonial pike and struck the stone floor twice, and at the ringing sound the doors swung open smoothly.

Keilan's breath caught when he saw what awaited within.

"Remarkable," Seeker Garmond murmured, "the legends do not do it justice."

The circular room was vast, a hundred steps deep, at least, lit by a dozen huge iron braziers. Keilan couldn't guess what burned within, as the flames were blue-tinged and gave off surprisingly little smoke. What shimmering coils there were twisted upwards and vanished through the circle cut out of the high domed ceiling; through the haze Keilan could see the faint sparkle of stars. The room's curving walls were covered with long tapestries, scenes from the most famous stories of the north picked out in bright glimmering thread. There was

Isabel reclining on the banks of the tumbling Serpent, being wooed by the River Prince in his vestments of foam and weeds. And there was the seventh son of the cursed lord of Pendreal, raising his lance high as the great dragon spread its wings above him, the tragic knight intent on avenging his six lost brothers. The artistry of the tapestries was remarkable, unlike any he had seen before, but it was not what awed Keilan now.

The Tree of Vis filled the center of the room, soaring toward the hole in the domed roof, great roots rippling into a patch of brown earth. Its bark gleamed silver, while the leaves bowing its limbs shimmered white and ghostly, almost translucent. Also speckling the branches were small dark shapes; as Keilan watched one hopped from its perch and fluttered higher. How many stories and great quests had started with a prophecy given by the oracular birds of Vis? He felt as if he was moving through a dream, and at any moment he might wake in his bed back in his village.

A table shaped like a horseshoe wrapped partway around the tree, and at its bend stood Prince Lynn, smiling and beckoning them forward. He gestured toward the empty chairs on his right; the ones on his left were already occupied by three people Keilan had not yet met. When they had seated – Vhelan beside the prince, then Garmond, Nel, and finally Keilan – the prince made the introductions.

"My friends from distant lands, please let me introduce three of the most distinguished citizens of my city. First we have the Lady Meredith, my beloved paramour." The tall, graceful woman next to the prince inclined her long neck, the yellow stones set into her silver tiara flashing as they caught the firelight. Hers was a beauty that belonged in the old tales, Keilan thought, and he felt a little thrill when her hazel eyes found his.

"And beside her sits Ghabrial Menoth Fen-Kiva, famed poet of *The Lay of Lost Starlight*, among many others. We in Vis consider him the greatest living writer in the world."

The wiry old man blew out his drooping gray mustache and rolled his eyes.

"Such kind words from you tonight, my prince. It makes me nervous about what we've all been invited here to agree to." Nevertheless, the old poet rose smoothly and offered them a bow.

"And the last is the head of our ancient order of librarians, Pelimanus Tarryn Voth-Anan." The man looked like a librarian: his unlined face made guessing his age difficult, and he was deathly pale, as if he rarely saw sunlight. He was dressed in long brown robes, unaccented by any trim or design, the cowl thrown back to reveal a head so hairless it reminded Keilan of a boiled egg.

The librarian stood and also bowed, lower than the poet. "Welcome to Vis," he said softly.

The prince swept his other arm out, encompassing Keilan and his companions. "I've spoken of you all already, of course, but allow me my moment, if you please. We have so few occasions for formal dinners here in Vis."

"Thank the gods," muttered the old poet and took a hearty swig from his wine glass.

"My old friends, here we have Vhelan ri Vhelus, a magister of the second rank in the Scholia of her majesty, Cein d'Kara. Beside him is the Seeker Garmond of the Reliquary. Then this enchanting creature is Nel, sworn in the service of our good magister, and here is Keilan, not so long ago of the Shattered Kingdoms."

Keilan glanced over and saw Nel's jaw tense when the prince introduced her. To his surprise, he also saw the poet Ghabrial wink across the table at her, and he suddenly wished Vhelan had convinced her to relinquish her daggers outside.

"All of Vis welcomes you, and pledges whatever aid we may after your recent troubles."

Introductions finished, the prince used his silver spoon to ring a small bell placed beside his wine glass. At the sound, doors cleverly hidden along the walls swung open, and servants entered the room carrying platters heaped with a sumptuous array of foods. The first plates were vegetables and fruits, slabs of roast pumpkin glistening with butter, long green strands of morning glory drizzled with purple sauce, a tiered pyramid of tangerines and plums, and a golden horn overflowing with grapes, apples, and other fruit he did not know. Then came the meats, capons with their skin crisped a beautiful brown, filleted river eels soaked in brandy, and a great haunch of beef, the outside of which was charred black, but when it was cut into the juices ran bright red.

Keilan had barely touched the feast before the main course arrived, a huge roast pig reclining on a great tray, which was carried in by two struggling servants. Conversations ebbed and flowed as the endless procession of food and wine continued. Garmond and the Visani librarian struck up a loud and lively discussion about the origin of wraiths, and whether they were a cursed tribe of men, as some claimed, or another species of animal altogether. The seeker seemed intrigued by one of the older legends of the north, which suggested that wraiths had once lived in cities of their own, great nests of tunnels and chambers that honeycombed some of the most forbidding peaks of the Bones. Keilan found himself imagining a horde of the creatures that had attacked their caravan creeping through the bowels of a mountain like monstrous ants, and couldn't suppress a shudder.

He shifted his attention from that conversation to what was being exchanged between Nel and the old poet. It seemed to be one-sided – whatever techniques employed by Ghabriel in wooing the good ladies of Vis were being wasted on the knife. She sat with a smile frozen on her face as the poet attempted foray after foray, sometimes offering up a tepid response when pressed.

"Lovely jewels, my lady. They suit your complexion perfectly."

A slight nod.

"Do you like poetry, my dear? You remind me of something I wrote in my youth, a simple little couplet about hyacinths in bloom."

Shrug.

"Have you ever tried Mire black eel? A true delicacy, and some say it contains certain aphrodisiacal qualities . . . not that a man of my virility needs such charms, of course."

A blank stare, brimming with immense boredom.

Finally the poet set his elbows on the table and leaned forward. When he spoke again the charming cadence to his words had vanished.

"My dear, you seem ignorant of how the world works. The old and rich are attracted to youth and beauty. The young and beautiful are partial to fame and pretty baubles. I am plenty famous and have collected many expensive trifles that I am willing to share – you should be at the very least pretending interest in what I am saying."

A hint of a smile tugged at the edge of Nel's mouth. "Master poet, if there's anything I want from you I won't waste both our time. I'll just steal it."

Keilan had to pretend to cough to hide his own smile at the look of shock on the poet's face. The expression passed quickly, though, and the old man slapped his hand beside his plate, abruptly silencing the table.

"Ha! Did you hear that, Lyn? You need to convince her to stay here as an advisor. I think she could breathe some life into this old embalmed city."

The prince stood, smiling. "Lady Nel certainly has her charms. And my heart would be gladdened if all our guests could stay a while in Vis. Unfortunately, Magister Vhelan tells me that they have pressing matters in Herath."

"But they want something before they go?"

The prince nodded slightly towards the poet. "Yes. I've already told you all about how their caravan was ambushed on the Wending Way by a clan of wraiths. There was something else, though. The beasts seemed to be under the control of a creature that had assumed the shape of a man. During the battle it shed its human guise, revealing its monstrous nature. Magister Vhelan believes that this thing had been dispatched to slay the servants of Dymoria, but by what agency he does not know. I would let him access to the Barrow, and see if any answers can be found within."

For a long moment the table was silent. Then the poet crossed his arms and sighed loudly. "My prince, I knew your father, and his father before him. They would never have even considered such a thing."

"I know. Our time is different."

"Three thousand years and no one save the librarians and the line of Adreth have descended into the Barrow. Now in the span of a season we would twice allow outsiders access to our greatest secrets?" The poet turned to the head librarian, who was leaning back in his chair with a thoughtful expression. "Pelimanus, how did the spirit take to the Crimson Queen's visit?"

The librarian sat forward, steepling his hands. "It was agitated. I do not know exactly what happened that day, as by the prince's order we did not accompany her majesty into the Barrow." Keilan thought he heard a hint of reproach in the librarian's tone. "But I have my suspicions. I believe that the spirit refused to help the queen in whatever it was she wanted . . . so she tried to bend it to her will, and force it to give up what was hidden."

"And did she succeed?" It was the first time Keilan had heard the Lady Meredith speak, and her voice matched her elegant beauty.

The librarian shrugged. "I do not know. But I would be wary about letting more strangers into the Barrow so soon. My order cannot guarantee their safety."

"I would not have them go alone," said the prince. "You would be with them this time. And I could not say no to the queen or her demands, you know that. She is not a woman to be refused."

The librarian bowed his head in acknowledgement of the prince's words.

"What is this spirit you are referring to?" asked Garmond, twisting strands of his long gray beard around his finger, a mannerism Keilan had seen before, and meant that something had caught the seeker's interest.

The prince and the poet shared a look. Finally, Ghabrial threw up his hands. "Go ahead, tell them then. I expect that fairly soon every peasant will know all our city's ancient secrets. Perhaps we can invite them into our most hallowed sanctums, charge a silver a visit, and make a goodly fortune."

The prince ignored the poet's outburst. "Seeker Garmond . . . the truth is that we do not know. It's always been there, as far back as our histories go, since the Barrow was truly a barrow and held only the first kings of Vis. That is why some think of it as a ghost, or a spirit. I am not sure it is indeed that. I think of it as a presence. Sometimes it helps our librarians when they are searching for something, sometimes it hinders them. Why, I could not tell you."

"To be truthful, in the Reliquary we have heard rumors of this spirit. Even that some deaths have been blamed on it."

The librarian frowned at the seeker's words. "Librarians have died before in the Barrow, and even one king, if the stories are true. Most became lost in the deeps and could not find their way out. One young adept was found just a hundred paces from the stairwell to the surface, dead from thirst, surrounded by the gnawed leather binding of books he had tried to eat. It may be that the spirit of the Barrow had some role in his passing . . . or perhaps not. The rows of books seem to twist in upon themselves, a shifting labyrinth, but I do not know if the spirit controls this aspect of the Barrow. In any case, good seeker, you need not worry. I would not allow a rival scholar from the Reliquary entrance to our most sacred halls."

Garmond stopped stroking his beard, shock and disappointment plain in his face. "Truly?"

"Truly." The librarian leaned forward. "Would you grant me entrance to your most hallowed sanctum?"

The seeker sighed. "Aye, we would not. None but those who have sworn their lives to the lore may delve into our innermost archives."

The poet cleared his throat loudly. "But you would allow a magister of the Scholia to descend into the Barrow? Pardon me if I do not understand."

All eyes now turned to the prince. The lord of Vis spread his arms, glancing at each of them in turn. "You all know that I believe the future of our city is bound up with Dymoria and her queen. Some of you disagree, and I respect your opinions. So I will leave the decision of whether to allow these visitors into the Barrow up to the ancient guardians of our city." He gestured towards the soaring tree. "Let us ask the starlings."

"You're going to have the birds decide?" Nel asked, clearly surprised.

"I am, as we have done many times before. That is why I asked the poet Ghabrial and Lady Meredith here today – there are none more respected in reading the murmurations." The prince withdrew a slim golden whistle from a pocket. "Are you ready?"

"We are," said the poet.

"Very well."

The prince placed the whistle in his mouth and blew, and though Keilan heard no sound the great mass of birds clustering the branches of the tree suddenly stirred, fluttering dark wings. Then, as if one great creature, the starlings threw themselves into the air, instantly blending together. They became like a great snake slithering around the trunk, looping over the branches, silent except for the susurrus of the leaves that came from the wind of their passage. Keilan could almost imagine that the tree itself was whispering to them.

Lady Meredith and the poet watched this with rapt attention, until the birds finally returned to their perches. Then they shared a long look.

"Magister, prepare yourself," said the poet slowly, "you shall enter the Barrow."

23: THE BLACK VIZIER

THE PEACH RAINS had finally come.

For weeks now Menekar had been swaddled in a shroud of late summer heat, heavy and suffocating. Along the Aveline Way, in the shadow of the aqueduct that channeled water from mother Asterppa to the cisterns and gardens of the city, the bare feet of children had slapped the marble as they ran shrieking to play in the crowded fountains. Past them matrons and maidens alike had walked swaying to market, their jokkas unbound and bared breasts gleaming, hair coiled atop their heads so that the faint breath of a breeze might cool their necks. And elsewhere in the city, in shaded villas along the banks of the sluggish, silty Pandreth, the painted wives of satraps summering in the capitol had reclined on velvet couches, fanned by great feathers held by the hairless men of the Whispering Isles.

As summer had waxed, the days had lengthened, becoming more languorous, colors slowly seeping from a city bleached by the heat.

Then the spell had broken. As happened every year, something in the swollen air had burst, and the peach rains had finally come, sweeping over the city in lashing torrents. The patter of children's feet had given way to the sound of falling raindrops; the hairless men of the Isles had set down their fans and bent to rub oils into the legs of their mistresses. The dust and filth of the hot dry summer months had been swept into the suddenly overflowing canals. Menekar had been reborn, cleansed – for a short while, at least.

The idea of cleansings had always fascinated Wen Xenxing. It was an essential aspect of this empire and its faith, but still after so many years he could not bring himself to embrace the notion that transgressions could simply be washed away. Mendicants brought sinners to the shores of Asterppa and submerged them in the blessed water, and when they broke the surface they were considered innocent again in the eyes of Ama – if not the law – no matter what their crimes. The Pure expunged the taint of magic from sorcerers in their most holy ceremony, and on occasion the Cleansed even rose again as paladins of Ama themselves, blazing with the god's sacred light.

The Shan did not believe in rebirths. There were no second chances in this life, no possibility that what had come before would be overlooked or forgotten. If you could not accept the shame of your actions than death – not a new life – was the only honorable outcome. Wen had found that this made it much easier to live with his decisions. And he would have a great many important ones to make in the coming months, he was sure. The slow pulse of history had quickened recently. He remembered an old curse of his homeland, inflicted only upon true enemies – 'may you live in interesting times.' Interesting times had indeed come to these lands.

The decision he had to make at this very moment held great importance to him, if no one else. Wen Xenxing, the black vizier of Menekar – spymaster, assassin, whisperer – hovered above the unrolled scroll that spanned the length of his chamber, unsure where to paint the cranes. There, between the mist-threaded crags? Or perhaps swooping low over the unruffled lake, with its lone sampan and cluster of stilt houses? Maybe – and this offended the purist in him – this landscape should lack for cranes, despite what meaning that would impart. Cranes were symbols of fidelity. Of loyalty.

Whatever else Wen was, he was loyal to his adopted home. So how best to serve it? How could he protect his emperor against the shadowy forces he felt gathering? There was a pattern there, hidden in the events of the past few months, a revelation that would lay bare the threat to the empire. What was it?

A powerful sorceress arises in the west, wielding magics that render Menekar's greatest weapons impotent. Meanwhile in Tsai Yin the Betrayers escape – or were freed? – from their ancient prison, and hunters from Shan spread across the land trying to recapture them. The High Mendicant dispatches a disgraced paladin and a shadow-blade to steal away a boy whom he believes could become Ama's holy champion. What was the connection? And why did he feel, against all reason, that the emperor's favored concubine was somehow at the heart of this unfolding drama?

A cool breeze slipped into the chamber, fingering the edges of the heavy scroll. Wen straightened and glided over to the open window. He stared out into the darkness for a long moment, listening to the rain as it fell upon his garden, the staccato drumbeat of drops striking broad palm fronds, the sound the water made as it trickled down the rocks he had so carefully sculpted. He could close his eyes and envision exactly what his garden must look like in this downpour. The curve of every plant's stem, the placement of the mosaic tiles that inlaid the paths, the colors that patterned the koi fish in the pond – he had carefully arranged everything. The men north of the Broken Sea preferred their gardens wild, unkempt, truly more nature than civilization. But the Shan desired spaces to find peace and harmony, and wise men understood that those qualities could only be attained when you were able to control every aspect of your surroundings. Wen could have closed his eyes and walked out into his garden, his jeweled slippers perfectly following the twisting paths. *Ja-nin*, the old masters had called it, the inner peace that mastered the outer tumult.

He must guide events, shape the future rather than react to what had already happened. But how? And how did this Alyanna fit into what was unfolding?

Wen remembered the peacock in the garden dipping its head to her, almost as if it was paying obeisance. Could she be a sorceress, a servant of the Crimson Queen disguised from the Pure, just as the emissary had been that had died in the audience chamber? The other concubines in the harem seemed either infatuated with her, or terrified beyond reason. None had been willing to divulge much about the emperor's favorite. And then there was the matter of the man in black . . .

One servant had reported seeing a strange pale man with long, dark hair in the pleasure gardens, speaking with Alyanna. He had set aside that whispering as inconsequential, but then the same servant had seen the stranger again, in the company of the disgraced paladin as they had left the temple on their mad quest to recapture the boy the Pure had lost to the servants of the Crimson Queen. And then Wen had learned from his sources in the temple that the man was kith'ketan!

What was an imperial concubine doing consorting with a shadowblade? How did it all connect to the Crimson Queen and the Betrayers?

Wen's gaze traveled the length of the painting spread before him. The landscape of vanished Shan, preserved in pine-soot ink. Gnarled trees clinging to rocky bluffs, cliffs that plunged precipitously down into placid gorges, the gentle scrawl of birds in flights above pagodas. Bent-back old women laboring along steep mountain paths, glimpses of tigers prowling within bamboo groves.

They had stolen this beautiful world away. The Betrayers. They had brought the Raveling, had ended the Heavenly Kingdom and driven the Shan into the sea. Now only these paintings remained, a fading echo.

When he had learned from his spies in Tsai Yin that the Betrayers were loose again he had been shocked beyond words. It was like a terrible nightmare had bled from the dream world into the waking. Why had the mandarins not dumped that cursed chest into the ocean during the years of the Empire of Wind and Salt?

There. Wen hurried over to a section of the scroll, retrieving a fine horse-hair brush from the collection on his desk. With a few deft strokes a crane materialized above the ancestor shrine he had painted atop one of the vertiginous peaks. Yes, that was fitting. Fidelity to the ghosts of the past – he would avenge his ancestors, find the Betrayers where they had fled, and use the powers of the Pure to exorcise those demons from this world once and for all.

A tentative knock on his chamber's door. "Yes?"

His servant's muffled voice came from the other side. "My lord, your newest visitor has arrived."

"Good," called back Wen as he crossed the room to return the brush to its ivory container. "Make sure she is washed this time."

"Of course, my lord," replied the servant, and a moment later Wen heard the footsteps receding.

Gone to prepare his girl for the evening. Wen crouched and carefully rolled up the long landscape painting. Once his passions had become so inflamed that he had bitten one of his playthings too hard, and blood had splattered his chamber's floor. He could not risk such a thing happening again, not while his painting was exposed.

His heart began to beat faster. In another life, in another world, the Shan would not have lost at the Shivering Stones and the legions would never have overrun the camp where he had been awaiting his old master's triumphant return. He would have continued his education in the Jade Court, and very likely would have been selected to ascend to the Phoenix Throne. His manhood would have been removed, his passions cut away for the greater good of Shan.

It was times like these that he appreciated the twisting thread of his life, and where it had brought him.

Another knock at his door, so faint he barely heard. He stood, excitement building in his chest. Tomorrow he would visit the pleasure gardens again, this time with several of the Pure. He would discover what secrets, if any, this concubine was hiding.

He gripped the carved ebonwood handle of his chamber's door and pulled. The child standing outside shrank away as his huge bulk filled the entrance. Wen quickly stepped back, offering a comforting smile.

"Come in, my dear," he murmured, sweeping his arm out to usher the child inside. He glanced down the hallway, looking for his servant. Where was the fool? This girl was too young, even for him. And hadn't he specified a golden-haired one this time, not this ragged little thing with its tangle of black hair?

Realization came to Wen just as he closed the door. He turned slowly. He would not scream, he told himself, no matter what it did to him.

In the end, he screamed.

24: ALYANNA

WHEN THE MISTS cleared, she found that she was flying towards the glittering emerald spikes of the Star Towers.

Far below her rippled a patchwork blanket of terraced farmland, small rivers like stray threads twisting between the hills. Here and there she saw clusters of tiny dwellings, rude little houses, the occasional mill or barn.

She had come from one of those hamlets. She had slept on a dirt floor, covered in rags. An old mangy cat had curled beside her, and from its closeness she had drawn strength and comfort as she had listened night after night to her father beating her mother senseless. A long time ago.

This was not part of his dream, she knew. Alyanna did not understand everything about dreamsending, as the power was relatively new to her, but she had quickly come to realize that when you entered another's mind your own thoughts and images intruded into what they were experiencing – particularly if you were familiar with what they were dreaming about. Somewhere in the city ahead was Demian, and as she approached him the memory of her own life in a village outside one of the Mosaic Cities was filling in the blank spaces she traversed.

Then abruptly she was there, passing between the forest of towers, drawn inexorably toward the one she had come to find. This rapid stuttering of movement was common in the dreamworld, especially when one neared the other dreamer, and the link between the minds strengthened. The pale green light filtering through the tower's glass made her feel as if she floated underwater. Green – she was in Kashkana. In each of the Imperium's major cities the color of the Star Towers had been different, and the sorcerous orders unique to each had identified by the same hue. She had been a Yellow Wizard, from Mahlbion. Demian had been a Green.

There. Of course it would be that one. The tower was different than the rest, smaller. The tapering, luminous swordpoint that topped each of the other Star Towers soaring around it had been sheared off, destroyed in a long-forgotten sorcerous duel. Now the remnants of its uppermost walls were simply ragged shards of green glass. A platform had been built at the highest point where the walls still held, open to the air. This had been the dueling ground for the swordsingers of Kashkana, in the glory days of the Kalyuni Imperium.

Demian was there, spinning across the platform, his sword a flashing blur. He was not dressed how she had come to think of him, in the somber garb of the kith'ketan – rather, he wore traditional swordsinger attire, loose blue pants cinched by a golden belt, a red vest open to reveal his muscled chest. He gleamed with sweat. His opponent was clad similarly, and moved with the same effortless grace. Their swords were simply too fast for Alyanna to follow, flickering like lightning as they spun together and came apart again and again.

"Demian!" she cried, alighting on the platform.

The swordsinger paused, breathing heavily, and turned to her. For a brief moment confusion passed across his face, and then it was gone.

"Ah. I am dreaming." He sheathed his sword in his golden sash.

His opponent faded, and then blew away in tatters of gray mist. Before he vanished completely Alyanna glimpsed his face.

"Your brother."

Demian's eyes narrowed. "Yes. I dream about him often. He was the only swordsman I knew better than myself. I never bested him. My magic was of course the greater, but his bladeskills were unparalleled."

"And still you contest with him, a thousand years after his death."

Demian rested his hand on his sword's ornate golden hilt. "No one can escape their past, Weaver. Particularly us."

Alyanna turned slowly, staring at the glittering crown of Star Towers rising up around them. "They were glorious, weren't they?"

Demian said nothing.

"Have you ever visited them?"

He shook his head curtly.

"I have. Once. Perhaps six hundred years ago. I traveled to the edge of the Broken Sea, and I dispatched my sending into the depths. Deeper and deeper I pushed, the blackness so total it was like I was lost in some fathomless cavern. But I remembered the way."

He was listening intently now.

"Then I saw them, glimmering in the distance, tiny points of light. It was this city, actually. They glow, you know, these towers – some vestige of sorcery I suppose. And there are things down there, attracted to this luminescence. Sea-creatures I have no name for, great schools of blind fish, lacking eyes yet somehow, for some reason, they are drawn to the lights. And there are other things. I saw, wrapped around one of these towers, a great sea wyrm large enough that it could crush a ship in its coils. It slept, savoring the light and the faint warmth in the cold darkness. I've often wondered since then what it dreamed of."

"Now that you can dreamsend you could find out."

Alyanna shook her head sharply. "No. I can only dreamsend to humans, and even then they must be someone I am familiar with."

"You know me that well, Weaver?"

"I do, Demian. Even in your new guise as a kith'ketan. And from you I can know others."

Understanding filled his face. "Ah. That is why you have come. You wish me to make the introductions we spoke of."

"I do."

The swordsinger sighed. "They are not like us, Weaver. Not like any of us. Whatever you propose in return for their aid, they will refuse it if it does not fit their . . . pattern."

Alyanna squinted into the bright sun. "They are mortal. There is one thing I promise you that they desire."

His eyes widened. "You cannot . . . you cannot promise that, Weaver. It took nine true Talents before, and it still nearly consumed us. And we would need another cataclysm."

She flung out her arms. "Look where we stand, Demian. In the detritus of the past, in the world we destroyed. In your dreams! Do you question what I can do? We *must* perform the ceremony again. The sand in our hourglasses has nearly run out."

He gripped her arm. "Hear me, Weaver. If you lie to them to gain their aid, it will be your end. They will come after you. And even with all your guile, all your sorcery, you could not escape the vengeance of the kith'ketan. I lived among them for five hundred years. They can call upon powers you do not understand."

Alyanna pulled away from him. "And I command powers they cannot comprehend." She willed herself into the air, coming to hover above the swordsinger. "I am not lying, Demian. The sorcery I crafted a thousand years ago, it was rough-hewn, simple, a fumbling attempt to recreate what the Warlock King had almost achieved. I have had a very, very long time to refine the magic. Now it is far more elegant, more powerful. I believe only three true Talents will be needed for the ceremony."

He drew back a pace, his expression thoughtful. "Three true Talents . . . you, myself, and the Bard?"

Alyanna shook her head fiercely. "My cunning may be legendary, but even I could not fool the Bard a second time."

"Then you mean to use this child. I wondered if you had special plans for him."

"Now you know his importance. With his help we can halt our aging once more. How goes the journey?"

Demian shrugged. "We are a week out from Menekar, about to enter the Bones. At our pace, we will reach Herath in a month."

"And what of the Pure?"

"Tediously righteous. He does not care for me or what I am."

Alyanna chuckled. "And rightfully so. But his help is necessary. There will be at least thirty sorcerers in Saltstone, and the queen must be a true Talent. You will need Ama's gift to seize the boy."

"Just pray we do not kill each other before we reach Dymoria."

"If there's one thing I've learned in all my years, Demian, it's never to rely on prayer."

"In that, Weaver, we are in agreement. But there *are* powers beyond men. Something infuses the Pure with their poisonous light. The kith'ketan's abilities likewise derive from an entity beyond our ken. Are you sure you wish to grant immortality to the daymo? He would make a powerful ally, to be sure, but if he turned on you as Gengris and that Visani fop, Querimanica, did after the first ceremony . . ."

"I told you, Demian, that I have refined the magics. Now what I give, I can also take away."

That surprised him. "You could withdraw the gift? Then they would be beholden to you forever."

Alyanna smiled sweetly. "Exactly. We must gather together the most powerful in Araen, and infuse them with an endlessness that we can snatch away at any time . . . we will create a cabal of immortals, kings and emperors and archons, and us ruling over them like gods."

Something in Demian's face almost looked disappointed. "I thought better of you, Weaver. I had hoped you'd transcended such trivial things as lusting after dominion."

Alyanna sighed. "Truly, Demian, I am not so arrogant. I do not need peasants to throw themselves in the dirt as I pass. I do not wish to deal with the petty banalities of ruling. I do not want to be an empress! But, my old friend, I am tired of skulking in the shadows of the world, hiding from those who would destroy me if they knew what I was, what I had done. I want to feel secure, and having the rulers of the world beholden to me forevermore is the perfect way to assure my own survival."

He was quiet for a long moment, studying her without expression. Finally he shook his head. "You are mad, Weaver. But it was your madness that granted me the last thousand years. I will help you, as you knew I would. I will bring you before the daymo of the kith'ketan."

Alyanna was surprised at the relief she felt. Had there been any doubt, truly, that Demian would aid her? He had always been her steadfast ally. Friend, even? She held out her hand, and he reached up to take it. "Good. Now I want you to close your eyes, and imagine the daymo. Paint in your mind the most complete picture you can of the old man. The cadence of his voice. The tremor in his hands. His smell. Do you have it?"

"I do."

In her mind's eye an image was forming, pulled from Demian's thoughts. "And now it is mine," she said excitedly. "Keep holding onto my hand. I will try and bring you along with me into his dreams."

"What if he is not sleeping?"

"Then we will try another . . . wait. I have it, I think. Prepare yourself, Demian. We go."

Together they rose smoothly into the air. They passed quickly out of this pale reflection of lost Kashkana, the towers blurring around them. Then they were over the farmland again, while ahead of them, in the distance, a mountain like a fang swelled larger. She could sense a presence within, waiting.

Alyanna glanced down. Far below, a familiar girl in tattered, threadbare clothes watched them pass.

"You've returned."

The voice was raspy, a snake's belly sliding over rock. It reverberated in the chamber, seeming to come from everywhere and nowhere.

That is, if this was indeed a chamber. The blackness was total, all encompassing. She could see nothing, not even the faintest outline of what surrounded her.

"I have," Demian said, and Alyanna was surprised at the relief she felt knowing that he stood beside her.

"And you have brought your . . . old friend you spoke of before."

"In truth, she brought me."

The faint slither of cloth shifting. "Did she? You must have led her here, at least. Though this is not where we dwelled together for so long. You have intruded upon my dreaming mind, Undying One."

"Yes. She has a proposition for you, and we did not have the time to travel in person to your mountain."

Alyanna heard movement, a faint scraping. She raised her hand, preparing to summon forth wizardlight, but Demian caught her wrist. How had he seen her do that in the darkness?

"A proposition." The voice was closer now, but off to her side, as if the presence had somehow circled around her.

She shivered, clammy air brushing her neck. Was that the daymo's breath? If so, what kind of a man was he?

"We only ask that you bring it before your master," Demian said. "I believe that it will fit his pattern."

"Are you so sure?"

"No. But I have descended into the darkness and stood before him. I have bargained with what coils in the shadows, and returned into the light. I believe there is no other living man who can claim the same."

A long silence. Alyanna half-thought the daymo had abandoned them, but then he spoke again.

"What do you propose?"

Alyanna mastered her fear and spoke into the blackness, making certain that there was no quiver in her voice. "A death, for life eternal."

Another pause. "What use do we have for life, sorceress?"

"Do you not wish to live forever, to serve your master through years without end?"

"You would make me an Undying One?" The disembodied voice had a strange inflection now, almost as if tinged by wry surprise.

"Yes."

A dry chuckle. "This I do not want."

What man did not yearn for eternal life? "Very well," Alyanna said, tempted to flood the chamber with light, even if it upset Demian. She did not enjoy being kept at a disadvantage. "But there is something you desire. What is it?"

Again, silence. Alyanna suddenly realized that the daymo was not using these lulls to gain some advantage; rather, he was conversing with someone else. Someone, or something.

"Bring us one like you. A youth, unformed, but with the same depth of power."

"A child with Talent?"

"Yes."

Alyanna heard a sharp, indrawn breath from Demian. Did the daymo somehow know about the child that had nearly destroyed the genthyaki? The very child Demian had been sent to claim?

"I can give you this."

"It would please us. Who do you wish to receive our master's dark kiss?"

Alyanna did not hesitate. "Cein d'Kara. The queen of Dymoria."

25: KEILAN

KEILAN WAS COLD.

He stood with Nel and Vhelan inside what resembled a large stone tomb, its outer facade carved with florid but fading designs that evoked the changing seasons, in one of the many small orchards within the grounds of the Visani royal palace. A pair of guardsmen had brought them here from their chambers and now stood outside, refusing to set foot within the ancient structure. In the center of the chamber where they waited, instead of a bier or burial mound, a dark hole had been cut into the floor. There seemed to be an almost other-worldly chill seeping from the darkness below, and he shivered.

"What exactly are we looking for, boss?"

"Knowledge, my trusted knife."

Nel crouched beside Keilan, peering into the black. "And what do they have here that you can't find in the library of the Scholia? Or the Reliquary? I'm sure Garmond would help you, if you asked."

Vhelan sighed. "The Barrow of Vis is perhaps the oldest library in the world. It predates even the founding of the Reliquary in Ver Anath and Menekar's Baskilium. Just the opportunity to venture into its fabled depths is reason enough."

Nel snorted. "So in other words, it's your damn sense of curiosity yet again. I was hoping you'd have learned a lesson in Uthmala, but I suppose I know you well enough to realize that *that* will never happen."

Vhelan clucked his tongue at her. "Nel, Nel, Nel. This isn't some haunted ruin that has been abandoned for a thousand years."

"No, it's a haunted ruin that foolish people go into regularly, some of whom don't come back out. Didn't you hear the librarian talking about the ghost that inhabits this place?"

Vhelan waved away her words. "A ghost. Hardly – more like a friendly spirit."

"Friendly spirit," Nel repeated sarcastically. "Well, I don't want to hear 'even I'm wrong once in a summer snow' from you later."

"I promise nothing," said Vhelan, winking at Keilan. "Now, where is that librarian? He said the seventh bell, and it must be approaching the eighth."

"Maybe the ghost got him."

"He's coming," said Keilan, relieved to hear the sound of hurrying footsteps.

A fat man dressed in the same simple brown robes as the librarian they had met at dinner the night before burst through the doorway, his face flushed. He flashed them a broad smile, even as he struggled to catch his breath. "Well met . . . friends. I am . . . Brother Challindris, senior librarian. Brother Pelimanus cannot be here . . . unfortunately. He has been called away by the Lady Astrallia. Her childbirth goes poorly, and he is known as one of the finest chirurgeons in . . . Vis. Oh, by the Silver Lady." The librarian mopped his brow with a long sleeve. "I came here as quick as I could, yet I am still late. My apologies."

Vhelan waved away his words. "Nevermind, Brother Challindris. We greatly appreciate your company today."

The librarian smoothed his robes. "It is highly irregular," he admitted, "allowing guests into the Barrow. But I suppose times change. Shall we go down?"

Keilan glanced from the librarian to the gaping black hole cut into the floor. "Shouldn't . . . shouldn't we light some torches?"

The librarian blanched. "Gods! No, lad, we would never bring fire into the Barrow! Thousands of books and scrolls, all piled together in close confines . . . why, if a stray spark should ignite a blaze . . ." He shuddered, unable to finish the thought.

"Then how will we light our way?" Nel asked.

"Wizardlight," the librarian answered matter-of-factly.

Vhelan shrugged a hand free of his own long sleeves and summoned a small glowing sphere. "Of course I can help, Brother Challindris. But I think my knife's question is: what do you do when a sorcerer is not here?"

The librarian furrowed his brow, and then his eyes widened. "Ah, by the Silver Lady! I assumed you knew." With his finger he sketched a shimmering circle in the air, and when he had finished the light coruscating along the edges of the disc seeped down to fill the center, until a ball of wizardlight hovered in front of him as well.

Nel and Vhelan watched in open-mouthed surprise.

"Yes, well, let's be off," the librarian said, moving past them to start on the ancient stone steps. The glowing sphere preceded him, sending the shadows skittering deeper down the stairwell.

Vhelan hurried to follow, his robes flapping. "Wait! Brother Challindris! You are a sorcerer?"

"Of course," the librarian said over his shoulder as he descended. "We all are. I have to admit I'm surprised – the queen knew about us before she came. I assumed she had told her magisters."

"She did not," Vhelan replied, sounding slightly perturbed. "So as you must imagine, this is a great shock to me. How did you keep this secret from the Pure all these years?"

Nel and Keilan shared a quick glance and then fell in behind Vhelan. The steps were cut into the side of the wall, spiraling down around a shaft of blackness so intense it seemed to drink the wizardlight. Keilan tried not to imagine how deep it went, and what would happen if he lost his footing on the crumbling stone steps.

"With great care," the librarian called back to Vhelan. "That's why the prince has thrown his support behind Dymoria, you know. He believes it is time for the wizards of Vis to come out into the light again, and that will only be possible in the new world envisioned by your queen."

"But the Cleansing . . . I knew there was an ancient sorcerous order in Vis before the cataclysms – it raised the great iron walls, of course – but how did it survive when the armies of Menekar spread out over the lands hunting wizards?"

The librarian chuckled. "You are standing in the very reason, my friend. Yes, the armies of Menekar camped outside our walls a thousand years ago. They knew of our ancient order, and they demanded we give up to them all those we sheltered with the gift, even though we had taken no part in the cataclysms that had wracked the old world. Despite the power of the Pure and their mighty siege weapons, they likely could not have breached our iron walls, but such fanatics would have continued their siege until we had all been reduced to eating each other. And the king in Vis and his advisors knew this. So with a heavy heart they were poised to order the sorcerers of Vis to give themselves up, which would have spelled the end of a proud tradition that stretched back for nearly two thousand years."

"But they did not."

The fat librarian shook his head emphatically at Vhelan's words. "Before the king could issue the decree, the sorcerers of our order offered to sacrifice themselves to save the people of the city. They drank poison, and their bodies were hung from the walls for the paladins to see."

"Yet some survived."

"Yes, some did. The leader of our order hid a few of the most promising apprentices deep within the Barrow. He commanded them to stay until the armies of Menekar had long departed."

"The Pure must have scoured the city."

"Oh, they did. The paladins insisted on searching every cranny in the city for hidden sorcerers. They even descended into the Barrow. But somehow the ancient spirit of the library kept the apprentices hidden deep down in the darkest recesses. There was talk from the Pure of burning the library, in case it contained any sorcerous tracts, but by some great good fortune the general in charge of Menekar's armies was a learned man, and he did not want to see one of the world's great stores of knowledge destroyed. So the wizards of Vis survived, unbeknownst to all save the high nobility of this city."

"We must share our sorceries," Vhelan said excitedly, "I am sure both our orders have much to teach each other."

"Certainly, certainly," the librarian said, stepping off the final stair into a small antechamber. "And here we are, the Barrow." Keilan could hear the pride in his voice.

They passed through a wide arched entrance, into a vast chamber filled with row upon row of stone bookshelves that vanished beyond the farthest edges of the wizardlight. Keilan walked forward, as if in a trance, brushing his fingers along the spines of a collection of tomes bound in cracked red leather. He pulled one of the books out, savoring the heft of it, whispering the title to himself.

"The Flora and Fauna of the Sunset Lands, Volume III."

Brother Challindris grinned. "A fascinating study conducted by one of the first seekers to cross the Derravin. He writes of turtles as large as aurochs, and vines that can strangle a man who tries to pass through them." The librarian reached out to affectionately stroke the binding of one of the volumes still on the shelf. "I can see you truly appreciate books."

Keilan slid the tome back into its place. "This . . . this is what I've dreamed of. To be in a place such as this."

"Then welcome, my boy."

Vhelan's wizardlight had drifted deeper between the rows, but the boundaries of the chamber had not yet resolved from the darkness. "How do you find anything in here?"

Brother Challindris turned to him. "This section of the library is well-catalogued. Any book that has come into our possession in the past three hundred years or so is here, and if you give me a title or author I could almost certainly pull it from the shelves within a quarter-turning of a glass."

"And beyond that? What about older texts?"

The librarian smoothed his robes. "Ah, there are members of my order who are familiar with certain sections of the Barrow. Brother

Tellimanchus is an expert in the chamber that houses most of our Min-Ceruthan writings. I myself have spent much of my adult life translating and ordering the collected philosophies of the pre-Warlock King ethicists of old Menekar. Those are located quite a bit deeper than where we stand now."

Vhelan eyes widened. "You mean there are chambers other than this?"

"Oh my, yes. There are seven passages leading off from just this room. And each empties into another large chamber, and so on and so forth. Generally they slope down, so as you continue you go deeper and deeper. The age of the manuscripts increase – on this level it is all books, most bound with modern processes. But two levels below us the texts are much more rudimentary, and many are falling apart. By the fourth level it is nearly all scrolls, many so aged they crumble at the slightest touch – some of my brothers spend their lives treating the brittle paper and papyrus with solutions we've developed to help preserve them. And there's even deeper levels, the original Barrow itself. Not many of us venture that far. There are tablets in writing we cannot decipher, piled within niches cut out of the walls. And the floor is strewn with bones mounded about huge stone caskets that we believe contain the remains of the first kings of Vis, laid to rest over five thousand years ago. The presence is strongest in that place, and there is always the sense of being watched."

Nel shivered. "I feel like I'm being watched right now. Why don't you remove all these books and put them above ground, away from whatever thing haunts this place?"

The librarian shook his head emphatically. "No, no, no. The presence in these halls is as much a part of our order as the Barrow itself. It protected us from the Pure a thousand years ago, and it often . . . assists us in finding books."

"How does it do that?" Vhelan asked, and Keilan could hear the interest in his voice.

Brother Challindris shrugged. "It simply seems to know what we are looking for, even if oftentimes we do not have a clear sense of the same. That is why the Prince thinks you may be able to find answers down here – certainly, on your own, if you searched for a year you would come up with nothing. But perhaps the presence will lead you to the answers you seek. It has happened many times before."

"And did the queen find what she was looking for down here?"

The librarian swallowed hard at Vhelan's question. "Ah. That was . . . interesting. Sometimes the presence helps, and sometimes it does not. Why, I could not tell you. And if the queen found what she was looking for I do not know. None of us were allowed to accompany her. But when we came later, after she had ascended again . . . you could feel the agitation in the air. It made the skin prickle and the hair on your arms stand up. And the chamber where the tracts from the days of the Kalyuni Imperium are stored was in complete disarray. Scrolls and books had been torn from the shelves and tossed about, as if a great wind had swept through the hall. It was almost like . . . almost like there had been a contest of will between the queen and the spirit. I cannot hazard a guess as to who triumphed. I would not have thought that anyone could bend the spirit of the Barrow to their desires . . . but I have never met anyone like the queen before."

Nel smirked. "She certainly wouldn't have taken a refusal well, even from a ghost. I wish I could have seen what happened down here that day."

The librarian cleared his throat. "Yes, well, hopefully your presence here won't cause anywhere near the same disruption."

Vhelan clapped his hands together loudly, the sound echoing in the vast hall. "Excellent. How do we begin?"

"I would suggest we separate. I will go with young Keilan here, and you and your . . . bodyguard can search elsewhere. In what age do you think the answers to your questions might lie?"

Vhelan rubbed his chin. "Seeker Garmond claimed to have seen references to creatures like attacked us from around the same time as the cataclysms that consumed the old sorcerous empires of the world. We could begin then."

"Very well. If you go that way," the librarian gestured between two long rows of shelves, "you'll come to a passage that leads to where we've stored most of the Menekarian writing from that era. Some of it is a bit archaic, but you should be able to understand most of what's there. It's divided by subject, so I would hunt around for the section devoted to the natural world, strange beasts and what-not."

"And where will you go with the boy?" Nel asked. Keilan saw that she was unconsciously stroking one of her tunic's long sleeves, where he knew one of her two favorite daggers was hidden, strapped to her forearm. The Barrow clearly made her uneasy.

The librarian furrowed his brow. "Not much of Min-Ceruth's writing survived the ice, but we do have a few hundred of the bones and shells upon which they laid down their wisdom. I cannot claim to be an expert, but I do have a passing familiarity with the ancient runes of the north – the language of old Vis used similar symbols. Now, we have a far more extensive collection of Kalyuni books and scrolls – the sorcerers of the Star Towers competed to see who could produce the most scholarly works, we think – but I'm afraid we would have to ask Brother Yeb to come down and translate for us, as he and his two apprentices are the only members of our order well-versed enough in the language of the Mosaic Cities."

"The boy can read it."

Brother Challindris whirled on Keilan. "Truly? You understand High Kalyuni?"

Keilan felt his face flush, and he ducked his head. "Yes, well enough I suppose. My mother taught me."

"Humph. A fledgling sorcerer with great natural gifts who reads the most obscure and difficult – yet also the most useful — of all the old wizardly languages. If you decide you do not like the Scholia, please consider returning to Vis and joining my hallowed order. Just imagine the joy of a life spent immersed in the knowledge contained within these halls . . ."

Vhelan coughed loudly. "Once Keilan meets the queen and sees what we've established in Dymoria he'll never want to leave. It is a place where we can work together openly to awaken our powers, rather than hiding underground like burrowing voles –"

"Burrowing voles?"

"He means it in the politest way possible," Nel said, pulling Vhelan in the direction of the Menekarian archives.

Brother Challindris harrumphed again and smoothed his robes, a mannerism that Keilan had already seen several times when the librarian appeared agitated.

As the wizardlight of the Dymorian magister and his knife melted into the Barrow's far reaches Keilan turned towards the Visani wizard, who was still staring off into the distance.

"So where should we start?"

"In the great sorcerous empires of old, my dear boy, as I said. Min-Ceruth, and then the Mosaic Cities."

Brother Challindris took the lead, and together they passed through the huge chamber, the shelves soaring like cliff-faces around them. Keilan guessed that they must be at least twice the height of a man, and he was about to ask the librarian how they reached the highest tomes when he spied a rickety wooden ladder that had been left leaning against one of the shelves. The sheer number of books was intoxicating – Keilan caught only glimpses as Challindris hurried him through the stacks, but every shelf appeared to be bursting with the accumulated knowledge of the world: dusty grimoires bound in leather, slim folios of travel writing, weighty ledgers that claimed to contain the complete genealogies of the Visani noble houses, and even sheaves of wooden plates that had been held together with string or catgut.

Finally, they reached the far wall and entered a low passage that sloped downwards. After a few twists and turns they passed into another chamber filled with shelves, and this was repeated several times, until at last they entered a large room quite unlike the others. Instead of row upon row of shelves there were many what looked to be stone troughs, radiating like spokes out from some kind of squat white stool set in the chamber's center. Brother Challindris paused beside one of these channels and gestured for Keilan to look inside.

What he saw surprised him. Laid out in neat rows were cracked and yellowing bones covered in tiny, squirming black runes.

"The saga bones of Min-Ceruth," Brother Challindris whispered reverentially. "In the holdfasts they did not write on vellum or parchment – instead, they inked bones and other animal parts with everything necessary for the functioning of a great civilization: the legends of their heroes, the records of compacts between merchants, lists of possible transgressions and the punishments for each, and so on and so forth."

"What kind of bones are they?"

"From all different animals. Aurochs, wolves, elk. Most of the heroic tales are inscribed on wraithbone, as the greatest of their old stories involve wars with those creatures. We've also identified a few bones that contain spells, though we have never managed to replicate the sorceries they contain. The magic of Min-Ceruth seems incompatible with our own."

"What are the spells written on?"

Brother Challindris smoothed his robes again. "Human, every time. We suspect they laid down their sorceries on the bones of dead wizards, though there's some disagreement about that."

Keilan knelt down to more closely inspect the saga bones. "May I hold one?"

"Yes. These bones have all been coated with a lacquer that helps preserve them."

Gingerly Keilan pulled what appeared to be a long thin femur from a stone trough. He studied the tiny jumbled runes etched in spiraling rings around the bone.

"Can you read this one?"

Brother Challindris bent closer and squinted at the crabbed writing. "Let's see, it's some sort of proclamation regarding the awarding of noble titles. It reads: '*let the mountains witness, on the seventh day of the seventh moon of the year of broken horns, the high queen did raise up to the title of jarl the following bondsmen who demonstrated great valor in the war against the eastern tribes . . .*' and then there's a long list of names and deeds."

Keilan set the bones back down carefully and stood. He began to walk beside the trough, peering intently down at the hundreds of bones set so neatly in their rows. The familiar pang of wanting to *know*, to *understand*, kindled again in his chest, so intense it was almost a physical ache. What secrets had the Min-Ceruthans possessed? Where had their great power come from? How could they have been so utterly destroyed? And why? One day, Keilan promised himself, he would learn their writing, and return here to read about this lost people in their own words. He shivered in anticipation at the thought.

No, he was shivering from something else. It almost felt like there were ants crawling on his skin, and the air suddenly seemed to shimmer around him.

"Brother Challindris," he cried, looking around in alarm, "what's happening? Is it the Barrow ghost?"

The librarian hurried to him. "No, no. I should have warned you. It's that." He pointed at the white stool from which the stone troughs radiated. There were runes etched into it as well, thousands of incredibly dense layers of lines.

"What is it?" Keilan whispered, scratching at the prickle creeping up his arms.

"Dragonbone," Brother Challindris replied softly. "A single vertebrae torn from the back of a great beast. In every holdfast the ruling queen or king sat on one as a throne – most people would feel nothing strange standing before them, but to the gifted such as us the very air seems to warp and weft. Dragons are creatures of great power, and it lingers in their bones."

Keilan backed away from the throne, the feeling of crawling wrongness gradually receding. "I wouldn't want to have to sit on that every day," he said with a shudder.

"And yet the queens of Min-Ceruth were always sorcerers. Perhaps over time the feeling grows more familiar."

Keilan gazed around the chamber, with its dozens of long stone troughs, suddenly daunted by the task set before them. "How can we find anything here?"

Brother Challindris shrugged. "We must rely on the spirit to guide us. If we sense nothing, I suggest we move on to the Kalyuni archives. Yes?"

Keilan paused for a moment, hoping to feel a pull towards something in this room, but now that he was outside the radius of the dragonbone throne he felt nothing strange. "All right."

They passed through more twisting corridors and rooms filled with shelves. In these chambers, mounded pyramids of scrolls were piled on the stone slabs instead of proper books, reminding Keilan of the Kalyuni scrolls they had discovered underneath Uthmala, and he briefly wondered what secrets would be discovered when those could be more thoroughly studied in Herath.

They were definitely moving deeper: the air, already chilly, was growing even colder, and the musty smell of earth and ancient parchment thickened, until he had to fight back the urge to sneeze.

At last they arrived at the Kalyuni archives, and at once Keilan noticed that there was something different about this chamber.

"As you can see," Brother Challindris said, ushering him inside, "we haven't managed to re-organize everything since the queen's visit. She truly did leave it in utter disarray."

The librarian spoke the truth: where in most rooms a sense of order pervaded, here chaos prevailed. Books and scrolls were jumbled together on the shelves, as if they had been scooped from the floor and dumped haphazardly wherever space could be found. There were even a few stray pieces of parchment strewn about the floor, evidently ripped from the books during whatever struggle occurred here between the queen and the spirit of this place. Keilan gingerly stepped over them as he approached the closest shelf.

Brother Challindris made a disappointed clucking noise with his tongue as he surveyed the mess. "That woman . . . her visit was certainly interesting, but I don't believe many within my order want her to return too soon."

Keilan carefully sifted through a mound of ancient tomes. "What was she like? Magister Vhelan talks about her like she's almost a living god. Nel doesn't feel the same, but she speaks respectfully of her."

Keilan didn't turn from his search, but he could be almost sure the librarian was again smoothing out his robes.

"She was beautiful. And intelligent. She had this way of speaking to you . . . she would stare into your eyes so deeply it seemed the rest of the world just faded away, and she could strip away any pretenses you tried to hide behind. I only spoke to her a few times – but once, for example, I slipped in a small falsehood, some simple white lie about why she couldn't visit the Barrow at night, and she seemed to just *know* that I was lying to her. It was disconcerting. Especially from one so young – she couldn't be much older than Magister Vhelan, and yet she just seemed to radiate power and confidence."

Keilan felt a slight breeze stir his shirt as the librarian finished talking. "Is there a passage to the surface near here?" he asked, glancing around the room. "I feel a wind."

He heard the librarian suck in his breath. "Ah! My boy, we are no longer alone."

Keilan froze. It did feel like there was something else now in the room, hovering just out of sight. Coldness crawled up his spine as the sense of being watched deepened.

"What should I do?" Keilan whispered, afraid to even turn his head slightly.

"Just relax. If the spirit wishes to help us, it will."

Keilan concentrated on his heartbeat, trying to will himself calm. He felt a trickle of cold sweat trace a line down his back.

The breeze came again, playing with the hem of his tunic, and there was a slight tug, as if ethereal fingers were pulling him away from the shelf he stood beside.

"It feels like it wants me to move."

"Let it guide you!" Brother Challindris hissed back excitedly. "There is something it wants you to see!"

Keilan stepped hesitatingly in the direction he thought the spirit was leading him. The tugging came again, more insistent, as if frustrated by his slowness, and he quickened his pace, passing three more rows until the feeling suddenly ceased and he was left staring at a shelf cluttered with ancient books. One caught his eye, and he felt a sudden, overwhelming certainty that it was this slim black volume that it wanted him to take. Just as he picked up the book another on a lower shelf seemed to shift of its own accord, and he also pulled it free, sensing that it also held some importance.

As abruptly as it had come the presence departed. Brother Challindris hurried closer, straining to see the books the ghost of the Barrow had bequeathed upon Keilan.

"What are they?" he asked, his voice brimming with almost boyish excitement.

Keilan studied the title of the second book he'd found, struggling to make sense of the flowery script. "I believe this book is named *Searching For* . . . no, no, I'm wrong . . . *Hunting the Hidden Ones*."

"That sounds exactly like what you're looking for! The hidden ones must be the creatures that can assume the shape of men! And the other one?"

The thin black book had nothing written on its cover, so Keilan gingerly flipped through its brittle yellow pages. He noticed that there were many incomprehensible diagrams and formulas set within the text. Finally he found a page near the beginning that contained but a single phrase in large black lettering. *"The Dream of the Warlock King,"* he said slowly.

"Some study of the old sorcerer kings of Menekar? I wonder why the spirit felt you should have that?"

Keilan shrugged. Then he noticed a name in a small elegant hand at the bottom of the title page, and he glanced again at the cover of the other book.

"Oh, interesting. I believe the same author wrote both these books. Perhaps that's the connection."

"And what's the name?"

"Alyanna ne Verell."

26: JAN

THE CORMORANT WAS a lively inn and tavern, particularly in the evenings when the day's work on the docks was done and the boats that fished the bay returned to port. Big, broad-shouldered laborers who earned their wages unloading cargo from trading vessels would arrive just as twilight was fading into night, their tunics darkened by sweat, and were followed soon after by the men and women who crewed the crab-boats and trawlers. Sprinkled among these regular patrons was always a shifting assortment of sailors from the visiting merchant ships: most were Dymorians themselves, or from the Gilded Cities just down the coast, Lyr or Seri or Ver Anath, but there were sometimes a few from farther and more exotic lands. Several of the ships had crewmen who hailed from the Eversummer Islands, tall and dusky sailors dressed in shawls of shimmering feathers. There were also hairless men from the Whispering Isles, veiled Keshian merchants, and on one occasion a small group of Shan from the great junk moored in the harbor had visited the tavern, their glistening black hair bound into top-knots. They had watched the noisy revelry without expression, smoking their twisting pipes and picking with slim metal sticks at the spiny, long-legged crabs set before them.

Serving girls would circulate around the large eating room during the supping hours, ladling out fish stew or pouring fresh mugs of grog or ale, evading with practiced grace the hands that tried to pinch and grab them. And there were always a few tables playing cards or tzalik, or enjoying the squat metal contraptions that dispensed dreamsmoke by means of serpentine tubes.

It was generally a merry and friendly atmosphere, but Jan understood why the Cormorant's owner, Fendrin, had wanted a minstrel here, as arguments and fights were far less likely to break out if much of the crowd's attention was trained on the raised stage in the center of the common room.

For the most part he played tavern favorites like *One-Shoe Suli* and *Faye the Long-Haired Maid*, fast-paced songs that caught the listeners up in their skirling melodies and carried them along like skiffs in a swift-running river. There was also a skilled piper who had been the sole entertainer before Jan had arrived, and they often performed together in racing harmonies that left the crowd pounding the tables for more. The remembered joy of playing to a large and boisterous crowd, the embers of which had first been stirred in the Demon's Mouth weeks ago on the Wending Way, quickly was fanned into a full blaze. For a few days he allowed himself to set aside the task that had brought him to Herath and enjoy the simple but intoxicating pleasure of being a bard again.

While performing, he sometimes caught glimpses of the red-haired woman from the docks, Selene, sitting along the far wall at crowded tables full of young folk. While the others around her laughed and carried on their conversations, she always watched Jan carefully, her head slightly tilted to one side and the hint of a wry smile playing at the corners of her mouth. On several occasions he had tried to speak with her after he had finished his set, but each time when he had managed to get off the stage and push through the heaving crowds she had vanished.

There were other interesting visitors to the Cormorant, as well. When he had first sensed their presence in the tavern the surprise had caused him to stumble on the strings, which drew a few curious glances from the crowd – he had quickly earned a reputation as a near-flawless player. While working to recover from the misstep he had scanned the room, searching. He found them quick enough, a man with a forked black beard, and two young women, one with long straight hair the color of straw, the other more heavyset, her broad cheerful face framed by tight auburn curls.

All of them were gifted.

Carefully he tucked away every stray thread of his power, making sure that none of these sorcerers could accidentally notice what he truly was, and watched them closely as he continued playing. The man was nodding his head in time to the music and tapping the beat out on the table, while the two ladies were whispering quietly to each other as they watched Jan perform.

When he had finished the song he slipped from the stage to a scattering of applause and looked around for Fendrin. He found him leaning against a wooden post surveying the busy room.

"Good playing," the tavern owner rumbled as Jan approached. Fendrin was an imposing figure, a giant of a man who, like his nephew, had once been in the city guard, though in the years since retiring he had gradually softened and gone to seed.

Jan nodded to show his thanks. "I'll finish up with a few more once I get some ale in me. It's thirsty work up there tonight."

"Aye, it's hot. Summer's last gasp, I hope."

A serving girl materialized beside Jan with a foaming mug, and he accepted it gratefully. "Ah, that's good," he sighed, after taking a deep draught.

For a few long moments they were silent, watching the swirl of people. Finally, Jan cleared his throat and gestured with his mug. "Say, who are those three over there? I haven't seen robes like that before. Scribes? Clerks?"

Fendrin shifted, the post he leaned against creaking alarmingly. "Them? They're from the Scholia. Green means they're apprentices, I think, not full magisters yet – we've had them in a few times before. The fellow there appreciates a good tune; when we had another bard come through here a few months back he came near every night. Must've just heard about you."

"The Scholia?"

The tavern keeper glanced at him in surprise. "You don't know it? Hmm, I thought they were talking about it all over Araen. It's a new academy founded by Queen Cein," Fendrin knuckled his brow in deep respect when he spoke her name, "dedicated to churning out learned men and women like that big place down in Ver Anath. The magisters they produce have pretty much taken over the running of the city, and they're a good deal fairer than the old leeches who used to govern around here and shake me down for bribes. So I like them, and give a good discount on their drinks."

"A prudent man curries favor with the magistrates," Jan said, quoting some tract on governance he'd read a long time ago – probably well before Fendrin's great-great-grandfather was a squalling infant – then he drained his mug and placed it on the tray of a passing serving girl. "Ah, I feel the music bubbling up again. I'll do my best to keep those apprentices coming back."

Jan returned to the stage, settling back onto his stool. There were a few suggestions shouted at him, most of them bawdy, but he smiled and waved them away. "A new one for you," he said loudly over the din, "though in truth it's very old."

With a brief glance to make sure he had the attention of the sorcerers, he began to play one of the ballads of the old north, a haunting tale of a spurned lover's terrible revenge. He sang in the lost language of Nes Vaneth, the dialect of Min-Ceruth that he had grown up speaking, and by the time the last note faded away the tavern had fallen almost silent. Whether they had enjoyed the song or were simply bewildered by its strangeness he could not be sure, but he suspected probably a little of both.

Across the room he caught the eye of Selene, and she smiled; she was seated beside a handsome young man wearing a rich doublet of yellow silk slashed with red. He leaned close to her and whispered something into her ear, and she laughed, covering her mouth. To Jan's surprise he felt a flicker of jealousy. How was that possible, when he had spoken to her only briefly?

Ah, he had such a weakness for strong and clever women. Leaving his lute leaning against the stool to show that he'd return soon, Jan hopped down again from the stage and began threading his way between the tables and knots of standing patrons, trying his best to keep Selene in sight. She smiled when she noticed him approaching and moved a bit closer to the man beside her, who glanced at her in surprise. After a slight hesitation he slipped his arm around her shoulders; she winked at Jan and wriggled into the embrace.

So that's how it's going to play, Jan thought, feeling pity for the clueless fop at her side.

He was almost to her table and just opening his mouth to say something when he felt a tap on his shoulder. He turned. It was the apprentice, the man with the forked black beard. The Scholia sorcerer smiled broadly and knuckled a respectful greeting.

"Master bard, excuse me please."

Jan cast a quick glance behind him; Selene now wore an amused expression, her eyebrows raised in mock surprise.

"Of course, young scholar," Jan said, turning back to the apprentice.

"Yes, ah, my name is Malichai d'Kalas. I had the great good fortune of hearing you sing tonight. Wonderful! Particularly that last piece – tell me, was it from the old north? Min-Ceruth, perhaps?"

Jan bowed slightly. "It was, learned master d'Kalas."

Malichai pounded one hand with the other, grinning. "I knew it! I told my companions I thought it was and they scoffed at me. Truly remarkable. Master bard . . ."

"Jan."

"Master Jan. I must know – where did you learn those words? Can you speak the language? I had been told there was no one alive who knows the tongue of Min-Ceruth."

Jan ran a hand through his hair, trying to figure out a way to disentangle himself quickly from the apprentice. "Just a few songs, I'm afraid. I studied in Vis for a time, and the lore masters there have preserved a handful of the old ballads of the ancient north."

"Then it is amazing how well you sing it. Such passion, such feeling. Even though I did not know what the words meant the song still stirred something in me."

"Yes, well, I'm pleased you appreciated it."

Malichai reached out and grabbed Jan's arm in a fierce grip. "Master Jan, I would like to extend an invitation to you to come perform at Saltstone tomorrow, in the queen's own dining hall. There will be many magisters from the Scholia in attendance, and I believe they would find your mastery of the old songs of Min-Ceruth as fascinating as I do. What say you? I can promise the compensation for such a performance would be rich indeed."

That took Jan back. Here he had been expecting a long, arduous journey from tavern minstrel to performing before the queen, with the slow accretion of fame bringing him from the Cormorant to a finer eating house frequented by the city's elite, to a noble's private function or perhaps a post as a house bard, and then once enough people were speaking of the new minstrel in Herath he might – if he was fortunate – receive an invitation to perform at a dinner hosted in the royal palace. A few months, at the very least. And yet here he was, only several days in Herath, and by some great stroke of luck he had already been given an opportunity to see the queen in person. It was almost like Alyanna was still pulling strings from a half a world away.

Jan bowed deep. "I would be most honored, Master d'Kalas."

Malichai clapped him hard on the shoulder. "Excellent! Present yourself tomorrow at the gates to Saltstone before the sixth bell and tell the guards I have invited you. Show them this." The apprentice passed him a small bronze medallion stamped with an image of an eagle in flight, a writhing snake in its talons. "My family crest. I will let them know you are coming. Until tomorrow, then!"

Still bemused by his sudden good fortune Jan watched Malichai shoulder his way back to his table, where the two sorceresses were waiting.

"Until tomorrow," he murmured to himself, idly stroking the medallion as he turned back to Selene's table.

She was gone.

The castellan who greeted him at the entrance to Saltstone's servant quarters did not seem impressed. He sniffed disdainfully, his gaze lingering on the new damask tunic Jan had spent much of his savings on that afternoon, his lip actually curling in disgust when he noticed his well-worn traveler's boots. Jan sighed inwardly. Of course, his shoes – he had not bought a new pair. It had been too many years since he had performed in a royal court, and he had forgotten which articles of clothing the nobility and those that attended to them always checked first to see if there was an imposter in their rarified realm.

"Good evening. The guards at the gate said I should come here and speak with you. I was invited by Master d'Kalas."

The castellan's eyes did not soften. "Yes. He told me you would come. When I heard he was going slumming down at the docks I wondered what riff-raff he would bring back this time."

Jan flourished a courtly bow. "This riff-raff is very honored to be here."

"You should be." The castellan turned sharply on his heels and began walking briskly down the corridor. Jan hurried to catch up. "Payment will be fifty silver kitari, and you may collect them from me here at the end of the night. You are the third and final performer, and you will continue playing until the dinner is finished, or the queen bids you stop. If your playing displeases her you shall receive no silver, and I will have you beaten and thrown back into the gutter from whence you came. Understood?"

"I can see the legends of this hall's kindness were not exaggerated."

The castellan did not reply, but his footsteps echoed a little louder as they passed through the maze of twisting servant's passages. These were the corridors the queen and the nobles would never see, the ways by which the servants scurried to their tasks without disturbing the high-born. Occasionally they passed men and women wearing the livery of House d'Kara, a sinuous red dragon on a white field, and every time the pace of those servants quickened noticeably when they realized it was the castellan approaching. Finally, they stopped at the entrance to a small room and the castellan gestured for him to enter.

Inside, a beautiful woman with a small golden harp waited on a bench beside an oaken door banded by iron. Nothing adorned the bare stone walls of the chamber save for a single guttering lamp.

"Wait here until a servant comes to fetch you," the castellan said, then after a final withering look whirled around and strode away.

"A pleasant fellow," Jan murmured, finding a seat on the edge of the bench.

The woman's laughter tinkled like the ringing of musical bells. "Geramin isn't so bad, really. He's strict but fair, and if you please the queen tonight the next time you're invited to the palace he'll be much kinder."

Jan unslung his lute and began tightening the strings. "You've been here before, then?"

The woman nodded slightly. "I have that honor. I've been invited up to perform at least once a month for the past year."

"You must have a great gift. My name is Jan Balensorn, of the Shattered Kingdoms."

"Rhianna ri Numil, once from Lyr."

Jan knuckled his brow. "A high name. Excuse me, my lady."

The harpist waved away his words with an exquisitely pale and long-fingered hand. "No apologies, please. I've kept my name because it puts me in better graces with the nobles here, but I left my family a long time ago. They could never understand a musician's calling."

"I wager they regret all those harp lessons they forced upon you when you were young."

Rhianna laughed again. "Almost certainly, master Jan."

The door suddenly swung open, the mournful final notes of *The-Brother's Lament* preceding a boy in Dymorian livery as he slipped quietly into the room. Behind the servant Jan glimpsed a huge chamber filled with long trestle tables, many of which were crowded with men and women wearing a riotous assortment of colors and dresses, including some in the same green robes the apprentices had worn the night before at the Cormorant.

"Lady Rhianna. The lutist is nearly finished. Please come with me."

The harpist rose and spent a moment smoothing her dress, making sure her beautiful blond curls were artfully arranged with the help of a small silver mirror.

"Luck be with you," Jan said, and she smiled.

"To you as well, master bard," she replied, then followed the serving boy through the door, which swung shut behind them.

Jan finished tuning his lute and plucked a few simple ditties to make sure everything was to his satisfaction. Then he leaned back against the stone and sighed, feeling the familiar tingling begin in his fingers as he reviewed which songs he would play tonight. A half-dozen or so fast and familiar melodies, to put the audience in a good mood and to demonstrate his skill, then something slow to show the depth of his passion. And to finish, a Min-Ceruthan ballad that should pique the interest of the scholars – hopefully it would earn him another invitation to the palace.

Jan stood and went over to the door, pressing his ear to the wood. It must have been thick, as he could just faintly hear the ethereal notes of a plucked harp. She did have a great talent, Jan decided, after listening for a few moments. There was no handle on the door, so he could not open it a crack and spy on the performance. For a brief moment he entertained the thought of magically forcing it open, but quickly discarded that idea when he remembered Alyanna's beliefs about the queen's strength. Jan was sure he could conceal simple magic from the Scholia's sorcerers, but if Cein d'Kara was a true Talent then it would be far more difficult to keep such an act secret.

He returned to the bench and closed his eyes, sifting through the fragments of his past as he waited. He did this often, hoping for some new shred of knowledge to surface that would be the pebble that started the avalanche of his memories. He remembered vividly his life as a crofter in the Kingdoms, and perhaps a decade spent wandering as a minstrel before that, but the rest still remained shrouded. He could conjure up names from long ago and match them to faces, but he had no sense of his own relationship to these people. It was almost like he had read history books rather than having actually lived through those times. If Alyanna was to be believed, he had intentionally excised himself from his own memories. Why would he do that? What was he trying to forget?

The door opened, and the liveried boy again stepped into the waiting room. "Master bard, the harpist is finished. Please come with me."

Jan stood and followed the serving boy into Saltstone's great dining hall. As he had briefly glimpsed, the lower level was filled with dozens of long trestle tables, around which sat scores of gaudily dressed nobles. They had obviously been feasting for some time, as the servants were just now clearing the platters and plates and refilling goblets of wine from large decanters. Great white banners emblazoned with the dragon of Dymoria hung from the high rafters. Jan noticed one table closest to the tier of steps that led up to the hall's second level where everyone was wearing the green, red-trimmed robes of Scholia apprentices. He searched briefly and found Malichai's smiling bearded face, nodding slightly in his direction. There was an almost palpable crackle of sorcery emanating from that table. Despite his fractured memories, Jan knew he had not sensed such a gathering of magic for many ages.

Jan paused before ascending the steps to the dais where the queen and her favorites sat facing the rest of the room. He bowed deep, trying not to stare at the assembled high lords of Dymoria. He saw, in his brief glance, those who must have been the magisters of the Scholia, seven or eight men and women wearing robes of deep, almost wine-dark red. The waves of power flowing from these sorcerers was greater still than the combined strength of the table of apprentices below. There were also a few richly-dressed nobles, their faces showing the carefully cultivated air of bored indifference that was the mark of the truly high-born. And in their midst was a Shan, Jan noticed with some surprise. He was dressed in a simple gray tunic, but around his neck a scarlet cloak was clasped with a golden dragon broach. While the others at the table fidgeted with wine glasses or gesticulated with their hands as they spoke, the Shan sat in absolute stillness, his uptilted black eyes watchful. Here was a warrior, and a dangerous one.

Then there was the queen. She sat, like the Shan, without moving. Her skin had been whitened by some cosmetic, so that she almost could have passed as a marble statue, save for the rich red curls that fell past her shoulders. Her dress was dazzling, faintly shimmering and a lighter shade than the red of the magisters seated beside her, its neckline inset with moonstones the size and shape of quail eggs. A twisting silver diadem studded with emeralds rested on her brow, matching the green of her eyes. She did not look at Jan when he glanced at her, but seemed to be staring at something past him.

Jan realized, with a shock, that he felt no sorcery flowing from her, and since she was seated between several of the magisters that absence was jarring. There could be two explanations, Jan thought as he was led by the serving boy up the steps to the far side of the dais, where a beautifully carved chair awaited him. Either she truly had no power, and there was another sorcerer lurking somewhere behind the throne, or she had mastered the difficult art of hiding her strength, even from a Talent such as Jan. And that would mean she was very powerful indeed.

His performance passed in a blur. He played well, although he had to strain his voice to be heard over the constant hum of conversation in the hall. A few of the tables closest to him began stamping their feet and singing along to the most popular songs. He imagined he saw a few wet eyes when he sang of the tragic tale of Llewyn Tir. But before he even had a chance to start singing one of his Min-Ceruthan ballads a horn sounded somewhere nearby, and instantly every table quieted, the assembled nobles turning towards the dais. Jan paused his playing as well, uncertain what was happening.

Without saying anything the queen stood, and the others at the high table rose with her. They remained standing as she turned and stepped from the dais, vanishing through an arched doorway. The

Shan followed close behind her, graceful as a hunting cat, and a moment later most of the Scholia's magisters filed out as well. When they had all departed the feast hall the horn blew again, and the nobles at their trestle tables turned back to their conversations. Jan resumed his playing, but his thoughts were elsewhere, circling the strange conundrum that was the Crimson Queen.

By the time he had finished his last song, *The Lament of the Raven Prince,* all of the tables had emptied save for the one where the Scholia apprentices sat. They clapped loudly as the last tremulous notes faded, led by Malichai, who leaped to his feet in obvious excitement.

"Remarkable!" he cried, looking for affirmation among his fellow apprentices. "The songs of lost Min-Ceruth, preserved against all hope. Please, master Jan, you must come again. I will send a summons to your quarters at the Cormorant soon, yes? We at the Scholia are holding a feast next month to mark the summer's end, and I deeply hope you can perform for us."

Jan stood and bowed. "I would be honored, Master d'Kalas."

The Scholia apprentices began to disperse, talking and laughing among themselves. As if by magic the liveried serving boy appeared again at Jan's side.

"Master bard, I will lead you out."

Jan nodded and followed the servant, but they did not return by way of the performer's door set into the side of the great hall. Rather, the boy led him through the same arched entrance the queen and her retinue had vanished into earlier. This was no servant's corridor – intricate stone carvings graced the ceilings and the frames of the doorways they passed, and great tapestries depicting dragons flying over rolling forests hung from the walls.

"Are you sure this is the way?" Jan asked as the servant led him deeper into what he was starting to suspect were the royal apartments.

"I was told to bring you here, master bard."

Could the queen or one of her sorcerers have penetrated his disguise? Impossible – Jan had learned his arts in a much more refined age, and not even the strongest of the remaining Talents in the world would be able to sense his sorcery at this moment, given the depths he had hidden it. Or could this be some sort of illicit rendezvous? It wouldn't be the first time that a noble lady had summoned Jan to her quarters after a performance. He decided he liked that possibility much better than the first.

They paused in front of a large door fashioned from beautifully aged red wood. The servant hesitated briefly, as if unsure if they should enter, then pushed hard on the door. It swung open easily despite its size, and the boy stumbled inside, nearly falling over.

He glanced back, red-faced. "Master bard, enter please."

Jan stepped carefully into the silent room, his boots sinking into a plush Keshian carpet patterned with red and white diamonds. It appeared to be some kind of audience chamber. A large, elegantly wrought throne of gleaming golden wood sat on a raised dais at the end of the long chamber, the carpet running all the way from where he stood to the base of the steps. There were windows of stained glass set high up on the walls, although with the night sky beyond them he could not tell what images they held. And the light in the room came from great candelabras placed along the path to the throne, each holding a dozen flickering candles. Shadows skittered across the numerous statues of crowned men that stood in heroic poses against the length of the walls.

"Please wait here, master bard. Someone will be with you soon."

"Who?" Jan asked, but the serving boy was already pulling the doors shut behind him.

Alone in the room, Jan wished he could summon his wizardlight or extend a tendril of sorcery to probe the chamber's shadowed recesses. But he did not. Instead he walked halfway to the throne and waited. His hand ached to stroke the fire opal set into his sword's hilt, but he had left Bright hidden back in his quarters at the inn.

The attack came without warning, precisely coordinated.

Waves of sorcerous power billowed from different points in the room, smashing into Jan and sending him staggering to one knee. Gritting his teeth and trying to focus through suddenly blurred vision he saw three robed figures step out from behind different statues, their upraised arms coruscating with blue light. The hollow echo of wizard's chanting filled the chamber, rising and falling, each thunderous peak a fresh explosion of power. With effort Jan climbed again to his feet, and the onslaught strengthened, wrapping him in coils of sorcerous energy.

They were trying to immobilize him.

He tested their strength, straining against the constricting bonds, and they gave slightly. He had their measure, and it was wanting.

But he was curious to see where this would go, so he let his struggles falter and give out. Immediately his arms and legs seized up, his muscles and bones aching at the sudden pressure. Only his head remained untouched – below his neck his body felt like it was now being held in a slowly crushing grip.

"Who are you?" Jan managed hoarsely, but the sorcerers ignored him and continued their chanting, shuffling closer.

"The question is, who are you?"

The voice came from the direction of the throne, and with some effort Jan twisted his neck to see who had spoken.

Surprise hit him like a cold wave.

Selene sat on the chair, dressed again in the frayed blue shift he had first seen her wearing at the docks, one leg draped carelessly over an upswept armrest.

"Selene?" he whispered numbly, trying to organize his suddenly scattered thoughts.

She smiled crookedly, leaning back in the throne. Something impossible hovered at the edge of his understanding. The hair, those eyes, if the whiteness was scraped away . . .

A second shock, greater than the first. "You're . . . you're the queen."

She clapped her hands together slowly three times, in mock congratulations. "Very good Jan Balensorn, once of the Shattered Kingdoms. And now that you know my secret, I believe it is time for you to give up your own."

Jan raised his eyebrows, in imitation of the last look she had given him the night before in the Cormorant. "Very well, if we are dispensing with pretenses."

He gathered his power, forming it into a tight ball of raw sorcerous strength, and then thrust it outwards against the waves of energy binding him. The three magisters were flung through the air; two tumbled hard to the stone floor and slid backward, while the third, who had been standing too close to the wall, was smashed against it hard. She cried out sharply and crumpled into a heap.

The queen's confident expression did not change, but Jan saw her grip on the throne's armrests tighten.

The two magisters who had not struck the wall scrambled to their feet and began fluttering their hands and chanting. Jan grinned tightly when he saw the fear in their faces and began readying his own counterstroke.

"Stop!" cried the queen, rising. "Jonus, Kyrin, see to Eleria. Make sure she is all right."

The two magisters shared an uncertain glance, but they stopped chanting, their forming magic dissipating.

"Now!" The queen stepped forward, fists clenched, and the cloak she had used to hide her own power suddenly fell away. She blazed like a fallen star, and the candles guttered before her shining strength.

Jan sucked in his breath, awed. She was a great Talent indeed – Alyanna was right to fear her.

The magisters hurried over to their colleague, who was moving feebly and moaning, and bent down beside the fallen sorceress.

"Your Majesty," one called out after a moment, "Eleria will be fine. A few broken bones, perhaps, and she's addled from striking her head on the stone. But there's no blood in her hair, so I think her skull is intact."

"Good," the queen said, the glow of her power dampening. She settled back into her throne, her back as straight as when Jan had seen her in the feast hall, and turned to him, her gaze flat and hard. "Tell me who you are."

"My name is Jan, as I said. But it is not Jan Balensorn. I have been known by many names, but I was born as Jan duth Verala."

"Duth Verala. I do not know this name."

"Nor should you. It is very old, from a place long vanished."

"How old." It was a command, not a question.

Jan thought briefly of lying to her, but he suspected she would somehow know if he did. "My lineage can be traced back over two thousand years. I am only half that age."

Her stony expression did not change, but there was something different now in her eyes.

"You claim to be a thousand years old?"

Jan swept into a formal bow. "I was born in Nes Vaneth, Your Majesty, only a few decades before the ice swallowed the north."

She blinked unsteadily, a tremor passing across her face. "The song you sang last night . . . it was in your own language."

"It was."

"You are Min-Ceruthan."

"I am."

For the first time she looked shaken. "Are there others like you?"

Jan hesitated. "I come on their behalf."

"For what purpose?"

"To discover more about the Crimson Queen that has in such a short time remade the world. To ascertain whether you are a true Talent."

"A Talent?"

"One who summons great sorcery instinctually, without the need of shaping it with words or gestures. The rarest kind of wizard."

"And am I?"

Jan nodded slightly. "Most certainly."

She studied him thoughtfully, her lips pursed. The moments dragged on as Jan watched her consider something carefully, and then reach a conclusion.

"Jan duth Verala, I wish to learn more about you and the past of which you speak. Will you stay awhile in my court?"

Jan allowed the sorcerous power he had been holding inside him to subside. "I will."

27: SENACUS

THEY RODE OUT of the spine of the Bones to find that autumn had arrived in the west.

Senacus and Demian had left the furnace of the plains behind them when they first climbed into the mountains, and there the treacherous paths that threaded between rocky gorges and clung to the side of sheer cliff-faces were high enough that when they awoke, frost often dusted the grass near their campsites. It was jarring, to see the peaks thrusting into the blue vault of the sky around them covered in snow, when just a few days past Senacus had been forced at times to ride without his armor, a cloth soaked in water wrapped around his head. And it was equally strange when they descended again expecting to be submerged once more in the heavy pall of late summer, and instead found brisk winds and an endless forested expanse just starting to blush with the changing of the seasons.

Entire days had passed in silence; Senacus had actually forgotten the sound of the shadowblade's voice until they parlayed with a troop of imperial soldiers guarding a narrow defile in the Spine. The legionaries had not recognized them, as they had shed their traditional garments. Both of them were now dressed in leather and mail, pretending to be just a pair of sellswords heading west to find themselves a lord in the Shattered Kingdoms, and the white armor of the Pure was carefully packed away in Senacus's saddlebags. The relic of Tethys hung around his neck, and it had been a shock for him to speak with the legionaries as a mere man, instead of as a paladin of Ama.

While they rode, Senacus studied his mysterious companion. The kith'ketan were the stuff of stories told to frighten children. Assassins who walked in shadow, the servants of a dark power who dwelled beneath a mysterious holy mountain. Many did not believe they even existed, yet here one was, eating legion hardtack and checking his mare's hooves for stones every night. A few of the legends swirling around shadowblades Senacus could already disprove: sunlight did not harm them, and animals did not shy away from their unnatural nature. However, he did feel a creeping sense of wrongness the longer they rode together, even with his powers dampened by the relic he wore. It wasn't emanating from Demian himself, he realized eventually, but from the ancient sword at his side.

They had left the spine three days past and started on the Wending Way when Senacus finally broke the silence.

"I don't like your sword."

The kith'ketan did not look at him. "It doesn't like you, either."

Senacus started to say something in response to this, but then snapped his mouth shut. How could one answer such a statement? He settled back on his horse and watched the forest, wondering how he had found himself in the company of a madman.

The shadows lengthened as they rode on, dappling the ancient road. He was just drifting off into some pleasant daydream when Demian spoke again.

"Paladin, do you remember your life before?"

Senacus glanced curiously at the shadowblade. "Before what?"

"Before they made you into what you are."

"You mean before I became Pure?"

"Yes," Demian replied, and Senacus could hear the edge in his voice. "Pure."

Senacus had never discussed such things. It was considered rude for the paladins of Ama to talk about their former lives between each other, or of what little they could recall, and the common folk were so intimidated by the holy warriors that none had ever dared to ask. But this long silence had started to weigh on him, and he had a few questions of his own for the shadowblade.

"I remember fragments. Standing in a golden field, watching a man that might have been my father thresh wheat. A newborn calf pressing its wet nose into my hand. The taste of milk freshly churned."

"You were a farmer."

Senacus shrugged. "Perhaps. The Cleansing burns away our past lives, as it burns away the taint. We are reborn in the light."

"Can you speak of the Cleansing?"

"Not . . . completely. It is pain beyond imagining, and our minds cannot stay strong during the ordeal. I remember being strapped to the altar by an old mendicant with a kindly face. He had brushed back my hair and kissed my brow and given me Ama's blessing. Then the flash of a knife. Pain. And not just from the cut, as I've been wounded similarly many times since. It was like there were lines of fire snaking out from the wound, racing through my veins, until I was burning up from the inside. Then I saw a light of such perfection that I wept, and I was enveloped by it, and the flames in my body were replaced by cool water, and when I awoke I was in a bed with clean white sheets, and I had become Pure."

"How old were you?"

"I don't know, but perhaps ten?"

"Do you ever wonder about your family? Your people?"

Senacus fingered the relic around his neck. "I have a family, and a bright father who wants for the world to be perfect again for his creations, like it was before the taint of sorcery seeped in from the Void."

Demian shifted in his saddle, turning to look at Senacus. Was that pity in his eyes?

"And what about you? How does a man enter your order? I can't imagine the initiation is any less terrifying."

Demian chuckled. "I imagine not. I never suffered through a childhood spent under the mountain, thank the gods."

Senacus blinked in confusion. "Then you are not kith'ketan?"

"Truly, I am not."

"But the High Seneschal said . . ."

Demian held up a hand to forestall him. "He believed I was. And to most the difference would be academic. I have lived under the mountain. I have bargained with what . . . persists down there, and been given certain abilities that are usually reserved only for those that bear a shadowblade."

"Which that sword is not? I thought it must be."

Demian chuckled, the ghost of a smile touching his lips. "Be careful, paladin – Malazinischel does not forgive insults easily."

Now it was Senacus's turn to grin. "That's the sword's name? Malazith . . . Malazid . . . surely a better one could be chosen. Night's Kiss – there's a good name for an assassin's sword. Or how about Blood –"

The shadowblade lunged from his horse, grabbing Senacus's shoulder and wrenching him from his saddle. Something hissed through the air above him as he fell. The shock of hitting the ground knocked the wind from the paladin, but still he managed to push Demian away, scrabbling for the knife at his belt. The shadowblade ignored him, holding tight to the reins of his horse while keeping himself crouched behind its flank.

"What –"

"Archers. I heard bows being drawn."

"But there were no –"

Demian pointed to a tree a few span behind them, just off the Way. An arrow fletched with gray feathers was stuck in it, still quivering slightly.

Senacus moved to take cover behind the other leg of the assassin's horse. "Can you see them?"

Demian peered under his horse's belly at the line of trees fringing the far side of the road. "Yes. Two archers, both with arrows nocked. Another three men with swords. One of them is coming out into the open."

Senacus risked a glance around the horse's leg. A bald man armored in a motley assortment of battered plate and leather now stood a few dozen paces away, his hand on the hilt of the greatsword strapped to his back.

"Hail travelers, and welcome to our forest!" he called out, and harsh laughter rose up behind him. "That was an impressive little tumble you took, and it leaves us all in a bit o' pig mud, as I'm sure you can see. We want that there horse you're hiding behind, but we also want to kill you. So in my great spirit of generousness," more laughter at this, "I'm gonna say you both can run on down the road, so long as ya leave your horses and your bags behind. Either that or we start shooting again, take your stuff from your corpses, an' have horsemeat for dinner. I'm not fussed, honest, however this plays."

Senacus glanced at the assassin. "Ideas?"

Demian drew his sword. The aura of menace radiating from the cracked, curving blade made the hair rise on Senacus's arms. "Yes."

He straightened and walked calmly toward the trees overhanging the road. Senacus heard the twang of bowstrings and cried out to Demian, but as the assassin passed into the shadows cast by the branches he vanished, and the arrows sliced the air where he had been.

"Bright sun," Senacus whispered, sketching the holy symbol of Ama in the air.

A cry of fear and pain from the woods, cut short. Another scream, a different voice. The bald man started back toward the forest, his sword in his hands, then hesitated.

"What sorcery –" he said hoarsely, his words dying away as Demian walked unhurriedly from the woods. In one hand he held his strange curving sword, and in the other he carried four heads by their long hair. He tossed them on the ground in front of the bandit.

The man dropped his sword, staring wide-eyed as a trickle of blood reached toward him from the closest head. He fell to his knees, clasping his hands together.

"Mercy! A shadowblade . . . gods, please, we did not know . . ."

Demian stepped closer and pressed the tip of his sword into the man's throat. A bright red point blossomed, then blood slid down his neck.

"Please, lord." The man was crying now. "We have gold, jewels, back at the ruins. Slaves to sell . . ."

"Slaves?"

The bandit seized on this. "Aye, slaves. A boy and two girls, one is very fetching. We took them from a family of pilgrims on this road, not a week ago. They're unspoiled, would bring a good price in Menekar."

"Where are the ruins you spoke of?"

"Please, lord, my life."

Demian withdrew his sword and the man rubbed his throat, smearing his hand with blood. "I will not cut you again. Now, where is your hideout?"

The bandit gestured at the woods behind him. "Back there you'll see a deer trail; follow it till you come to a stream. The ruins are south of that a little ways, near the willows."

"Thank you," Demian said, stepping away from the man and sheathing his sword. He went over to his horse and gathered up the reins.

"You are not going to kill him?" Senacus said, coming to lay his hand on the assassin's arm.

Demian led his horse off the road and tied it to a low-hanging branch. "Malazinischel has tasted him. He is already dead."

Senacus glanced back at the bandit, who had begun writhing in the dirt clutching at his bloody throat. Spidery black lines were spreading from where the sword had nicked him, creeping up his face; when they touched his eyes it was like ink had been dropped in water, darkness rising up to fill his sockets. With a final death-rattle, the man convulsed and was still, black tears streaking his face.

"By the Radiant Father," Senacus murmured, appalled.

"Nothing by his hand, I can assure you," Demian said, slinging a bag over his shoulder. "Bring back your horse and tie it next to mine. Take whatever possessions are most important to you, in case the horses are gone when we return. Let us go pay these bandits a visit."

Senacus went to fetch his mount, which had cantered down the road a ways after the attack. When he returned he unlashed the pack containing his holy armor and hefted it. "Are we really going to attack a bandit stronghold?"

Demian's dark eyes glittered. "I hate slavers."

"Truly?" Senacus said as he followed the shadowblade into the forest. "Why?"

"I was a slave once."

Senacus crouched in the forest clearing and waited. He was tempted to don his Pure armor and unwrap his sword, since the mercenary garb he now wore seemed as flimsy as paper, and the hunk of poorly-forged steel at his side had none of the exquisite balance of his white-metal blade, but in the end he did not. If any of the bandits happened to escape, then the story of a paladin and a shadowblade traveling west together would spread like wildfire across Araen, and would most certainly arrive quickly in the court of the Crimson Queen.

Senacus started as Demian stepped from the shadows. "That is unnerving," he said, shaking his head.

The assassin knelt beside him and with a stick began quickly sketching out the bandit's hideout in the soft forest loam, using pebbles to mark where he had seen men. "There are at least eight in the ruins -"

"So you didn't kill them all already?"

Demian ignored the sarcasm. "No. I thought you would want to join me."

Senacus sighed and shook his head.

The assassin tapped a series of large squares in the corner of what he had drawn. "These buildings are mostly intact, and quite possibly more bandits are inside. I did not see anyone going in or out, but I only watched for a brief while. It is the remains of a town, Myrasani most likely. The forest has reclaimed much, but some of the stone structures still stand. Here were some large casks under a tarp," he pointed to another crudely-drawn shape, "probably ale or wine, but it could be oil, so have care. There's also a long table here, and as you can see most men were clustered around it. They were playing some card game that involves having to stab quickly between the spread fingers of a hand. It looked interesting."

"Any archers?"

"None had bows with them."

Senacus sat back on his haunches. "Well, that makes it easier. Do you have a plan?"

Demian shrugged. "We have wasted enough time already. I do not want to try any elaborate ruse to lure groups of them out into the woods. I propose we walk into the camp and kill them."

"Eight men?"

"If there's another eight in the ruins we might actually have a proper fight."

Senacus stood, brushing dirt from his legs. "You don't lack for confidence."

"These are not trained soldiers, if the men we met on the road are any indication. Most likely a group of peasants driven from their land in the Shattered Kingdoms, or perhaps local Myrasani reduced to banditry because of famine."

"Yet you have no sympathy for them."

"Whatever simple farmers they once were, they no longer are. Murderers, thieves, and slavers."

"If that bandit had not mentioned that they had slaves they planned to sell in Menekar, would we be here now, or a few leagues down the road?"

Demian said nothing, and Senacus nodded. "As I thought. So in your eyes slavery – a practice condoned in the Tractate itself – is worse than murder."

The kith'ketan's flat eyes were unreadable. "It is."

"Why? Most slaves are well-cared for, fed, given clothes and a place to sleep. There are many in the world who can only dream of such things."

Demian swept his hand through the loam, obliterating the drawing he had made. Senacus took a quick step back, surprised. It was the first true emotion he had seen from the assassin.

"There are no gods, paladin. There is no afterlife, no eternal reward. You, in fact, are a slave to a creature you cannot even comprehend." Demian stabbed the stick he still held into the ground. "All that a man has in this world is his own will, the freedom to do what he desires. Taking away that is the greatest crime one can inflict upon another. Murder – it is terrible. But it is over in an instant and the dead never can truly understand what has happened to them. They are simply gone. But slavery – day after day, year after year shackled to another's whims – it is the most heinous of crimes."

Demian rose, his hand on the hilt of his sword. "Come. It is time."

The ruins were as Demian had sketched, a low shattered wall surrounding a handful of crumbling stone buildings. A large courtyard had been cleared of debris, and two great trees dragged into the center of this space and shaped into a long table. As the shadowblade had said, men were gathered around it, intent on some game. Most were dressed in ragged, frayed tunics, though a few were clad in bits and pieces of stolen armor. As they strode into the ruins Senacus saw that a number of the bandits wore dented legionary helms; they must have ambushed a small patrol or a diplomat traveling west with an imperial escort. If that was true, it was only a matter of time until the legion sent out a proper force to root them out.

The bandits were so engrossed in their game that the shadowblade and the paladin had almost reached the table by the time one of the men noticed them and cried out. Senacus glanced at Demian to see if they should attack during the confusion, but instead Demian folded his arms and waited as the outlaws fell into chaos. Cards fluttered up in the air, and piles of coins scattered as they stumbled away from the table, reaching for their swords and axes.

"Who in Garazon's black balls are you?" yelled a man wearing a plumed legion helm.

Demian offered a humorless smile. "We are the men who are going to kill you."

The bandit shared an uncertain look with his companions. "We heard that Telemach had put a bounty on our heads. You come to claim it?"

"No."

"Are there more of you out in the woods?" he asked, straining to look past them.

"No."

"Just you two?"

"Yes."

"Then either you want to die, or you're both damn fine warriors." The bandit cleared his throat and spat. "Well, just so happens we have our own damn fine warrior. Benjin."

A thin boy in a dented cuirass much too large for him stepped forward. "Yeah, boss?"

"Go wake the Skein."

The boy grinned, showing a mouthful of missing teeth. "Aye." Then he dashed away, vanishing inside one of the listing stone buildings.

The bandit leader shook his head slowly. "You two are just as brazen as the last bunch. Marchin' down the road, blowing their horns an' telling us to come out and meet imperial justice." Senacus could see the tension draining from the other outlaws, the shock of seeing him and Demian stride from the woods fading. "Well, might be a few months ago our heads would've been on pikes back at their fort. But they didn't know about the Skein." A ripple of laughter from the outlaws. "Born killer, that one. So vicious he had to leave the Frost-lands, if you can believe that. We took him in, give him plenty o' chances to slake that blood-thirst of his. Tore through that imperial patrol like he was a wolf in a chicken house, he did."

A deep, gravelly voice boomed from inside the building the bandit had entered moments before, harsh words spoken in a language Senacus did not know.

"Well, here he comes."

A giant stepped from the shadowed interior, stooping to avoid striking his head on the doorframe. Senacus steeled himself to avoid taking an instinctive step backward – the Skein was huge, two heads taller than any of the other bandits, and at least half again as broad. He looked to be armored in the full skin of a black bear, its head hanging down from his shoulder and its clawed paws laced across his stomach. Tied into his wild blond beard were three shrunken gray heads; Senacus thought they must be wraiths, though he had never actually seen those monstrous scavengers of the north. The Skein's bared arms were roped with muscle, and he held two giant battle-axes, which he clashed as he moved blinking into the light.

"Why wakes me?" he bellowed, his face flushed.

"Ah, Golgeth, these men say they have come to kill you." The bandit leader pointed at Senacus and Demian.

Still holding his battle-ax, the Skein wiped his nose with the back of his hand. "They? Only two?" He uttered a string of harsh syllables, punctuated by smashing his weapons together again and stalking toward the waiting shadowblade.

"I will slay this one," Demian said calmly to Senacus. "Keep the others from helping him."

Senacus stepped away to give the assassin room to move, then turned his body so that he could both watch the fight and make sure none of the other bandits attacked Demian from behind.

The Skein's pace quickened as he approached Demian, who drew his strange sword with a flourish. The giant lunged forward, lashing out with startling quickness, and the shadowblade leaned backward as the first ax-blade whistled a half-span from his neck, then brought his sword up to block the second. He staggered slightly under the tremendous force of the blow, and Senacus feared for a moment that the ancient blade would shatter, but it held with a rending shriek and a scattering of silver sparks. Demian leaped backward as the Skein continued surging forward, his ax-blades flashing. Several times Senacus thought the giant had actually caught Demian in one of his sweeping cuts, but each time the shadowblade managed to twist away or duck beneath blows that would have chopped a young tree in half. As Demian retreated before the onslaught, Senacus found himself holding his breath, afraid that a slight misstep on the uneven ground could doom the shadowblade.

Then something changed. Suddenly it was the Skein who was stumbling back, desperately attempting to ward off Demian's flickering blade. A line of red appeared on the giant's arm, then he reeled away as the shadowblade's sword scored his side. Demian paused his advance as the Skein tripped and fell backward, one of the axes flying from his grip. The shadowblade followed, and snorted derisively. Screaming in rage, the Skein heaved himself from the ground and leaped at Demian, his axe a silvery arc. The shadowblade nimbly sidestepped the blow and struck out with his sword and the Skein's head separated from his shoulders, spinning through the air.

Before it had even landed Demian charged the stunned bandits. Senacus joined the shadowblade, and together they easily cut down the outlaws as they cowered or turned to flee. After a few bloody moments only the young bandit who had awakened the Skein remained, Senacus's sword at his neck. He blubbered incoherently, his face deathly pale.

"Boy, do you have prisoners here? Ones you planned to sell as slaves across the spine?"

The boy swallowed, nodding.

"Go bring them out."

Still sobbing, the bandit scrambled away and entered another of the collapsing buildings. Soon he returned herding three dirty children in ripped clothes that might once have been of fine make, their hands bound together. Bruises stained their pale skin. They blinked, wide-eyed at the carnage before them; the eldest girl looked at Senacus and Demian with hope.

"Cut their bonds," Senacus said to the bandit. Demian busied himself wiping his sword clean with a piece of cloth torn from a dead man's tunic.

The boy took a knife from his belt and slashed the ropes, then dropped the blade, as if afraid by merely holding it the paladin would have an excuse to kill him. The children rubbed their wrists, still unable to stop staring at the scene laid out before them.

"You're free," Senacus said in his most comforting voice. "I'm sorry for what has happened to you and your family, but these men have been punished for their sins."

"Who are you?" the smallest child asked, a tow-haired boy with large dark eyes.

"Warriors of good who do not like bad men," Senacus said, bowing his head slightly to the boy.

"He should die too," the eldest girl suddenly interrupted, pointing at the last bandit. "He hurt me. He . . . did things to me."

"I agree," Demian said, moving toward the boy, who shrieked and shrank away.

Senacus caught his arm. "Wait. He is barely more than a child himself. Surely there is mercy for one so young."

Demian shook off his hand. "He is old enough to understand what he has done. All free men must accept the responsibility of their actions. The boy was no slave." His blade lashed out again and the bandit tumbled back, clutching at his cut neck. As he writhed on the ground, blood seeping from between his fingers, the girl stepped over him and spat in his face.

Senacus frowned, then sheathed his own sword. "Come. We will take you to the nearest town."

The girl went over to the other children and gathered them into an embrace. She spoke to Senacus from over the boy's shoulder. "These men have some money hidden here. My father was a rich man, and he was not the first they robbed."

"Then we will take it with us, and you may use it to start a new life for you and your siblings. We have no need for riches."

The girl pursed her lips, watching them. "Thank you. I prayed to Ama to be saved, and he sent you. You are truly blessed."

Senacus smiled. "You are more right than you know, child."

Demian snorted and kicked at the Skein's severed head.

28: KEILAN

"**WRITING, CONTENDS THE** *great sage Jeniphus, is the most arrogant of all the solitary arts. This statement resonated with me, for some strange reason, when I first encountered it as a young student while exploring the textual borders of the saffron crèche. Certainly the old master dispensed far more enigmatic platitudes – this one, by contrast, required only a moment's reflection to draw forth its meaning: a book is the pinnacle of arrogance for it demands to be heard, but it cannot listen. It desires to communicate, yet it refuses conversation. I thought that was the extent of its profundity.*

"Now, as I write this volume, a book that will either be kept under lock and key forever, never to be read by any except the greatest of our Orders, or simply destroyed, I have another interpretation. A slight reformulation, perhaps, but as I sit here laboring to recount what has happened, how the world has changed, my new understanding of the old master's words has affected me deeply. The arrogance of writing comes not from the finished creation, but from the very act itself. What hubris is required for a single mind to believe that its thoughts should populate the world? What unbridled arrogance is it to disperse ideas like the petals of a dandelion in the wind, allowing them to float free, to germinate in the minds of others like an invasive weed?

"Accordingly, I do not consider my writing of this book to be an act of arrogance, as only a handful of people, if any, will ever read it. And I accept this. It is the way it must be. For if the truth was known among the great, giftless masses – the truth that I am about to lay before you – the very fabric of our society might tear under the immense strain.

"Could you imagine how quickly terror would spread if the common people knew that until recently they were feed animals for another, more powerful species? And that this species could mimic our own form with such uncanny precision that even friends and husbands and mothers could be fooled?

"Have you ever stopped outside a pen and stared into the great, wet eyes of a cow and wondered if the poor beast had any slight premonition as to what fate lay in store for it? No simple animal could, of course, and for many thousands of years – our race's entire history, even? – humans were no better. We were livestock in our pens, oblivious.

"But then we woke up.

"This book is a telling of the war against the hidden ones, the genthyaki, a war that was conducted in the shadows by the united sorcerers of the Star Towers of the Mosaic Cities and the holdfasts of Min-Ceruth, a war that has resulted in our liberation after millennia of secret enslavement.

"This book may never be read, but it must nevertheless be written. It is better, certainly, if all memory of these creatures is expunged. Yet something drives my hand along. Perhaps, someday, you will know what that is."

Bleary-eyed, Keilan forced himself to look away from the cracked and yellowing pages. The flow of the writing was almost hypnotic, burrowing into his brain as he worked to parse meaning from what he had read. Many times he had found the words washing over him without truly understanding what he had just finished – that was the true challenge of High Kalyuni, and he suspected the reason why there were only a few scholars who could still read the language. Learning the fifty-eight letter alphabet was easy enough, but unlike Menekarian, which had seemingly been designed for clarity, passages in High Kalyuni often resembled an intricate puzzle, full of word games and linguistical feints that all had to be understood for the final meaning to become apparent.

It was like the very act of writing was a competition, and the sorcerers of the Star Towers demonstrated their intelligence by fashioning nearly impenetrable tracts. The author of this book, Alyanna ne Verell, wrote with a level of complexity far beyond the two books from which he had learned to read High Kalyuni. He could sense the vast intelligence looming behind the words, and found it daunting – he wished his mother were here to help him pick apart Alyanna's tangled knots of meaning. Trying to understand what she had written on his own was exhausting, and left his head tingling.

"Keilan! How goes it, lad? Uncover any ancient secrets yet?"

Garmond and Vhelan also looked like their heads were tingling, but for a different reason. The magister and the seeker were huddled like a pair of thieves at Garmond's desk, ostensibly searching through a few of the old books Vhelan had found in the Barrow . . . but the near-empty bottle of scholar's milk between them suggested that they had instead spent the evening pursuing a less productive venture.

"Did you hear me, lad? Uncover any ancient –*'hic'* – secrets?"

Keilan shook his head at Vhelan to forestall hearing the question a third time. He pushed himself away from the small table where he sat, and as he did this a thought struck him. *This is where I taught Xin to read. This is the very place where Xin last saw one of his brothers alive.* Keilan felt a pang of sorrow in his chest as he considered that.

No wonder the Fist warrior had chosen to ride by himself during the day as they traveled, and laid out his bedroll far away from the campfire when they halted for the night.

He can't escape the ghosts of his brothers. They call to him still.

"I'm tired. I'm going to find my bed."

Vhelan lurched from his chair, steadying himself with a hand on the desk. Garmond made a clucking sound as the magister knocked over the bottle, but righted it before the silty dregs at the bottom could manage a sluggish escape.

"Wait, Keilan. I'll go with you."

The seeker made a shooing motion with his hand. "Fine, then, run away young magister. I suppose we have an answer to our little wager, and it is the Reliquary that wins, as I knew it would."

Vhelan snatched his hand from the desk, affronted, and stood there swaying. "Nonsense. You've just developed a tolerance for that devil water. Next time we'll see who can polish off more bottles of firewine."

Garmond winked slyly at Keilan. "I await the chance."

Vhelan snorted and turned away from the scholar, staggering slightly. Keilan rushed forward and grabbed the magister's arm.

"Thank you, lad," Vhelan slurred, patting Keilan's hand. "You're a fine friend. And let me tell you, you're going to be a great sorcerer some day. I'm sure of it. The queen, she's been waiting for one like you. Someone to challenge her. Someone to delve into the true mysteries with . . . I wish we could, the other magisters. But we don't have the gift like she does. Like you do. Aye, keep hold of me lad and get me to my bedroll."

"Of course." Keilan gently guided Vhelan through the flap that now hung in the entrance to the seeker's wagon. The dark fabric, embroidered with the white candle of the Reliquary, was the replacement for the door that had been ripped from its hinges by the wraith during the ambush. Keilan couldn't hold back a shudder at the memory of that terrible night.

They had circled their wagons in a shallow bowl clear of trees, just off the Way, a place that from the charred patches of grass had served as a waystop for caravans before. The shadowy bulk of hills rose up around their camp, rippling into the blanket of stars spread across the sky. It had been a night very similar to this when the last attack had come, but Keilan was not worried now. An entire cohort of heavily armored Visani royal cavalry was spread out in the woods, keeping watch with the few Dymorian rangers who had survived the wraiths. Among them was Captain d'Taran – Keilan had felt a rush of relief when he had met him again before they had departed the Poet's City. The ranger had been bedridden for the weeks they were in Vis, recovering from a wound in his side, but he had been well enough to ride by the time they had bid farewell to Prince Lys.

Keilan led Vhelan down the wagon's steps and toward the camp's central fire. There were a few knots of people sitting together and talking quietly, but most of the travelers accompanying them to Herath – the rangers, the few merchants who still lived, and a delegation from Vis – had already retired, their bedrolls forming concentric circles radiating out from the fire. He was surprised to see that Nel's sleeping spot was empty, despite the lateness of the hour; usually she was snoring away by now, an arm's length from Vhelan's bedroll.

"I can't see Nel," Keilan said as they approached.

Vhelan stopped for a moment, blinking. He furrowed his brow, as if trying to work through some intractable problem. Then a slow smile spread across his face.

"Ah. I don't think we should worry about it, lad."

"Do you know where she is?"

Vhelan cleared his throat. "Perhaps. Tell me lad, can you see the Fist's bedroll?"

Keilan scanned the camp site, looking for Xin's distinctive red rucksack. "Yes, I see it."

"Tell me please, my eyes are bad: is the Fist there?"

"No . . ."

Vhelan patted his arm again. "Then don't worry about Nel, lad. I think she may be trying to convince our Fist friend that he has a reason to live."

"Oh."

They arrived where they'd laid out their bedrolls earlier, and the magister flopped down, not even bothering to disrobe or work his way under the blankets. His breathing softened almost immediately, and he murmured something unintelligible.

Keilan watched him for a moment, lost in his own thoughts. The idea of Nel and Xin together . . . it did make him happy, certainly, as they were both his good friends. But even still there was a niggling sliver of envy when he thought about it, about the way Nel had looked at Xin when they had gone together to visit him in his room back in Vis.

Of course she had every reason to care for the First warrior in that way: Xin was handsome, and confident, and a skilled warrior. He had shown patience and kindness when they had trained together in the evenings before the ambush, and his dry humor had left them with aching sides many times. But still it hurt, thinking of Nel's impish smile and sparkling eyes, and the effortless grace with which she did everything, from riding a horse to spinning her daggers.

Keilan sighed and slipped out of his tunic. He kept his spidersilk shirt on – he almost never took it off now, except for his infrequent baths when their camp was pitched near a stream wide and deep enough for swimming. It was so light that he hardly noticed its weight, and the spidersilk was cool and smooth against his skin.

He wriggled inside the bedroll's seam and pulled the cloth up until he was virtually cocooned within. Nel. He had to stop thinking of her that way. She was older, and far more worldly than him. To her he must be just a fisherman's son, a simple peasant who for some unknown reason had been given a great gift by the gods. He squeezed his eyes shut, willing himself to sleep. But it didn't come easily, and after a little while he opened them again.

His breath caught in his throat. Nel and Xin were emerging together from the trees. They were just two shapes, but nevertheless he could tell it was them: the distinctive broad shoulders of the Fist warrior loomed beside the knife's lithe shadow. They weren't touching, but it looked to Keilan like she was leaning in toward him.

They separated, Xin moving to where he had made camp. Keilan squeezed his eyes shut, feigning sleep as Nel approached. He heard her light footsteps coming closer, then some rustling, and finally a hissing sound as she dragged her bedroll away through the grass.

He cracked his eyes, watching Nel as she pulled her bedroll over to beside Xin and laid it out. Then the Fist warrior and the magister's knife sat facing each other, crosslegged, talking softly until a brief peal of laughter burst from Nel. Keilan noticed Xin's hand was on her leg.

He was happy for them. Truly, he was. He closed his eyes again and wished for sleep.

29: JAN

JAN'S FIRST AUDIENCE with the queen had not gone quite as expected, and he found that he was eagerly anticipating the second. Two days passed while he waited patiently for the summons to come.

It was the castellan who finally came to fetch him in his new suite of rooms in the palace, knocking deferentially and then ducking his head when Jan opened the door. Jan couldn't hold back a grin when he saw the head servant's embarrassed flush.

"My lord," the castellan said, "the queen wishes for you to attend her."

"Me?" Jan said in mock surprise, "I'm honored."

The castellan cleared his throat and shuffled his feet. "Yes, my lord. Will you please follow me?"

"Of course. But wait." Hanging in his chamber was a large gilt mirror, and Jan spent a moment making sure he looked presentable. He wore a doublet of pale blue silk embroidered with twining flowers and a pair of what he assumed were fashionable black breeches, one of the many outfits that fit him well enough that he had found hanging in his bedchamber's large armoire. He leaned in closer to the glass, checking to see that his face was clean and nothing was in his teeth. Sandy-blonde hair, lightly tousled. Dark blue eyes the color of the northern sky. If it weren't for the crow's feet around those eyes, he thought he could still pass for not having yet seen thirty winters.

"All right. Lead on."

Jan had assumed that the castellan would bring him to an audience chamber, either the small one in the royal apartments where he had last seen the queen, or perhaps to whatever more formal chamber she used when she received large delegations. Instead, the servant led him outside and onto the grounds of a sprawling garden – not nearly so grand or elaborate as the imperial pleasure gardens of Menekar, but still impressive.

The emphasis here seemed not to be on wild profusions of dazzling blossoms, or showcasing exotic creatures culled from far away lands, but rather on carefully-cultivated beds of flowers, many of which Jan had in fact noticed while traveling through the hills outside of Herath. The garden was almost geometric in its design, and he guessed that it was a reflection of the queen's ordered, practical mind. There were also elaborate stone fountains scattered about, lions and pachyderms and leaping fish carved from granite or pink marble.

He found the queen sitting on the edge of a pool beside one of these fountains. It was shaped into a rearing dragon with wings outstretched, but instead of fire spewing from the beast's roaring mouth a stream of water splashed into the basin. The queen was staring at something in the pool, a slight smile on her lips. Beside her the Shan warrior from the feast hall stood motionless with his hand on the hilt of his sword, watching Jan approach without expression.

When they had come within a dozen paces the castellan dropped to one knee and bent his head, and after a moment's hesitation Jan did the same.

"Your Highness," the castellan said, his voice sounding slightly strained, as if he did not introduce visitors to the queen very often, "may I present Jan Balensorn, of the Shattered Kingdoms."

The queen did not look up from the pool, but her smile deepened. "Of the Shattered Kingdoms. It is a necessary fiction, I suppose – such panic the truth would create." She sighed. "Geramin, my thanks. Now leave us. And Jan, you may rise and approach."

With hurried grace the castellan stood, bowed again deeply, and then backed away. Jan rose as well and moved a few steps towards where she sat; the queen glanced at him and frowned, then beckoned him closer. He came to stand beside the pool, only an arm's length from her. This close he could see that her skin was flawless, without any blemish or mark. She was dressed in a simple blue shift that echoed what she had worn that first day on the docks, though this one was obviously of much finer make, and she wore no jewelry save for the twisting silver diadem set with emeralds he had seen before in the feast hall.

"Look," she said, gesturing into the pool.

The water was not as clear as he would have supposed: clumps of algae floated on a surface pocked by lilies, and the flower's tangled roots trailed down into the murky depths. The queen was pointing at a rock with strangely colored striations – no, not a rock, a large turtle shell patterned with whorls. Its black head poked from the water, unblinking yellow eyes fixed on the queen. Jan tried to sense if she had it under a compulsion, but felt nothing.

"A handsome beast," Jan remarked, unsure of what exactly he should say.

The queen laughed, high and free. "Handsome? I'm not so sure. This fellow is Belgariod, named by my great-grandfather after the river spirit of the Serpent. He's lived in this fountain for almost a hundred years, by my reckoning." The queen glanced at Jan, humor glinting in her eyes. "A fledgling, you must think."

"Just a babe," Jan replied, shrugging.

The queen studied him for a long moment, her face suddenly serious. "If a century-old turtle is a babe to you, what must I be? A mayfly on a summer's day?"

"No, your Highness."

"You say you are a sorcerer like me. We both share this Talent you spoke of. Does that mean that I could discover a way to arrest the ravages of time, as you have?"

She did not fence with words, Jan thought, shifting uncomfortably. Straight to the point. "Your Highness, I must admit my ignorance. I have a . . . condition, and there are gaping holes in my memories. I cannot remember the details of how I achieved immortality – only that it involved a great act of sorcery, and the combined strength of many wizards like us."

The queen considered that, chewing her lip. "I see. Assuming that I believe your rather unlikely tale, you did say that there are others like us?" She motioned for him to sit, and Jan joined her on the lip of the basin.

"I know of only one other. It was she who sent me to you, so I might ascertain what you are."

"You must tell me more about this sorceress. But later. First, this condition you claim to have – how did it come about?"

Jan shrugged helplessly. "I wish I knew, Your Highness. I thought for decades that I was just a simple crofter, but then something happened that awakened part of me. And though I know now who I was and many details of the world, I can remember only a few random fragments from my past. Sometimes I feel strongly that I have been somewhere before, or tasted the same food long ago, but the sense is fleeting, and carries with it no real knowledge."

"Is it possible that this other sorceress made you forget?"

"She claimed I did it to myself."

The queen snorted. "As would I, if I had done it. Come here." She patted the stone beside her, and Jan slid closer. "Let's see if I can help."

She reached out and lightly touched Jan's temple, furrowing her brow in concentration. "I don't notice anything strange," she murmured softly as a warmth spread from her fingertips, making Jan feel lightheaded.

Suddenly she breathed in sharply. "Wait! There is something, like a dark stone rolled across a cave's mouth. I would wager that behind it are the answers to your past."

Jan tried to temper his excitement. "Can you remove it?"

The queen's mouth thinned as she concentrated. "It feels like it gives a bit when I push, but not nearly enough. No, I think I would need some kind of lever." She withdrew her hand, and the tingling sensation in his head gradually faded. "I will devote myself to this problem. I very much want your memories returned to you, Jan."

"As do I, Your Highness."

The queen suddenly stood, smoothing her dress. "Good. Now walk with me – oh, but first, I haven't introduced you to Kwan Lo-Ren." The Shan standing beside them bowed stiffly from the waist. "Kwan is the captain of my Scarlet Guard, the most elite warriors of Dymoria. He was trained at Red Fang mountain."

Jan blinked in surprise. "Red Fang mountain? Is he still a member of their order? I didn't think they swore themselves to anyone, even the Phoenix Throne of the Empire of Swords and Flowers."

"No, they do not," the Shan said haltingly. "I am not of the mountain anymore. In Shan I would be called a Tainted Sword, one who has left Red Fang in disgrace."

"Oh," Jan said, meeting Kwan's glittering black eyes. "Then I'm sorry for whatever happened."

The Shan's expression remained composed, his voice even. "Do not be."

Jan expected some further elaboration, but Kwan said nothing more. Finally, Jan turned back to the queen, who had watched this brief exchange with some interest.

"When I accepted Kwan into my service the one condition for his loyalty was that I would never command him to reveal why he had left the mountain. I've kept my part of the bargain, but I must admit to being a bit curious."

The Shan warrior bowed again. "I am sorry."

She waved away his words. "It is fine. How dull life would be without mysteries." She glanced at Jan mischievously and winked. "Now, master Bard from lost Min-Ceruth, I have something to show you. Come with me."

They left the garden and entered the palace again, the queen leading them down twisting passages of dark stone lit by gilded wall-sconces. Behind a few of the doors they passed Jan could sense strange sorcerous reverberations, and his skin prickled.

"My private quarters," the queen said. "No doubt you can feel some of the artifacts I've gathered. My magisters have scoured the land looking for the magical detritus of the old world – books, weapons, jewelry, whatever has survived. It is a depressingly small amount, really. But there are a few wonders."

They paused before a large door inscribed with the twisting dragon of Dymoria. The queen pressed her palm against it and closed her eyes and a moment later the door swung smoothly open, revealing a vast, darkened chamber. Another filament of sorcery leapt from the queen and a great glass sphere suspended from the ceiling suddenly brightened, bathing the room in a golden light.

"This is my homage to your people."

Dazed, Jan stepped forward, his gaze traveling over the relics of the past. Of *his* past. There was a fragment of the Winding Stair, silvery steps lustrous in the globe's light. Beside it lay a chunk of dark stone roughly carved into the shape of a dancing girl – the fierce sorcery bound up in this statue made his eyes water. Silver urns overflowing with rune-carved saga bones lined the walls. His eyes darted from wonder to wonder: there was a device that resembled a ballista, there a contraption made of glass tubes containing several glimmering blue sparks, there an ancient two-handed sword with a black blade encased within a block of crystal. And in the center of all these ancient artifacts was one of the holdfast thrones, a seat carved from the bone of a great dragon. Magic swirled about the chair like silt stirred up from the bottom of a muddy stream.

Cein approached the throne and gently lowered herself onto it. The sorcery seemed to settle around her, giving her an aura of radiant power. She watched Jan carefully. "What do you think?"

"I think . . ." he began, his mouth suddenly dry, "I think you look like a queen of my people."

"Like the queen of Nes Vaneth?"

Jan shook his head. "No," he said softly, speaking as if from a great distance, "she had golden hair, and eyes like the ocean."

"So you remember her?" Cein leaned forward, interested.

"I remember . . . something." Jan sighed in frustration. "I am sorry, Your Highness."

The queen set her elbows on the throne's cracked armrests, steepling her fingers in front of her mouth. "Such an interesting pair we make. You, a relic of a glorious, vanished past, and I a harbinger of wonders that may come again."

"Then you believe that our world's twilight is ending? That sorcery will return to these lands in strength?"

The queen nodded. "I am certain of it. Just a few months past I sensed another like us, a young boy with great sorcerous ability. He must also be one of the Talents you spoke of."

Jan blinked in surprise. "Truly? And where is he now?"

"I dispatched a magister to fetch him – I am expecting their return any day now. I received a bird from Theris that the boy had been found, and that they were returning along the Wending Way."

Jan was silent for a moment, considering this. A single Talent appearing after so many centuries could be considered chance . . . but two? No – Alyanna had been right, the pulse of sorcery was indeed quickening once again. But why? What had changed in the world?

Slowly his gaze traveled over all the marvels the queen had gathered. "Your Highness, forgive my impertinence, but how did you learn magic? Who was your master?"

The queen studied him thoughtfully. "I had no master."

Jan remembered the waves of power he'd felt in the queen's audience chamber, tendrils of sorcery expertly woven together and lashed to her will. Such mastery required years of careful study at the feet of other sorcerers. No matter how strong her Talent, the queen could not have spun her sorcery out of whole cloth!

"I find that incredible, Your Highness. Apprentices might develop their own small, unique cantrip, or put some twist on a larger spell, but the great sorceries were far too complex to learn independently, and required the instruction of a master."

The queen shrugged. "And where did the master's master's master get the ideas for his spells? Someone, somewhere developed the sorceries of the old world. After all, the magic is always there, formless, inside of us. We simply must be creative in how we use this infinitely malleable tool."

Jan was stunned. She spoke as if it were as simple a matter as embroidering a blanket or painting a picture, but he knew that what she was describing was almost beyond belief. Cein d'Kara was creating her own unique school of magic, distinct from what had existed in the Star Towers or the holdfasts.

"And there are guides. I have found several spell scrolls and saga bones inscribed with ancient magics, and many other ancient books give descriptions of lost sorceries. With some effort I've managed to craft my own approximations."

It beggared belief. Jan had assumed that there had been a coven of sorcerers that had persisted here in Dymoria, or perhaps that even there was another mysterious immortal aiding the queen. Instead he had found that she was laying the foundation for her own unique strain of sorcery.

He shook his head in wonder. "I am impressed, Your Highness. Truly you are a wonder of this age." Something occurred to him. "Is that how you sensed my approach? I had been trying to hide my Talent when I was traveling to this city, yet still you noticed me. Whatever ward of yours I tripped was not a spell I've encountered before."

The queen smiled. "Yes, it was one of my own devising. You had wrapped up your sorcery quite well – when you were performing in the feast hall I could feel nothing. But I had spent some time weaving spells into the roads running to Herath, so that I would sense even the most cleverly disguised sorcerer approaching."

"And then what? You threw on some rags and hurried to meet me at the docks?"

The queen leaned back in the throne, chuckling. "I wanted to take your measure, it's true. I'd never felt a power like yours before, and that's why I spent some time watching you at the inn."

Pieces slid together in Jan's mind. "And the invitation to the palace – you arranged that."

She nodded slightly, still smiling. "I'd seen enough. You were not here to assassinate me, and I wanted us to meet."

"Magister d'Kalas should be a mummer," Jan said, feeling slightly annoyed at having been fooled.

"If it's any consolation, master bard, he was truly impressed with your playing."

"Hmmm. And Selene of the Tides?"

"An old fiction. My father brought me here when I was very young, only ten years old. Before that I had lived in a small village on the coast of the Sunset Lands, spending my days exploring the fields and forests. The idea that I could not wander where I wished when I arrived in Herath was infuriating. Very soon the walls of Saltstone became like a prison for me. So I used to slip from the castle and descend into the city, exploring the alleys and markets and eating houses. Selene of the Tides was my disguise – I learned more about my future subjects on those excursions than a hundred history lessons in my father's study."

"There's a song in that story, Your Highness."

The queen laughed again. "Perhaps. I hope by the end of my reign that they'll be plenty of songs to be sung."

30: KEILAN

KEILAN SMELLED the sea.

It slithered on the wind between the red-leafed trees pressing along the road, a faint briny sharpness that summoned forth memories of seaweed drying on jagged rocks, and endless breakers rolling toward a desolate shore.

The sense of home came upon him so powerfully, so suddenly, that Keilan almost thought that the forest around them would dwindle away as they crested a ridge, and he would gaze down on the mud and thatch huts of his village. He knew, of course, that they were instead nearing the Derravin Ocean, which was hundreds of leagues from the Broken Sea. But something clutched at his chest, a deep longing to see his father and Sella and the others in his village who had shown him kindness. Mam Ru, gnarled and ancient as the Speaker's Rock, who had slipped him freshly-boiled cockles and told him stories as he'd sucked their salty flesh straight from the shells. And Big Benj, who had taught him how to tie a bowknot that never loosened and had gathered him into an embrace in the days after his mother's death, something even his father had never done, and let him sob into his broad chest.

He had last seen them only a few months ago, but it seemed like a lifetime had passed. Would he choose to return to his village, if that was possible? Could he, after all that he had seen and done?

"We're almost to Herath," Vhelan said, smiling. The magister had donned wine-dark robes that looked of finer make than his other garments.

"I thought we must be. I can smell the sea."

Vhelan breathed in deep. "You're a fisherman's son, so I'm sure you can. Me, I can smell sorcery on the breeze."

Sorcery.

Keilan shivered at the word. The idea that he would be taught to become a sorcerer had seemed so remote during their travels. Now they were on the verge of completing their long journey, already well within the borders of Dymoria, and somewhere through these woods and over these hills waited the Crimson Queen on her dragon throne. Months ago she had sensed him, and sent for him, and now he had nearly arrived. What would he find?

"Cold, lad?" Vhelan asked, eyeing him carefully.

"No, it's just . . . I mean, my whole life I've been told that sorcerers . . ."

". . . are evil," Vhelan finished, "and that they brought about the cataclysms that destroyed the old world."

Keilan glanced at Vhelan uncertainly, shame flushing his cheeks. Hadn't the magister shown him only kindness? How could he still doubt the motives of him or his queen?

Vhelan nodded slowly. "And, of course,there is your mother."

Keilan blinked in surprise. "My mother?"

"She was murdered under the suspicion of being a sorceress, by men you'd loved and trusted. They killed her for the crime that you are poised to willingly commit. Perhaps you feel some guilt about this?"

Keilan swallowed and looked away from the magister, his eyes stinging. "Perhaps," he said softly.

"You have a choice, you know."

"What?"

"No one can force you to nurture your gift, not even the queen. She would not want anyone to come fully into their power if they truly believed that the sorcery within them was evil. It would be all too easy, then, for the sorcerer to abdicate responsibility for their actions. To blame sorcery itself for the crimes committed."

"I would not do that," Keilan said, his voice barely above a whisper.

"I know, lad. Or I think I do. Do you remember what Captain d'Taran said in the ruins of Uthmala?"

Keilan shook his head.

"He said that just as some men are good and some are bad, so the same is true of sorcery. But he was wrong. Sorcery is a tool, nothing more. Like a sword, it can be used to take from others, or to protect your family."

"And I have a choice? If I fear what I might do with sorcery, then your queen would understand if I decided not to develop this . . . gift?"

"She would be disappointed, I'm sure, as we all would be. But she would understand. *That* is the difference between the sorcerers of Dymoria and the fanatics of Menekar. The Pure who took you from your village, who saved us from the spiders, he had no choice. He was Cleansed and filled with that poisonous light against his will. *That* is evil. Do you know what the paladins of Ama truly are? Or perhaps *were* would be a better word."

"No."

"They were gifted, like you and me. Children that were born touched by sorcery. The ceremony they suffer through does not simply cut away their magic . . . it inverts it. Where we may draw sorcery from the Void and fashion it to serve us, they leach it from the world and throw it back into the beyond." Vhelan shuddered. "They are abominations."

"Why does their god hate magic so?"

Vhelan shrugged. "Who can know the whims of gods? Or perhaps Ama does not even exist. After all, the Pure's powers come from the corruption of their own gift for sorcery, not a divine wellspring. But whether Ama is real or not, I do know that there are things out there, in the Void. The queen has glimpsed them, and she has spoken of them to us magisters. Are they demons? Gods? I suppose it depends at which temple you pray. But I will tell you something that I strongly believe, Keilan. They did not make this world. They do not sit in judgment of us. Our souls will not be consigned to the abyss because we are gifted, so do not let that frighten you, or dissuade you from pursuing sorcery."

Keilan considered this as they rode on, and the magister left him to his thoughts. After a while the trees did thin, but it was not a village like the one he had left far behind that could be glimpsed in the distance.

A great city spread below them, its tangled streets hemmed by buildings of wood and brick. There was nothing orderly about the way it sprawled beside the bay, as if it had been allowed to grow without any guidance or plan, like a garden left untended. The city's northern flank swept up a steep hill, upon which perched a great fortress of dark stone. Keilan knew, without being told, that the Crimson Queen waited inside. He could almost feel her, and gooseflesh prickled his arms. But that *must* be his imagination.

They descended a hillside cleared of trees, the road twisting around great jagged chunks of white rock that emerged from the long grass like shards of broken bone. As their horses began to pick their way down the steep slope horns sounded from the distant walls, and the few rangers who had survived the horrors beneath Uthmala and the wraith ambush let out a ragged cheer. Captain d'Taran unslung his own silver horn and returned an answer, just as a pair of horsemen passed out of the city's closest gate and spurred their mounts toward them.

When the riders arrived at the vanguard of their host they clasped forearms with Captain d'Taran and inclined their heads toward Vhelan. Keilan was close enough that he heard one of the Dymorian guardsman questioning d'Taran about their Visani escort, but d'Taran shook his head and brusquely told the young warrior that such news was for the queen's ears first.

They entered Herath accompanied by another pealing of horns. Of the two large cities Keilan had already seen, Theris and Vis, the

Dymorian port more resembled the Shattered Kingdom's largest city. Vis had been encircled by walls of gleaming black iron, and its buildings were soaring edifices carved of basalt and limestone. Its people had seemed to move slower, and with more gravitas, as if they were players upon a stage or minstrels before a crowd. Herath, like Theris, was a riot of activity, the streets of churned mud filled with hawkers and performers and bleating animals. Vividly dressed men and women turned the streets into a swirl of colors as they hurried on their daily business, and many stopped to knuckle their brows and dip their heads when they caught sight of Vhelan in his dark robes riding among the warriors of Dymoria and Vis.

As they progressed through the city their small host gathered a retinue of ragged children, who ran alongside and begged the warriors astride their horses to draw their swords or throw them treasure. Vhelan winked at Keilan, then tossed out a handful of small coins. The crowd of urchins scattered, laughing.

"Their lives are much better under the queen," Vhelan said, leaning towards Keilan. "Before she ascended to the throne, they were treated like vermin by the city guard. The queen constructed several orphanages and poor houses to shelter them, and gives enough silver to keep hot food in their kitchens. Several members of the city watch have been flogged for treating the waifs harshly."

Keilan felt some of his apprehension about meeting the queen subside. How could a ruler who cared so much for the least among her subjects frighten him?

The dirt beneath their horse's hooves gave way to cracked tiles, and the houses along the street grew in size and grandeur. Many boasted elaborate porticos and balconies. The urchins trailing their company gradually fell away, and Keilan suspected that despite the queen's largesse they were still not welcome here, in the richer districts of the city.

The great fortress swelled larger and larger, until it filled the sky with battlements and soaring turrets. Keilan's mouth had gone dry, and Vhelan must have caught him staring, because he nudged his horse closer.

"Saltstone. Herath has been sacked by the Skein a dozen times over the centuries, but never have the barbarians overrun these walls. Your new home."

My home. The thought made him dizzy.

They entered the fortress though a massive gate, then dismounted in a courtyard that could have easily contained his entire village, with room to spare. Vhelan motioned for Keilan to follow him through a set of double doors twice the height of a man and carved with the twisting dragon of Dymoria. Captain d'Taran and Nel fell in beside him, while the rest of the rangers and the Visani royal guard stayed behind. As they departed, a horde of stableboys and servants swarmed the courtyard to take care of the horses and unload their baggage.

"Nervous?" Nel asked, jabbing him in his side with her elbow.

"Should I be?"

She shrugged, as if to say *perhaps*, and Keilan felt his heart take a little jump.

Vhelan led them down a wide corridor lined by armored warriors, their long spears angled so that the barbed points formed an arch for them to pass beneath. Windows of colored glass set high up on the walls drenched everything below in shades of green and blue and red, and the light made the guard's plate flash.

Another massive door swung open, and they entered the audience chamber of Cein d'Kara, the Crimson Queen of Dymoria.

She was like a statue upon her golden dragon throne, her back straight as a sword, her skin unnaturally pale. Fiery red curls tumbled around her long white neck and lay upon the ruffle of her scarlet dress. A dozen men and women in wine-dark robes clustered at the base of the steps leading up to the throne on its dais, and they gave way as the four of them approached.

Vhelan dropped to one knee, and Keilan followed suit. "My Queen," he said, his eyes fixed on the chamber's floor, "I have returned."

There was a rustling as the queen shifted. "You have," she said. Her voice carried a tone of command that Keilan had never heard before, not even from the prince of Vis. "But you are late."

"Yes, Your Majesty, we encountered the Pure and –"

"Silence."

Vhelan's mouth snapped shut, so abruptly that Keilan heard the click of his teeth coming together.

"My cousin in Theris dispatched birds telling of the Pure. And Prince Lyn sent riders before you that informed me of the ambush along the Wending Way." The queen rose from her throne and began to descend the steps. "I am pleased that you have completed the task I set before you."

She halted a few span from where Keilan knelt, and he had to struggle to control his breathing. There was a palpable warmness emanating from her, as if her bright red hair truly was aflame.

"Keilan Ferrisorn," she said, and he forced himself to look up at her. "Will you pledge fealty to me, and enter my Scholia?"

He swallowed away his fear, his fingernails digging into his palms."Yes, Your Majesty. I will."

31: KEILAN

TAP. TAP. *Tap.*

Magister d'Terin's staff guided him as he descended the odeon's limestone steps, toward where the tree of knowledge spread its pale limbs over the apprentices. They waited for him upon stone benches, six in all, their gray robes dappled by the early morning light. Behind d'Terin, rising above the topmost tier of the amphitheater, Saltstone bulked dark and jagged against the cloudless blue. The fortress was a gnarled fist raised in defiance at whatever sky-gods held sway in Dymoria. A few months past, Keilan had believed heaven to be the abode of the Shael, the great titans who cast down spears of lightning at the sea when they warred with the Deep Ones. Now, he wasn't so sure. Ama, the Silver Lady, the Ten, the spider-demon of Uthmala – it seemed that every city and town they'd passed through on the way to Herath venerated different gods and spirits. How to know which one was the truth? Or did they all exist side by side, yet intangible to each other, like reflections in a hall of mirrors?

The cowl had been pulled back from the magister's age-spotted head, wispy strands of gray hair stirring in the breeze, and as he approached the apprentices he slowly turned so that his milky eyes passed over them all. D'Terin was blind, yet in the fortnight that Keilan had spent in the Scholia he had never seen the magister stumble, or fail to realize when one of his students had not appeared for his lessons. He seemed to possess an almost magical sense of when the attention of his charges was wandering; more than a few times, Keilan had felt the sting of the magister's ashwood staff on his arm while he had been gazing up at the crenellations of Saltstone, or watching clouds drift between the tree's skeletal branches.

Magister d'Terin passed close to the bench where Tamryl sat beside Halix Keviling and reached out to trail his fingers in her dark hair. Tamryl's silver eyes blinked in surprise, but she did not flinch away at his touch. Then he was past her, within the crescent of stone benches facing the tree. Slowly he shuffled closer, laying his palm upon the ghostly white bark of the trunk, and bowed his head, as if in communion with the spirits hanging from its branches. The wind suddenly strengthened, causing the silver skulls dangling on their silken cords to spin and dance, a few even clicking together in a faintly musical clamor.

Past the magister and the tree was a low stone railing, and beyond that was the edge of the white cliffs, which plunged down more than a thousand span to where the ocean endlessly gnawed on the rocks below. The first time Keilan had recognized the magister's blindness he had spent half the lesson on the edge of his seat, prepared to dash across the odeon if he strayed too close to the edge. But very quickly he had come to realize that d'Terin was more aware of his surroundings than every one of his students.

Including Keilan.

He tried, he really did, to concentrate on what d'Terin or the other instructors were lecturing about, but invariably he found his attention drifting away like the shreds of clouds in the wide blue sky. It was just so much more interesting to disappear into the rabbit hole of his memories, reliving the terror below Uthmala, the soaring beauty of the silver tree in Vis, or the tingling awe he had felt while floating in the presence of the godlike creature he'd found in the ocean's depths. Rambling explanations of the Lyrish political structure, or the great

Keshian contest that determined who became padarasha – delivered in desiccated husks of statements, all energy leached from them – simply could not compare with his adventures over the summer months.

That, and the boys who sat behind him were quite distracting. There were three of them, all around Keilan's age: big, broad-shouldered Karik, smaller Sevanil with his quick smile and laughing eyes, and the darkly handsome Belin Sorelsorn. Karik and Sevanil both hailed from the Gilded Cities, Ver Anath and Lyr. Belin was from Theris in the Shattered Kingdoms, and intensely proud of it, though it seemed like he had lived in Dymoria for more than a few years. They called themselves the Tradesmen, as all three were the sons of skilled workers – Karik's father had been a mason, Sevanil's a tailor, and Belin came from a long line of famous goldsmiths. He had looked almost affronted when Keilan had claimed to have never heard of his father, since they were both from the Shattered Kingdoms. By his account, every noble and merchant in Theris thought Sorel to be the finest jewelry-maker of his generation.

Even though his father was just a simple fisherman the boys seemed well-disposed toward Keilan; maybe it was because he shared the same homeland as Belin, or perhaps because he said little during the morning lectures. Most of their whispered attentions were directed at the two students sitting in the benches directly in front of the magister, Tamryl and Halix. Every time the dark-haired girl rang her little bell – they'd all been given one, to alert the instructor that they wished to speak – an audible groan would rise up behind Keilan. It must have been loud enough for Tamryl to hear, though she never showed that she had.

She did ring her bell often, Keilan had to admit. And when she spoke her accent and diction suggested that she was high nobility, born far above the rest of them. But now they were all apprentices in the Scholia, and their past titles had been set aside. In the court of the Crimson Queen, at least, they were all considered nobility. Keilan had wondered why anyone born into wealth and power would trade their damask and silks for the simple gray apprentice robes of the Scholia

– but then he remembered the sorcery he had seen Vhelan perform, and he suspected he knew the answer.

Not that they had learned any magic yet. Instead there had been an interminable series of lectures on history, philosophy, ethics, botany, astronomy . . . Keilan knew he wasn't the only one of the new apprentices who was aching to be instructed in some real sorcery.

But as had been explained to him weeks ago, knowledge must come before power. A sorcerer ignorant of the world and its workings was a threat to all.

This morning's lecture was on the final days of the two great magical empires, Min-Ceruth and the Kalyuni Imperium. Keilan struggled to focus on what the magister was saying.

"And so," Magister d'Terin said, his voice like the crackling of dry paper, "a balance was reached after centuries of rivalry. Two distinct streams of sorcery had diverged in the years following the dissolution of the Warlock King's kingdom in Menekar. The northern holdfasts – cold, aloof, dominated by tradition and honor – could never understand the wild, unrestrained south, where the sorcerers in their Star Towers pursued every avenue of magical study. Indeed, the internecine strivings between the various schools of the Mosaic Cities were often even more intense than their conflicts with the wizards of the far north. Though greater in number, the sorcerers of the Imperium were so riven by these internal arguments that they had never managed to unite themselves and establish the magic of the Star Towers as preeminent in Araen."

"But perhaps the greatest deterrent to outright war between these two people was the knowledge that both the holdfasts and the Star Towers had developed a spell of such cataclysmic power that it would utterly destroy their rival. Who would dare cast such a sorcery, when the counter-stroke ensured your own destruction?"

Ring-ring.

"Yes, Apprentice Tamryl?"

"Magister, how did the Sundering come about, then, if both sides knew casting that final spell would doom them as well?"

D'Terin paused, reaching up to cup one of the silver skulls hanging from the tree. "Child, in the end they were not as wise as they thought they were."

"What happened?"

The magister spun the skull on its silken cord. "There is only speculation. Perhaps the most authoritative account came from one of the few Min-Ceruthans to escape the fall of Nes Vaneth, the greatest of the holdfasts. He wrote that an emissary from the Imperium had been found guilty of murdering the beloved royal princess, and in her rage and sorrow the queen unleashed the spell that sent the Derravin Ocean flooding into the Imperium, and thus creating the Broken Sea. But even as the water thundered toward their Towers the greatest of the Kalyuni sorcerers sent their own counter-stroke hurtling north, and the black ice crept down from the northern wastes to swallow the holdfasts."

"Why would this emissary have done such a thing?" Tamryl continued.

Keilan heard the boys behind him shift and mutter. They certainly didn't want the history lesson to go on any longer than necessary, as almost every day the boys slipped outside the Scholia to eat their midday repast. But Keilan found himself interested in what the magister was saying. He had been told various stories about the fall of the old empires, but this was the first time any had been imparted by a true scholar.

The magister shrugged. "Who knows, child? Revenge, madness . . . the human heart is often guided not by reason, but by these fraught and dangerous emotions."

Another bell sounded, and d'Terin turned slightly toward the boy sitting beside Tamryl.

"Yes, Apprentice Halix?"

"M-m-magister d'Terin," the boy said, fighting through a stutter. Keilan had wondered before how Halix would be able to cast magic with such an affliction, but he supposed the magisters must have believed it still possible, otherwise he would not be here.

"Excuse my im-mpertinence, but my f-f-father's seeker once told me that some in the Reliquary believe that it was the sorcerers of the Star T-t-towers that struck first. They had thought they'd gained some advantage, and that they could destroy the holdfasts b-b-before any response was made."

"My f-f-father's seeker," Belin whispered mockingly. "Too bad the little rich boy can't buy himself a new v-v-voice. He'll cast every spell in triplicate." Karik and Sevanil sniggered at this.

Magister d'Terin nodded. "As I said, there are several theories as to what happened. Various factions within both the Reliquary and the Scholia believe different things. But whoever struck first, the lesson here is the same – power, no matter how great, does not ensure wisdom. It is a stark reminder of why we fill your head with knowledge before we teach you any real sorcery." The magister raised his head so that he seemed to be looking at the boys clustered towards the back benches. "A prudent decision, do you not agree, Apprentice Belin?"

The low laughter stopped as suddenly as if a bolt of lightning had flashed out of the blue and struck the odeon's tree. Belin cleared his throat. "Oh, aye. Of course, Magister d'Terin. Very prudent."

"I'm glad you concur," the old man said dryly, a slight smile playing at the edges of his mouth as he turned away.

Following the morning's lecture Keilan was so lost in his thoughts that he did not notice Nel until she came up beside him in the corridor and hooked her arm through his.

"Nel!" he cried, fighting back the urge to hug her.

"Keilan," she said, lacing her hand in his and giving it a small squeeze. "How are you finding the life of a Scholia apprentice?"

"It's . . . it's good."

"Three meals a day and all the boring history you can cram into your skull?"

Keilan laughed. "Yes. Something like that."

"Well, I remember Vhelan complaining about the same. But there's good reason for what they do, don't worry. They want to take your measure before they start teaching you real sorcery. A fair number of those they bring here with ability never end up becoming magisters, and instead are returned to their families."

"Oh." Keilan hadn't known that. He'd supposed that sorcery was so rare that the Scholia would strive to never turn any away they found with the gift.

They walked together in silence for a time. "It's so good to see you," he finally said. And it was. He hadn't met any of his old companions – Nel, Vhelan, or Xin – since the ceremony in the great hall where the queen had welcomed them and taken his oath of service, though Garmond had sought him out before the seeker departed for Ver Anath, gifting him with his beautifully illuminated copy of *The Tinker's Bestiary*.

Nel patted his arm. "I'm sorry I haven't been around. Vhelan has kept me busy running all over the city attending to different things, and he's spent quite a bit of time with his fellow magisters poring over the scrolls, books, and other treasures we gathered in Uthmala and Vis."

"Did they discover anything?"

"Yes, but progress is slow because only a few of the magisters have any ability in High Kalyuni. Vhelan had me find some scholars in the city who claimed proficiency with the writing, but even still –"

"Keilan!"

They turned to find the Tradesmen approaching. The boys had changed into tunics and breeches since the lesson ended, so they must have been planning to go out into the city. Belin had remarked a few days ago that more than a few winehouses and taverns refused to let them gamble if they were dressed in their apprentice robes.

When Sevanil noticed Keilan and Nel together he elbowed Karik and whispered something that made the larger boy leer. Belin sauntered closer, making a show of looking Nel up and down. "Keilan Ferrisorn! Not two weeks in the Scholia and already you've made friends with the prettiest serving wench. I knew you were a proper Kingdom man."

Nel quirked an eyebrow. "I'm no serving wench, boy. Run along."

Belin chuckled, but his eyes had suddenly turned hard. "Well, are you a noble? A magister? One of the queen's handmaidens?" At each shake of Nel's head he edged closer, until he was looming over her. "Then we're running out of things you could be."

Nel gazed up at him, untroubled by his attempt to intimidate her. "I'm the personal assistant of one of the senior magisters."

"Personal assistant? I've been looking for one of those. I had to leave all my 'personal assistants' when I moved into the Scholia. How about it, girl? Tired of 'assisting' some dried-up old man?"

Karik guffawed loudly at this.

Anger rose in Keilan, and he took a step forward, but Nel tightened her grip on his arm. "Such sweet words you sing. If you'd prefer to sing them in a much higher octave, I encourage you to keep talking."

Belin stepped back a pace, blinking in surprise. "Did you just threaten me, girl? I'm a magister and the son of Sorin Derrilsorn!" He snarled and reached out for her, but clutched empty air. In an eye-blink Nel had twisted free of Keilan and sidestepped Belin, a dagger appearing in her hand as if plucked from the air.

"An APPRENTICE magister," Nel said amiably, spinning the onyx pommel in her palm so that the blade glittered in the flickering light from the wall sconces. "And not so far from being the gelded son of Sorin Derrilsorn."

Belin mouth worked soundlessly, an enraged flush creeping up his neck.

Nel tapped the side of the dagger against her chin. "Tell me, do you think your father would still introduce you as his son if I –" and now Nel made a clicking noise with her tongue "– disposed of whatever passed for your manhood? Care to find out?"

"I'll have you flogged for this," he whispered hoarsely. Keilan couldn't imagine that Belin's bulging eyes could get any bigger.

"But then you'd have to tell everyone how you scampered away from a little girl like a dog with its tail between its legs. And you'd have to say that this happened."

The dagger flashed, too fast to see clearly. Belin made a strangled sound, but no dark stain blossomed anywhere on his tunic. The boy let out a shuddering breath, then glared at Nel. "I'll take that knife and shove it in your –"

His breeches fell down.

For a brief moment everyone froze. Keilan couldn't hold back a hiccup of laughter at the shock in Belin's face.

Nel's brow crinkled as she studied him critically. "If that's all you have to offer, apprentice Belin, I think I'll pass on your offer."

At that the two boys behind Belin laughed as well. The boy from the Shattered Kingdoms lunged down and gathered his pants, holding them up after he had straightened. With as much dignity as he could muster Belin backed away, his face pale but his chin held high.

"I'm going to find out who you are, girl," he muttered. "And when I do . . ."

The dagger vanished as quickly as it had appeared. Nel pointed at Sevanil. "You. You're from Lyr, yes?"

Sevanil nodded slowly, glancing at Karik beside him.

"Do you know who Col Temis was?"

Another nod. "Aye. The Warren King."

"Do you know what happened to him?"

"He died. On the Night of the Black Masks."

"He died with a knife in his belly. My knife. So I would advise you to enlighten your friend here what that says about me. *Veniche, amini*?"

Sevanil swallowed hard. "*Veniche*. I will talk to him."

"Good, do that," Nel said, then as if dismissing the three boys she took Keilan's arm again and turned away, leading him further down the corridor.

When Keilan glanced over his shoulder he saw their retreating backsides vanishing around a bend in the passage, Belin almost hopping as he tried to both run and keep his pants up.

He looked at Nel, and she sighed and shrugged. "You've seen me fight giant spiders and shape-changing demons. Do you really think I'm going to back down in front of those little toads?"

"No . . . but aren't you afraid he'll tell one of the senior magisters?"

Nel patted his arm. "Don't worry – I know all of them quite well. And none would take his word over mine."

"And that story about the Warren King?"

"Yes?" There was a mischievous twinkle in Nel's eye.

"Is it true?"

She chuckled. "On the Night of the Black Masks I was doing the same thing as every other sensible thief – keeping my head down behind the stoutest door I could find. It is still a mystery who killed dear old Col, so I'll use that to my advantage. I like having a few whispers going round about how dangerous I am."

Keilan shook his head. "I've never met anyone remotely like you."

"Nor will you again!" she said, then was quiet for a moment. "Keilan, I didn't come here simply to say hello or scare a few beardless boys. There's something I need your help with."

"Tell me what it is and I'll do it."

Nel smiled – almost sadly, Keilan thought – and patted his arm. "I knew you'd say that. Keilan, it's about Xin."

Ah.

"I was hoping that time would heal the wounds he's carrying. Time and . . . me. And you. Being around friends who could replace his brothers. But . . . but he's still slipping away, Keilan. Bit by bit, a fragment at a time. I can feel it."

"How can I help him? Do you want me to talk to him?"

Nel turned to him with glistening eyes. "That helped before. It did. I think he would have killed himself in Vis if you hadn't reminded him of his debt to you. But I was thinking of something else. Do you remember those evenings we spent training together? I would demonstrate a knife trick or two, and then Xin would lead us through some simple sword-fighting patterns, and finally you'd take him off to the seeker's wagon to teach him how to read?"

"Of course I remember. Those were some of the best nights of my life."

Nel gripped his arm hard. "I think so, too! Only with Vhelan had I felt so free before, so accepted . . . and I know Xin enjoyed those evenings as well. Keilan, I've spoken with the magisters in charge of educating the newest apprentices. I've convinced them that it would be to the great benefit of you all if you received some basic training in weaponry. Nothing so intense, just enough that if you find yourself without the strength to cast a spell – or have your sorcery drained away by a paladin of Ama – that you are not as helpless as babes."

"And Xin will teach us?"

"Yes! I hope it will be another reason for him to continue living in this world. What do you think? Can you help?"

Keilan nodded, and Nel gathered him in a quick embrace.

"Thank you, Keilan. Together we can save him, I know it."

32: KEILAN

THE REACTIONS OF the apprentices when they had first been told that they would be beginning weapons training surprised Keilan. He had thought that the mere mention of the Fists would have sent ripples of excitement through them, but most seemed bemused that those preparing to learn how to summon fire and lightning would ever find themselves in a situation where they needed to jab someone with a thin piece of metal. Tamryl had blinked her large silver eyes slowly and pursed her lips, as if in disapproval of the thought of violence. Her friend and constant shadow, Halix, had demonstrated the attitude Keilan had expected: more interested in the Fists themselves than the idea of swinging a sword. He had peppered the magister who had informed them about their new instructor with questions about how one of the legendary slave-soldiers had found his way to the Scholia. Belin and Karik had affected bored indifference, as if this was just another demand on their time, which they would rather spend in the gambling dens and taverns of Herath. Sevaril had snorted contemptuously and remarked loudly that his older cousin, a celebrated bravo of Lyr, had already taught him the dueling arts.

All these conceits had been shattered and swept away before the first lesson was even finished. Xin had come before them in the wine-colored leather cuirass of the Fists, his long black hair – which he had allowed to grow since his brother's deaths – swept back and bound into a top-knot. Two others had accompanied him, Magister d'Terin and a solemn-faced Shan wearing the red cloak of the queen's personal guard. The two warriors had stood stiff-backed beneath the gently swaying silver skulls hanging from the odeon's tree as d'Terin had introduced them to the apprentices: Xin, third of five, from the Lapis Stables, and Kwan Lo-Ren, once of Red Fang Mountain, and now the commander of the Scarlet Guard. Then the blind magister had stepped aside to make room, and without a hint of ceremony a demonstration had commenced.

Keilan had felt a change in the attitude of the apprentices within moments of watching these two master swordsmen come together. There had been an audible intake of breath as the Shan had leaped forward, drawing his curved blade with such speed that it seemed to simply materialize in his hand. For the briefest of moments Keilan feared that Xin would be unprepared for this lightning-like attack – but with a quickness at least equal to the Shan the Fist warrior had met the flashing sword with his own, and the shriek of steel coming together had shivered the air.

Cut and parry, lunge and block, the blades had flickered like striking serpents as the two warriors had moved around the odeon's tree, stepping carefully over exposed roots and buckled stone. The spectacle had been hypnotic, the swords weaving patterns as they came together and separated almost too fast to follow, and when Keilan managed to tear his attention from the duel he had found the other apprentices watching wide-eyed. Finally the two swordsmen had stopped, sheathing their blades simultaneously as they turned to their audience, and the apprentices had burst into applause at the display.

Xin's class quickly became the most exciting time of their morning lessons. After d'Terin or another of the senior magisters had finished their daily lecture, Xin would lead the students to an ancient section of the battlements with enough room to accommodate swordplay.

He began simply, as he had with Keilan: the first few sessions were dedicated to improving the apprentice's footwork, their balance and the grip they used. The boys learned with the heavy wooden practice swords Keilan and Nel had once trained with; these were roughly the same weight as the Fist's preferred weapon, a double-edged sword most suitable for slashing and hacking. But for the slight, reedy Tamryl he introduced a thin, piercing blade, similar to the swords favored by the bravos of Lyr. After a late morning spent struggling with the heavy Fist sword, a sweat-soaked Sevanil had also adopted the more slender blade, claiming that this was in fact the weapon for any true Lyrishman.

Keilan felt the apprentices drawing closer under the Fist's tutelage. After a few sparring sessions, Sevanil started teaching Tamryl some of the tricks and techniques his cousin had once shown him, and soon whatever animosity had arisen from her constant questioning of the magisters disappeared. Even Belin grudgingly accepted her when his friends welcomed her into their group. They started eating together, and a few times talked long into the night about their families, and of their hopes and dreams for the future. Tamryl was part Kindred, Keilan discovered – her mother had been a famous physician among that itinerant people. When their caravan had passed through Ver Anath many years ago, her mother had been summoned to the manse of a powerful merchant family and had saved the life of their eldest son. The merchant prince and the Kindred chirurgeon had fallen in love, and Tamryl had been born the following year, causing a great scandal in the city.

Halix's father was also wealthy and famous, one of the greatest of Seri's artificer lords. At first his family had been aghast when his sorcerous gift manifested itself, for the artificers prided themselves on harnessing the natural, measurable forces of the world, and most felt that relying on sorcery recalled an earlier, more barbaric era that deserved to be forgotten. But his father had seized upon it as an opportunity: perhaps his son could learn how to merge the clockwork genius of the artificers with the wild and chaotic power of sorcery. And so he had been sent here, to Herath and the Scholia.

As they spent more time together the sneering bravado of the Tradesmen was revealed to simply be the insecurity of boys thrust into a situation they didn't truly understand. Belin even apologized to Tamryl for his earlier rudeness, giving her a twisting golden bracelet he had fashioned in his father's workshop. Tamryl, in her generosity, had smiled shyly and accepted Belin's words and gift with good grace.

The improved mood among the apprentices was not the only benefit that came from the sword training. To Keilan's great relief and happiness he quickly noticed an improvement in Xin's demeanor as well – when their lessons had first begun the Fist warrior had rarely grinned, his face sallow and his eyes almost lifeless. But after a few sessions Keilan thought he saw some color returning to Xin's cheeks, and he started moving with more purpose. Ten days after the morning trainings had started, Keilan had been surprised to hear the Fist's laughter erupt while helping Tamryl and Sevanil refine their technique. He never did learn what the Lyrish boy had said to elicit that reaction from Xin, but his heart had soared at the sound.

Weeks passed, and Keilan embraced the rhythms of the Scholia. Study and swordplay in the mornings, afternoons spent exploring Herath with the other apprentices. Every day brought new and interesting experiences. He drank firewine and listened to minstrels with Belin in the taverns near the docks. The next day he visited a Kindred encampment with Tamryl when a string of their brightly painted wagons had passed through Herath, trying their bitter tea as dancers whirled to the sound of racing fiddles. Later he had watched in breathless fascination as Halix had shown him his collection of small copper automatons shaped like animals, and how simply winding a key on their backs could send them stumbling forward, as if animated by sorcery.

After months of turbulent storms, the sky was finally lightening, and the shoreline had appeared on the horizon.

And then came the summons from the Crimson Queen.

Her presence loomed over Saltstone and the Scholia, even if the apprentices never saw her, save for when they were invited to dine in the palace's great feast hall. During those dinners she hardly seemed to eat or talk, a goddess of pale white stone watching with an unknowable expression as the nobles and magisters of the Scholia drank and cavorted. Once she had caught him watching her, and he thought – for the briefest of moments – that the corners of her thin mouth had quirked slightly. But whatever emotion, if he had not imagined it, had been fleeting, and she had not looked at him again.

"Strength," Nel had told him, a few days after Xin had started teaching the apprentices. She'd visited him to ask about how the others were taking to the weapon training, and he in turn had wanted to know more about the queen, and why she seemed so aloof during the feasts. "It's a show of strength. Because of her age, she's still just a girl in the eyes of many of the kingdom's nobles. If she had been anyone else there'd have been a regent, most likely, and eventually Cein would have been married off to one of them. There are a half-dozen families in Dymoria with a claim nearly as strong on the Dragon Throne as the d'Karas, and since she was born out of wedlock, and spent her childhood in the Sunset Lands, that only puts her on more uncertain ground. A few years ago, you know, a group of powerful nobles tried to overthrow her. The results were as you could imagine, but there are still mutterings, in the manses on the Slopes, that she's leading the kingdom toward ruin. So during feast days, when everyone can see her, she has to be cold and hard and strong. Any sign of weakness might inspire another attempt to seize the throne. But she's not as emotionless as she might appear – in many ways, she's fired with more passion that anyone I've ever met. She'd have to be, to accomplish all she has while still so young."

The summons came in the form of a prim young servant wearing a shimmering satin doublet emblazoned with the dragon of Dymoria. His eyes had seemed to be fixed on a point just above Keilan's head as he commanded him to immediately attend the queen in her study. There was an audible intake of breath from the other apprentices sitting around the table, and Sevanil even dropped his wooden spoon into his porridge bowl, splashing the hem of Karik's sleeve.

With his breakfast sitting like a stone in his stomach, Keilan swallowed hard and pushed himself away from the table. He forced himself not to glance back at his friends as he followed the servant out of the small hall near the kitchens where the apprentices usually took their meals, and through the passages that led from the wing of the palace that housed the Scholia and into the section set aside for the royal apartments.

Here the stone was older, pitted and worn, and in places it looked to have even been scarred by ancient fires. How many times had men fought and died in these halls, or assassins slipped through the shadows cast by flickering torchlight? Keilan wondered if sorcery could be used to summon forth the ghosts of past events, like an echo returning from a well. If it could, he would wager these halls would have more than a few interesting stories to tell.

The corridor they followed emptied into a courtyard decorated by a collection of worn statues that Keilan recognized as representing the various Aspects of Ama. One was a fierce warrior, brandishing a broken sword at the gulls jostling for space along the higher battlements; another was a mysterious robed figure with arms outstretched, features hidden in the depths of its cowl. Evidently these statues had not been very well cared for, as many were cracked or stained by lichen, and a few were even missing limbs or heads.

They passed between the statues, approaching a tall domed building with an imposing set of doors carved with a faded sunburst. Huge, round windows of colored glass were set above this entrance, each faceted ring growing smaller and more intricate until they reached the center, a perfect disk of pale, white metal. It looked to Keilan like the temple of Ama in Theris where Vhelan and the Dymorian rangers had given over the wounded paladin to the surprised mendicants.

"The queen follows the Light?" Keilan asked the servant as they approached the ancient building. The very thought seemed preposterous.

The servant shook his head. "No. This temple is a relic from a much earlier time. It was built by one of the first d'Kara kings, after he had been converted by wandering mendicants. Despite the king's fervor, the faith never took root in Dymoria, and the temple stayed empty for centuries. The queen repurposed it as a shrine to her own god a few years ago."

"Her god?" Keilan hadn't seen anything else in Saltstone or the Scholia to suggest that the queen was devout.

The servant pushed open the large doors and motioned for Keilan to enter first. "Yes."

His breath caught in his throat as he slipped inside the ancient temple. Between the pillars that supported the ceiling's soaring dome high shelves of gleaming black ebonwood had been constructed, filled with books of every size and shape. Tall ladders leaned against the shelves, many of which reached nearly three times the height of a man, and a wizened little person – male or female, Keilan couldn't tell – clung to one of them, sifting through the books cramming one of the highest shelves. In the center of the temple, upon a dais that he assumed had once held some kind of altar, was a black table covered with unrolled scrolls and open books. The light from the circular stained-glass window above the entrance bathed the table and its jumbled mess in a faint rainbow of colors.

A young woman sat at the table, her head bent over a large, leather-bound grimoire, absently twisting a strand of red hair around her finger. With a start Keilan realized that this was the queen herself, and he quickly dropped to one knee, his heart hammering in his chest. He had met Cein d'Kara only once before, in the audience chamber when he had first sworn allegiance to her throne. At that time she had been dressed in a shimmering red gown, a diadem of emeralds the size of swallow's eggs glittering in her hair. But here she wore only a simple blue shift, he could see no jewels at her throat or on her brow, and she wasn't caked with whatever cosmetic had given her the appearance of living stone.

She glanced up as the servant softly cleared his throat. Her eyes met his, and the ghost of a smile tugged at the corners of her mouth. "Keilan Ferrisorn," she said, in a voice far different than the one that had filled the audience chamber, "I bid you welcome."

Keilan ducked his head, hoping she couldn't see the blush burning his face. How could he be here, in the presence of a queen? "I am at your service, Your Majesty."

"Stand and approach," she said. Keilan climbed to his feet, his gaze still fixed on the tiled floor.

The queen sighed. "Look at me, Keilan."

With a great effort he lifted his eyes. "Forgive me, Your Highness. I don't . . . I'm not accustomed to coming before royalty."

"I'd say you're handling it all very well. At the beginning of the summer you were a boy from a small fishing village. Since then you've explored a ruined city infested with black sorcery, slain a demon who wore the skin of a man like a cloak, and communed with the spirit of the Barrows. Now you stand before a queen. Honestly, I feel that this should be almost boring, given your accomplishments."

Despite the lightness of her tone, Keilan's palms were slick with sweat. "It is not, Your Highness. Everything that has happened to me occurred while I was trying to come here, to your court. I feel like what came before was but the prelude, and now my real story begins."

The queen watched him in silence for a long moment. "That is an interesting thought. It implies that we are all part of some grand tale, directed by some higher power for the whims of others." She closed the large book in front of her, raising a cloud of dust that glittered in the light slanting down from the window. "I reject such a notion."

Cein d'Kara rose, placing her splayed hands on the gleaming black wood of the table. "We make our own destiny. Believing otherwise abdicates responsibility for what happens, and I refuse to do that. Failure or glory, the result belongs to us. Do you understand?"

Keilan felt dizzy, but he managed to nod. "I . . . I think so."

"Good. We are the harbingers of a new age, Keilan. But before we can shape the future we must know what happened in the past. That is why I summoned you here today."

"You did?"

"Yes," The queen swept out her arm, indicating the scrolls and books spread across the table. "Do you recognize these?"

Keilan approached slowly, still hesitant to get too close without her permission.

With a frustrated sigh the queen came around and grabbed Keilan's arm, pulling him next to the table. "Everyone acts like I have the plague. Now look."

A few of the books were familiar, Keilan realized, as he noticed the two slim volumes written in High Kalyuni that the spirit of the Barrow had bequeathed to him. "Those are the ones I brought out of Vis."

"Yes." The queen picked up *The Dream of the Warlock King*. "And that you were given these two books I find very interesting."

"Why is that, Your Highness?"

She opened the book, carefully turning its cracked and yellowing pages. "Because I have been searching for this book for many years. In fact, only a few months past I traveled to Vis to try and find it in the Barrow, but the spirit refused to give it up to me then. And now you appear, bringing it to my court. What does it mean?"

"Perhaps the spirit decided you should have it after all?"

"But why? I wanted the book because it is referenced in other sources as the definitive account of the sorcery that the old Warlock Kings of Menekar employed when they tried to achieve immortality, before the Pure cast them down. And now it arrives on the heels of another echo from the past, another link to the sorcery of ever-lasting life . . ."

The queen set down the book and stared intensely into Keilan's eyes. "I need to know what is in these books. The scholars of High Kalyuni in Herath are fumbling incompetents, and I do not have the time to invite one of the seekers from the Reliquary who specializes in the history of the Imperium to come here. I've looked at what you translated on the road from Vis, and it is far better than anyone else I've given that task to has produced. I want you to continue what you started. Every day when you finish your lessons in the Scholia you will come here and assist me. Do you understand?"

Keilan nodded, swallowing hard.

"Good. Then you may go."

He bowed deep, his mind whirling, and turned away . . . only to nearly collide with a man who had come up behind him, and was staring with the same look of surprise Keilan felt. He didn't appear to be a servant of the queen – his clothes were fine, but he lacked the deferential air Keilan had noticed almost everyone in Saltstone carried. He had a tangle of sandy hair and piercing blue eyes. At his side was a sword with a blazing jewel in its pommel, the first weapon Keilan had seen in the queen's presence.

"Ah, Jan. You're late."

The man kept his eyes on Keilan, his shock still plain. "I am sorry, Your Highness. I was in the gardens, and the servants had trouble finding me."

"Very well. Jan, I wanted you to meet Keilan Ferrisorn. He is the boy with the gift that my magisters recently brought to Herath. It was he who the spirit of the Barrow gave the books I've been trying to have translated."

Jan looked Keilan up and down slowly. "Surely, my Queen, you can see the same thing that I can."

The queen slipped into one of the chairs, resting her chin on her laced fingers. "I believe so, but I wanted to hear it from your lips first."

"The boy is a Talent."

A satisfied smile spread across the queen's face. "I thought so. He looked to me just as you do."

"And the same as how you look to me," Jan said.

"A Talent?" Keilan whispered, feeling himself blush under the scrutiny of the queen and the strange man.

Jan nodded. "Yes. Those with Talent and some training can always recognize each other, unless great pains are taken to hide the trace of sorcery. While one who is merely gifted is a flickering candle flame, Talents are like torches blazing in the blackest night."

The queen drummed her fingers on the table. "An untrained Talent arrives in my court bearing two books of ancient knowledge I have long sought, both written by someone with whom you are *very* familiar with, Jan. The spirit is trying to tell us something important."

"I think it is trying to tell us to beware of Alyanna and her schemes."

Keilan's ears perked up at the name. "Alyanna? Alyanna ne Verell, the writer of those books?"

The queen and Jan glanced at him as if they had forgotten he was still there. "Yes," the queen said, watching him carefully.

"She's alive?"

There was a long pause, and then Jan answered. "Yes."

Keilan blinked in surprise. "But the books looked so old. No, they *must* be ancient, from before the cataclysms, at least. How could she still be . . ." Pieces slid into place in Keilan's mind. "The book is a treatise on the sorcery of achieving immortality."

Jan and the queen shared a long look. "Well, you're no fool, Keilan," Jan said with a sigh. "Yes, Alyanna achieved what the Warlock King of Menekar could not."

"How?"

Jan pinched his brow, as if the question pained him. "I don't know. Or perhaps I do, but . . ."

Both Keilan and Jan jumped as the queen struck the table hard with the flat of her hand. "I must know what secrets are in your head! Everything I've built here in Dymoria might depend on it!"

Jan spread his arms out helplessly. "I know, Your Highness, I'm sorry. I . . ." something dawned in Jan's face, his eyes widening in excitement. "Wait! You said you could feel what was blocking my memories shift in my mind when you tried to push it aside?"

The queen nodded slowly, and Jan continued. "There is something else that is special about those with Talent, outside of their great power and the ability to summon sorcery without relying on incantations and gestures. Unlike those who are only gifted, Talents can share their strength between themselves. Many of the greatest acts of sorcery were accomplished by powerful, Talented sorcerers linking their magic together. Perhaps if you could draw upon Keilan's strength you could destroy the prison holding back my memories!"

The queen glanced at Keilan dubiously. "But he is so young, and untrained."

Jan clapped Keilan on the shoulder. "He just needs to open himself to you and allow you to draw from the well of power within him. It is simpler than you think, as you will be the one actually shaping the sorcery."

Keilan's head was truly spinning now as he tried to understand what Jan and the queen were proposing.

"Why do you not lend me your strength, if all Talents can do this?"

Jan shook his head at the queen's question. "I cannot, if the spell is being performed on me. It would rip my mind to shreds, channeling power out of me and then feeding it back inside. Such loops are impossible."

The queen was silent for a long moment, watching Keilan. "Very well. I need to make some preparations. We will try tomorrow night."

Keilan felt his knees wobble at the queen's words. How could this be happening?

33: ALYANNA

THE TREES WERE singing to the stars.

It was a lament, Alyanna decided, as she stood in the clearing and listened to the mournful dirge rise and fall. At first she thought the sound came from the gusting of the wind, perhaps even that these trees were hollow like giant pipes, but as she watched the branches sway and tangle above her she realized that their movement was disconnected with the constant wailing. Could a tree feel sadness in this place? She imagined idly that they envied the cold beauty of the stars, fastened far above her like jewels in the Void's terrible emptiness.

Vast and ancient, the trees towered over her, their scarred trunks crusted with patches of luminescent moss. She glimpsed creatures in the darkness scurrying along the boles and branches, their eyes glimmering when they caught what little light there was.

Suddenly, as if the forest had taken an indrawn breath, the trees quieted. Alyanna listened intently to the silence, waiting. For a moment all was still, and then there was movement above, beyond the canopy, a great shadow that stalked with inhuman grace across the night sky, occluding the blazing firmament. It paused, as if it sensed her presence below, and a thrill of apprehension made her shiver. Then it continued on.

After it had passed, the song swelled again, rising with renewed vigor to the heavens. In response, bright glittering threads of light began to fall from the sky, twisting slowly as they drifted down. Were the distant stars unspooling, like balls of fiery twine? She watched as some became caught on branches, the tree-animals shrinking away from them, while others continued on to the ground, where they writhed in the grass like shining serpents.

"What is this place, Weaver?"

Alyanna turned to find Demian standing in the forest clearing with her, gazing at the falling threads uneasily. She plucked one from the air, letting it wrap around her arm.

"This is my dream, Demian. Welcome."

The shadowblade stepped away from one of the threads as it groped blindly toward him. "You have a vivid imagination."

Alyanna laughed, and the sound sent a rainbow of colors shimmering up the trunks of the trees nearest to her. "Others have said the same."

"This is a new aspect of dreamsending, is it not? I have never heard of a sorcerer pulling others into their own dreams."

"It was an experiment, and it seems to have worked. Unless, of course, you are simply a figment of my mind as well."

Demian offered a tight smile. "I am real, I assure you."

Alyanna unwound the thread from her arm and let it fall. "Good. Events are moving rapidly now, and I need your assurances that everything is ready."

"Ready for what?"

She ignored his question. "Have you arrived in Herath?"

He nodded curtly. "We have. And as you told me to, we've taken a room in the closest inn to Saltstone, on the Slopes, only a stone's throw from the outer gates and with a view of the fortress."

Alyanna gestured, and in an eyeblink a mound swelled from the forest moss, shaping itself into a crude chair. She sank into it, watching him closely. "Tell me what you've found in the city. Can you sense the queen's Talent?"

"Not . . . directly. But there are traces."

Interest sparked in her face. "So she's discovered how to hide her Talent, but not all the residues from her spells. Well, that is to be expected – rubbing every sorcerous blemish from the world is difficult, even for us. But it suggests that she is not as far along in her learning as I had feared."

The shadowblade shook his head. "You misunderstand. It was not I that noticed the stain of her magic. It was the paladin."

That disturbed her, and Alyanna found to her surprise that she was holding a clump of the chair's moss in her hand. She didn't even remember pulling it loose. "Tell me."

"We were on the road leading to Herath, perhaps a league out from the city. The Pure was riding in front, and he suddenly reined up his horse and turned to me in confusion. He had sensed something strange – across the road was a kind of sorcerous filament, an invisible tripwire of sorts. It was ingeniously wrought and virtually undetectable, even when I knew something was there. I would not have noticed it without it being brought to my attention by the paladin. I walked between the shadows to avoid it, and so I do not think the queen knows that I am here." An emotion passed briefly across Demian's guarded face. Respect? Awe? "It was beautiful, Weaver. You would have appreciated the subtlety and the magnificence of the spell's composition. I have not seen an original sorcery such as this since the sundering of the world."

Alyanna was silent for a long moment, lost in thought. "Then that must be how she knew about the Bard."

"The Bard is also in Herath? And his true nature has been revealed to the queen?"

"Yes."

"How do you know?"

"I have felt her touch upon the barrier in Jan's mind that separates him from his memories."

Demian rubbed his chin thoughtfully. "Then it *was* you who took away his past. I suspected as much."

"The partitions in his mind that I constructed were done at his behest a long, long time ago, and if I had not agreed to his wishes then he would have surely ended his life already. There were two layers to the spell – the outer one shielded him from any recollection at all of the past, essentially turning him into someone else, while the inner only protected him from the truths he was trying to avoid confronting. The outer layer degraded slowly, memories seeping through gradually, and over the centuries I've had to repair it many times, in each instance essentially giving him a new mortal life to live. The inner has never been breached in a thousand years, although I suspect that some reverberations from these hidden memories have indeed trickled into his consciousness. Surely that would explain his recurring fascination with women who bear some resemblance to Liralyn."

"Why do you not dreamsend to him, Weaver? If the queen has discovered the Bard, then surely a conversation now could illuminate much about her intentions and capabilities."

Alyanna dismissed the idea with a wave. "No. The spells woven into Jan's mind make that idea untenable. It would be like trying to cross a room high in a burning building, where the floor has been weakened by fire. Everything could collapse at any moment, and I do not want his memories flooding back while he is in the Crimson Queen's clutches."

Demian crossed his arms. "Then why send him to her in the first place, Weaver? What if she manages to tear down the walls in his mind and learns about us? If what truly happened a thousand years ago becomes common knowledge in the world we will be hunted down and destroyed . . . Dymoria, Menekar, Shan – all the powers of Araen would unite against us."

Alyanna sighed, shaking her head. "My simple friend. Of course I expect her to breach the spells holding back the Bard's memories – though, to be honest I did not expect her to make as much progress as she has so quickly. But now that you are there the game can well and truly begin. Do you remember what I told you to do?"

"Of course. You said that the Pure and I were to sneak inside Saltstone using my powers. Then we will follow the paladin's senses to the boy Keilan, and escape with him. You promised there would be a distraction to keep the queen and her servants from pursuing us."

"And what else?"

"I was to bring the riftstone with me and use it when I was within the walls."

"Good."

"Weaver, how will I know when to enter the fortress? Will you send a signal?"

Alyanna smiled. "Yes. Keep watching Saltstone. When the signal comes, you will know it."

34: KEILAN

THE MAGISTER WHO came to fetch Keilan the next evening seemed familiar. He had high, aristocratic features and a dark pointed beard that had been stylishly forked, and he carried himself with the casual arrogance of high nobility. Keilan thought that he had seen him sitting at the royal table during feast days, and only a few places removed from the queen herself. Magister Kyrin, he believed was his name, a high-ranking sorcerer in the Scholia, and a scion of one of the most powerful families in Dymoria. Belin had pointed him out, as well as many of the other men and women at the high table, since being from Herath he was familiar with most of them.

When Kyrin arrived at Keilan's door in the apprentice's quarters of the Scholia he frowned and arched his eyebrows.

"So you're the boy who has impressed the queen?"

"I suppose so, my lord," Keilan replied softly, his eyes darting to the two warriors flanking the magister, both tall and stern-looking and wearing red cloaks.

"You are summoned now. Follow me."

Keilan barely had time to mutter "Yes, my lord," before the magister turned on his heels. The two guardsmen stayed behind, waiting for

Keilan as he hurriedly donned his robes, and then fell in beside him as he scurried to catch up with the magister's long strides.

"My . . . my lord," Keilan managed between gasping breaths, "pardon me, but where are we going?"

The magister did not glance at him. "The queen is preparing some sorcery in Ravenroost. She has requested your presence, although how *you* could be of any help when she has several magisters of the first rank in attendance, I have no idea."

Ravenroost. The tallest tower in Saltstone, and according to the whispers among the apprentices the one where the queen pursued her own magical studies. No one save the most senior among the magisters, the Scarlet Guard, and a handful of older servants were allowed within, but still rumors had trickled out of rooms filled with strange and ancient sorcerous artifacts, stairs that led into walls of solid stone, and even the ethereal presence of demonic spirits that the queen had summoned to give her counsel.

Nothing of the sort presented themselves to Keilan or the magister as they made their way up the tower's great spiraling staircase. At each landing there were several very ordinary-looking doors, and though Keilan strained to see inside one that had been left ajar he glimpsed only in the light of a candle an elderly servant folding cloth and placing it in a basket.

Possibly the rumors were exaggerated, he decided.

The stairs ended in the middle of a great room that filled the entire top floor of Ravenroost, its soaring domed ceiling crowned by a cupola. The queen was there, dressed in the same simple blue robes Keilan had last seen her wearing, bustling between several long tables strewn with strange silver instruments and opened books. Globes filled with softly glowing mist hung from rafters by glimmering golden strands, and they illuminated so well that it was almost as if the night outside had turned to day. Several other magisters were assisting her. Keilan noticed Magister d'Terin speaking softly at the queen's side, and he was the first to turn his milky eyes towards them as Keilan emerged from the stairwell into the chamber.

"He is here, Your Majesty," Keilan heard him murmur to the queen, and she set down the silver sphere she was examining.

"Ah, good. Thank you, Kyrin, for bringing him, now go assist Eleria with the preparations. I want those tinctures ready in case he starts to wake before we are finished."

Kyrin bowed smoothly to the queen and moved over to where a woman with a bandage wrapped around her head was measuring out some liquid into a small metal flask.

"And Keilan, come to me. We should discuss your part in all this."

Keilan hurried to attend the queen, and when he had moved around the tables he saw what had been hidden from him: the man from the queen's study, Jan, lay upon a raised stone dais,covered by a red blanket. His eyes were closed and his hands clasped upon his chest, which rose and fell in the slow steady rhythm of sleep.

"Is he all right?" Keilan blurted, and the queen smiled.

"He is fine. I had him drink some nightblossom tea laced with shaelinic extract – given what we are attempting, I thought it best if he was in the deep dreamless sleep of the moonflower. Nothing will wake him for several hours."

"What *are* we attempting?"

The queen picked up a small, thin stiletto from the table beside her. She gently pressed her thumb against its tip, testing the sharpness. "Surgery."

Keilan glanced from the knife to Jan lying motionless on the dais, his eyes wide. The queen saw this and chuckled.

"Not surgery on his physical body, Keilan. On his mind. Someone or something has imprisoned his most personal memories behind a dark barrier, and together we shall destroy those walls and restore Jan to who he was before."

Keilan swallowed hard, his wide eyes taking in the high-ranking magisters bent to their labors, the piles of ancient grimoires, and the arcane instruments scattered across the tables. "Your Majesty, I haven't even been taught how to summon wizardlight. I don't think I'll be able to help you."

The queen approached Jan holding the stiletto and a glass vial, beckoning for Keilan to join her. "Do you remember what happened in my study? Jan claims you are special, a Talent like he and I. And by his account, Talents can share their strength when they need to achieve some great act of sorcery. Jan has explained to me how the process works, and you will have to do nothing save open yourself, and allow me to draw upon the power within you. Hold this." She passed him the glass vial, and then pressed the stiletto's blade to her lips, frowning.

"Your Majesty? What is the problem?"

"I'm trying to think where it would be best to cut him."

Keilan nearly dropped the vial. "But, Your Majesty, you said we wouldn't be doing the surgery on his body!"

The queen crouched down beside Jan and took his hand in hers. "I did. And we won't be. But an opportunity like this – the chance to harvest an immortal's blood – is simply too good to waste. Who knows what secrets it might contain?" She pricked his forefinger with the stiletto's point, and Jan murmured and shifted in his sleep. "Be careful," she said, "don't let any spill."

An immortal's blood?

Hurriedly, Keilan positioned the vial so that the blood welling from Jan's finger dripped inside. A fleeting look of discomfort passed over Jan's face, but the queen pressed a hand to his forehead and whispered something soothing, and he quickly relaxed.

What sorcery could be done with someone's blood? This was like the stories in the Tractate of wicked sorcerers, who used black magic to summon demons or bind spirits to corpses and bring them to life again. Keilan felt a creeping unease watching the falling drops collect at the bottom of the vial.

Finally satisfied, the queen wrapped the finger in gauze, then motioned for Keilan to pass her the vial. She studied the blood for a moment, holding the vial up to the light of the hanging globes of mist, then carefully she placed it in a small black pouch and slipped that inside one of her shift's pockets.

"Now," she said, placing her palm on Jan's brow and beckoning Keilan closer. "Let's see what we are capable of." She took Keilan's hand, lacing their fingers together, and closed her eyes. Keilan gasped as he suddenly felt the queen's power, a vast roiling sea plunging down into great depths, a sensation not unlike when his sending had hung suspended in the waters of the Broken Sea. The queen was there, far below, an immense presence that waited and watched in the calm of the Deep, just as the Ancient had, while far above the surface above was lashed by rain and lightning. He gasped as a tendril of her sorcery slipped inside him, and he felt his own strength flow into her, a river of power that fed into the churning maelstrom that was Cein d'Kara –

Jan lay on a bed under a shimmering silver cloth. Above him motes of light floated through the air like stars tumbling slowly across the night sky. He watched them etch faint patterns on the chamber's ceiling, seemingly in accordance with the spare, ethereal notes playing somewhere far away.

His side hurt, and gently he traced the puckered scar that curved along his ribcage. How could he have been so foolish, blundering into a wyvern's nest? He'd been lucky he hadn't ended up as meat for screeching hatchlings – lucky, really, that his display of power had caught the attention of the others here in their hidden mountain fastness.

At least it seemed to be healing well. The fallowmancers of Vis must have made some advancements in their restorative sorceries, if the spell Querimanica had laid upon him had taken such quick effect. He tried to sort out what exactly had happened, but his memories were hazy, obscured by the veil of pain that had descended over his thoughts after the wyvern had scored his side with its barbed tail. He remembered clambering over tumbled boulders, excitedly following the faint scent of sorcery he had caught that morning after weeks of searching. Then the stone had shifted beneath him . . . except it hadn't been stone, but the pebbled hide of a sleeping wyvern. Pain had lanced his side, and he had fallen; he had forced himself to his feet, Bright singing in his hand as he had desperately tried to keep the beast's snapping jaws at bay.

He had slain that one, but others had come, drawn by their mate's death cry. He had struck out with dreadfire, turning the largest male into a blazing comet that had crashed into the cliffs above, which had started a cascade of stones that smashed into his flickering wards and driven him to his knees.

A red mist had seeped across his vision as he had fought to keep himself conscious, and he had been sure that his death was upon him, that his fate was to be torn to shreds atop this barren mountain.

But then they had arrived, clawing the wyverns from the sky with their glittering sorceries and sending the beasts fleeing deeper into the Bones. *She* had been foremost among them, lashing out with blazing strength, her long black hair dancing in the charged air. Alyanna. The one he had come to find.

Then, darkness. He could faintly recollect a few moments of clarity after that: the tall, gaunt Visani sorcerer straining to staunch his wounds and knit his broken bones, a great door carved into the rock of the mountain swinging open, warm broth dribbled between his lips by a young servant girl.

But, in truth, he had little idea of where he was or how long he had been asleep. Was he a prisoner, or a guest? He would suppose the latter, considering the chamber he found himself in . . . though when sorcery was involved, of course, a prison did not require iron bars or manacles. There could be all manner of restraints waiting to be tripped if he tried to leave the room.

A faint tapping came from the chamber's door. "Enter," he said, sitting up in the bed.

Alyanna slipped inside. She wore a flowing white dress hemmed by silver, and her long black hair was bound up in the latest Kalyuni fashion. The floating motes of light brightened as she approached his bed, a few drifting down to dance around her head.

"What an unexpected surprise this is, Jan. Welcome to my hall."

He shifted, grimacing from a sudden stab of pain. "Alyanna. Thank you for rescuing me. How long have I been asleep?"

"Three nights and two days. I was afraid you might never awaken, but Querimanica has a rare talent for healing."

"So that *was* Querimanica. I recognized him, but I also thought I might be delirious. I'm surprised he's joined with you."

Alyanna nodded. "He is here, and Hepheus and Demian and Xillia, among others. I've gathered the greatest collection of Talents since the Pure put the court of the Warlock King to the sword." She raised her thin eyebrows. "But I had not thought you would come. You never answered my invitation."

Jan put a hand to his temple as a wave of dizziness washed over him. "Your message was quite cryptic, as I'm sure you intended."

Alyanna sat on the edge of his bed. "So now you think you know what we are doing here?"

Jan nodded. "The note you sent was a puzzle, but after I'd picked apart the meaning I realized you were asking me to join you in some great endeavor, the purpose of which could be found in your writings. I was intrigued, so I gathered all the books of yours I could find – your canon really is quite impressive for one so young."

Alyanna smiled, the motes dancing around her head flashing. "Too often those of us with Talent rely solely on our natural gifts. True power comes from knowledge, and I find researching and writing books gives me the clarity I need to make new discoveries."

"Then you've done it."

"I believe I have."

"How? It has eluded the greatest sorcerers throughout history."

Alyanna shrugged. "Perhaps I am the greatest sorcerer in history."

Jan shook his head. "If you are right . . . then you very well might be."

Alyanna ran a finger along the shimmering silver blanket, tracing the outline of Jan's leg. "So I can assume that your presence here means that you've decided to join us?"

Jan tried to ignore her touch. "I was intrigued enough to spend weeks searching for where you'd hidden yourself. Whether I decide to –" Jan swallowed and shifted as her fingers traveled up his thigh – "to join you will depend on the . . . the details of what you are attempting."

Alyanna leaned closer and he caught her familiar smell, spices and lilacs and that other, almost animal scent that had so inflamed him a year ago. "I still think of our night in Kashkana, Jan, after your performance in the crèche. Tangled together in the Lesser Gendern's own bed, with the stars swirling above us. It was why I invited you here."

Jan put his hand on hers, stopping it from going any further. "I am heartsworn to Liralyn. That night was a mistake."

Alyanna pinched him lightly, but he saw a slight hardening in her eyes. "A mistake? It was a beautiful night. How can you be heartsworn to a queen who is forbidden to marry? And doesn't she have a daughter from some high lord?"

Jan tightened his grip on her fingers. "That is our way, Alyanna. Providing an heir with the proper bloodlines is more important than any personal desires."

Alyanna snorted and withdrew her hand. "That is the problem with our species. Tradition binds us as tight as any chains. We must break those bonds if we are ever to realize our true greatness."

"And you can do that, Alyanna?"

The hint of playfulness vanished from her face. When she spoke the intensity in her voice sent a shiver through him. "I can, and I will."

Jan gradually gained strength over the next few days. To his slight surprise, he was allowed to wander freely through the mountain redoubt Alyanna and her mysterious cabal had constructed. It seemed to have been built over the ruins of an ancient wraith nest – the passages soared nearly twice the height of a man, curving and twisting in upon themselves in the distinctive labyrinthine style wraiths employed to keep their king and his harem safely hidden in the deeps. But workmen had obviously spent quite some time here, carving human-sized steps where needed, setting doors at the entrances to chambers, and furnishing those same rooms in the lush style of the Mosaic Cities, with pastel strips of knotted silk hanging among chairs and tables of finely-wrought copper and glass. Jan found himself wondering what had happened to the workers who had made this secret fortress so comfortable – but, knowing Alyanna, he had his suspicions. She wasn't one for leaving any loose ends untied.

In his explorations he occasionally came across one or more of the other Talents. Some he had met before, while others he knew only by reputation. He stumbled upon the Eversummer Islander Hepheus in the redoubt's well-stocked library, poring over some ancient text. Jan had greeted her warmly; ten years ago he had traveled to the great tree-towns of her homeland and spent a month singing for their lords and drinking her people's famous numbing sap as he sailed from island to island. Hepheus had been but a girl then, the apprentice of the legendary sorcerer-vizier who advised one of the archipelago's kings. Jan had sung for the court and danced with her in the slow style of Min-Ceruth, and as he had held her close he had seen in her adoring gaze the glimmer of a girl's first love.

He couldn't find that same spark in her eyes now when she finally dragged herself from the tome she was reading. Hepheus had regarded him coolly, then stood and offered him a formal greeting. They had talked of the islands and the north, but skirted any topic that might shed light about how Alyanna planned to accomplish her impossible task.

Jan had also sought out Querimanica and offered him thanks for his healing magic. The gaunt Visani had accepted Jan's words with grace, but he had also been coy when Jan tried to turn the discussion toward what had brought him to this forsaken corner of the world, in the company of those he once had considered his bitter rivals.

The swordsinger Demian practiced for hours each day in one of the empty great halls, and Jan spent some time watching the Kalyuni's flashing routines. He had fought and bested his share of warriors from the Mosaic Cities, but he had to admit that the technique and ferocious speed of the swordsinger would make him a dangerous opponent. Jan had thought himself hidden in the shadows, but at the end of one of Demian's spinning attacks he had suddenly stopped, staring at where Jan stood in the upper galleys. The swordsinger had not moved or said anything for a long, tense moment, and then abruptly he had turned on his heels and strode away.

On the third day inside the mountain, the world changed forever. Jan was inside his quarters, idly plucking out a tune he'd been toying with on his lute, when something happened very far away that made him clutch at his chest, gasping. It was a reverberation, like the tolling of a distant bell, but with such strength and power that he felt like one of the vibrating strings of his instrument, his bones thrumming with the echoes of some distant sorcery.

He stumbled from his room, reeling against the wall to try and steady himself before he toppled over. Jan pressed his face against the cold, rough stone, his thoughts scattered.

He wasn't sure how long he slumped there, half-conscious. Finally he felt someone pulling on his arm, and slowly, he surfaced, blinking to try and focus on his surroundings.

It was Alyanna. Her eyes were wide and her black hair hung in tangles, as if she had just been pulled from her bed. "Jan! Wake, curse you! We need to go now!"

"What . . . what is happening?" he slurred, pushing himself from the wall.

"It has begun! What we've been waiting for!"

She led him stumbling through twisting passages, until they came upon a small chamber he had never seen before. A circular table of gleaming black ebonwood filled the room so completely that there was no space for chairs, and the seven men and women clustered around it had been forced to stand. Hovering above the table was a huge multifaceted jewel the color of a fading bruise, blemished by drifting shreds of darkness that almost looked like ribbons of smoke uncoiling in a twilit sky.

He saw Hepheus and Xillia and Demian and Querimanica, and three others he did not know – one a grossly fat bald man with copper-colored skin, another a small mousy sorceress in gray robes, and the last a beautiful silver-haired woman who –

His mother! Keilan surfaced from the tumbling rapids of Jan's memories, gasping for air. The pale skin and silver hair, like moonlight on water . . . no, no, he realized after the initial shock had faded, it wasn't his mother. But close, so close, the hair was the same but the cast of her face was very slightly different – the resemblance was uncanny, though, like glimpsing a ghost . . .

"Weaver, we are ready."

It was Demian who had spoken, his voice an oasis of calm in the room. The swordsinger seemed unaffected by the roiling sorcery crackling in the air, but the others looked how Jan felt. They swayed slightly, their faces ashen and drawn.

Alyanna moved to the edge of the table and took a deep breath. "There is no time for ceremony. The moment has come when we will either seize the world, or lose everything. Open yourselves to me, and prepare to become what we were destined to be."

Around the table the sorcerers reached out and clasped each other's hands. Alyanna gestured for him to join them, and with a slight hesitation Jan stepped forward, completing the circle. Immediately he felt the power of the others flowing through the chain, feeding into Alyanna, whose chest heaved as the strength of seven of the world's greatest Talents filled her.

"Jan! Join us!" she cried, her fingers tightening in his grip, her long nails digging into his flesh and drawing forth a trickle of blood.

And he did.

He unclenched his power, allowing Alyanna to siphon it from him like how a waterspout draws the ocean up into the sky. He gritted his teeth as he felt her sucking him dry, leaving him a husk of himself, every drop of sorcery wrung from his body.

Alyanna's face was flushed, and power crackled in her eyes. Her hair writhed in the air, a nest of coiling snakes.

He gasped when he saw the spell she was weaving, its beauty streaking his face with tears. How could she do this thing? What mind could create such a masterpiece of dizzying complexity?

Across from Jan the small woman in the gray robes slumped forward, her neck lolling to one side, as if broken.

"She's dead, Weaver," rasped the fat man with copper skin, his face gleaming with sweat, "you've drained too much!"

"Close the circle!" Alyanna commanded, "or we'll all follow her!"

The man let go of the gray-robed woman and reached over her motionless body to take Demian's hand.

Something was approaching. A vastness, greater than Jan could comprehend. He saw in the wide eyes of the others that they also sensed its coming, a rolling, unstoppable wave as tall as a mountain and as broad as the sky –

It washed over them. Alyanna screamed, her hand spasming in his grip. Jan held on, desperate to keep the chain intact, knowing that if he let go – if any of them let go – that their minds would be shredded, just like the poor, dead woman slumped across the table.

The tendrils of darkness within the jewel hovering before them pulsed, swelling larger. It was drawing this great force like a lodestone, and Alyanna was deftly manipulating the energy as it filled the jewel, fashioning it into something else and feeding it back again into the gathered Talents.

It rushed into Jan, the terrible power that Alyanna had drawn here, until he felt like he might burst from the strain. What was it? Not raw sorcerous energy like those with the gift drew from the Void; it was something else entirely, although equally as powerful and magnificent. He drank greedily.

A flicker within the flood, a glimpse of another place through the eyes of someone else. Jan was a woman standing in the doorway of a sod house somewhere in the far south, wisps of clouds uncoiling in a mauve sky. A girl – the woman's daughter, he knew – was playing in the long grass with a wooden horse her husband had carved. Jan watched as a great shadow fell over the small girl, and she looked up curiously, squinting into the distance. Something was building beyond the treetops, a mountain where there had been no mountain before. With a numbing shock he – no, the woman – realized that it was a wave approaching them, a wave even though the sea was hundreds of leagues away.

Another stuttering image, from a balcony in a tower in a distant city. Dark waters surged through the streets below, rising to cover tiled roofs where men and women had gathered; they reached imploringly to the heavens as the sea rushed up to swallow them. With a jarring shock Jan realized that this was the great sorcery the Min-Ceruthans had fashioned, the cataclysmic spell that could obliterate their rival to the south. Why had they unleashed it now? And how had Alyanna known they would?

Then he was in a place he was familiar with, in a city of gleaming black stone crouched in the shadow of the Bones. Nes Vaneth, the greatest city of his people. He was running, his boots slipping in the snow as a terrible dark ice blossomed around him, rushing up to cover the buildings, the ground, his screaming countrymen.

Memories. This torrent of power Alyanna was drawing to them was filled with the final moments of countless lives – thousands of lives, perhaps even millions. The victims of the unimaginable sorcerous stroke and counterstroke the wizards of the north and south had long held over each other. How could Alyanna be channeling these lives into the jewel, and then feeding this river of souls into those gathered around the table?

This was how she planned to realize the dream of the Warlock King, and turn them all into immortals?

Jan felt swollen, gorged on the lives of others – he cried out, trying to pull himself from the rippling chain of power, but he could not break free now . . . and that's when he felt it, a familiar spark buried within the onslaught of souls coursing through him, the final, radiant memory of the woman he loved more than life itself – ice was creeping into the throne room of Nes Vaneth to claim her as she sat on the dragonbone throne, and for one terrible moment she *saw* him, and she knew what he had done –

The queen gasped and reeled away from where Jan lay on the stone dais, clutching at her hand. Keilan returned to himself with a jarring shock, collapsing onto his knees as the room spun.

"Majesty," he said hoarsely, trying to keep himself from slipping into the darkness. Then the queen was there, surprisingly gentle, helping him to stand.

"Keilan, are you all right?"

He glanced at her: a vessel had burst in the queen's eye, staining it with a bloom of red. The rest of her face was bloodless.

"I'm . . . I'm . . ."

On the dais beside them Jan suddenly contorted, his back arching, as if he had been lanced by great pain. Green fire trickled from his nose, and his eyes snapped open, blazing with power. But he did not see them; instead, he stared emptily at the domed ceiling. Sorcery was building within him, faster than Keilan had ever felt before, until Jan's body was a dam ready to burst before the surging energies –

The queen reached out towards Keilan as the world erupted around them.

35: SENACUS

A FLOWER OF green flame bloomed in the darkness.

Moments later a wash of sorcery like a great wind came rushing down from Saltstone, battering Senacus where he stood on his balcony staring out into the night. The paladin staggered, and if he hadn't been leaning against the railing he might have fallen, such was the unexpected force of the magical explosion.

"By the Radiant Father," he whispered, blinking away the spots the green flash had left in his eyes. What had just happened?

He peered up at the shadowy crenellations and towers picked out against the star-spattered dome of the sky, but the light had vanished completely, as if it had never been.

He heard the door open and close behind him and he turned away from the darkness. Demian had slipped inside and was hurriedly donning a shirt and pants of some shimmering black cloth.

"Did you feel that?" Senacus murmured, moving as if in a daze into the room they shared at The Twisted Serpent.

The shadowblade thrust his sword through a silken tie at his waist. "I did, paladin. That is our signal, I'm sure of it. We should hurry – it will be chaos in the fortress for only a short while."

"The horses –"

"Are saddled and ready in the inn's stables. Once we have the boy we must move quickly. If we are lucky, they won't realize he's missing for a few days, and that will be the start we need to escape pursuit. Now, take up your sword. Every moment is precious."

"What was that sorcery up in the fortress?"

Demian paused for a moment, his eyes passing beyond the Pure to stare at something distant. "A trap, paladin. It was a trap laid long ago, baited with something Cein d'Kara could not resist." He shook his head, and Senacus had the sense that the shadowblade's next words were not intended for him. "Always spinning your webs, Weaver. Games within games."

Weaver? Senacus started to ask another question, but then snapped his mouth shut. Demian was right – they should move quickly, and there would be time for answers later. Ama himself had set him on this path for redemption, and he was not about to disappoint the Radiant Father a second time.

Hastily, he buckled on his sword-belt, replacing the scarred leather scabbard with its ill-balanced iron longsword with the sheath of twisting filigreed silver that held his white-metal blade. Wearing his Pure armor while in the streets of Herath would certainly be too conspicuous, but if he was forced to draw his weapon in Saltstone he wanted the perfect balance of his own sword.

Demian's gaze lingered on the blade's copper hilt, but he said nothing. Perhaps the shadowblade realized that if they were discovered they would need every possible advantage. Senacus's hand went to the relic of Tethys, dangling on its chain around his neck. He dearly hoped he wouldn't have to shed his disguise while inside Saltstone; if he used his holy power it would be like a candle of bright white flame flaring in a darkened room. He doubted they could escape from a thousand elite Dymorian warriors and dozens of enraged sorcerers if their presence was revealed.

"Stay close to me," said the shadowblade, and vanished out the door. Senacus hurried to follow him, sketching the circle of Ama in the air and murmuring a prayer imploring for his lord's favor this night.

They left the inn by way of a small side door used by the servants; it emptied into an alley littered with clumps of nightsoil and refuse from the kitchens. Senacus grimaced as his boot heel skidded on something soft. He wondered how many other paladins of Ama had been forced to creep through muck in order to demonstrate their loyalty and faith. Very few, he guessed.

They pushed deeper into the alley, until they came to a stone wall that soared twice as high as the nearby buildings. This was the outer curtain wall of Saltstone itself, the first of three layers that protected the inner fortress and its towers.

Demian had chosen The Twisted Serpent because it was so far up the Slopes that it nearly hunkered in Saltstone's shadow. How he planned on getting over these imposing walls he had been rather coy about, though, when Senacus had asked just that question.

He had imagined climbing spikes or some kind of grapple, but Demian merely went right to the wall and started pulling himself up smoothly, almost like a spider. Senacus gaped in surprise, hurrying over to run his hands along the smooth stone, noting how tiny the grooves were where the great blocks fit together. He concentrated, trying to ascertain whether this was sorcery, but felt nothing. Perhaps it was some strange shadowblade power, like walking between the darknesses.

It took only a few moments for the shadowblade to reach the top and vanish over the battlements. Senacus was still staring up after him, wondering if he should try and follow, when a length of black silk struck his shoulder. So that's how he was supposed to get up. Gripping one of the knots tied into the silk he started to climb, his boots scrabbling for purchase.

By the time he arrived at the top his arms were aching, and Demian had to help pull him over the parapet. He collapsed on the walkway, breathing hard.

The shadowblade retrieved his rope, coiling it tightly while Senacus recovered. When Demian had finished, he secreted the rope away and crouched down beside him.

"Can you feel the boy?" he whispered.

Senacus cast out with his senses, sifting through the tempest of sorcery swirling within the fortress. "I can. His signature is unique, so bright and strong. The other sorcerer is here as well, the one who first stole him away from me."

The shadowblade patted his shoulder. "Good."

Crouched low so that he was not visible over the battlements, Demian began moving quickly along the walkway, motioning for Senacus to follow him. They had only gone a few dozen paces when there was noise ahead: a guardsman making his rounds. Light from his upraised lantern puddled around him. He appeared nervous, Senacus decided, as he kept glancing over his shoulder at the tall tower where the green flash had erupted from earlier.

Senacus tensed, his hand going to his sword hilt, but Demian turned back and shook his head curtly. The assassin crept closer to the battlements beside them, and when he passed into this deeper patch of shadows he simply vanished. Like before, there was no ripple of sorcery. Senacus gritted his teeth. How could his brothers protect the emperor and Menekar from men with abilities such as this? Where did he get his powers?

The approaching guardsman paused, as if distracted by something. He turned slightly just as Demian swelled behind him. Steel flashed in the light from his lantern, the assassin slicing his throat with a curved dagger. The guardsman's knees buckled, and a wash of blackness flowed from the cut. Demian snatched the lantern from the guardsman's slack hand before it could fall; at the same time, he gently guided the twitching body to the ground. He placed the lantern on one of the wall's crenellations, as if it had been set there purposefully, and then dragged the guard outside of the circle of light it shed.

A cold wave washed over Senacus. Was this what the Radiant Father wanted, murdering an innocent from the shadows? How could a paladin of Ama accept such a thing? Was he being tested again?

"They will find him soon enough," Demian hissed at him, "we cannot linger." Then the shadowblade dashed to a set of stairs clinging to the side of the wall and hurried down toward the inner courtyard. Senacus followed, trying to keep his holy senses fixed on the distant spark of sorcery that was the boy Keilan. It flickered strangely, like a flame guttering in the wind. He half-thought the alarm would be raised before they reached the bottom, but soon they were standing on grass again. Senacus wondered how long their luck could hold.

Keeping to the shadows he started towards a large door set into Saltstone's inner walls, peering everywhere for signs of more guards. He couldn't imagine that there were normally so few; the sorcerous explosion earlier must have pulled many from their duties. He glanced back when he reached the door, but Demian had not followed him; rather, the shadowblade had retreated deeper into the shadows, and as Senacus watched he pulled something from a hidden pocket and held it out in front of him.

Now Senacus could feel the creeping tingle of sorcery. What was happening? Was Demian some kind of sorcerer? Did the High Seneschal know this? A circle of air near the shadowblade began to undulate like cloth caught in a strong breeze, until it had become a window to a very different place. Gone was the utter blackness of the stone wall, replaced by a tangle of tree limbs silhouetted against a sky dusted with distant stars. Shapes moved beyond this doorway to elsewhere, but Demian did not stay to see what came through. He turned and jogged to where Senacus waited, taking his arm. "My brethren are coming, and they will provide the distraction we need. Take me to the boy."

36: KEILAN

THE BLACK ROCKS were slippery today. A storm had flailed up from the south the night before, lashing the coast with rain and wind, churning the sea until waves smote the beach and washed over the ragged line of tumbled boulders that reached out into the bay.

Sella seemed unaware of the danger, however, leaping like a mountain goat from rock to treacherous rock, pausing occasionally to examine what had collected in a tidal pool, or poke with a piece of driftwood at one of the large, blue jellyfish that had been stranded when the waters receded.

"Kay! Kay, come look at this!" she called back to him, gesturing frantically for him to hurry. She was straddling a crevice where two of the rocks came together, staring down at something.

Sighing, Keilan stretched out his leg, trying to find purchase on the closest boulder without falling into the water below. He threw himself forward, grimacing slightly as his hand closed around a jagged fin of rock, and he was forced to hold on tight so he wouldn't slide into the frothing sea. Why had this seemed so much easier when he'd been younger?

"Kay, you need to come right now! It's gonna swim away real soon!"

"I'm coming Sella, I'm right behind –"

Keilan's foot skidded on the wet stone; his arms pinwheeled as he tried to catch his balance, but it was too late, and he toppled backward. Sharp pain bloomed in his back as he bounced off a rock, and his wrist twisted when he threw his arm out to stop his fall.

Bracing cold enveloped him as he hit the water, his head striking a submerged stone. Numbness spread from his skull down his neck, to his arms, and though he struggled to swim he could only thrash weakly, a great weight pulling him down, down, down . . .

Into the darkness. Into the Deep.

There was light above, the bright sun dancing on the surface of the water, but it was receding quickly, fading into blackness . . . and then something grabbed his wrist. He screamed, sending up a stream of bubbles and flooding his mouth with seawater.

Small fingers clutched at him, pulling at his tunic, and there was Sella floating beside him, her long hair coiling in the water.

He kicked his legs and pushed upwards. His lungs were burning, but the light was brightening above him as he surged towards the surface . . .

He gasped, returning to himself. A hazy sun was set into the shadowy dimness above, turning slowly – no, not a sun, it was a cracked crystal sphere dangling from a golden thread, still faintly glowing with shreds of luminescent mist. Other threads hung down, but their globes were gone. They twisted in the wind like stalks of seaweed gently drifting on the ocean's current.

Wind?

Keilan struggled to sit up, grimacing as waves of pain tried to force him back down. He moaned when he saw what surrounded him.

The top of Ravenroost had been utterly destroyed. Much of the cupola that had crowned the tower had collapsed, and great chunks of stone now lay among the blackened tables that had once held the queen's magical instruments. The cold breeze playing with the hanging threads came from gaping rents in the ceiling; the wind reached down from the now-visible night sky, stirring Keilan's hair and fluttering the pages of an ancient tome that had fallen open near him. Another book beside that one was burning, slowly being devoured by ghostly green flames.

All was silent, save for the wind's moaning and the hiss and crackle of the still-smoldering pockets of fire.

"Your Majesty," Keilan cried, stumbling to his feet. Frantically, he cast about for the queen, and quickly found her body just paces away, splayed among the rubble. He staggered towards her and knelt down, clutching at her wrist.

A pulse, faint but steady. Her beautiful pale face was smudged with dirt, and there was a red bump on her brow that was already starting to purple. Gently he squeezed her hand. "My Queen, wake up. Please wake up." He searched her face, but saw no sign that she could hear him.

What had happened? He had been there, inside Jan's mind, watching his hidden memories unspool. Then there had been a flash . . . they had tripped something, down in the deepest recesses of his mind, triggered some fell sorcery. Power had erupted from Jan, and the last thing Keilan remembered was the queen lunging towards him and throwing up her hands, a blue barrier materializing in front of them just as waves of green fire had filled the chamber. For a moment the shield had held, but then it had threaded with cracks, and the queen had cried out as it shattered, sending them sprawling backward.

Keilan touched his head, wincing from the pain. How long had he been lying here? Why had no one else come yet? Perhaps only moments had passed since the explosion of flames.

He had to get help. Keilan stood, swaying slightly. He had to find the magisters and bring them up here. They could save the queen, surely.

Magisters. Keilan's eyes darted around the darkened room, searching for the others who had been assisting the queen. A shadow in the dimness. He took two stumbling steps towards it, then cried out in horror.

Etched against the wall was the charred outline of a man, his arms upraised as if he was trying to ward away his onrushing doom.

Keilan put his hand out to steady himself on the edge of a table, the blackened wood crumbling to soot beneath his touch. Was this . . . could this be Magister d'Terin? Memories of the old man's kind smile and gentle voice brought stinging tears to his eyes. Why had this happened?

The chamber tilted, righted itself. Darkness lurked at the edges of his vision, waiting patiently to drag him back again into oblivion. With a wrenching sob Keilan shook his head, trying to clear it, then stumbled toward the stairwell.

He passed the man – the immortal, the queen had called him – lying motionless on the dais. The red cloth beneath him had been burnt to ashes; just a few ragged black scraps remained. His eyes were open, staring at nothing, and his bloodless lips were slightly parted. He looked dead. Keilan staggered past, not pausing to see if he was alive or not.

With a pained grunt he squeezed past a huge chunk of the cupola that had fallen and now partially blocked the entrance to the stairs. One foot after another, both hands on the marble railing he descended step by shuffling step. Tremors coursed up his legs, causing him to nearly fall several times.

A commotion from below. Several men, some in the robes of magisters, others wearing red cloaks, were hurrying up the stairs. They cried out when they saw him.

"Boy!" said the first Scarlet Guardsman to reach him, a Shan with jet-black hair and uptilted eyes. "What has happened? Where is the queen?"

Keilan swallowed and shook his head, pointing with a wavering hand back towards the highest floor. "Sorcery . . . an explosion. The roof came down –"

The Shan warrior grabbed him by his shoulders. "The queen!"

"Alive," Keilan gasped, "but hurt."

A moment later the warrior was gone, bounding up the stairs. Keilan could only clutch at the railing as the others pushed past him.

He pressed his brow against the cold stone of the balustrade, feeling his strength seep away. The pain in the back of his head was sharpening, an incessant pulsing that blotted his vision with floating spots of color. He doubled over, retching up the supper he had eaten hours ago

His friends. He had to find his friends. Nel and Vhelan would know what to do.

Keilan pushed himself away from the marble baluster and started down again. He reached the bottom, passing from Ravenroost and back into the lower reaches of Saltstone. The corridors of the great fortress blurred together as he stumbled down them, leaning heavily against the walls; occasionally others would rush past, boots pounding the floor, but they paid him no heed. Horns sounded in the distance.

Finally he could not hold back the darkness anymore. "Nel . . ." he whispered, sliding to his knees. The Deep rushed up to claim him once again.

37: ALYANNA

A FUNERAL SHROUD of silence draped the gardens this night. No animals rustled the underbrush, no birds called out their songs, no laughter or the plucked strings of keppas issued forth from the pavilions of the emperor's concubines. Even the wind seemed to be holding its breath, the chimes hanging like silver fruit among the branches.

A new presence had invaded the imperial pleasure gardens, something not entirely of this world. She had invited it; she knew the source of this unease. But to the others who shared these grounds with her – the beasts and the birds and the flawless courtesans – it must be terrifying. They could only huddle together and stare out into the night and imagine what moved in the darkness.

A tremor from the riftstone, tingling numbness spreading from where she clutched it tight in her palm. Her heart quickened – it was almost time. Between two of the soaring quartz monoliths the air began to ripple and twist. Glimmering points of fire appeared, slowly resolving into torches, the light they cast puddling on the dark stone of some distant fortress.

Saltstone.

A man in black stood just on the other side of the rift, looking out at her. Demian. He said nothing, only nodded slightly and turned away, quickly vanishing beyond the edge of the floating portal.

Alyanna swallowed. She had told Demian, months ago, that without taking risks the world could not be seized. This was one of those risks, where her fate and the fate of all Araen hung in the balance. Either she would emerge triumphant, a sorceress without peer once again, or she would be destroyed, her thousand years of glittering life finally snuffed out.

"Are you ready?" she spoke into the night. There was no sound or movement, but she knew that they had heard.

"I know you are here. I can feel you."

A presence emerged from the deeper shadows pooled beside one of the monoliths. Alyanna summoned a faint ball of wizardlight and the darkness around her fled, painting the grass silver and making the quartz sculptures shine like they were the great bones of giants sunk into the earth.

As the night melted away they were revealed. Two-dozen warriors garbed in black, veils drawn across their faces. The one who had stepped forward first addressed her in a voice soft and cold.

"Greetings from the daymo. We have come to uphold his part of the bargain you struck." The eyes of this shadowblade were uptilted – he must be Shan.

Alyanna allowed her wizardlight to float closer to the assassins. The black cloth they had wound around their bodies seemed to drink the light, but it was the swords at their sides that interested her. The blades appeared to be carved from the night itself, gleaming fragments of darkness, each surrounded by a penumbra that her sorcerous light could not penetrate. So these were shadowblades, the famed weapons of the kith'ketan. Alyanna had glimpsed the Void before, had stared out into that terrible emptiness where great beings surged and contested in the endless dark, and these swords gave her the same creeping chill she had felt then. They were not forged on this world.

"You are the dagger with which I will cut out the heart of Dymoria," she said, loud enough that all the gathered assassins could hear her.

"The queen and her senior magisters must not survive this night. When they are dead, return to your master and tell him that he will have what was promised. Keilan will be given up to him, after the boy assists me in one great act of sorcery."

The shadowblade began to turn away, but then hesitated. "What is that?" he asked, pointing beside her. There was a strange edge to his voice, an emotion she could not place.

Alyanna glanced down. One of the Chosen crouched in the grass, its head lowered so that its snarled black hair obscured its face. This one was a girl, she thought.

Alyanna smiled affectionately and reached down so that her fingers rested lightly on its bony shoulder. "My beautiful child."

The assassin's gaze lingered on the Chosen for a moment longer. "That thing does not belong here, sorceress."

Alyanna quirked an eyebrow. "She and her brothers are coming with us tonight. They have special talents that could prove useful."

"Keep it by your side," the assassin spat,"and away from us." Then with preternatural grace he moved quickly toward the floating rift and passed through it. Without the slightest noise the others followed, a stream of dark shapes that soon vanished, leaving Alyanna alone in the garden.

"I do not think he likes you," she said to the ragged creature hunkered beside her.

we know the one he serves. Their echoing whispers seemed to come from everywhere and nowhere.

"The daymo?"

Dry, rasping chuckles. *No, the one that dwells farther beneath the mountain, the one whose black tears now hang at their sides.*

Alyanna tamped down her surge of curiosity. Another time she would investigate what her new servants knew about the kith'ketan and their mysterious dark lord. She could afford no distractions tonight. If the queen had survived the trap she had laid within Jan's mind then she must be prepared for a contest of equals. Surely her own sorcery was the greater, nurtured and refined over a thousand years, but she would be confronting her rival in her own fortress, in her sanctum, and who knew what spells the queen had woven into the fabric of Saltstone and could call upon for aid.

Enough. No more hesitating. Had she become craven, after so many creeping centuries? She had stolen the Chosen from the warlocks of Shan. She had bound the soul of the last genthyaki to her own. She had descended into the dark and taken the eye of the mountain from the hall of the wraith king. She had dueled with a dozen Talents over her endless wheeling years and bested them all.

She had conquered death itself.

For a time, at least. Alyanna restrained herself from touching the wrinkles that had appeared at the corners of her eyes. With Keilan and Demian beside her she could recreate the ancient ceremony, she was sure of it. She could make herself immortal again. She just needed to arrange another cataclysm.

Alyanna stepped through the hanging portal and into a courtyard somewhere within the walls of Saltstone.

The coldness of the flagstones seeped through her thin, silken slippers. Demian had vanished, presumably along with the paladin. It had been a risk, she knew, appearing in the High Mendicant's dreams and compelling him to dispatch the disgraced Pure with the swordsinger. The paladins of Ama commanded great powers – powers that despite her best efforts she had not fully plumbed. But she needed this new Talent, the boy Keilan, and the Pure could follow his magical scent in this fortress like a bloodhound, despite the miasma of sorcery that hung heavy and thick over everything here.

She glanced about. A door, slightly ajar. She passed into the fortress proper, and followed twisting corridors until she came upon two guards in the livery of House d'Kara.

"Where are the queen's quarters?" she asked the two stunned warriors.

The older guard regarded her brazenly, no doubt taking in her apparent youth and simple shift of diaphanous green cloth.

"Who sent you, girl? Are you one of Chastian's playthings?"

Alyanna sighed. "I don't have time for this, fool. Tell me where your mistress conducts her sorcery."

The guard stepped forward, looming over her. "Look here, wench –"

Alyanna gestured and an avalanche of force slammed into the guard, smashing him against the wall. Blood erupted from his mouth, and his face crumpled under the tremendous pressure, his scream trailing off into gibberish.

Alyanna turned to the other guard, who gaped at her with wide eyes as his friend slid to the ground in a mangled heap. "Where are the queen's quarters?"

His mouth worked soundlessly for a few moments before he finally found his voice. "Follow . . . follow this corridor until you come to a set of double doors. Through them, then left. Past the gardens and you're there. Ravenroost. Her tower."

"You have my thanks," Alyanna said, then made a cutting motion with her hand. The guard tumbled backward, clutching at his slashed throat.

Careful to avoid the rapidly spreading pools of blood Alyanna stepped daintily over the twitching bodies of the two guardsmen.

She didn't meet anyone else as she followed the guard's instructions to the queen's tower. She heard distant horns, and once even the sound of swords clashing from a nearby passage. That must be the shadowblades, sowing chaos. While the magisters and the Scarlet Guard dealt with the assassins, she would be able to confront the queen directly, without interference. She dug her nails into her sweat-slicked palms, reveling in the anticipation of what was coming. For a thousand years she had been without equal. The chance to prove herself the greatest still was making her almost giddy.

Finally, she stood at the base of Ravenroost's great spiraling steps. She could sense the residue of sorcery above, redolent with her own unique flavor.

"Attend to me," she said, and the Chosen appeared beside her, stepping out from wherever it was they lurked in the ragged fringes of the world.

Mistress.

"Guard these stairs. Kill anyone who tries to take them to the top." Alyanna paused on the first step, glancing back at the demon child. "Oh, and anyone besides myself who comes down."

Rasping laughter followed her as she started the ascent.

38: XIN

THE DARKNESS ENVELOPED him. Xin stood on a floor of uneven stone, someplace far underground. He knew he was deep beneath the surface because the blackness was so total, so encompassing, that he could not even see his hand when he passed it in front of his face. Also the air was clammy and stale, redolent of earth and rotting things, the smell of a tomb opened after many ages left undisturbed.

The silence pressing down on him was just as seamless as the dark, but he knew he was not alone. He could feel them, standing in a circle around him, just beyond his reach. They did not breathe – they did not need to breathe anymore. They said nothing, did nothing.

His brothers waited with the patience of the dead.

A sound shivered the stillness. He felt himself being pulled away, his spirit receding from this terrible place. A glimmer of light kindled in the distance, swelling as he hurtled closer.

Xin awoke.

He lay in a soft bed in a chamber lit by flickering candlelight. His racing heart gradually slowed as the memories of his dream faded. He had been somewhere dark, surrounded by the ghosts of his brothers.

Every night was the same – he could never remember the exact details, but he knew that they had been there, watching him. Watching and waiting.

Nel squirmed against his chest, muttering something in her sleep. Xin pressed her slim body to his own, feeling her relax into his embrace.

He wasn't ready. His brothers would have to wait. Even with a fractured soul he still had reason to live.

He drowsed beneath the silken sheets, not wanting to descend again fully into the dreamlands. His fingers played with Nel's hair as she began to snore softly.

The sound that had dragged him from the darkness came again, a horn's faint pealing. Nel grunted awake, her body tensing.

"What was that?" she murmured, pulling away from him.

"This one doesn't know. A horn. That's at least the second blast – the first woke this one a few moments ago."

Silk whispered as Nel sat up in the bed. "What's the hour?"

Xin glanced at the candle on the bedside table; the wax had barely melted. "Perhaps the eighth? We've been sleeping only a little while."

Nel slipped from the bed and scooped her tunic from the chamber's floor. "I've never heard horns blow this late. Something is happening outside."

Xin drew his knees up to his chest, not quite ready to relinquish the warmth of the blankets. "Surely the Scarlet Guard can handle whatever it is."

Nel frowned, buckling onto her forearms leather bracers studded with throwing daggers. She pulled on her tunic and bent again to retrieve her pants. "The Guard will defend the queen, surely. But there are others in Saltstone that need protection."

"The apprentices. Keilan."

"Yes."

Xin threw back the blanket and stood, the chill air licking his naked body.

Nel's gaze lingered on him appraisingly. "Let's hope it's nothing, and I can get you back in bed quickly."

Xin smiled back at her, but his expression changed when the faint sound of clashing steel carried into the chamber.

He snatched his leather cuirass and swordbelt from where they hung on the wall and quickly donned both, while Nel reached under her pillow and pulled out Chance and Fate, the daggers vanishing into hidden folds in her clothes.

"Vhelan?" Xin asked as she headed for the door.

"I'll wake him," Nel replied, then disappeared into the hallway. Xin followed her, his sword in his hand.

"Wake up, boss!" the knife yelled, pounding on the door to the magister's chamber. While she tried to rouse the sorcerer Xin listened hard, hoping to catch the sounds of battle again.

Finally, Vhelan opened his door a crack. "Garazon's black balls, Nel," he slurred, swaying slightly in the entrance. "What is the matter?"

"Saltstone is under attack. Get your robes on."

The sorcerer blinked bloodshot eyes, as if he was struggling to understand what his knife was saying. "Attack? That's impossible."

"Listen," Xin said sharply. A scream, suddenly cut short. Again came the shriek of steel, and not from very far away.

Vhelan vanished back into his chamber, then emerged moments later in robes that nearly matched the color of his bloodshot eyes. He groaned and rubbed his temple, shaking his head as if to clear away the cobwebs. "I hope there's a Skein warband camped outside that I can call down the wrath of the gods upon. I have an overwhelming desire to inflict pain on whoever is forcing me to be awake right now."

"They are inside, not outside," Xin said, motioning for them to follow him.

"Come, the sounds came from this direction."

He led them down corridors hung with faded tapestries and lit by torches set into iron brackets. After a few twists and turns they nearly collided with a hurrying older servant. The man's watery blue eyes widened in fear when he saw them, but he relaxed when Vhelan stepped forward in his magister robes and held up his hands placatingly.

"Calm, we are friends. What is happening?"

The old man pointed back the way he'd come. "There!" he cried, his voice cracking, "Hennus and Thale are dead! I – I – I saw it kill 'em, knives comin' out of the darkness –"

Again the rending sound of steel from farther ahead, and Xin pushed past the stammering servant. He rounded the corner and skidded to a halt, trying to process what it was he was seeing.

Two servants in Dymorian livery were sprawled at the end of the corridor, blood soaking their white tunics. A tall warrior wearing the red cloak of the Scarlet Guard stood above them, turning frantically as if trying to catch sight of a hidden enemy and slashing his sword at empty air. Briefly Xin thought this man must be the murderer, either a disguised assassin or simply crazed, but after a moment he realized that no blood darkened his blade.

"Guardsman!" he shouted, and the man whirled to face him with wild eyes. "Who killed these two?"

The warrior continued to wave his sword like a madman, thrusting at nothing. "The night!" he screamed at Xin. "The night is alive, we must warn the queen –"

Something emerged from the man's chest, his steel breastplate parting like silk. It was a length of blackness, the way it tapered to a curving point reminding Xin of the sword wielded by the Shan from the caravan, the one who had been slain by the monster that had murdered his brothers. The man dropped his sword, staring in numb shock at what was protruding from his body. His mouth worked soundlessly, a flower of blood blooming on the tabard that covered his breastplate. The spreading darkness quickly obscured the sinuous red dragon of Dymoria.

Then the unearthly blade withdrew from the Scarlet Guardsman, and he crumpled to the stone floor. Standing behind him was a man dressed all in black, the lower half of his face covered by a silken veil. Xin was certain, madly enough, that moments before this man had not been there. It was like he had simply stepped from the shadows cast by the guttering torches.

"Kith'ketan!" Vhelan gasped, and the shock flooding Xin momentarily rooted him to the ground. Could it possibly be one of the legendary assassins? Here? *Why*?

The man regarded them calmly for a moment and then stepped backward into the shadows, vanishing. Xin started forward, his grip on his sword's hilt suddenly slick with sweat. Where had the assassin gone?

Instinct saved his life. He heard a faint sound, like surf hissing on a sandy shore, and he threw himself forward, rolling when he hit the floor and then coming again to his feet. The man in black stood behind him, his shadowy blade still extended where Xin had been a moment ago, the eyes above his veil round with surprise that the Fist warrior had avoided his strike.

Nel lunged forward, daggers flashing, but the man faded again into the darkness, and her blades cut nothing.

"Stay away from the shadows!" Xin cried, moving closer to one of the torches while his gaze roamed the corridor, alert for any sign of movement.

One of Nel's daggers disappeared back up her sleeve and she grabbed Vhelan's arm, yanking the sorcerer towards Xin. "This isn't very fair," she said, and Xin almost smiled at the annoyance he heard in her voice.

Something occurred to him in a flash of insight. "Vhelan! Summon wizardlight, as bright as you can!"

The sorcerer blinked slowly, as if trying to comprehend what Xin had said, then realization dawned and he began muttering an incantation. A brilliant white radiance flooded the passage, overwhelming the torchlight and banishing every shred of darkness . . . and also revealing the kith'ketan, sliding along the wall toward them with his blade of shimmering black poised to strike.

The Fist warrior surged forward, screaming a battle cry, and the startled assassin barely had time to bring his sword up to meet Xin's attack. The force of his blow staggered the shadowblade, and Xin pressed the advantage by following his initial strike with a series of sweeping cuts that the man in black just managed to parry. He was quick and skilled, but Xin doubted that the assassin ever had to fight like this, without the advantages conferred by his strange powers.

The hilt of a dagger sprouted in the shadowblade's shoulder, and his sword-arm faltered. Xin took advantage of this opening and stepped inside his guard, burying his steel in the assassin's stomach. The eyes above the veil widened again, this time in pain, and when Xin wrenched his weapon free the shadowblade collapsed soundlessly, the ebony hilt of his sword slipping from his fingers as he tried to use his hands to keep his entrails from spilling out. He slumped forward, the dark blade on the floor beside him beginning to glimmer faintly. A moment later it fell apart into a sword-shaped outline of fine black dust.

The pounding of many boots approached, and suddenly the passage was flooded by Dymorian guardsmen. The red-cloaked warrior leading them blinked, shielding his eyes from the blazing wizardlight, and took in the sight of the three of them standing over the crumpled assassin and the slain Scarlet Guardsman. He bowed his head when he noticed Vhelan's robes.

"My lord, are you all right?"

The sorcerer let his wizardlight fade. "Yes. This man was a shadowblade, as incredible as that sounds. I saw him walk between the darknesses myself."

The Scarlet Guardsman nodded. "There is more than this one. They are killing magisters all over Saltstone. We were coming to your quarters in the hopes you yet lived."

Vhelan ran a hand through his sleep-mussed hair. "The queen?"

The Scarlet Guardsman swallowed. "I'm not sure . . . rumors are flying. There was an explosion in Ravenroost, the top of the tower was destroyed. Kwan Lo-Ren went to find her. Then these assassins emerged from the shadows, hunting down magisters, and we've been trying to catch them, but when we do they just melt into the darkness."

"Wizardlight," Nel said, rolling over the dead assassin and retrieving her dagger. "Have magisters accompany every group of guardsmen. When you find one of these bastards summon enough light that they cannot disappear into the shadows."

The Scarlet Guardsman's eyes brightened. "Yes, of course." He addressed the warriors behind him, most of whom were staring at the dead shadowblade with unease and dread. "Delion, Malachai, Vix. Run back to the hall where we've gathered the magisters. Tell whoever is in command what Lady Nel just said. Now go."

He turned to the magister as the three warriors hurried back the way they'd come. "And what shall we do, my lord?"

Vhelan bit his lip. "Nel, you and Xin should make for the apprentice quarters. Find Keilan and keep him safe."

"And where will you go?" his knife asked.

"To Ravenroost, with the captain here and his men. I must see to the queen."

Nel snorted. "I'm coming with you."

Vhelan shook his head firmly. "No. If these assassins are hunting those with the gift then they will also come for the children."

Nel's face twisted, but after a moment she nodded grudgingly. "Very well – be careful, boss. I'll see you soon."

Vhelan reached out and gripped her arm affectionately. Then he glanced at Xin. "Keep her safe."

"You have this one's word that I will, sorcerer."

39: ALYANNA

ALYANNA SUCKED IN her breath when she reached the top of the spiraling stairs and saw what devastation her sorcery had wrought. The summit of Ravenroost had been cracked open like an egg: great chunks of the cupola that had crowned the tower had fallen, and now were strewn among shattered tables and charred corpses. The night sky was visible through these massive rents in the ceiling, and a chill wind reached down to sweep over the scattered debris. The walls were likewise riddled with gaps where the magical energies had punched through the stone, and the one section of the tower where she could see no obvious holes was still fissured by deep cracks.

Sometimes she didn't know her own strength.

The light from the lone mistglobe still hanging from what remained of the ceiling was completely subsumed by the blazing white radiance of the three spheres of wizardlight suspended over the devastation. The magisters who had cast those spells were clustered a ways off, turned from her and intent on something on the ground. Alyanna could guess what lay there.

She began to pick her way carefully through the rubble towards them. A tall warrior in a red cloak standing near the magisters noticed her approaching and hailed her. "Girl!" he cried in the clipped accent of the Shan. "Did Terys find you? Are the healers here?"

Alyanna lifted up the hem of her skirt as she stepped over the still-bubbling body of a magister, the remnants of his – or her – robes fused to blackened flesh. "No. The healers are not here."

The Shan warrior flinched at her tone, and she saw his hand stray to the hilt of his sword. "Then what are you doing here, girl? Who are you?"

"I've come to pay my respects to your queen," she said lightly, and made a dismissive gesture in his direction.

An invisible wind lifted the Scarlet Guardsman from his feet and flung him against a wall with bone-shattering force. As he tumbled to the floor, leaving a smear of blood upon the stone, the three magisters whirled around, incantations spilling from their mouths as sorcery coalesced around their fluttering fingers.

Those without Talent were just glacially slow.

Alyanna stretched out her hand and willed into existence three crackling lances of blue energy. She flung the bolts across the chamber, and though one magister managed to finish his chanting and erect a rudimentary ward the lance pierced it like it was a soap bubble and all three magisters collapsed, fist-sized holes burned into their chests.

Too easy. Alyanna shook her head as she approached where the magisters had been gathered. What she had told Demian was true: the queen and her plans to rejuvenate sorcery posed a very real threat to those who had survived the breaking of the world. Only a Talent like the queen with a school of wizards behind her could eventually discover Alyanna and what she had done. Thus she must be destroyed – but, if Alyanna was honest with herself, she had hoped that Cein d'Kara would prove a worthy adversary. It had been a long time since anyone had truly challenged her. Instead, her carefully-laid plans had come seamlessly to fruition, every piece on the gameboard fulfilling its role perfectly.

Alyanna realized that what she had thought was a corpse sprawled across a chunk of the fallen ceiling was actually the body of the Bard. What a tragic fool. She had given him the greatest gift anyone could possibly receive, and he had rejected it, choosing to cling to the etiolated memories of a vanished past. But Alyanna did feel a flicker of emotion as she came to stand over his body, and she gently closed his staring eyes. The world would be less beautiful after this night.

"Goodnight, my Bard," Alyanna whispered, bending down to brush his lips with her own.

He tasted the same as he had a thousand years ago, when they had kissed for the first time in the vaulted, marmoreal hall of the Lesser Gendern, while the dancers swirled around them and the stars floated above crooning their mysterious sad songs. Soft, full lips. Warm lips and warm –

Alyanna straightened in surprise, her hand going to her cheek. He breathed. He still lived. How was that possible? His mind should have been shredded by the release of all that sorcery. But perhaps . . . perhaps only his body persisted, reduced to a hollow shell. Yes, that must be it.

"Are you still in there, Jan? Can you hear me? How did you survive my gift to the queen?"

"I protected him."

Alyanna summoned her strongest wards as she turned toward this voice. A girl stood among the rubble. Her simple blue shift hung in tatters, and blood and grime smeared her face. She looked like a servant – but Alyanna had no doubt who this was. The girl held herself high, matching Alyanna's gaze.

"Welcome to my home, sorceress. Please excuse the mess."

A thrill went through Alyanna. She smiled and spread her arms out wide. "Your Majesty. There's nothing to apologize for."

She could sense the wards flaring around the queen, a shimmering bubble of prismatic energy. Different than what she had felt before – Demian had been right, Cein d'Kara was creating her own unique strain of sorcery. Remarkable. But was it the equal of lost Kalyuni?

"You protected him? How did you do that?"

The queen stepped towards her, staggering slightly. Alyanna could see that she favored one of her legs. She was injured, but how badly?

"I channeled the energy away from him as best I could as it was being released – otherwise, yes, it would have scorched his mind to cinders. It really was quite clever of you. I never imagined it was possible to nest such a trap inside someone's mind. And the power it unleashed when tripped . . ." The queen glanced around the shattered chamber. "I still have so much to learn, it appears."

"Pity about that, really. You do have such potential. I almost regret having to extinguish it."

The queen's eyes hardened. "Why did you do this? We should be working together to return sorcery to this world, and bring back the glory that was lost."

"Who do you think destroyed that glory in the first place?"

The queen looked taken aback. "You? You caused the cataclysms?"

Alyanna grinned. Why not tell her the truth? One of them would be dead soon enough. "Not directly. I had my servant – I believe you know which one, the shape-changer who ambushed your servants on the Way – assume the form of a Kalyuni diplomat, and murder the beloved child of the Min-Ceruthan queen. As I expected, her grief led her to unleash the sorcery that flooded the Mosaic Cities; she believed that this act of revenge would destroy those who had ordered the death of her daughter. Then the wizards of the Star Towers – faced with their destruction rushing towards them – did the only thing they could before their deaths: they struck back, bringing the black ice down upon the holdfasts."

"Why would you do that?" whispered the queen. Then her eyes widened. "You needed the lives," she continued softly. "What I saw in Jan's memories . . . the great spell that filled you with your immortality, it required a vast number of souls as fuel. The cataclysms provided them." Alyanna saw revulsion in the queen's gaze. "You're a monster."

"They were already doomed. It was inevitable that the fools would destroy each other – I merely decided the time, so that some benefit might come from it."

"Benefit. You are swollen with the lives of countless innocents."

Alyanna threw back her head and laughed. "You see? This is why we can't work together. And also why you are a threat to me – for all your strength and ingenuity, you are still constrained by petty morals."

The queen ignored her words. "Bloated like some blood-sucking insect. But what do you do with eternity? Murder and manipulate. Skulk in the shadows. Jan told me that you are posing as a concubine. You should be an empress, and instead you spread your legs like a common –"

"Enough!" snarled Alyanna, her temper fraying. "I live my life as I choose, as I always have. I do not need the condemnation of one born in a royal birthing chamber. I suffered every depredation and injustice you could imagine, queen. I knew how rotten and depraved those sorcerous empires you fantasize about actually were. Sorcery is power, and power blackens all souls. Yes, I murdered empires. But I freed the rest of mankind from the yoke of sorcery, from those who dominated and enslaved and sucked pleasure like marrow from the bones of their inferiors."

"Then you are a hero. A mad, misunderstood hero."

Alyanna mastered herself again. The queen was trying to anger her and make her control slip – she knew such an advantage might be the difference in the coming contest. Of course, the queen didn't know that Alyanna could summon the Chosen if she somehow proved her equal. The conclusion of this little drama was already scripted. "A hero? We are all heroes in our own story."

"Your story has finally come to an end, witch!"

Power billowed forth from the queen, smashing into Alyanna's wards. She gritted her teeth and reinforced her shields. By the gods, what strength! The queen was not only the greatest Talent of this faded age – she might have been the most powerful even if she'd lived during the glory years of the Imperium.

But Alyanna could also lay claim to that title. Dreadfire erupted from her outstretched hand, a river of green flame. Rather than letting the torrent wash against her wards – which would have been like trying to hold back the tide – the queen instead nudged the dreadfire wide, diverting it so that it flashed harmlessly past and melted a gaping hole in the wall behind her.

The remaining stones buckled inward, then with a rending crash collapsed onto the queen, sending her to her knees as chunks of debris shattered across her wards. Alyanna pressed this advantage, striking out with whips of pure sorcerous energy, lashing the queen as she struggled to maintain her protective sphere.

It should be breaking. No wards could withstand such a battering.

And yet . . . and yet the queen was climbing to her feet again. She was actually *pushing back* against Alyanna's onslaught!

She reached deep within herself, plumbing the depths of her power. Her will was the strongest! Her strength was the greatest!

The waves of sorcerous force smashing together stabilized, then began to creep toward the queen. Blood filled Alyanna's mouth, and she spat it out, redoubling her efforts. A child! She would not fall to a spoiled child!

The space separating Alyanna and the queen roiled with magical energies, the very air shimmering and twisting; the stone floor convulsed, cracking, and began to melt and run like wax. The mistglobe hanging above them exploded, showering Alyanna with shards of glass and burning silver sparks.

There was no elegance to this duel. No subtlety. Just raw power and will crashing together.

The Chosen. She needed the Chosen. "Come to me, slaves," she hissed between ragged breaths.

She spared a quick glance over her shoulder, towards the stairs, hoping to see the vicious little demons emerging from below.

That saved her life; otherwise, she never would have known that a pair of magisters had entered the chamber, until they had already struck her down.

"No!" Alyanna screamed, buttressing her wards as coils of energy smashed into her from behind.

"Gendril! Vhelan!" The queen cried over the roaring crackle of sorcery. "Throw everything you have against her! She must not escape!"

Escape. Alyanna fell to her knees, blackness pressing at the edges of her vision. She must escape. Her wards shuddered, cracked. The Chosen. How did they get past the Chosen?

She swooned, struggling to keep herself conscious. A flash of movement among the rubble. Her heart lifted when she saw a creature of tangled black hair and tattered rags crouched on the shattered remnants of a table. "Help me," she mouthed, reaching imploringly toward the Chosen. But the demon child faded into the darkness and was gone, leaving only the whispering echo of its hoarse laughter.

She was alone. Could she call upon Demian? No time. Her wards would be breached in moments, and then she would be consumed by the queen's sorcerous wrath.

Alyanna sunk her hands into the churning gray mud that had once been the floor. One chance. She would almost certainly die . . . but she would die anyway if she did nothing.

Alyanna channeled what remaining strength she had into the viscous stone underneath her. She reached down, feeling the solidity below this melted layer, and thrust out with all her power.

The floor shattered beneath her, and she fell into darkness.

40: XIN

THE TWISTING CORRIDORS of Saltstone blurred together as Xin and Nel raced through the fortress. Every dancing shadow made him pause, his hand on the hilt of his sword, but they did not encounter any more of the assassins. Several times he heard the distant sounds of screams, and once the passage shook with the force of some far-off explosion, dust sifting down from the ceiling.

"How much farther?" Xin asked between heavy breaths. Even after more than a month here the fortress was still a maze to him.

"Not far. Up ahead there's a small kitchen and a hall where the apprentices take their meals, then the –"

Nel was slightly in front of him, and as she rounded a bend in the corridor she gasped and threw up her arm to stop Xin.

"Keilan!" she cried, the fear in her voice making his heart drop.

The boy was there, sitting slumped against a wall, his legs splayed out in front of him. He raised his head groggily at his name, but he could only blink unsteadily a few times before a tremor of pain passed across his face, and he closed his eyes again.

Two men crouched beside him, and at first Xin thought they might have belonged to the queen. One had striking silver hair and was dressed in the leather and mail of a warrior, though the lack of any coat-of-arms on his tabard implied he was a sellsword, rather than one of Saltstone's guards. Xin's eyes were immediately drawn to the sheath of filigreed silver that hung at his side, and the gleaming copper-colored hilt of his sword. This was no common mercenary.

The other was more troubling. Darkness seemed to drape him, as it had the assassin Xin had slain earlier. But though he was also dressed all in black he wore no veil across his strikingly pale face, and the sword in his hand was not anything like the unnatural shard of gleaming shadow that had been wielded by the kith'ketan.

Xin wasn't sure whether they were friends or foes, but Nel seemed to have no doubt; her throwing daggers were already tumbling through the air as the two men turned from Keilan and stood.

Then the impossible happened. For a drawn-out moment the black-clad warrior did nothing, watching the dagger's glittering approach with a slight frown, then he slashed the air in front of him with his long curving sword. Metal shrieked as the daggers skittered past him into the shadows.

Xin gasped at the casual skill with which the warrior had knocked the daggers *out of the air*. He had trained with the finest swordsmen in the city of Gryx, retired Fist soldiers whose bladework was legendary among the Fettered, and he had never seen anything like that before. A coldness settled over Xin as he adopted the third form of the One Who Waits, leaning forward on the balls of his feet with his sword-point extended toward the man in black.

The man's eyes widened in shock as he watched Xin assume the fighting stance, and then his face twisted in anger, as if he had just been grievously insulted. The silver-haired man beside him was also staring in surprise, but at Nel rather than Xin, his hand having gone to some charm he wore around his neck.

"I know –" Nel started to say, but her words trailed off into a strangled yelp. Xin glanced over at her to see what was the matter . . . or tried to. His neck refused to turn; in panic he struggled to move his arms or legs, but it was like every part of his body was bound by invisible bonds that wrapped him more tightly than iron chains. What sorcery was this? The man in black stalked closer, staring at Xin with a look of intense concentration, his lips pursed. Xin's heart thundered in his ears as he watched the man's sword. This was not how he wanted to die, slaughtered like a trussed pig.

The silver-haired man approached the man in black and grabbed his arm. "What did you do? Why aren't they moving?"

The warrior who had cut the daggers from the air said nothing, continuing to study Xin.

"Is this some kind of shadowblade trick? I don't feel any sorcery."

He doesn't feel any sorcery? Was the man one of the Pure? He had the silver hair of the paladins, but not their golden eyes or white armor.

"It is some kind of trick," the man in black said softly. He reached toward Xin and touched his elbow, twisting his arm slightly inward. Then he gently turned his wrist so that his blade was parallel to his body. Another tingling wave of shock washed over Xin as he realized what he was doing. This was the second form of the One Who Waits. How did this man know the stances?

The silver-haired man spoke again. "Demian, listen to me. I recognize this girl. She saved my life months ago, after I disgraced myself beneath Uthmala. You cannot kill her."

"She would kill us."

"To save the boy. She does not deserve to die."

The warrior in black – Demian – tore his gaze from Xin and turned to the silver-haired man beside him. "There is something I must do here. Take the boy and leave the fortress. Make for the inn and saddle the horses. I will find you there before the tenth bell strikes, paladin."

Paladin! The Pure, in Saltstone, allied with shadowblades? It seemed the wildest of fantasies. The queen must be warned! Xin strained against the invisible chains holding him, his muscles aching.

The Pure grabbed the man in black's arm again, more roughly. His eyes narrowed in anger. "Promise me you will not kill her."

"Every moment you waste increases the chances that the magisters will find us. I don't think your god would be pleased."

"Promise me!"

A slight smile ghosted across the man in black's pale face. "Very well, paladin. The girl will live. Now go."

With a last lingering look at Nel, the silver-haired man turned away, and moved to where Keilan still slumped against the wall. With surprising tenderness he scooped the boy into his arms.

"The inn, Demian. I will see you shortly. And then I want answers about these powers of yours."

The man in black grunted something unintelligible in reply as the paladin vanished down the passageway carrying Keilan. Xin thrashed against his bonds.

The man in black watched him calmly; the anger Xin had seen in his face only moments ago had vanished, as if it had never been.

"I am going to relax what binds you, warrior. I have questions. If I feel that you have answered me truthfully, I will give you the chance to prove your worth with a sword in your hand."

Xin felt the invisible chains wrapped around his limbs and neck loosen, though he still could not move freely.

"What . . . what did you do?" he rasped, his throat raw.

The man in black blinked, as if surprised by the question. "I thought it would be obvious. I held you immobile with sorcery."

"But the Pure said –"

"I learned long ago how to hide my gift from the paladins of Ama. It is simple enough for one with Talent."

"Who are you?"

The man in black waved his question away. "Answer me this: where did you learn how to fight?"

"It is . . . it is the way of the Fists. This one learned it in the red sand pits of Gryx."

"No," the man in black snarled, anger rippling his voice like a pebble dropped in calm water. "It is not. Your first stance was the third movement of the blue cantata. I changed it to the second, and I saw in your eyes that you knew what I was doing."

Xin swallowed uncertainly. "The Fists . . . it was said to this one that the secrets of our technique came from the swordsingers of the lost Mosaic Cities. Are you also familiar with their fighting style?"

"I am the last swordsinger!" the man spat, his eyes blazing. "You make a mockery of us! Our beautiful bladesongs, aped by the slaves – slaves! – of some festering cesspool of a city."

The man in black breathed deep, mastering himself. When he spoke again, his voice was once more shriven of emotion. "Long ago, if any warrior not of our order dared to imitate our bladesongs he would be hunted down and dragged back to our hall in Kashkana. There he would be given the chance to prove himself worthy, by dueling the finest among us, with his life as the prize."

Demian retreated back a few paces and settled into the first form of The One Who Waits. "Your people have stolen from me, and I demand retribution."

The bonds holding Xin fell completely away, and he staggered forward. "You're a madman," he said, quickly completing a simple combination of sword strokes to try and return feeling to his numb arms and wrists.

"I am the sanest person I know," the man in black said, another small smile touching his lips. "Though in truth that might still make me mad."

Xin felt like he was moving through the thickened air of a dream as he adopted the first form, mirroring the man in black. "Remember what you told the paladin. The girl lives, even if I die."

Demian's lip curled and he lunged forward, smoothly shifting from The One Who Waits to the fifth form of The One Who Strikes. Xin stayed in his stance, meeting the long curving blade with his own. A flurry of blows followed, almost too fast to see. Only his familiarity with these forms allowed Xin to parry the swordsinger's flashing routines. He had spent a decade dueling his brothers and the Fist veterans in the Pits, mastering this fighting style, but he had never seen such speed and precision.

Xin leaped backward, trying to put some space between them. The man in black followed, his eyes flat and hard.

"You know the counters," he said in words that dripped with cold fury. "But you've changed their edges. You . . . slaves . . . have lost the elegance, the beauty."

Another dazzling combination, two slashes that Xin turned aside, then a lightning-quick jab that almost skewered him. He spun away, feeling the blade lightly score the side of his cuirass.

He needed to get closer, to try and counter the advantage in reach the man in black received from the length of his strange, cracked sword. But it flickered like a striking serpent, so fast that Xin knew if he made only the slightest mistake that it would be the end of him.

And Nel knew it, too. Xin spared a glance at her; she was still held frozen by the swordsinger's spell, but the glistening tracks of tears scarred her cheeks.

Again the man in black surged forward, and again Xin fell back before him, desperately warding away his flashing sword. The fourth form of The One Who Strikes, shifting fluidly into the seventh, then the first, then the fourth again, all done with an effortless grace that would have awed Xin and his Fist brothers if they'd seen it in the Pits. Cut and slash and thrust, Xin only a moment away each time from having the sword bite deep into his flesh.

But a pattern was emerging: the same forms, the same combinations, just done with blazing speed. He could not hope to keep up for very much longer . . . his only chance was if he could guess what was coming next and use that to his advantage. Third, second, third, sixth. Ninth, first, second, third, sixth, first. The swordsinger always followed the second form of The One Who Strikes, a downward slash, with the third, a quick thrust. It was a devastating combination – twice it had nearly caught Xin, and really only blind luck had allowed him to throw himself from the blade's path each time.

If he could just survive until he used the second form again . . . Xin parried the curving blade, trying to make himself appear a fraction slower and goad the swordsinger into returning to the sequence that had almost finished him.

There! The second form, sword slicing down, but before the man in black could halt his strike and thrust out, Xin spun inside his guard and slashed. His stubby Fist sword bit deep, raking across the man in black's ribs, and the swordsinger stumbled back holding his side, his eyes wide with shock. Xin followed him, stabbing his swordarm, but the man somehow kept holding onto his sword's hilt as he collapsed against the wall. His blade wavered as he tried to hold it up; blood was already starting to pool on the stones below him, dribbling steadily from underneath his shirt. Xin lunged forward, but with a last effort the man in black took a faltering step and threw himself to the ground directly behind Nel.

When he touched the edge of her shadow he vanished.

Xin spun around, searching the other patches of darkness created by the corridor's flickering torches. But the man in black was gone, and as if to assure him that this was indeed true Nel suddenly drew in a shuddering breath and fell to her knees. Xin hurried to her side and helped her stand.

"Keilan," she gasped, clutching at Xin's arm. "We have to follow that paladin. Gods, you were amazing." She grabbed behind his neck and pulled his mouth to hers, kissing him hard. After a long moment she let him go, flashing one of the lopsided smiles he loved so much. "You've earned more than that, but that's all we have time . . ."

Nel touched his arm lightly, turning it so she could get a better look at something. "Are you all right?"

Xin glanced down. A spot of blood had appeared on his shirt. "Barely a scratch."

Nel frowned and rolled back his sleeve so that she could see the small cut on his forearm.

"This one is fine, it's nothing." He looked away, peering into the shadows, wondering where the man in black had vanished.

"Xin . . ."

The concern in her voice made him look again. Spidery black lines were creeping under his skin, spreading from the tiny wound. He watched in numb fascination as they reached his wrist and branched out into his palm.

"Oh!" he cried, slipping to his knees. His arm was so cold; it felt like he had thrust it through the ice of a frozen pond. So cold it burned like fire.

"Xin!" Nel was screaming from very far away, shaking him. Something black pooled in his eyes, rising up to blot the light, and he was falling backwards from a great height.

He reached out, grasping desperately for Nel's hand, and he felt strong fingers close around his wrist. They were too rough to be hers, calloused by endless hours of swordplay. Xin knew whose hand it was. He smiled.

His brother Delon pulled him further into the blackness.

41: ALYANNA

CROUCHED IN THE shadows, Alyanna peered between the wooden spokes of an ox-cart's wheel and silently cursed her luck. Across the courtyard from her a pair of guardsmen stood near the deeper blackness cast by Saltstone's wall, their hands on the hilts of their swords as they watched the night warily. Behind them, she knew, recessed farther back and hidden from her vantage, was the rift leading back to the imperial gardens. It must have escaped notice in the swirling chaos of the attack, or this whole courtyard would be crawling with guards. Still, the two that were here were more than she could overcome in her weakened state.

Alyanna let out a long, shuddering breath and rested her head against the wheel. The pain in her chest swelled again, and she coughed as quietly as she could into her hand, speckling her palm with blood. She suspected that the grating ache in her side was a broken rib, and that it had punctured her lung. It was getting harder for her to breathe, and every time she allowed herself a ragged cough more blood was coming up. That was not her only injury, either: her ankle throbbed, and she had been forced to half-run and half-hop during her frantic dash back through the fortress.

Then again, she supposed it was a minor miracle that she still lived. She had collapsed the floor beneath her as her wards were breaking atop Ravenroost, falling into the empty chamber below in a shower of dust and stone. Her faltering shields had taken the brunt of the impact, and then before the queen could follow she had scrambled for a window and thrown herself out into the night. She had hoped that she could muster the strength to fly, but when she had tried to summon forth the sorcery she had found herself completely hollow, drained of every last shred of power. Plummeting through the darkness, the cold night air washing over her, she had almost resigned herself to death. It would have been over in an instant, bone and flesh shattering on flagstones, the darkness finally rushing up to claim her.

But that was not who she was. Somehow, as the ground swelled larger below her, Alyanna had found a tiny reserve of untapped power. Not enough to allow her to climb again into the sky, but she had managed to slow her descent so that when she struck the ground she had not died or slipped into unconsciousness. Still, the fall had broken bones and driven the wind from her. Climbing to her feet and hobbling through Saltstone had been one of the most painful experiences of her long life.

Yet she had done it, through sheer force of will. And now she was just a hundred steps away from freedom – but how could she slip past the guards without sorcery? Alyanna reached deep within herself, hoping beyond hope that she could scrape together enough power to cast even a tiny cantrip that might distract the Dymorians. But there was nothing. She would have to rest and let the well of power inside her refill with the Void's sorcerous dribbling. Perhaps if she pretended to be a terrified scullery maid she could get close, and then dash for the rift . . .

She saw the guards stiffen. They shared a quick glance, and then relaxed as a ragged creature darted across the courtyard, legs and arms flailing in a mimicry of a child's awkward running gait. The Chosen. What was it doing here?

One of the guards crouched down and reached out a hand to corral the Chosen, evidently thinking it was some refugee from the kitchens fleeing the chaos in the fortress. The Chosen grabbed the guard's wrist in its tiny hand and pulled hard. Pain and shock filled the guard's face as he was yanked forward, his shoulder wrenched from its socket. In the same motion the Chosen thrust its other hand into the guard's stomach, ripping out a handful of his entrails.

He slumped forward, screaming as the demon surged past him towards the other guard, who was now desperately fumbling with his sword. The Chosen took two quick little steps and leaped, clawed fingers sinking into the man's shoulders. The guard let go of the hilt and tried to pry the creature loose, but it was fastened tightly, and it took only a moment for the demon's mouth to find and tear out his throat. The Chosen leaped away, landing on all fours like some predatory beast. The guard collapsed, blood spurting from his ravaged neck.

Alyanna found she was holding her breath, her fingers clutching the wooden wheel-spoke so hard that splinters had broken off in her hand.

The Chosen slowly stood and turned to face where she was hidden. It gave her a blood-spattered smile as it chewed and swallowed what it had torn from the guard's throat, then raised its childlike hand and beckoned toward her.

It wanted her to come with it.

Her thoughts, coldly analytical even when swamped by pain and stress, considered what this meant. She held no control over it now – in retrospect, Alyanna wondered if it had ever actually been bound to her, since the day she had first stolen away the chest from the warlock's tower in Tsai Yin. When she had commanded it to strike down the queen atop Ravenroost the creature had effortlessly slipped its leash, suggesting that it could have disobeyed her at any time.

Why had it and its siblings pretended to be her servants? And why did it want her to come with it now?

The queen. If Alyanna was captured, then the queen would certainly interrogate her and discover that the Chosen existed. She might even contact the warlocks of Shan, and inform them as to where their wayward demons had gone.

The Chosen turned and sauntered into the shadows that concealed the rift.

Alyanna considered her choices. If she stayed here, the queen and her magisters would discover her, and she would be captured or killed. But if she passed through the rift and returned to the imperial gardens she would have to contend with the Chosen. Would the demons kill her? Enslave her? Could they be allies? She had not mistreated them. Perhaps they could come to some accord.

The guard whose entrails had been torn out by the Chosen had regained consciousness. He began to keen, a high-pitched wailing that sounded more like an animal than a man. Alyanna glanced at the passageways that emptied into the courtyard. The sound would bring others here, and soon.

She made her decision. Climbing unsteadily to her feet, Alyanna began limping towards the dying guardsman and the rift beyond him. He did not seem to see her as she passed him, his bloody hands clawing at the stone as he writhed in agony.

A shout came from behind her. Alyanna glanced over her shoulder and saw guardsmen spilling from a doorway, all wearing the red cloaks of the queen's elite warriors. Two women in robes were with them as well, and Alyanna stumbled faster as she felt their sorcerous reverberations. Her ankle shrieked with pain, and she blinked away tears, her breath coming in ragged gasps. One bolt of sorcerous energy, and she would be finished.

She passed into the shadow of the wall and found the rift. Within it she could see the looming quartz monoliths of the garden and bright stars burning in the sky. Incantations rose from behind her, prickling her skin as the magisters formed some sorcery. With a final effort she leaped forward through the rift, throwing out her arms to break her fall. Jarring pain blossomed as her elbows struck the ceramic tiles of one of the garden's many paths. Alyanna rolled onto her back, fumbling for the riftstone in her pocket. She had to shut the portal. Her fingers closed around the small white circle and she tried to summon the tiny shred of sorcery necessary to use the riftstone. At first there was nothing, nothing at all, but she continued to strain, and in her desperation she found a spark deep within herself and channeled it into the stone.

The portal rippled and vanished.

Sobbing in relief, Alyanna rolled back onto her stomach and lay her cheek down upon the cool tiles. She had survived. She should have died a dozen times that night, yet she still lived. And where there was life, there was hope.

She needed to get back to her pavilion. There she could collapse among pillows and silks, and have the concubines fetch healers to tend to her.

Alyanna tried to stand, but her body betrayed her, and she collapsed again. Fine. She would crawl, if she had to.

Grunting in pain, Alyanna dragged herself through the grass. Silken sheets. A silver bell to summon strong wine. Graceful hands to massage her aching body. A soft lap on which to pillow her head.

Soon. Soon.

She crawled through a stand of shimmering ghostweed, which made her face and arms prickle. Beyond the grass she found herself in a bed of faintly-glowing nightblossoms, and she tried her best to avoid the thorned stems of the flowers. Suddenly her hand fell upon a silken slipper, and she glanced up in alarm. A huge dark shape towered over her, occluding the stars. Who could this be? A gardener, perhaps, tending to the nightblossoms?

"Help me . . ." she whispered.

Robes swished as whoever it was crouched down beside her. In the faint light of the nightblossoms she saw a pale face, round as the moon, with uptilted black eyes.

Wen Xenxing.

What was the black vizier doing in the gardens at night?

"Oh, my lord," she gasped, reaching for the hem of his long robe. "Please, I fell and hurt myself."

"Did you, Alyanna?" he said in a voice dripping with wry amusement. "And where did that happen?"

"The quartz sculptures. I . . . I tried to climb them."

The black vizier clucked his tongue. "In the dark? How very foolish. I would have expected more wisdom from someone as old as you."

Coldness settled in her chest. "What are you talking about, my lord?"

Wen Xenxing seemed to ripple in the light of the nightblossoms. It was just a momentary tremor, but in that instant she glimpsed a monstrous scaled face, one of its cheeks reduced to a glistening patch of burned flesh.

The genthyaki. Alyanna moaned.

A huge grin split the face of the false vizier. "I always wanted you to crawl before me."

"The Chosen. I told them to kill you."

The genthyaki wagged a plump finger in front of her. "Ah, you did not. I remember your words very well, for they are seared into my memory. '*You may do as you wish*' you said, and so they did. The Chosen had another use for me, to take the place of this empire's black vizier. Unfortunately, I don't believe they have such a use for you. You're too dangerous, you see."

The false vizier reached down and cupped her chin in his hand. "But I begged a boon from them. I asked them to give you to me, for a little while at least. And they said yes. So now, mistress, you are mine, until your body or soul breaks. I should warn you, I've dreamed about this moment for a thousand years." He tenderly wiped away a tear as it trickled down her cheek.

"Now, let us begin."

42: SENACUS

HE PASSED THROUGH the dark and silent city, keeping to the puddles of light beneath the streetlamps. In the gloom, the buildings rising up around him had transformed into leering faces, the pockets of deeper blackness created by recessed doors and windows becoming gaping mouths and eyes. Eyes that watched him and judged him. It was as if the city knew of the crimes he had witnessed this night, the innocent lives Demian and his brother assassins had brutally ended with their monstrous powers. He had seen the bodies of the servants and guardsmen sprawled in the corridors of Saltstone as he had fled carrying Keilan. Murdered by the kith'ketan.

Senacus knew the stain was on his hands, as well. He had led Demian through the fortress, following the thread that had bound him to Keilan ever since he had first touched the boy in his village, all those months ago. And then he had abandoned the girl who had saved his life and nursed him back to health after the horrors of Uthmala, leaving her to the mercy of a shadowblade. No, something more than merely a shadowblade. Something worse.

Now he was stealing away like a thief in the night, the boy

(the innocent)

slumped in front of him, wrapped in a shawl, so weak and drained he would have slipped from their horse if Senacus had not been there to steady him. The striking parallel between this moment and that day on the road to Chale could not be ignored. Was Ama giving him a second chance? The possibility of redeeming himself for losing the boy once before to the Crimson Queen's servants?

If he believed that, what was this terrible, gnawing guilt he felt?

Senacus watched the shadows, half-expecting Demian to materialize from the darkness. But he did not. The assassin had not joined them in the inn's stables, as he had said he would, and when the tenth bell had come and gone Senacus had struck out into the city without him. Chaos would grip Saltstone for a while still, but he knew he needed a significant lead if he was to have any chance of reaching the Gilded Cities before the hunters caught up.

"I saw him."

The voice was thin, reedy. For a moment Senacus didn't realize who had spoken, and he glanced around wildly. But then Keilan shifted slightly, his head rising, as if he was just coming awake.

Senacus reached out and gripped the boy's arm. Not hard, he meant it to be comforting.

"Who did you see?"

"Him."

Perhaps the boy was delirious. Senacus didn't know what the boy had suffered that night, but something terrible had happened before they had found him slumped in the corridor.

"The man in black."

A chill stole through Senacus. He was speaking of Demian.

"That is impossible, Keilan. I traveled from Menekar with him to find you."

"No," Keilan croaked, and then coughed. "I saw him from before."

"You mean, when you were in your village?"

"No. The queen . . . we used sorcery. I helped her to catch a glimpse of the past. The deep past, hundreds and hundreds of years ago. Before the cataclysms."

Senacus let go of Keilan, realizing that he was gripping the boy's arm too tightly. "You are not well."

"He is a sorcerer."

"No," Senacus whispered, "that is not possible."

"How can the paladins of Ama ally themselves with sorcerers?"

"He is not a sorcerer!"

Keilan coughed again, wet and hacking. "I remember . . . I remember his name. From my vision. Demian. He was a swordsinger of the Kalyuni Imperium. And a wizard."

"He is a shadowblade now," Senacus murmured numbly, his thoughts whirling. Suspicions that he had fought to suppress since their assault on Saltstone rose again, demanding to be heard. Demian scaling the walls like a spider. Demian in the courtyard, opening a shimmering portal to somewhere else, where his dark brothers waited. Demian holding Nel and that swordsman immobile, as if he had turned the very air around them to stone. The mysterious powers of a shadowblade . . . or a sorcerer?

"But I could feel nothing," Senacus said softly.

Keilan was quiet for a long moment. "Where is your holy light? Perhaps just as you can hide your power, so can sorcerers."

The lightning-strike of this truth exploded in Senacus's mind, and suddenly the events of the last few months seemed clearer, etched stark against the darkness through which he had been struggling.

The Crimson Queen had learned how to hide the power of her servants from the Pure. Why could another not do the same?

But if Demian was a sorcerer . . . the thought was almost too horrific to entertain. The High Seneschal, the High Mendicant, could *they* be unwitting pawns in some unfathomable game between wizards? Was he delivering Keilan from the queen to another sorcerer far more wicked, one who employed such vicious servants as the kith'ketan?

His hand had gone slack on the reins, and his horse slowed its pace, cocking its head as if it sensed its master's uncertainty.

One of Herath's night gates loomed in front of them. There were only a handful of these set into the city's walls, kept open for the caravans or travelers who arrived after the last blush of twilight had faded from the sky. Barely large enough for a wagon to trundle through, and guarded at all times.

The soldiers flanking the door regarded him curiously as he approached, but none hailed him or questioned his purpose for leaving at this late hour. Senacus stared into the deep blackness beyond the gate, trying to order the feverish rush of his tumbling thoughts. His palms were cold and slick.

Why would a shadowblade serve the will of Ama?

The High Mendicant had seen Demian in a dream, and then he had appeared the next day, as if summoned.

A sorcerer. Could it be true?

Green fire in the night. *That is our signal, I'm sure of it.*

But who had sent the signal?

Always spinning your webs, Weaver.

Webs . . . Senacus felt the old cuts upon his legs begin to itch. Spiders, an endless horde rushing out of the darkness, razor-sharp mandibles slicing his flesh, black ichor splashing his armor and trickling beneath his mail to burn his skin . . .

Senacus nudged his horse closer to one of the slumping, half-asleep guardsmen. Then he gripped Keilan and lifted him from his horse, handing the limp boy down to the surprised soldier.

"The boy is an apprentice in the Scholia. Return him to Saltstone."

The guardsman gaped at him. "Who . . . who are you?"

Senacus clutched the relic of Tethys hanging upon his breast. "I don't know," he said, then kicked his horse's flank and plunged into the darkness beyond the walls.

43: KEILAN

WE BURNED HIM *this morning.*

Nel's voice, echoing in the darkness.

He's with his brothers now. He's whole again. Or I hope so; I never believed in an afterlife, to be honest. The Abyss. The Golden City. The Pale Fields. Just fictions to give comfort for weak minds. But Xin . . . he was so certain that he could still feel them out there, in the beyond, that I almost started to believe they were really waiting for him.

Keilan groped towards consciousness.

Do you think he'll wait for me?

Golden light, leaking through latticed shutters. Keilan struggled awake in sweat-damp sheets, his head throbbing. He was alone, in a richly-appointed room striped by shadows and sunlight.

But Nel had been here, he was sure of it, sitting on the edge of his bed and waiting for him to wake. As she had once before, in Vis, so that together they could go visit Xin.

Xin was dead.

Keilan knew this to be true; it was a hard stone of certainty lodged in his chest, pressing upon his heart.

Xin. His easy grin as he'd flourished a wooden sword. His laughter as Nel had used some blackguard trick to disarm him while practicing in a forest glade. The joy in his face as the mysterious squiggles on the page they'd hunkered over in the seeker's wagon had magically transformed into a word he knew.

Keilan groaned, struggling to sit. The air in the chamber was heavy, fetid. It smelled like a sickroom.

What had happened last night? He remembered the flash atop Ravenroost, green fire rushing over the queen's wards. Then stumbling through twisting corridors. Two men looming over him; one who was, impossibly, the Pure who had first kidnapped him from his village. The other . . .

Keilan shuddered. A pale man, wrapped in darkness. But also familiar. He had seen him before, in the memories of someone from an ancient, vanished age. Demian, swordsinger of the Kalyuni Imperium. An immortal sorcerer, who like Jan had drunk greedily of the lives of thousands. And there had been others who had done the same.

A beautiful sorceress, blazing with power and purpose. Alyanna.

A tall, gaunt man, who had healed Jan as he lay injured from the wyvern's ambush. Querimanica.

A woman with shimmering silver hair, her face flushed as she strained to control the sorcery surging around the table during the ceremony. She had fed this power into Alyanna, allowing her to shape it into the spell that would render them all eternal.

His mother.

No, it hadn't been. But the resemblance was too close to be a coincidence. If his mother had lived another ten years she would have looked exactly the same, he was sure of it.

Who was she?

Keilan swung his legs over the side of the bed and found a pair of gray cloth shoes waiting. He slipped them on. There were two doors in the room, and Keilan moved sluggishly toward the one with sunlight trickling around the edges of its frame. He needed some fresh air to clear his head.

Keilan opened the door, and had to blink and shield his eyes from the brightness. He stood at the edge of a sprawling garden, on a stone path that wended among sprays of colorful blossoms and carefully sculpted hedges. Scattered among the beds of flowers were statues carved into the shapes of fantastical creatures, some of which he recognized from his reading of *The Tinker's Bestiary*.

Slowly, he shuffled out onto the path, the aches in his body melting away as the warm sunlight washed over him. Keilan reached down to cup a blue, bell-shaped flower that hung out over the path. He knew this flower. Sella had brought him a bouquet of them once, a fortnight after he'd lost his mother. She'd held them out shyly for him to take, tears starting to glimmer in her mis-matched eyes. Then they'd gone down to the rocks together and thrown them into the water, one by one, and watched them drift away.

Soul's Tears. That's what they were called in his village. Flowers for the dead.

Keilan gently twisted the blossom from its thorned stem, then resumed walking. He could hear the faint gurgle of running water, and moved in that direction, until he passed through an arched silver trellis and found himself standing before a huge stone dragon. The beast was rearing back on its hind legs, as if poised to lunge upon some helpless prey. Water leaped from its mouth and fell into a pond of murky green water, which was pocked by lily pads and the black shells of sunning turtles.

Keilan went to the edge of the pond and tossed in the flower.

"Goodbye, Xin," he whispered as the ripples formed by the falling water pushed the blossom across the pond's surface. It spun slowly as it floated, until it came to rest against the huge, mottled shell of an ancient turtle.

Keilan was just about to glance away when he saw the petals of the flower shiver, as if stroked by invisible fingers. The blossom lifted from the water, dripping, and Keilan gasped, rushing to the edge of the pond. As if annoyed by the unwanted commotion the old turtle slipped beneath the surface and vanished.

Keilan watched, dumbstruck, as the flower drifted over the pond, borne by a wind he could not feel. He turned to follow its path as it floated past him, only a few span from his head. Then it was plucked from the air by the slim white fingers of Cein d'Kara.

The queen leaned against the silver trellis, studying the flower in her palm. She let it fall, watching it flutter to the ground with a thoughtful expression.

When it had come to rest, she raised her head and met Keilan's surprised gaze. The realization of what he should be doing struck Keilan like lightning.

"Your Majesty," he cried, dropping to one knee.

"Rise," she said, motioning for him to stand. "Get up."

There was an edge to her voice he hadn't heard before. She sounded almost . . . frustrated?

He stood, and she pushed herself from the trellis, coming closer. The queen looked so young, barely older than Nel. She hadn't applied whatever it was that she usually used to whiten her skin, and her hair, always perfectly brushed when he'd seen her before, now hung in tangles. It seemed like she had just awoken. Keilan realized with a start that he probably looked the same, and had to fight back the urge to smooth down his hair.

"I am sorry about your friend, Keilan. He was one of many we lost last night."

Keilan swallowed away a lump in his throat. "Thank you, Your Majesty."

"They wanted you," she said, reaching up to brush away a red curl that had fallen across her face. He noticed that she had been cut above her left eye, and a bruise darkened her cheek.

"I'm so sorry if this is my fault."

She waved away his words. "Do you know why they came for you?"

He shrugged helplessly. "I don't. But do you think it could be related to what we saw in that man's memories? The terrible sorcery they did?"

"You remember that."

"I do. Your Majesty . . . I saw something when we were in his mind. There was a woman, with silver hair. Did you notice her?"

The queen nodded, her eyes narrowing slightly.

Keilan knew he must sound crazy, but he pushed on anyway. "She looked almost exactly like my mother," he blurted, and then the words came tumbling out. "I never knew her family, where she'd come from. My father pulled her from the sea after a storm. But that sorceress in the man's mind *must* be related to her. Has Jan recovered? I want to ask him about her."

Something flickered in the queen's eyes. "Keilan," she said softly, "Jan . . . he did not survive." Her words were like a blow to his stomach. *No, I must know!*

"His mind was destroyed by the sorcery unleashed, and though he did live on for a while last night, in the end his body couldn't endure by itself. I'm sorry."

"It's not your fault, Your Majesty." His voice seemed to come from very far away.

"But it is," the queen said bitterly, running a hand through her tangled hair. She let out a shuddering sigh, glancing down – and for the first time, Keilan thought, she looked like the young woman she truly was.

"I brought him into Saltstone. My desire to *know*, to *understand*, made me push caution aside. How I've wanted to know the secrets of the glorious past! All these deaths are on my head, so many of my old friends . . ."

"You couldn't know, Your Majesty."

Cein d'Kara looked up, her eyes blazing. "I am the queen, the mother of all my subjects. They pledge their lives to me, and I pledge my life to them. Never again will my weakness cause them harm. This I promise."

Keilan found Nel in the stables saddling her horse. Several bulging travel bags lay beside her in the straw; it looked like she was prepared for a long journey.

"Nel," he said, and she turned. Her eyes were red, her mouth set in a thin line.

"Keilan, you're awake. How do you feel?"

"All right. My head still aches, but the rest of me is much better."

"Good." Silence stretched between them for a long moment. "Did you . . . did you hear about Xin?"

"Yes."

Nel blinked away tears, wiping at her cheeks. "He died fighting to save us."

Keilan took two steps toward Nel, then hesitated. "I know that's how he would have wanted to die. And he did save you – and me, as well, because if that man in black had lived I'm sure he would have met up with the Pure later, and the paladin would not have abandoned me at the gate."

"I'm not sure if Xin killed him," Nel said, sniffling. "I think he did. He put a span of steel into his side, but we never found the shadowblade's body."

"He wasn't a shadowblade. Or at least, that's not all he was."

Nel shuddered. "Yes. He used some sorcery on me so I couldn't move. I've never felt so helpless."

Keilan gestured at the bags she'd piled in the straw. "You're leaving?"

Nel lifted one of the bags and secured it to the horse's saddle. "I'm going after that paladin. He must know more about what happened last night. I want to know who ordered the attack, and where I can find them."

"And then?"

Nel flicked her wrist, and Chance appeared in her hand. "Then I'm going to show them a bit of Warren justice."

"I want to go with you."

Nel snorted. "The queen would have my head on a spike. Whoever is behind this attack tried their best to get you out of Saltstone. You'll be vulnerable outside these walls."

"I'm vulnerable within them, apparently."

Nel shook her head. "You can't come."

"They know I'm here. Can the queen protect me if the shadowblades return? Or another sorcerer? I would be safer with you, on the road."

Something wavered in Nel's face, and Keilan pressed on.

"I think the paladin knows something about my mother. The shadowblade he was with, I saw him in a vision with a woman who looked so much like my mother that they could have been sisters."

Nel eyed him skeptically. "Your mother? A vision? Keilan, is your head addled?"

"A sorcerous vision. The queen summoned me to Ravenroost last night to conjure it forth. What I saw was true, I'm sure of it."

The knife chewed on her lip, considering what he had said. Finally, she reached into one of her travel bags and tossed him a cloak.

"Wrap yourself in that and pull down the cowl so no one can see your face. The queen dispatched rangers this morning to hunt down the paladin, and I want to catch up with them before they reach him. Go saddle your horse – we have to ride now."

EPILOGUE

A DOOR creaked.

Shadows moved behind the cloth covering his eyes, and his jaw ached from being forced open by the piece of metal shoved between his teeth.

Footsteps, coming closer.

He shifted, trying yet again to lift his manacled hands and remove the thing in his mouth. But the chains connecting him to the wall went taut before he could reach far enough.

A vague shape loomed over him.

He thrust within himself, scrabbling for his power, but the sorcery trickled through his cupped hands like water.

Fingers touched the edges of his blindfold and lifted it off. The Crimson Queen squatted beside him, her face impassive. There was no warmth in her eyes. No mercy.

"Jan," she said. Her long red curls were tangled, and a bruise was spreading over her cheek.

He tried to ask her what was going on, but with the bit in his mouth his words came out as gibberish.

She pursed her lips. "You must be asking why you are bound like this."

He managed a slight nod, the thick metal torc around his throat cutting into his chin.

"It is because you are an assassin. You were dispatched to kill me, with a weapon hidden inside your mind."

He tried to think back, but the last thing he remembered was drinking the cup of moonblossom tea the queen had handed to him atop Ravenroost. What had happened after?

"Nearly a hundred of my subjects died last night, including some of my closest friends. That creature Alyanna nearly killed me."

Alyanna had come to Saltstone? If the queen was still alive, did that mean that she was dead?

"I know your great crime, Jan. What you wanted to forget. I saw it in your memories."

And he knew, too. Jan moaned as the images came flooding back. Liralyn on her throne, crying out in agony as the ice rushed up to claim her. Her soul, her life, dragged across the world by Alyanna's monstrous crystal, then twisted and driven into the sorcerers around that table.

They had fed on her. *He* had fed on her. Jan slumped to the stone floor, a hollowness spreading in his chest.

The queen stood. "The torc around your neck is an ancient artifact from the Imperium. It was called a collar, I believe, and I'm sure you know of it."

He did. Sorcerers accused of crimes had been bound by them. He would not be able to reach his sorcery while wearing it.

She lingered for a moment, looking down at him. "Perhaps one day I will trust you enough to free you. But that will not be soon, I think."

Then she bent again and slipped the blindfold once more over his eyes.

Darkness swallowed him.

ACKNOWLEDGMENTS

Many wonderful people helped me to realize this book.

Thank you to Rebecca Lynn Nicholson, who read my first chapters and gave me the support to persevere.

Thank you to Gerald Warfield, for his wisdom and sage advice.

Thank you to my readers, Sarah K. Wilson, Dominic Dimech, Samuel Schmoker, Inna Hardison, David Paulk, Arthur Dorrance, Cara DiGirolomo, Grant Starr, and Karen Rochnik.

And thank you to Shining Chen, for allowing me to pursue this dream.

ABOUT THE AUTHOR

Alec Hutson was the Spirit Award winner for Carleton College at the 2002 Ultimate Frisbee College National Championships. He has watched the sun set over the dead city of Bagan and rise over the living ruins of Angkor Wat. He grew up in a geodesic dome and a bookstore and currently lives in Shanghai, China. *The Crimson Queen* is his first book.